On the Edge

Michael Ridpath spent eight years as a bond trader at an international bank in the City of London. He is the author of six other novels – *The Marketmaker*, *Free to Trade*, *Final Venture*, *Trading Reality*, *The Predator* and *Fatal Error*. He grew up in Yorkshire and now lives in north London with his wife and children.

If you'd like to know more about the author and his work, log on to www.michaelridpath.com.

On the Edge

MICHAEL RIDPATH

MICHAEL JOSEPH
an imprint of
PENGUIN BOOKS

MICHAEL JOSEPH

Published by the Penguin Group
Penguin Books Ltd, 80 Strand, London WC2R 0RL, England
Penguin Group (USA) Inc., 375 Hudson Street, New York, New York 10014, USA
Penguin Books Australia Ltd, 250 Camberwell Road, Camberwell, Victoria 3124, Australia
Penguin Books Canada Ltd, 10 Alcorn Avenue, Toronto, Ontario, Canada M4V 3B2
Penguin Books India (P) Ltd, 11 Community Centre, Panchsheel Park, New Delhi – 110 017, India
Penguin Group (NZ), cnr Airborne and Rosedale Roads, Albany, Auckland 1310, New Zealand
Penguin Books (South Africa) (Pty) Ltd, 24 Sturdee Avenue, Rosebank 2196, South Africa

Penguin Books Ltd, Registered Offices: 80 Strand, London WC2R 0RL, England

www.penguin.com

First published 2005
1

Set in 13.5/16 pt Monotype Garamond
Typeset by Rowland Phototypesetting Ltd, Bury St Edmunds, Suffolk
Printed in Great Britain by Clays Ltd, St Ives plc

A CIP catalogue record for this book is available from the British Library

ISBN 0-718-14676-X

For my father, Andrew

Prologue

Flying Officer Alex Calder watched as the Tornado he was piloting flew itself at five hundred miles an hour two hundred and fifty feet above the Herefordshire countryside. His left hand rested on the throttle and his right on his lap as the aircraft made tiny corrections to heading and altitude prompted by messages from the Terrain Following Radar in the nose. Farmland sped by in flashes of green, gold and brown and in the sunshine the lone Tornado's shadow trickled along the ground a few yards to the right, like a loyal but ghostly wingman.

A chimney approached, rising two hundred feet above a cement works, a white sore on the landscape. 'Waypoint B,' announced Jacko, the stocky Scouser navigator in the rear cockpit, and the Tornado lurched to the left, obeying the instructions on the cassette that Jacko had carefully programmed back in 13 Squadron's Personnel Briefing Room at RAF Marham. 'Nothing on the RHWR.'

There were five reconnaissance targets programmed on to the cassette, and Calder and Jacko were also expecting a visit from a pair of fighters somewhere along the way. The Radar Homing Warning Receiver would give them some indication that the fighters were up there looking for them with their own radar, if the fighters chose to switch it on of course. Otherwise they would have to rely on their eyes.

The brown flanks of the Welsh hills lurched towards them, guarded by a bank of slate grey clouds.

'Brace yourself, Jacko,' warned Calder as the Tornado surged and bucked over the first ridge. Despite his five years' service as a navigator, Jacko still suffered from airsickness, and the movement in the back played havoc with his stomach, especially when flying on the TFR.

Now the aircraft was ducking and weaving, hunting the contours of the hills and valleys, the on-board computer instructing it to skip over each obstacle as it showed itself on the TFR. Even after a year of flying Tornados, Calder still found it difficult to restrain himself from giving the aircraft a helping hand.

Over the crest of a tree-covered hill, and the first target appeared – a dam at the end of a narrow lake. Calder took control of the aircraft, approaching the dam with an offset of about a hundred yards or so to get the best picture possible for the photographic interpreter back at base. The Tornado's infra-red video system was running, and as they flew past the dam Jacko called out a description of the structure. On the flight back to Norfolk he would edit the videotape, and this together with the cockpit voice recording would be given to the photographic interpreters as soon as they landed.

The dam behind them and on to the next target, deeper in the Welsh mountains. This was the flying Calder loved, the high mountainsides providing a ground rush even at three hundred feet. Calder's concentration was focused on the hills outside the cockpit, seen through the little green markings of the Head-Up Display, with only an occasional glance inside at the moving map.

'Buster! Kick sixty left!'

Instantly Calder jammed the throttle forward as far as it would go and threw the aircraft sixty degrees to the left, his g-suit gripping his legs and abdomen to counteract the gravitational pull from the turn and the acceleration. He kept low, hugging the mountains.

'Bogey four o'clock high, descending, about five miles.'

Calder glanced at his RHWR and could see a trace of the fighter's radar. It would be an F3 from RAF Coningsby, the fighter variant of the Tornado, attempting to close near enough to fire its heat-seeking missiles. The F3 was much faster than the GR.1A that Calder and Jacko were flying, and in open country they wouldn't have stood a chance, but in the mountains they might just be able to shake the fighter before it reached the stern range needed to fire its missile. Despite the wonders of modern electronics, the scientists hadn't invented anything yet that could see through rock.

'There's a valley that runs perpendicular to this one just over that ridge on the left – we'll lose him there!' Jacko called.

Calder turned the aircraft hard left, banking it all the way to inverted as he crossed the mountain ridge into the next valley, trying to keep the minimum height and time above the crest of the ridge where the fighter might make visual contact with them. The heather shot by above his head. Flying upside-down, he pulled the stick back to push the nose of the jet down into the valley. He rolled out. As the world righted itself, he saw in front of him a narrow green strip of pasture dotted with sheep, following a winding river downhill. A road led down to a tiny grey slate village with a chapel. And in front of the village, suspended as if stationary, was an aircraft. A high-winged, single-engined aircraft: a Cessna.

Of course the Cessna wasn't really stationary, it just looked that way to Calder. Which meant the two aircraft were on course to collide.

'What the hell is that doing there!' Calder shouted. It was madness for a civilian aircraft to fly that low anywhere, but especially here, in the middle of the Tornados' playground. It takes ten seconds for the pilot of a fast jet to spot an aircraft, identify it as a potential collision risk, choose a course of evasive action, and allow time for the aircraft to respond to the controls. At a closing speed of six hundred miles an hour, ten seconds is the time it takes to travel nearly two miles. The Cessna was now less than a mile away.

Calder rammed in the throttle and pulled back on the stick. The Cessna seemed to explode in size as the two aircraft closed.

The Tornado's nose rose, but too late. Calder flinched as the Cessna hit them, just to the left of the cockpit. There was a bang, and the Tornado bucked.

'We're on fire!' Jacko shouted.

Calder looked out to the left. There was a chunk missing from the wing and flames engulfed the port engine. Red warning lights flashed and sirens sounded as the Tornado told its crew that they were in trouble. They knew that already. The controls were listless in Calder's hands and the aircraft, which had been about to climb, was levelling off prior to entering a dive. Outside the fire was spreading.

There was only one decision, it was a decision he had been trained to make and Calder made it.

'Prepare to eject! Prepare to eject!' He reached down for the black and yellow handle between his legs. The nose of the Tornado was already beginning to point downwards. 'Three, two, one . . . Eject! Eject!'

But just as he was about to pull the handle, he looked up. Ahead, growing alarmingly in size, was the village. His eyes focused on a playground, small figures scattered over a square of tarmac in front of him. Directly in front of him.

He removed his hand from the handle and pulled hard back on the stick. He heard the pop of the canopy as Jacko banged out behind him. The air roared past the now open cockpit. At first there was no response from the Tornado to his commands, but he pulled back as hard as he could, almost ripping the stick out of the cockpit. Movement, just a bit of movement, then, miraculously, the nose of the Tornado rose. Now, instead of the schoolyard, there was the flank of a mountain, perhaps a mile away. It took six seconds to travel a mile.

Calder held on for two of them, until he was sure that if he let go of the stick the aircraft wouldn't plummet into the village. Then he pulled the handle.

The straps around his body tightened. Then nothing happened. For the next half a second, half a lifetime, Calder feared he had left it too late. Then there was a flash of light as the rockets under his seat exploded, the restraints dragged his arms into his sides and he was thrust upwards, into the jet's slipstream, a wall of air moving at five hundred miles an hour. As he tumbled he heard the explosion of the Tornado hitting the mountain, and then the small drogue parachute opened and stopped the whirling.

A moment later he was stable and drifting downwards under the main parachute. He became aware of a twinge in his back. A couple of hundred yards away, the Tornado was burning strongly. He saw the flames licking around the squadron insignia, a lynx's head painted on the giant tailfin. He glanced across at the school, still in one piece, and then beyond that to another smaller fire in a field on the other side of the village, where the Cessna burned. That poor bugger didn't have an ejector seat, he thought.

There was definitely something wrong with his back.

The ground rushed up at him in the shape of a steep slope strewn with rocks. Surprised by the speed of his descent after the brief calm following the opening of his parachute, Calder barely had time to pull his ankles together for landing when he crashed into a large rock and oblivion.

PART ONE

I

The skaters swirled around the tiny rink in the middle of Broadgate Circle, gliding, weaving, twisting, spinning, stumbling, maintaining a relentless anti-clockwise motion. A gangling young man still wearing his pinstripe suit scrabbled on to the ice, barely managing to remain upright for more than a few seconds. He grabbed at the handrail. In his ignorance he tried to force his way clockwise against the current. It broke in front of him and re-formed behind. He fell, bewildered, blinking in the floodlights. Looked around. Understood his mistake. Pulled himself to his feet. Followed the flow.

Calder smiled as he sipped his champagne, embraced by the warm alcoholic fug of Corney and Barrow, the semi-circular bar that overlooked the ice rink. He knew exactly how the man felt. In the first two months of the year he had been fighting against the current, buying Italian bonds when everyone else was selling. Then he'd given up, changed direction, and made a quick two million euros in a trade which he had closed out half an hour earlier. Two million wasn't much – Calder's team had made over forty million for their employer in the previous year, but it was a start. It certainly warranted a bottle of champagne.

'Hey, that looks neat. Shall we try it later?'

Calder turned to Jen, his new junior trader. 'Not tonight. Maybe some other time.' He winced as the man in the suit took another tumble. That ice looked hard. Calder could almost feel the jarring in his fragile back. During his sudden exit from the Tornado eight years before, he had sustained a compression-fractured vertebra, an injury quite common in ejected pilots. In time it had healed to become barely noticeable, and it didn't interfere with his ability to pilot an aircraft, but his spine was weakened and could not be risked in another ejection. No more fast jets. He could have converted to slower aircraft, but that didn't appeal, and so he had requested to leave the air force early.

With trepidation, he had followed some of his Cambridge contemporaries into the City. It had been a good decision: he was a natural at trading bonds just as he had been a natural at flying, and several years on he had developed an intuition about the markets and risk that was earning him, and his employer, a lot of money.

At least he and Jacko were still alive, unlike the pilot of the Cessna, a thirty-year-old entrepreneur from Swansea with two hundred hours' flying time: enough to make him cocky, not enough to make him safe. He had been buzzing low over his uncle's farm and hadn't informed the local air-traffic controllers what he was up to, probably because he knew they would forbid him from doing it.

'Scared I'll show you up?' Jen smiled at Calder, challenging him.

'Can you skate?'

'You bet. Every winter when I was a kid we'd go out on to the fire pond behind our house after school and play hockey. I loved it. I whipped the boys' asses.'

'Well, I doubt you'd whip mine.' Calder had only skated a couple of times before, but he had confidence in his general athletic ability and he was sure he would be able to keep up with her.

'You mean because I'm only a girl?'

'Um . . .' Calder could feel himself reddening slightly. That was what he had meant, although he didn't want to admit it.

She grinned at him. 'Don't worry. I'll spare your embarrassment for now.' Jennifer Tan was American. Chinese-American. The Chinese part you could have guessed from the way she looked, but not from the way she spoke. Brought up in a wealthy suburb of New York, with a post-graduate degree from one of the most selective universities in Boston, she was a fully paid-up member of the East-Coast elite.

She sipped her champagne. 'That's the trouble with this country. No decent winters. What you guys need is some cold blue skies and some real snow instead of this miserable grey damp.' She shuddered. 'It's *so* depressing.'

'You'll get used to it,' Calder said.

'Now why do I find that even more depressing?'

'Oh, come on, London isn't all that bad.'

'No, actually, it's not.' Jen smiled at him over her champagne glass. 'I like my job, for instance. For the first time in a long time I actually look forward to coming in to work in the mornings.'

'I knew I was being too easy on you,' Calder said. 'But you're taking to it well. We'll have you making real money for us soon.'

Jen's eyes searched Calder's, checking for insincerity but finding none. Calder knew she was bright and she had shown a quick grasp of the reasoning behind the trades he put on. He ran the Proprietary Desk in London for Bloomfield Weiss, a large American investment bank. His team of four had the freedom to deal across the world's bond markets for the bank's own account. The trades were big, and complicated, and usually very profitable. Calder was one of Bloomfield Weiss's most successful traders, a rising star with a reputation for taking big risks that made big money. Jen had the potential to succeed too, although she lacked a key ingredient: self-confidence. That was why Calder was careful to encourage her, gently, subtly. She had arrived at his desk with her belief in herself badly damaged. Calder was willing to invest several months to discover if the damage was permanent. But if she didn't shape up by the summer, she'd have to go. There were a limited number of opportunities to make a big profit in the bond markets in any one year and Calder needed decisive traders to take them.

'Oh God,' Jen groaned. 'Look.'

Calder turned. Another group of Bloomfield Weiss employees had taken up their positions at a table a few feet away. They, too, were drinking champagne, which was being poured by a man with a curly mop of fair hair, a pale babyish face and delicate wire-rimmed glasses. Although he looked the youngest of the crowd, he was actually the boss. Justin Carr-Jones.

'Ignore them,' Calder said.

'I can't,' said Jen. 'Let's find another table.'

'There aren't any,' Calder said. The place was filling up. 'Besides, you can't let Carr-Jones scare you away.'

Jen shifted her chair so that her back was to the group. 'I just don't want to be anywhere near him.'

Calder stifled his irritation. 'So he's a jerk. But Bloomfield Weiss is full of jerks. You have to learn to live with them.'

'I guess,' said Jen doubtfully. She sipped her champagne. 'Doesn't that bother you?'

'What?'

'That the firm we work for is full of jerks?'

Calder hesitated. 'No. Not really,' he said. He was her boss, after all. But he could see Jen knew from his tone what he really thought.

'I guess I should have expected it when I joined,' she said. 'Bloomfield Weiss does have a brutal reputation.'

'Oh, I don't know. It's true the firm is known for being aggressive, but there are a lot of decent people who work here, people who would do anything for each other.' Calder couldn't avoid Jen's look of scepticism. 'Or at least there used to be.' He sighed. 'Maybe you are right. Things are changing. Sometimes I get the feeling these days we're outnumbered by the scumbags.'

'Like Justin Carr-Jones?'

'Like Justin Carr-Jones.'

'Doesn't that make you wonder why you work here?'

Calder shook his head. 'It's the same everywhere,' he said.

He realized he was slipping badly from his earlier plan of motivating Jen. 'Bloomfield Weiss is still the best bond house in the market. There's no better place to learn your trade.'

Jen smiled, but Calder could see she wasn't convinced.

Matt and Nils, the two other members of Calder's team, finished their discussion about the spread-betting options for Manchester United's European Champions League game that evening, put down their glasses and took their leave. Calder checked the champagne bottle, which was empty. He didn't want to abandon the warmth of the bar and make the trek back to his cold empty flat, a flat that had felt colder and emptier since Nicky had moved out. He glanced at Jen. 'Shall I get another?'

She nodded her agreement with what seemed to Calder genuine enthusiasm, although she could just be humouring the boss. They broke open the second bottle, and proceeded to get pleasantly drunk in each other's company.

Calder was pouring out the dregs into his glass when he became aware of a presence swaying gently above the table.

He looked up. It was Carr-Jones. Calder knew that Carr-Jones drank rarely, but when he did it went to his head. Quickly. Usually the model of self-discipline, he could lose control after a few glasses.

'Have a good day, Zero?'

'Not bad,' Calder replied, responding to the nickname he had been given by some of the Bloomfield Weiss traders after a particularly successful manoeuvre involving zero-coupon bonds a couple of years before. He felt rather than saw Jen stiffening next to him. 'You? It's rare to see you guys celebrating.'

'Perumal over there just closed a deal.' Carr-Jones nodded towards a slight Indian with skin so dark it was almost black, beaming amongst the crowd of Carr-Jones's traders. 'It was an elephant. A great big enormous fucking elephant. With great big ears and a great big elephant dick that could fuck a . . . could fuck a . . . I don't know what it could fucking fuck.'

'That big, eh?' Calder said.

Carr-Jones ran the Derivatives Group. Derivatives are highly complicated financial instruments, the value of which is determined by formulae based on the movements of different financial markets. Carr-Jones's group made huge profits from selling these derivatives to customers who didn't really understand them. Even allowing for drunken exaggeration, a trade that big must have made Bloomfield Weiss some serious money. Ten million at least.

Carr-Jones grinned and swayed, his normally pale cheeks flushed with two bright red spots. 'You shouldn't have left us, Jen,' he said.

Jen glared at him. 'I'm very glad I did. No matter how big your elephant is.'

'Yeah, you're probably better off now. Bond trading suits your talents.'

'What's that supposed to mean?' Jen snapped.

'Oh, nothing,' Carr-Jones said, his expression one of mock innocence. 'I was just agreeing with you, that's all. And let's face it, the numbers are less complex.'

'I had no trouble with the numbers,' Jen protested.

'No, of course not.'

'Don't patronize me! I've got a goddamned masters degree from MIT in statistics,' Jen said. 'You know that.'

Calder raised his hand to calm her. 'Leave her alone, Justin,' he said reasonably. There was no point in getting into an argument with someone as drunk as Carr-Jones. 'She's doing a great job for me. She'll make an excellent trader.'

'So glad to hear it,' said Carr-Jones. He tried to drink from his glass, but it was empty. He examined the bottles on the table between Calder and Jen. 'You two having a nice time?'

'Yes, thanks,' said Calder, his patience wearing thin.

'Are you shagging him, then?' Carr-Jones asked Jen.

'What?' said Jen in astonishment.

'I said, are you shagging him? You are. You are, aren't you?

I said this job suited your talents.' He grinned, as though pleased with a new discovery.

Jen's face reddened. 'Where did you get that idea?'

'Oh, people talk. Everyone knows.'

'Knows what?'

'About you and Zero. Hey, I'm not knocking it. Whatever works for you.'

Jen opened her mouth to say something, then shut it again. With a hurried movement she pushed back her chair, clutched at her coat and bag and rushed from the table, eyes lowered, letting her straight black hair hang down to hide her distraught face.

'Jen!' Calder shouted as he tried to follow her. But he was wedged in behind the table and by the time he was on his feet she had left the bar.

He turned to Carr-Jones. 'What the hell was that all about?'

Carr-Jones shrugged. 'She's too sensitive, that woman. Always was.'

Calder grabbed Carr-Jones's jacket and pulled him close. Carr-Jones tried to struggle, but Calder was bigger and much stronger. He lifted him almost off his feet. Carr-Jones's eyes widened in alarm through his glasses.

'I know you're pissed out of your brain, but there was no call for that,' Calder muttered through clenched teeth. 'Tomorrow morning I want you to apologize to her, OK?'

'But –'

Calder pulled the trembling banker an inch closer to him. 'I said, OK?'

Carr-Jones nodded his head.

'Now piss off out of here.' Calder pushed Carr-Jones away, just as the bar's manager arrived.

'They're leaving,' Calder said, glaring meaningfully at Carr-Jones's loyal posse of derivatives traders.

They left.

As Calder pulled out his credit card to settle the bill for five bottles of champagne, he thought back to Jen's earlier question.

Why was he still in this business?

By the time Jen's taxi reached her flat in Chelsea, she had calmed down. It had started to rain. The taxi stopped a yard from the kerb next to a huge puddle. She leapt it, and managed to reach the pavement with her shoes dry, only to have her pants drenched a moment later as a bus swept by. She took the ancient lift up to the sixth floor of her building and exchanged scowls with the old lady from the flat opposite, who she had learned from her mail was called Mrs Pinney. For a month Jen had tried to be neighbourly, but she had given up when the woman had physically flinched at her 'Hi, Mrs Pinney, how are you today?' and recoiled into her private lair, muttering something about manners. What was it about her that the woman objected to, Jen wondered. Was it that she was Chinese? Or American? Or just that she was friendly? Jen didn't know. But she began to dislike Mrs Pinney. And as over the course of the winter she returned from work more and more frustrated, the dislike turned to something uncomfortably close to hatred.

She let herself into her tiny flat. It was raining hard, the drops dancing angrily in the pool of yellow light spread across the narrow balcony outside her living-room window. As she drew the curtains, her cell phone beeped. It was a text message from her mother in the States telling her that Vivienne was appearing on one of the business cable TV channels at three thirty New York time, with her top three hot stock tips. Jen checked her watch. Eight thirty-three. She grabbed a tube of Pringles from the kitchen, and flipped on the TV set.

There she was, Vivienne, her telegenic elder sister, an equities analyst at a major New York stockbroker who in recent months had begun to appear on television with her weekly stock picks. Jen watched as Vivienne praised the investment qualities of a manufacturer of plastic plumbing supplies. Admittedly there was something attractive about the way Vivienne spoke, Jen thought sourly; she appeared to know what she was talking about and to believe it. But she wasn't smart. She wasn't nearly as smart as Jen. Yet somehow that fact, which seemed so obvious to Jen, had always been lost on her parents. Vivienne should have been a weather girl – at least then her predictions would have come right occasionally.

Justin Carr-Jones's words came flooding back. How could he really think she was sleeping with Alex Calder? It's true that she liked him: life was so much better now she was working for him rather than Carr-Jones. He was considerate, fair and he listened to what she had to say. Like Carr-Jones, he was very good at his job, but unlike Carr-Jones, he was willing to explain why. And she had to admit, he was kind of cute, with those calm, thoughtful blue-grey eyes, and that little V-shaped notch on his forehead. She couldn't help noticing his lean supple body, which exuded a kind of controlled energy and strength that set him apart from the other sedentary slobs on the trading desk. But she prided herself on her professionalism. She would never sleep with the boss.

It wasn't the direct accusation itself that offended her, but all the assumptions that lay underneath it. That Jen could never be as smart as Carr-Jones's other, male, traders. That the only reason that she had achieved as much as she had was because she looked good. That her principal asset to Bloomfield Weiss was the promise of sex that her very gender suggested. She remembered how just after she had joined his desk the previous year Carr-Jones had asked her to accompany him taking some important clients out for the evening. When she met him in the lobby she was wearing a two-thousand-dollar Armani trouser suit. He had taken one look at her and told her to go home and change into a skirt, a short one, and join him and the clients at the restaurant. To her subsequent regret she had done as he had asked.

Carr-Jones seemed to view all women this way. The only other female on his desk, a big English blonde called Tessa, had been happy to go along with this treatment, in fact she took advantage of it. But Jen just couldn't. What made it worse was that Carr-Jones had just come back from a two-year stint in Tokyo where the Asian hostesses he had met while entertaining clients had clearly made an impression. Jen sometimes thought she was supposed to be his tame geisha. She had hoped that she had escaped when she had transferred to the Prop Desk, but Carr-Jones was only a few yards away, and his taunts still had the power to enflame her with indignation and shame.

Vivienne laughed at her from a distance of three thousand miles. Jen flicked the switch on the remote, and dug out a CD. Rap. She used to hate that kind of music, but a few months after moving to London she had bought an album by Eminem, then another and then another. She liked to play it loud, letting the angry words wash over her.

She didn't like the woman she was becoming. Sour, angry, negative. So negative. With the exception of a female lawyer whom she had known at college and whose working life was as bad as her own, she had no friends in London. The weather was miserable, the nights were long, tradesmen never fixed what they said they were going to fix, work was a nightmare. She wanted to murder Mrs Pinney and the female radio presenter who seemed to find the daily forecasts of sodden gloom so amusing when she woke Jen up every morning. She couldn't believe now that she had told Calder things had changed since she had started working for him. Who was she kidding? Just herself.

She hadn't always been like this. When she had joined Bloomfield Weiss in New York straight out of MIT she had been an enthusiastic optimist, determined to work hard and succeed, but equally determined to enjoy herself as she did so. She liked derivatives. She found great pleasure in breaking down the most complicated of transactions into their component parts and rebuilding them. And she was good at it too. Which is why she had been given a plum posting to London to work for Justin Carr-Jones, one of Bloomfield Weiss's top producers.

She shouldn't have let Carr-Jones's taunts get to her. He was drunk, he didn't know what he was saying. He wasn't even her boss any more. She knew what her parents would tell her: ignore it, Jen. If she worked hard, eventually things would come right for her. They had for her father, who had arrived in America in the 1970s from the People's Republic of China as a graduate student in particle physics and was now one of the world's foremost experts on microwave filter technology at Bell Labs. Or even Vivienne, who had overcome mediocre exam scores to pull down a salary of several hundred thousand a year on Wall Street. You didn't complain. You put your head down and showed them who was best.

But Jen wasn't just Chinese, she was American. At the liberal-arts college she had attended in the wooded hills of western Massachusetts she had been taught that women had a right to be treated the same as men. More than that, they had a duty to demand that right. It wasn't weak to complain, it was strong. Unless strong women stood up for themselves, men like Carr-Jones would take advantage of the weak.

Dammit, she thought, what he was doing was wrong, it was as simple as that. She couldn't let him get away with it.

She should have listened to her parents. Then she might have lived to see them again.

2

Calder was sitting at his screens, processing information. The information was coming from many different sources. Four flat screens, each in turn broken into several windows containing broker's prices (green on black), Excel spreadsheets (red and blue on grey), news from Bloomberg (orange on black), and Reuters (black on off-white), a trading blotter, an e-mail 'in-tray', a web-browser and real-time feeds of futures prices from exchanges on three continents. Numbers blinked and flashed, or even beeped as they changed. The occasional crackle and terse announcement came from two squawk boxes, one connected to the bond brokers Calder used most often and the other to Bloomfield Weiss's trading desks dotted in half a dozen time zones around the world.

In the RAF Calder had learned to process information quickly. In addition to the standard fast-jet flight instruments, the Tornado he had flown had a Head-Up Display that etched green numbers and lines on everything he looked at, a moving map, a terrain-following E-Scope and radar-warning equipment. Behind him had been a navigator constantly relaying information from his own array of gadgetry. And outside the cockpit images of land and sky flew by at five hundred miles an hour. Then he had learned how to sort through information and take decisions in less than a second. He had hours now, but the decisions were no easier.

Homer Simpson grinned down on Calder as he watched and listened. A moronic, yellow, foam-rubber Homer, bearing the marks of the dozens of times he had been flung against walls and screens, trampled upon and, on one occasion, even bitten. Calder had never liked Homer Simpson. One morning he had come into work to find Homer staring down at him from behind the Bloomberg screen. He had ditched Homer in the nearest bin, only to find him back on his perch after lunch. He had left with Homer that night and dumped him in a skip over the road from the office. Still there next morning. He had even taken Homer back home with him and buried him in his own wheelie-bin, to no avail. It was clear that one of the other traders had bought a job lot of Homer Simpsons, and eventually Calder gave up trying to find out just how big that job lot was.

Homer had no clue what was going on in the Italian government bond market, and neither did Calder. Someone was selling Italian government bonds. Selling them and selling them. Whoever it was was willing to take a lot of pain. Because whenever the market bounced back, they sold more. Calder was plugged into the rumour mill, and the rumour mill suggested that the seller was a man called Jean-Luc Martel, who managed a hedge fund from a remote hideaway in the Rocky Mountains. Whoever he was, he was building a massive position.

Hedge funds were some of the most sophisticated players in the markets. They sold short as well as bought, and they played in any market they chose: bonds, equities, currencies, oil, pork-bellies, even weather. Many were tiny, many satisfied themselves by smoothing out market inefficiencies for small profits, but some took big bets in big size. Martel's fund was one of these: he was selling hundreds of millions of euros of Italian government bonds he didn't own in the hope that he would make money when the price fell and he could buy them back at a lower price.

But this guy made no sense. The prices of Italian government bonds, known as BTPs, were already low, much lower than their French or German counterparts. True the Italian economy was suffering badly. The European Central Bank had been raising interest rates over the previous twelve months, spooked by the sudden strength of the French and German economies and fear of the inflation dragon waking up from its twenty-year slumber. Italy was struggling, it was in the middle of a recession, unemployment was rising sharply, the budget deficit was out of control and high interest rates were the last thing it needed.

But there was nothing Italy could do. It was a member of the euro zone, its debt was denominated in the same currency as France, Germany and the others, its interest rates were set in Frankfurt by the ECB. There was no way out. A couple of maverick economists and a disgraced former finance minister had urged the Italian government to ditch the euro, but that was a fantasy. In fact Bloomfield Weiss had paid for numerous legal opinions at the time the euro was established that had proved it was a fantasy. The promise never to quit the euro had been enshrined in the treaties of Maastricht and Amsterdam and hence into European law, which took precedence over the laws of the individual member states. Italy was stuck with the euro and the euro with Italy.

And as long as Italy remained in the euro zone, its bonds shouldn't trade far out of line with their French or German equivalents.

The Prime Minister had just announced his resignation amidst a corruption scandal and the governing centre-right coalition had fallen apart. As a result there was an election looming in a month or so, and elections unsettled bond markets. But Italy was always having elections and Calder couldn't see what was so special about this one.

Calder stared at his screens. So BTPs looked cheap. Should he buy some more, and risk getting burned yet again? He felt a dull ache at the base of his spine. His old injury warning him. Be careful.

He looked around for Jen, with the intention of posing the question rather than discovering the answer. She wasn't in yet. He checked the big clock hanging beneath the Bloomfield Weiss logo on one side of the trading room. Nine thirty. That was late. For a dealing room, that was very late.

'Matt? Heard anything from Jen?'

'Nope,' said Matt, who was tapping prices into his computer.

'Nils?'

The flabby Dane shook his head while still speaking on the phone. On a trading desk it was taken for granted that you could carry on at least three conversations at once.

Calder frowned. Bugger Carr-Jones. After all Calder's own gentle stroking of Jen's ego, Carr-Jones had screwed the whole thing up in five minutes. Unless Jen could forget him, she was never going to be any use on Calder's desk. Which would be a pity.

Calder glanced across to the Derivatives Group, only a few desks away. Carr-Jones was standing with a telephone receiver close to his ear, calm, sober, cufflinks shining through pink shirtsleeves, tie fastened tight, trousers pleated and pressed. He still looked young, like a schoolboy, but one of those eighteen-year-old self-assured public-school prefects, not the product of the south-Wales comprehensive that Calder knew he had actually attended. By a quirk of dealing-room geography the derivatives desk was slightly apart from all the others, an impression of distance that the group tried to cultivate. They saw themselves as the elite of Bloomfield Weiss's London office, the innovators, the financial engineers of the twenty-first century and, most importantly, the people who made the really big money.

Which was true. In his first year back in London, Carr-Jones's group had made profits of one hundred and thirty-two million dollars. An obscene amount.

Calder left his screen and wandered over to Carr-Jones, who ignored him as he continued his phone call. Calder waited.

Eventually Carr-Jones put down the phone and faced Calder.

'Justin. Remember last night?'

'I remember you physically assaulting me,' Carr-Jones replied.

'Do you remember what you said to Jen?'

'Would you excuse me, I've got work to do,' he said, turning back to his phone.

'You promised to apologize to her.'

Carr-Jones began punching out a phone number. 'You threatened me.'

'You were drunk.'

Carr-Jones leaned back in his chair, receiver pinned to his ear. 'So, I take it, were you. Which is why I will forget you attacking me. Oh, hello, Klaus,' he said, switching into smooth salesman mode and leaning forward. 'How are you today?' He smiled quickly at Calder, and then turned away from him.

Calder shook his head and returned to his desk. Jen was right. What was he doing working with people like that?

Ten minutes later she arrived, dressed as usual in a white top and expensive black trouser-suit. She placed her slim briefcase carefully by her desk, which was next to Calder's, sat down without taking her jacket off and turned on her screens. There was an air of quiet determination about her.

'Morning, Jen,' Calder smiled.

'Sorry I'm late.'

'That's all right. When you've checked the market, I'd like to have a chat about Italy. It's acting weird again.'

'OK,' she replied, without moving her eyes from her screens.

Calder stared at her. 'Are you all right?' he said. It was clear she wasn't.

Jen turned to him. 'Can we talk?'

'Sure.'

'In private?'

Calder frowned and led Jen away to one of the small glass conference rooms that edged one side of the dealing room. Occasionally these were used for meetings with clients. More commonly they were used for internal manoeuvring, rumour manufacturing and distribution, politics, conspiracies, corporate assassinations. Calder hated them. He was also concerned that Jen brought her briefcase with her.

They sat down on either side of a small table. 'Shoot,' said Calder.

'I want to make a complaint against Justin Carr-Jones,' Jen said.

Calder winced. This was bad. 'An official complaint?'

Jen dug into her briefcase and came out with a green ring-binder entitled *Bloomfield Weiss Human Interaction Protocols.* Calder winced again. She flipped open the ring binder to a page marked with a yellow sticky note. *Section 11: Sexual harassment and discrimination.*

'It says here that I must make the complaint in the first instance to my line manager. That's you.'

'Don't do it, Jen.'

'Here.' She handed him a single sheet of paper. Calder scanned it. It described succinctly the incident of the night before. It made the claim that this was the latest of many similar incidents that Jen had suffered. And it demanded that action be taken. Jen's spiky signature was scrawled on the bottom.

Calder carefully placed the sheet on the table between them. 'You don't want to do this, Jen.'

'I want Justin Carr-Jones disciplined.'

'I'm sure you do. But it's not going to happen.'

'Why the hell not? You were there. You heard what he said to me yesterday.'

'Yes, I was there. And I agree he was completely out of order. But this . . .' Calder flicked the paper towards her, 'this will just make things much worse.'

'Why?'

'Because Carr-Jones is the biggest revenue producer in the London office. He's one of the biggest revenue producers in the whole firm. And, as you well know, he's a shit. He'll make mincemeat of you. Your career here will be over. There will be nothing I can do to protect you.'

Jen looked at Calder in shock. 'I don't believe this. I thought you, of all people, would support me on this.'

'I will support you, Jen. I think you have a good future in this firm working with me as a proprietary trader. You've got a good brain and good instincts, and I'll make sure you get good training. Carr-Jones can't stop you from succeeding here unless you let him. This will let him.'

'You're just covering for him.'

Calder took a deep breath. 'I'm not covering for him. I'm being rational about it –'

'Meaning I'm not being rational?' snapped Jen.

'Meaning you're about to take a very bad decision and I want to stop you.'

'You want to stop me blowing a hole in Bloomfield Weiss's cosy men's locker room.'

'Come on, Jen, that's unfair, and you know it. What I can do is talk to Carr-Jones. Get him to apologize.'

'He'll never apologize.'

'He might have to.'

'If he did he wouldn't mean it. Anyway, I want him disciplined. Officially.'

'It won't work.'

'I want you to pass my letter on to Human Resources.'

'I won't do it.'

'It says here,' Jen said, stabbing the folder in front of her, 'that if I don't get satisfaction from my line manager, I should go to HR directly myself.'

Calder looked at the sheet of paper and at Jen. 'I'm sorry. I'm not going to help you blow up your own career. You can take this to HR if you want. But I strongly advise you not to.'

Jen glared at Calder. Without another word she snapped the folder shut and slid it and her letter into her briefcase. A moment later she was back at her desk, on the phone to HR, trying to fix up an immediate appointment. Calder glanced over to Carr-Jones, talking on his own phone, oblivious to what was going on. Bastard. Calder admired Jen's courage in standing up to him and if he had thought there was the slightest chance that she would succeed in getting him disciplined then he would have supported her. But of one thing he was sure: there was none.

As Jen picked up her briefcase and strode off to her meeting with HR, Calder felt a profound gloom settle over him. He hated to watch a potentially good trader throw away her career.

3

Jean-Luc Martel stretched his long, long frame and spun his four-thousand-dollar leather swivel chair away from the mess of the European bond markets towards the dawn. The delicate pink fingers of a sun which was still hidden behind the mountains to the east stroked the snow-covered tree-flecked slopes of the Tetons, and brushed the low-voltage luminescent blue of the sky above. The town of Jackson slumbered below, cosy in its 'Hole', the twenty-mile-long valley that followed the path of the Snake River through this stretch of the Rockies. Martel loved to come in this early, when the markets of London and Frankfurt were already active but the day had yet to begin in Wyoming.

Two decades before he had left the stifling restrictions of the Parisian financial establishment for the hurly-burly of New York's markets. After ten years he felt he had mastered them, and he began to find even the ruthlessly meritocratic investment bank he worked for too restrictive. So he had set up his own fund, in this mountain paradise, to take on the world's markets from afar. He had done well. Spectacularly well. A million dollars invested with his Teton Fund in 1994 was now worth nearly twenty million. He had been short the yen in 1998 and he had made money out of the hedge-fund disasters of that same year. He had ridden NASDAQ all the way up in 1999 and all the way down in 2001. He had sold oil in 2003 a couple of months before the invasion of Iraq. And he had done it all using leverage, borrowed money, the rocket fuel that turned a one-dollar movement in a market into a ten-dollar profit for the Teton Fund.

Martel fancied himself as a philosopher, a philosopher of

what he called behavioural evolution. He could quote Francis Galton, Daniel Bernoulli, Charles Darwin and Richard Thaler in bewildering combinations. He believed he traded fundamentals. Where other traders used this phrase to mean the fundamental strength of a particular company or market, Martel meant the fundamentals of human nature, especially the agglomeration of human nature that makes up a marketplace: greed, fear, euphoria, panic. But his most deeply held belief was one he had learned from the poker table as a young man. The player with the deepest pockets wins.

His successes had made him well known in the markets, but not outside. This frustrated Martel. He was the smartest investor in the world, and he was upset that the world didn't recognize it. Two men particularly irritated him. Warren Buffett, whose ability to accumulate billions by sitting on his hands and watching his investments grow placed him in a different category from Martel. And George Soros. Now there was a man Martel could emulate, and eventually surpass.

Soros was not trading actively himself any more, but he was still widely known as the world's most successful hedge-fund investor. His Quantum Fund had posted huge gains during the nineteen eighties and nineties, culminating in the rumoured billion dollars he had made when he speculated successfully against the Bank of England in 1992 as the markets ejected the pound from the European Exchange Rate Mechanism.

Like Soros, Martel was of Eastern European ancestry – his grandparents had come from Poland to France at the beginning of the twentieth century and his name had been Młotek before his father had changed it to Martel when he was twelve. Like Soros, he was a philosopher. Like Soros he was brilliant. Soon, the world would recognize these facts.

Perhaps very soon. The Teton Fund was short four billion euros' worth of Italian government bonds and Martel was selling more every day. Already his profit was twenty million euros, but he was expecting much more in the coming months.

He felt a discreet buzzing at his waist. He checked his Blackberry, a small mobile device that he always kept attached to his belt. It was an instant message from Walter Lesser, who ran a hedge fund in New York. Many hedge-fund managers would instant message each other all day long. They preferred it to e-mail, it was faster and it left no trace for regulators to examine later.

Hey Jean-Luc. You still shorting the BTPs?

Martel smiled, and flicked his fingers and thumbs over the compact keyboard of the Blackberry.

Yep. And it's got a lot further to go.

A moment later:

They say it's impossible for Italy to leave the euro. Unconstitutional.

Martel replied:

That's what they say. But I've got a law professor in Milan who says different. Do you want his report?

Martel waited, his excitement building. To his annoyance, the major hedge-fund players had never really accepted him as one of their number. Walter wasn't one of the biggest funds, but he spoke to the really big guys every day. If he could get Walter on side, then he'd tell his friends and Martel's trade would build up momentum.

It took a full minute before the response came back:

Send it.

Martel grinned and scanned the pile of papers in his office.

The room had started life as a plush executive suite with deep carpets and expensive art, but had since been overrun by a whirlwind of energy. Almost every inch of the walls was covered with newspaper cuttings, photographs, cartoons, aphorisms and white boards and flip charts sprayed with manic arrows describing trading strategies. The floor and desk surfaces were ninety per cent submerged below paper, although a medicine ball and some weights were strewn around the far corners. The Italian information overwhelmed a low steel and glass table and the carpet surrounding it. Martel picked out the law professor's report, which was on the pile next to one of his wife's Indian vases, scribbled a note and left it on his assistant's desk outside his office. As he returned to his own desk he glanced at the portrait of his wife, hanging on the wall opposite, a patch of serenity amid the chaos. It was a beautiful painting of a very beautiful woman. Perhaps he ought to commission the artist to paint him working here, in his office, on top of the world? At the very moment he was fashioning the trade that would change history. Worth a thought.

He stared at the nineteen-inch flat screen that dominated his desk. The prices of the Italian bonds were highlighted, gently ticking up and down. He knew it was a waste of time to stare at numbers, but sometimes, on mornings like this, he just liked to gloat.

Suddenly the price of the bellwether BTP flashed and gapped down three quarters of a point. He checked his Bloomberg screen to see why. Sure enough, there was a one-line item of news.

Leader of the right-wing Democratic National Party, Massimo Tagliaferi, announces that former finance minister Guido Gallotti had joined his campaign. Gallotti is a forceful advocate of Italy leaving euro.

Tagliaferi, the energetic owner of one of the country's largest industrial holding companies, was an outsider to win the coming election, but for the first time a credible Italian party was saying the unsayable, and in the process highlighting the fragility of Italian membership of the euro. The bond markets were spooked and Martel's trade was rolling.

Martel hit the button of his squawk box. 'Hey, Andy. Get in here!'

A moment later, Andy, his young but extremely smart bond trader, was in his office grinning from ear to ear. 'I guess you saw the news?'

'I did. And I have just spoken with Walter Lesser. He's interested.'

'Do we take profits?' the trader asked. 'We've got to be close to a hundred million up.'

'Do we take profits?' Martel repeated, his brown eyes bulging as he stared hard at his subordinate. 'Do we take profits? What do you think? *Hein?*'

Andy paused. He realized he had made a mistake, but there was no going back. 'Well, we've done pretty well, and I kinda thought . . .'

Martel threw himself and his chair back from his desk and leapt to his feet. 'You don't listen to me, do you?' He began pacing along his favourite runway by the window, which he kept clear of papers. He was just over two metres tall, and it took him only a few strides to reach the far wall. He might be forty-five, but he kept himself in good shape. With a tanned body well honed by fresh air and exercise and dark curly hair with only the first flecks of grey, he had the drive and the energy of a man ten years younger.

'We are not trying to make a couple of million here. Opportunities like this do not come along every day. This is the trade of the century. The trade of the millennium. Italy is going to crack. The economy is screwed, the government is screwed, the bond market is screwed. Within two months Italy will leave the euro.' Martel was speeding up, his long arms waving wildly. Once he got like this Andy always expected him to knock over some of the junk in his office, but he never did. Suddenly he stopped and stared at Andy with those bulging eyes. 'And once everyone realizes that, you know what will happen to Italian bonds?'

Andy was twenty-nine with an MBA, and one year he had pulled down a seven-figure bonus on Wall Street. He looked up at the towering Frenchman and thought how much he hated being treated like a five-year-old. But he had seen Martel in these kinds of moods before. There was no option but to humour him. 'Prices will fall.'

'Prices will fall. And fall some more. You know the Petersburg Paradox?'

'No,' said Andy. He was sure that Martel had explained it to him before but he hadn't listened.

'It explains everything.' Martel launched into a convoluted explanation of Bernoulli's Petersburg Paradox, something about the problems of valuing trading profits that increase exponentially. 'You understand?' he said when he had finished.

'Yes,' said Andy, although in truth he didn't see what relevance it had to the price of BTPs in the twenty-first century.

Martel turned towards the snow-covered mountain behind him, now glittering in the early morning light. 'So what do we do?'

This question Andy knew the answer to. 'We do more.'

'Exactly. I want to be short two billion more euros by tomorrow.'

'Two billion! The market's gonna move away from us on that size.'

Martel turned. 'Go to work, Andy.'

Andy went to work.

Martel smiled. He knew Andy was a good trader, his only problem was he just didn't know when to go into the market in size. Massive size. Very few people had the combination of skilful judgement and courage to be able to do that. George Soros had it, of course. And so did Jean-Luc Martel.

There was a tentative knock on the open door to his office.

'Hey, Vikram, you're back!'

'I got in last night.'

Vikram Rana was Martel's derivatives trader and one of his most loyal henchmen. Vikram had been born in India, but like Martel had taken to America with enthusiasm. At six foot three he was only four inches shorter than his boss, with a broad chest and flat stomach sculpted by many hours in the gym, skin that was no darker than Martel's skiing tan, and flashing black eyes. He was also very smart, one of those rare quants who was clever enough both to understand the most complicated of derivatives and to use that knowledge to work on the greed and carelessness of the other players in the market.

'So, we're done?' Martel asked.

'We're done.'

'That was one great trade.'

Vikram smiled, his white teeth gleaming. 'They fell for it. We've got them, like a tiger pouncing on the goat.' Vikram's American accent was much more authentic than Martel's. He'd worked hard at it.

Martel didn't give a damn about his. 'Do Bloomfield Weiss know what they've done?'

Vikram shrugged. 'I guess so. I dealt with an Indian guy called Perumal. I could see the only thing he was thinking about was how big a fee they'd be making from the deal. Fifteen million bucks, by my calculations.'

'Don't worry,' said Martel. 'If that's what it takes to hook them, that's fine. We'll make many times that when we've finished. Now what is it exactly we've bought?'

'It's pretty complicated. They call it an IGLOO note. It stands for Italian Government Lira Obligation Option. It's a bond redeemable in euros in twenty years' time if Italy stays in the euro, but if Italy leaves, then we get paid back in a year and the redemption price is based on a multiple of the devaluation of the new Italian currency against the euro. We also get paid a very high coupon if Italian interest rates rise above a certain level.'

'So we make some money if the Italian bond markets fall, and a shitload if Italy leaves the euro?'

'That's the idea.'

'Who's the issuer?'

'Doesn't matter. It can be any top credit. The first IGLOO note will be issued by the World Development Fund, I think. It's just a cheap way for them to borrow two hundred million euros. They don't take any of the Italy risk, Bloomfield Weiss lays that off elsewhere for them.'

'Bottom line?'

'I checked the numbers on the plane last night. If Italy does quit the euro, and the new currency falls like we think it will, then we make four hundred million dollars on our two hundred million investment.'

'And if Italy stays in?'

'Then we're left with a twenty-year note in euros paying us half a per cent. We'd lose about a hundred and fifty million.'

'But Bloomfield Weiss will give us eighty per cent financing?'

'They sure will. I told them any less and I'd do the trade elsewhere.'

'Nice, Vikram, very nice,' Martel said, rubbing his hands. And it was. This last concession meant that Bloomfield Weiss would lend the Teton Fund eighty per cent of the money to buy these IGLOO notes. So Martel only had to put up forty million of the two hundred million IGLOO notes he wanted to buy. If things went according to plan, that forty million dollars would become four hundred million. Ten times his stake, what was known as a ten-bagger in the trade.

And if it all went wrong? Martel didn't think about that. It wasn't an issue.

He looked out of his window, at the great wall of rock that was the Teton Range, and the chiselled peak of the Grand Teton at its eastern edge, wisps of cloud swirling in an ever changing dance around it. The mountain was new in geological terms, thrown up from the flat plain of the Snake River by a fault at its foot. It emitted a power, a kind of primeval magnetism, that enthralled Martel and inspired his greatest decisions. He had set up his Teton Fund in this mountain eyrie to give distance and perspective from the world's markets. In this pure air and pure snow, he could see clearly. And clarity of vision was what running a successful hedge fund was all about. In these days of optical fibre and broadband communications information travelled instantaneously anywhere on the planet. It was what you did with it that mattered.

Two thousand miles to the east was the financial sweatshop of New York, and a few thousand miles further on, Europe. He smiled as he thought of those finance ministers, those central bankers, those bureaucrats who didn't yet realize that the future of their beloved euro was in his hands.

His phone rang. He grabbed it.

It was his assistant, who must have just arrived for work. 'Jean-Luc. I've got Lawrence Baldwin of the *Wall Street Journal* on the line. Do you want to talk to him?'

'Of course,' said Martel, taking his seat. Time to tell the world what he was up to.

4

The room in HR had comfortable armchairs, potted plants and soothing prints on the walls, but the atmosphere was tense. Apart from Calder, there were five people present: Jen, Carr-Jones, Linda Stubbes the head of Human Resources, Benton Davis the head of the London office and Tarek al-Seesi, head of Fixed Income in London and Calder's boss.

Linda handed Jen's letter to everyone present. Calder took his without looking at it. He distrusted Linda Stubbes, if only because she was in HR. By its very nature HR dealt with all those aspects of corporate life that Calder hated most: recruitment policies, salaries, bonuses, reorganizations, redundancies. He knew that many of the employees at Bloomfield Weiss lived and breathed these issues, and it was Linda's job to involve herself in all the negotiating, plotting and back-stabbing that surrounded them. But he had to admit that in a world where loyalty was increasingly rare, Linda had plenty of it. She had joined Bloomfield Weiss's London office twenty years earlier, when it took up no more than one floor of a building near the Stock Exchange, and had worked her way up to the position of power she now occupied.

Benton Davis had also done his time at Bloomfield Weiss. He was an American, a tall, athletic black man in his late forties who had spent the last ten years in London. Always immaculately dressed, he affected an interest in higher things than the day-to-day money-grubbing activities of the firm he worked for. But the opera, the nice house in Holland Park, the expensive clothes, the 'cottage' on Martha's Vineyard, required big bonuses, and Benton never forgot that. Although Head of the London Office was a grand title, it meant that he was one step away from the revenue-generators, the likes of Calder and Carr-Jones. This was not necessarily good news at bonus time.

The third boss in the room, Tarek al-Seesi, was a friend of Calder and the likely owner of the job lot of Homer Simpsons. The third son of a Saudi merchant family, he was a canny trader and had run the Proprietary Desk before being promoted the year before to take over Fixed Income. He and Calder had made a powerful team when they worked together on the Prop Desk: Calder's aggression complemented Tarek's subtlety and intuition. The two men respected each other; Calder had learned much from Tarek and missed the way they used to toss trading ideas back and forth all day.

Tarek was still building his political base. Calder reported to him, as did all the other bond traders and salesmen in Europe, but Carr-Jones didn't. The Derivatives Group in London reported directly to the Derivatives Group in New York. Although he was nominally the big boss, no one who mattered reported to Benton Davis. As in some fifteenth-century royal court, power and influence at Bloomfield Weiss were constantly shifting. But if in the time of the Wars of the Roses power ultimately lay with the leader of the strongest army, in Bloomfield Weiss it lay with the man who produced the most revenue.

And that was Justin Carr-Jones.

'I've called you all here to discuss the complaint made by Jen in this letter,' Linda began. 'Very often it's possible to deal with problems like these face-to-face. This avoids the need for a full-scale investigation that can be painful for everyone.' She looked directly at Jen as she said this. Jen was perched on the forward edge of her armchair, legs together, hands folded on her lap, briefcase at her side. 'Perhaps you can tell us what happened?'

'It's all in the note,' Jen said. 'Justin accused me of sleeping with Alex. I found that deeply offensive. Especially since it was just the latest of many similar remarks.'

'Wait, this was in a bar, wasn't it?' Benton Davis said.

'Yes.'

'So it wasn't on Bloomfield Weiss property?'

'It's my understanding that that doesn't matter in cases like this,' Jen said, glancing at Linda.

Linda nodded minutely.

'And you had been drinking?' Benton Davis went on.

'Yes.'

'As had Justin? And Alex Calder?'

'Yes,' said Jen.

'You're a trader, aren't you? Isn't this the kind of comment that goes on in trading rooms all the time?' There was a note of distaste in Benton's voice. He came from the more cultured world of corporate finance, and was scarcely ever seen in the trading room.

'It does,' said Jen. 'But that doesn't mean that it should.'

Calder glanced at Linda Stubbes. She was looking increasingly uncomfortable at Benton Davis's questioning, but she kept her mouth shut. She was one of the few who did report directly to him, after all.

'Weren't you being a little over-sensitive?'

'I don't believe so.' Jen's reply was hoarse. Benton was an imposing figure and this was an important moment for her.

'Oh, come on. You live in the twenty-first century. You have to be tough to be a trader at Bloomfield Weiss, everyone on the street understands that. Now I know you've had a difficult patch these last couple of years, you didn't make the cut in derivatives, but you just have to put that behind you. Not let it upset you. Perhaps you should drop this complaint, take a couple of weeks off, come back and we'll see what we can do for you then.'

'No!' said Jen, her face reddening. 'I was doing really well in New York before I was transferred here. I would have gotten on fine in the Derivatives Group if Justin had let me. But he did everything he could to undermine me. He picked on me.'

'I can understand your frustration,' said Benton. 'We all go through bad patches in our careers. But you shouldn't let it drive you on to petty revenge.'

'This is not revenge!' Jen shouted in a voice an octave too high. There was silence as everyone in the room stared at her. She stopped herself. Clasped her hands in front of her. Her chin wobbled. A tear appeared in the eye closest to Calder. He desperately wanted to put his arm around her, but he feared that that would only make things worse, underline Jen's weakness. He had intended that he wouldn't get involved, but he had to say something.

'Jen's allegations are perfectly clear. Perhaps we should hear what Justin has to say about them.'

Benton frowned. 'At this stage we're exploring ways of avoiding an investigation.'

'Perhaps Justin would be prepared to apologize,' Calder went on.

'There's no need for that,' said Benton.

Calder ignored him. 'Justin?'

Carr-Jones sat still. 'I have nothing to apologize for.'

'Do you deny that you accused Jen of sleeping with me?'

'I don't confirm or deny anything,' Justin said. 'But I do know that this is wasting all of our time. It's been blown out of all proportion.' He checked his watch. 'Now, I don't know about you guys, but I have some deals to do. Can we wrap this up?'

'So you won't withdraw your complaint?' Benton Davis said to Jen.

'No I will not,' Jen said. Despite all her efforts, her eyes were watering. 'It's like you're accusing me. It doesn't make any sense . . . I haven't done anything wrong here . . . I . . .' She blinked once. A single tear slowly made its way down her cheek. She made no movement to touch it, as if by ignoring it none of the rest of the people in the room would notice.

There was silence. Jen was still sitting upright, her eyes

lowered, focusing on Linda Stubbes's shoes. Red blotches had appeared on her cheeks. The tear swerved into the corner of her mouth and she touched it with the tip of her tongue.

'Hormones,' said Carr-Jones. 'She'll be fine in a day or two. Let's just ignore it and go back to work.'

Jen sniffed and raised her eyes defiantly. Linda Stubbes glared at Carr-Jones. 'That was an inappropriate remark,' she said.

'It may be inappropriate, but you know it's true,' he replied with a knowing smirk.

'Linda,' Tarek said, speaking for the first time. 'It looks like we're not going to get agreement on this. Justin has made it clear he doesn't want to apologize, and it seems Jen doesn't want to withdraw her allegation.' All eyes turned to Jen, who shook her head. 'So where does that leave us?'

'The company policy on sexual harassment is clear,' Linda replied. 'We implement a formal investigation.'

'Thank you,' said Jen, managing a small smile.

Benton Davis frowned at Linda, and Carr-Jones raised his eyebrows, but Linda was busy writing notes on the pad of paper on her knee. 'If it's OK with Alex, I suggest that you don't spend too much time in the office until the investigation is over. As I said earlier, these situations can be difficult.'

Calder nodded, as did Jen.

She had won round one. But Calder somehow doubted she would last the distance.

'Benton? Simon Bibby.'

'Ah, Simon, old man, how the devil are you?' Benton Davis smiled as he spoke. It was a fake smile. Speaking to Simon Bibby, the Englishman based in New York who headed Global Fixed Income, was never any fun.

'I've just been talking to Justin,' Bibby said. 'I want you to make this problem with Jennifer Tan go away.'

'I understand, Simon,' Benton said. 'I was speaking with her only this morning and I suggested she think again.'

'Because there are rumours. Leipziger Gurney Kroheim are looking to hire a derivatives team. They'll pay top dollar. And they're going after Justin. If he goes and he takes his team with him, we've got at least a hundred-million-dollar hole in the P&L right there.'

'Hm. That would be a blow.'

'Too right,' Bibby said. 'Can't we just fire her? It's not as though she's any good anyway, is it?'

'You're right. We wouldn't miss her. I'll look into it, Simon.'

'You do that. Because if we lost London's top revenue-producer as the result of an HR cock-up, that would look bad. Very bad.'

'Of course, don't worry about a thing. I'll take care of it.' Benton's voice was deep and reassuring. 'You know, Simon, I did want to tip you off about the Mondrian exhibition. I went to see it at the Tate Modern the other day, and it's really jolly good. I understand it's travelling to New York next month . . .'

Benton paused as he heard a muttered 'Jesus Christ' and the phone went dead. He frowned and placed his own receiver into its cradle. He shut his eyes. His skills, which had won many a deal, were becoming obsolete. Benton was the master of the civilized conversation, the subtle prod, the gentle suggestion. He had charmed the British corporate establishment with his deep American voice peppered with Anglicisms, and his knowledge of the British cultural scene. He knew Glyndebourne, Covent Garden, Lord's, St Andrews and the polo fields of Windsor intimately. But the British establishment was changing. American-educated MBAs were taking over from the clubbable knights. Suddenly, at under fifty, he was too old.

There had been whispers about moving him back to New York, sitting him on a trading desk to win deal mandates from the black leaders of America's big cities. Benton shuddered. Because if they told him to, he'd have to do it. He needed the money.

He flipped the intercom. 'Stella, can you tell Linda Stubbes to come up here, please?'

Two minutes later Linda was sitting in the comfortable upright chair across the wide expanse of his desk.

'I just wanted to have a little chat with you about this problem with Jennifer Tan,' Benton began.

'I see.'

'It's a shame we have to launch an investigation.'

'It's unavoidable, I'm afraid. It was clear this morning that there's no chance of the two of them sorting it out between them.'

'Can't we just . . .' Benton paused, 'I don't know, get rid of her somehow?'

'No, Benton. We can't. We could be badly exposed on this one. If it went to trial we could be hit for hundreds of thousands. The publicity would be horrible. I've been in touch with our lawyers, and they say it's vital that we do things by the book.'

'I see. OK. Well, we'll have the investigation if you insist. By the book. But I've just been speaking to New York. It's very important that we don't upset Justin.'

'He should have thought before he said what he said.'

'What he is *alleged* to have said.'

'Whatever. But in the twenty-first century we can't afford to have bankers around who treat women like that.'

'In this case, Linda, we can't afford not to. Do I make myself clear?'

Linda looked at her boss. She had been in situations like this before. She knew how to deal with them. 'Yes. You do.'

'Wonderful,' said Benton with a smile. 'Wonderful.'

Justin Carr-Jones went to work. He could see trouble coming, but he was certain he could handle it. First thing was to gather his troops together. A dozen extremely brainy and extremely greedy young men, and one young woman, clustered around their leader.

'As you know, bonuses are paid at the end of this month. And as you also know, we had an outstanding year last year. Thanks to Perumal and the IGLOO transaction things are starting well again this year. So I think you can all look forward to good news. I just want to remind you all that I believe in rewarding individuals, but I also believe in rewarding the team. I think one of the truly best things about the Derivatives Group, and one of the reasons we are so successful, is that we all stick together.'

He smiled at the eager faces.

'On a separate note, you may know that Jen Tan has decided to pursue a complaint against me about some minor incident that occurred at Corney and Barrow the other day.' Everyone turned to stare at Jen, sitting at her desk a few feet away, just out of earshot. 'It's a silly thing, no big deal, I just mentioned the relationship between her and Zero, which, as you all know, is very close.' At this he winked, and was pleased to hear a titter in response. 'You might be asked some questions over the next few days by HR, who are carrying out an investigation. I'm sure you'll know how to answer them.'

He looked around his people to see whether they understood him. They did.

Next stop was Tarek al-Seesi's office, just off the trading floor. Tarek and Carr-Jones kept a respectful distance from each other. Neither really liked the other, but neither wanted the other as an enemy.

'It's a shame Jen Tan brought that complaint,' Carr-Jones said.

'It's a shame she had cause to,' Tarek replied.

'Oh, it was nothing. She's blown it out of all proportion.'

Tarek raised his eyebrows and reached for his well-worn worry beads.

'It's not going to do her career any good,' Carr-Jones went on. 'Those kind of things never do. It's a pity you couldn't have explained that to her.'

'Zero did try to talk her out of it.'

'Uh-huh. And what's your view?'

Tarek didn't answer straight away. In the quick-fire activity of the Bloomfield Weiss trading floor, he had learned the power of the pause. He was a slight man, balding, with a large moustache. Although he appeared to be in his forties at least, he was only thirty-five. He had a reputation as a top trader, a king of the bazaar, but actually his skills were more subtle than haggling for the best price. He had a highly developed sense of intuition, and an understanding of people. He also had a PhD in international relations from Johns Hopkins University in Washington, DC.

The worry beads clacked for several seconds. Carr-Jones sat, waiting.

'Actually, if she chooses to, I think that she has a right to be heard,' Tarek said at last.

Carr-Jones smiled. 'I'm sure she has a perfect right.' He stood up to leave. 'Oh, one of my team spotted something in one of the German papers last week. The police there are trying to track down a man called Omar al-Seesi. He was last seen in Hamburg. He's some kind of al-Qaeda activist, apparently.'

Tarek fiddled with his beads.

'No relation, is he?'

Tarek looked steadily at Carr-Jones, his soft brown eyes giving nothing away.

'Don't worry,' Carr-Jones said. 'It's probably just a coincidence. I doubt anyone at Bloomfield Weiss in New York reads the German papers anyway. And it was just a tiny paragraph. Good thing too. You know how touchy some of these Americans can be about terrorists these days.'

Tarek sighed. 'Thanks for stopping by, Justin.'

'No problem.'

As Carr-Jones turned to leave the room Tarek muttered under his breath a long and satisfyingly complicated obscenity in Arabic, which involved Carr-Jones's maternal ancestry, various anatomical combinations and a camel.

Justin paused. 'What was that?'

'You could say it was a kind of prayer,' Tarek replied with a small smile. 'Difficult to translate.'

When he had gone, Tarek wondered whether his mother knew that her wayward youngest son was now living in Hamburg. He decided not to tell her. Omar had caused them all enough heartache over the years.

5

Tagliaferi's Democratic National Party reduces gap in latest opinion poll. Rumours of possible alliance with the Northern League.

Jean-Luc Martel stared at the story for the twentieth time that morning. Now that really should have been good news for him. The Northern League was the right-wing Lombardy party who were pushing for more independence for the north. They held the balance of power in the Italian Parliament. An alliance with them should improve the chances of Tagliaferi winning power, especially with the opinion polls trending his way. He was cleverly outflanking the government's mildly anti-European stance, and the centre-left coalition, staunchly pro-European, were running a feeble campaign. Suddenly the idea of Italy leaving the euro was openly being discussed in Italian newspapers, although most commentators still thought it a bad idea. That should have hurt the Italian bond market. But prices hadn't budged.

Martel was having a bad day. In fact he was having a bad week. Following the brief spike down of the Italian bond market after the news about Gallotti joining Tagliaferi, prices had done nothing but strengthen. Slowly, relentlessly, powerfully, on steady volume. Martel had developed a feeling about markets, and this one felt like it was at the beginning of an upward move, which for Martel was not good. The market was rallying, a quarter of a point a day. And Martel was short. Short, short, short.

His unrealized losses on the Italy trade were now over five hundred million and rising. He had been forced to sell all his positions in other markets to cover them.

He glanced at the cutting from the *Wall Street Journal* which topped one of the piles of paper nearest him. 'Eagle Swoops on Euro from Eyrie in Rocky Mountains'. It was a flattering article, and a good *Journal*-style line drawing of him. He thought he had made a strong case for Italy leaving the euro. But no one seemed to have agreed.

He had held off bugging Walter Lesser, but he could stand it no longer. He sent him an IM.

Walt. Did you get my Italian law professor's report?

The response took a couple of minutes.

Sure did. Thanks.

Martel took a deep breath and tapped out:

Are you doing anything?

The reply was quick to come:

Nah. Not convinced.

Merde! If Walter wasn't convinced then his hedge-fund friends probably weren't convinced. Suddenly Martel felt a sharp pain throughout his body. It started in his stomach, then coursed like an electrical current through his limbs to the tips of his fingers and toes. Perhaps Walter and his friends were up to something after all.

He called Alberto Mosti, a contact in Harrison Brothers in Milan, and asked him the question. 'Have you seen any hedge-fund activity in the BTPs? Apart from ourselves.'

'No, Jean-Luc. Nothing.'

Martel ignored his denial. 'Because I know about Walter Lesser.'

There was a sigh on the other end of the phone. 'I'm sorry, Jean-Luc. You know how you hedge-fund guys are. Secretive as hell.'

Martel exploded. 'You listen to me! I've put billions of euros of business through you with this trade alone. I expect information for that. Good information.'

'But client confidentiality . . .'

'Bullshit, Alberto. I am your best client!' Martel was shouting. 'You treat me like your best client. Your only client. Always! Or I do no more trades with you. Not just that. Every time I hear you are trading I will trade against you. I will fuck you! Do you understand? Fuck you!'

'Yes, Jean-Luc. I'm sorry, Jean-Luc, I quite understand.'

Alberto sounded severely rattled. Which was just as he should be.

'OK, Alberto. I'm glad we've straightened that out. Now who else is buying? *Hein?*'

Silence.

'Alberto?'

'There is a rumour that the Bank of Italy is just about to order some of the big Italian banks to buy BTPs. In size.'

'When?'

'Tomorrow. The day after.'

Martel closed his eyes.

'Jean-Luc? Do you want to do anything? Close out some of your position?'

Martel just slammed the phone down.

The Italian government was fighting back. Once the banks started buying bonds, the struggle would really be on. The sharp twist in Martel's stomach reappeared, a twist that he recognized instantly. It was accompanied by a stiffening of the muscles in his shoulders and an increase in his heart rate. It was fear.

On good days, Martel thought he could read the markets. On bad days, he thought he was just lucky.

The first really large position the Teton Fund had taken was to sell the yen in 1998. The yen had continued to rise but Martel had kept selling. He would sell to anyone and everyone who would let him. Until he ran out of cash. His brokers demanded margin payments, daily transfers of cash to his account with them to cover his losses. Then two days before there would be no more cash to transfer the market had scrambled his way. After a month he looked like a genius. Perhaps he was a genius. Or perhaps he was just lucky.

A year later he had ridden the internet bubble up into the stratosphere. He held on to high-tech stocks far later than most of the other hedge funds thought made any sense, and made a killing. Then in late 1999 he too became bearish and began to sell. Selling internet stocks short was an expensive business, especially at that time. To sell the stocks, Martel had to borrow them from someone, a task that became increasingly difficult. Early in 2000, once again it looked as if he would have to give up, buy back his Amazons and E-Bays and Pricelines at much higher prices than he had sold them, get rid of the ranch and leave Wyoming. But then the market slipped and slid, and the Teton Fund lived to short again.

The Iraq war in 2003 was easier. The price of crude oil had soared over fears that Middle East supplies might be seriously disrupted in a messy conflict. But it was clear to Martel that the war would be a walk-over for the Americans, so he sold crude, tankers full of the stuff. A couple of months later American soldiers drove into Baghdad, oil prices crashed and Martel banked millions. Hundreds of millions.

The lesson Martel had drawn from these experiences was that he was always right, and sometimes he had to fight to buy himself enough time to be proved right. This was one of those times.

But what if he was wrong? What if the euro was as impregnable as every bond trader in the world seemed to believe? What if he had merely been lucky on those three previous occasions and it was now his turn to be unlucky?

His stomach flipped.

Insecurity ran in the family. His father was a civil servant in the Treasury in Paris, an educated and intelligent man who was frustrated by his inability to achieve promotion. Martel remembered conversations at dinner in which his parents blamed this on prejudice against his father's Polish ancestry. They had even gone so far as to change the family name, from Młotek, which meant hammer, to Martel, which was the ancient French word for the same implement, as well as being a surname of some distinction.

His mother realized that her gangling son was intelligent, and had pushed him as hard as she could academically. He had responded, winning himself a place to study mathematics at the elite École Normale Supérieure. But although he scored consistently highly in exams, his abilities never seemed to Martel to be recognized by either his teachers or his peers. Most of the time, he was convinced that this was to do with his Polish background. Despite the change of name, people knew. But occasionally, when suffering from those excruciating moments of self-doubt which assailed him even then, he worried that people didn't like him, thought him cocky, arrogant, uncouth, clumsy. Sometimes he even wondered if that had been the real stumbling block with his father's career: after all, the French finance ministry was riddled with people with Eastern European names.

So, after an uninspiring year in the trade-credit department of a French bank, he had turned his back on Paris, and headed for America. He had attended business school at Wharton, and then joined one of the top investment banks, avoiding a posting to Paris and staying in New York. There he had discovered the markets, or the markets had discovered him. He had been propelled by the success of his ever greater gambles from Wall Street to here, this valley high up in the Rockies.

They said that people who came to the mountains were escaping from something. If that was true, he wasn't doing a very good job of it.

He closed his eyes and took deep breaths. *Courage, mon brave.* This wasn't the time to give up. He had felt this way before and every time he had come through. The only thing to do was to fight it out.

He called Andy and Vikram into his office and discussed the situation with them. He wanted to short more BTPs. This was easier said than done. The Teton Fund was already short billions of Italian government bonds it didn't own. It had to borrow the bonds, usually from investment banks or brokers, so that it could deliver them to whoever it had sold them to. The problem was that every broker placed a limit on the amount of bonds that they were willing to lend to each of their counterparties, and the Teton Fund was up to its limits with everyone. No more bonds to be borrowed.

There was only one way left to increase the size of his position. Buy more IGLOO notes from Bloomfield Weiss.

'How many?' asked Vikram.

'Six hundred million.'

Vikram whistled. 'That would take us up to eight hundred. I don't know whether Bloomfield Weiss will do that much.'

One of the many beauties of the IGLOO trades was that it didn't involve borrowing any government bonds from anyone. But it did rely on Bloomfield Weiss lending the Teton Fund cash to buy the notes.

'I know investment banks,' said Martel. 'With the fees we'll let them make off this deal, they'll force it through their risk control department somehow.'

Vikram smiled. 'I'll call Perumal.'

Martel still felt tense as he drove the three miles or so out of town to his ranch. It had cost him three million dollars when he had bought it in 1994, but it was now worth several times that. The very wealthy who were serious about the outdoors had been flocking to Jackson Hole over the previous decade in a mass scramble to buy privacy and isolation. Teton County had the highest per capita income in the country, and it was rising fast. Jackson had become a wealthy cowboy town, a rich man's playground, with outstanding hiking, fishing, rafting, horseback riding, and some of the most challenging skiing in the US.

Martel's ranch was built of logs and river stone and set on thirty very expensive acres. It nestled in aspen and pine woods on the bank of the Snake River, right at the foot of the Tetons. What Martel liked most about it was the view of his beloved mountains, so close it seemed you need only to skip over the river to touch them, soaring seven thousand feet into the sky.

Martel parked the Range Rover in the garage and went looking for his wife. She was sitting in the great room, reading by a roaring log fire, one hand fiddling with a strand of her thick honey-coloured hair. She looked up as she heard him come in. Her blue eyes flashed, her cheeks glowed in the firelight, and the warmth of her smile drew him to her. Despite the horrible day he had had, despite the weight that seemed to be pressing in on his heart, his lungs and his intestines, his spirits lifted.

After six years of marriage, Martel was still very much in love with his wife.

They had met in Hamilton, Bermuda, where the Teton Fund was administered and legally located. She was a junior accountant in a business suit working for the firm that audited the fund. She captivated Martel the moment he saw her. She was so young, so innocent, so wholesome, so untouchable, so damn American. Martel had slept with many women, some gorgeous, some less so, but none like Cheryl. The partner of the firm had some quibble about the Teton Fund's accounting practices, which Martel had brushed off, but Cheryl wouldn't let it go. She had gone at him with an earnestness that had bewitched him.

He had to have that woman.

She was based in New York, so next time Martel was in the

city he had asked her to dinner. She had said no. Opera? No. Jackson Hole, skiing? Definitely not. But Martel didn't give up. He knew he wasn't being strung along. He could tell she liked him, he could tell she was intrigued by his Frenchness, his age, his experience, his wealth; he could tell she wanted to say yes. But there was a boyfriend in Wisconsin. And it wouldn't be proper – he was a client of her firm.

Eventually she cracked. He invited her boss and his wife and Cheryl to dinner on a yacht he had chartered in New York Harbor. He charmed her and played the perfect French gentleman throughout. At the end of the evening, when he had asked her to dine alone with him at Le Cirque the following week, she couldn't refuse.

Six months later, and Martel was further gone. It turned out that Cheryl's sexual appetite was just as healthy as the rest of her. But she still infuriated him, refusing to accompany him to certain social events. Then she tried to break off the relationship, saying she didn't want to become a rich man's mistress. Martel asked her to come and live with him in Jackson Hole; she said she had her career to think about. Martel had no choice. He asked her to marry him. But Cheryl did have a choice. There was their religion to consider, after all – he was Catholic and she was Lutheran. It took her three months to say yes.

At first Cheryl had enjoyed Jackson Hole. She had taken up skiing, and had quickly become proficient. She loved to ride her horse over the backcountry in the summer. And Martel had a pottery studio built for her, where she could indulge a passion for making American Indian-style jars and vases. Martel offered to open her own gallery in town, but she refused, saying her work wasn't good enough. Martel was willing to pay people secretly to come into her shop and buy her stuff, no matter how good or bad it was, but Cheryl had anticipated this. So there was a storeroom out back filling up with hundreds of pots and jars.

He bent down to kiss her. He smelled her perfume, mixed with the sweet aroma of the pinyon wood that was burning in the fireplace.

'Honey. You're all tense,' she said.

Martel nodded and collapsed into an armchair. Cheryl put down her book and swung her legs off the sofa. She was wearing tight blue jeans and a light blue T-shirt. He watched her as she moved behind him. She began to rub his shoulders.

'Aah! That feels wonderful.'

'Markets bad today?'

'You could say that,' Martel grunted. He was careful not to give Cheryl any details about what he did during the day. Not because she wouldn't understand it. On the contrary, she would understand it perfectly well and it would scare the hell out of her.

'You should quit, you know,' she said. 'The stress is doing bad things to you.'

'Maybe next year.'

'Why not now?' her hands ceased moving. Martel wanted to ask her to carry on, but thought his best bet was to keep quiet and hope she began again of her own accord. 'You've got all the money we could possibly need. There are lots of things you could do. Maybe raise money for the museum, for instance. It's all very well just giving them donations.'

Cheryl was on the board of the National Museum of Wildlife Art, a spectacular building a couple of miles north of Jackson. She was passionate about it. Martel did his best to indulge her passion, although his own private opinion was when you've seen one painting of a buffalo, you've seen them all.

'You don't understand,' he said. 'The trade I am working on at the moment. If it works . . . when it works . . . everyone will know that I am the master of hedge funds.'

Cheryl laughed.

'Hey! I want some respect from my wife,' Martel protested, reaching up to her with his long arms. She allowed herself to be pulled forward over the chair and they both ended up with a thud on the rug. She was still giggling when he kissed her. They undressed slowly in front of the fire. As her pale skin shimmered in the firelight Martel felt a surge of arousal. Eagerly he kissed her. And then . . . And then . . . And then, nothing.

She worked away, doing what she could to reawaken his ardour, and there was plenty that she knew how to do, but it was hopeless. They both knew it was hopeless.

In the end she gave up. Stopped. Abruptly. Pulled together her clothes. Began putting them on.

'I am sorry, *mon ange*.'

'You should see someone, you know. There are pills . . .'

'It will pass.'

'It's been six months. It's only because you're so damn proud. There's nothing to be ashamed of. So what if you're not the great French lover?'

'Hey, I used to make you scream with pleasure,' Martel protested, stung.

'It's hard to make babies without having sex first,' Cheryl said. 'They might not teach us much in Wisconsin, but they do teach us that.'

'Be patient.'

'This isn't just going to go away by itself,' she said, wriggling into her jeans. 'You're going to have to do something to make it get better.'

She pulled on her T-shirt and marched out of the living room towards her studio, banging the door behind her.

Martel lay on the rug, naked, his crumpled underwear only a few inches away from his nose. That ball in his stomach twisted again.

6

Calder let out the clutch and allowed the Maserati to crawl a few yards further up Heath Street in Hampstead. It wasn't far from his flat near Parliament Hill to his sister's house in Highgate, but it would take him twenty minutes through the bottleneck of Sunday morning traffic around the Heath.

The Maserati's four-litre engine growled softly in frustration. It was an early-nineties model, the Ghibli Cup, noted more for its performance than for its looks. Calder didn't care. He still craved the sensation of speed and power he had experienced in fast jets, and just occasionally, when he opened up the Maserati on an empty road, he came close to feeling it again. He loved the way it demanded skilful handling in corners, and the feeling that even if it was only crawling along at five miles an hour there was enough power under the bonnet to leave all the other cars on the road standing.

But the electrics were hopeless. Fortunately, it was starting without trouble at the moment, but he dared not lower the windows for fear of never getting them up again. Another trip to the specialist garage in Hertfordshire was required.

It had been a bad week. Not necessarily as far as the markets were concerned. Calder had kept well clear of the Italian situation, having decided he didn't understand what was going on. But Linda Stubbes had begun her investigation.

Her interview with Calder had given him some idea of Carr-Jones's line of defence. Calder had told Linda what had happened in the bar, which he remembered clearly. But then Linda had asked him to repeat the actual words Carr-Jones had said to Jen.

'"Are you shagging him, then?"' Calder said.

Linda wrote the words down on her pad and showed them to Calder. 'Are you quite sure this is what you heard?'

'Yes,' said Calder.

'Hm.' Linda studied her pad. 'Because, you see, it's different from what Justin and Jen say was said.'

'Really?'

'According to Jen, Justin said: "Are you screwing him, then?"'

'Well, that's about right,' said Calder. 'Screwing, shagging, it all means the same.'

Linda frowned. 'Possibly. But it shows the two of you have a slightly different recollection of what happened.'

'Oh, come on, Linda. Anyway, what does Justin think he said?'

She looked back at her notes. '"Are you two shagging?"'

'So what difference does that make?'

'He claims he said it to you. He says that he was pulling your leg. He says that if he meant to offend anyone, it was you, but that only in jest.'

'That's not right,' Calder said. 'He was definitely speaking directly to Jen. It was *her* he was accusing. And he was insulting her, not joking with her.'

'I see.' Linda was writing everything down carefully. But Calder could already see the way things were going. The investigation would boil down to his and Jen's word against Carr-Jones's that it was Jen that had been insulted and not Calder. He suspected Carr-Jones's next step would be to discredit him as a witness. This was turning into just the kind of political contest that Calder loathed and Carr-Jones excelled in.

Calder and Jen had scarcely spoken. As Linda had suggested, she had spent very little time at work while the investigation was under way. She still had to make herself available to talk to HR, but she wasn't involved in any of the trading on the desk. She seemed aloof and angry. He had tried to talk to her several times, but she had rebuffed him. It was as though she wanted to keep everyone and everything at Bloomfield Weiss at arm's length, including him. He was disappointed to be counted with the rest of the firm, but he could reluctantly understand it.

Eventually the Maserati chugged through the stop–start traffic to his sister's home. This was a large detached house in a road of large detached houses, and Anne and her husband William had lived there for only six months. It had been bought with the proceeds of some sizeable payouts William had received from the venture-capital firm of which he was a partner. Anne no longer worked: she had been a promising barrister but with the arrival of their second child she had given up the struggle.

Calder parked on the street. There were three cars in the driveway: his sister's suburban-warrior-woman Jeep, her husband's Jag, and an old red Volvo. His heart sank.

He rang the bell, clutching the bunch of irises he had brought with him. Anne opened it for him, and he entered the war zone, stepping over a couple of dolls, the plastic contents of a plastic supermarket and the lost spur of a wooden railway line.

'Lovely flowers, Alex,' said his sister, giving him a hug. 'Come through to the kitchen.' She looked as messy as her hallway, spiky black hair, denim skirt and a woollen many-coloured jersey.

'Anne! You didn't say *he* was going to be here!'

'I wanted to make sure you came,' she said, digging a vase out of a cupboard. The kitchen was still in good condition, and must have cost its previous owner tens of thousands of pounds. The Varcoe family had only just begun trashing it. Through the window he could see their fenced-in swimming pool at the far end of the garden, looking a hemisphere out of place in the grey February dampness.

'That's not fair. Of course I would have come.'

'Oh yeah? You didn't show up last time I asked him.'

'That was different. I had to go to New York on short notice.'

'Such an important man.'

Calder sighed. 'OK. You've got me.' He straightened up. 'Let's go.'

Brother followed sister into the living room. There was Anne's husband William, balding and middle-aged in his middle thirties. He was talking to a tall upright man with a craggy face and a shock of thick white hair.

'Hello, William,' said Calder. 'Father.'

'Alex.'

'Can I get you a drink?' said William. He and Calder's father were drinking very pale sherry.

'Yeah. Have you got a beer?'

William scurried off. From the next room a child, Phoebe, began to whine and Anne rushed off to her, leaving father and son alone. Calder hadn't seen his father in over a year. He was determined to prevent this meeting from ending like the last one.

'Och, that wee lass has Annie twisted round her little finger,' the older man said.

'She is quite demanding,' Calder admitted. Phoebe was a clever four-year-old who revelled in making her mother's life as difficult as possible. She was as sweet as anything to Calder, but a monster to her parents. William did his best to avoid her, but Anne was run ragged.

'They'll end up spoiling her, you know.'

'Things have changed since we were children, Father,' Calder said, taking the opportunity to back up his sister.

'That's rot. I see children in my surgery all the time. You can tell the ones that are well brought up. And it's got nothing to do with money or social class, I can tell you. Quite the reverse.'

Dr Calder's r's rolled with the resonance of the Borders, although Calder sometimes wondered whether his father's brogue strengthened as he travelled south. His own Scottish accent had softened considerably with time and distance, as had Anne's.

She returned, balancing a sniffling Phoebe on her hip. 'Come and show Grandpa,' she cooed.

Phoebe waved a dishevelled plastic pony at her grandfather. He took it, his grey eyes twinkled and he slipped Phoebe a secret smile, only for her. 'And what's this wee creature's name?' he asked her, his voice rumbling with gruff warmth.

Phoebe stopped sniffling. 'Popsy.'

'Popsy? That's a fine name,' lied her grandfather with all the conviction of the smoothest bond salesman. 'You run along now and give Popsy her oats.'

'Him. Popsy's a he. And he likes chicken nuggets.'

'That's grand, now,' said Dr Calder. 'And give him some extra ketchup from me.'

As Phoebe toddled off happily towards the plastic food strewn all over the hallway, Anne shook her head. 'I don't know how you do that, Father. Do you, Alex?'

'No,' Calder replied, repressing an irrational upsurge of resentment. He knew it was ridiculous, but he felt jealous of the little girl. Dr Calder was famous throughout Kelso, the small Borders town where he worked, for his smile and his kind words, but Calder couldn't remember the last time the doctor had smiled like that at his own son. Before his mother had died, probably. He felt a further surge of irritation that he let it bother him. He was thirty-four now. He had decided many years before that he could get by without his father's approval.

'It's a shame Nicky couldn't make it,' Anne said.

'Mm.' Calder glanced at his sister. 'She moved out last month.'

Anne's eyes widened in surprise. 'Oh, I am sorry about that, Alex. What happened?'

'You mean, did I end it or did she? She did. Said I wasn't

taking enough notice of her. The trouble was, we were both working such long hours. She'd managed to shuffle her shifts around to get a couple of days off so we could go to Paris together, and then I had to cancel. She wasn't impressed. The last straw, she said.'

Anne touched Calder's arm in sympathy. 'I know how much you liked her.'

Calder shrugged, pretending indifference. But he did like her. Loved her really, although he had foolishly never quite got round to telling her that. And Nicky was right that he had taken her for granted. Life had been pretty bleak since she had moved out of his flat. He had phoned her several times, but the conversations had been brief, and she had ignored his attempts to discuss rekindling the relationship. He had tried to invite himself round to the studio flat she had rented in Tufnell Park but she was having none of it.

'Pity,' said his father. 'She was the girl you were with the last time I saw you, wasn't she? Sensible woman. Thought she'd make an excellent doctor.'

'I'm sure she will,' said Calder. 'She's certainly dedicated enough.'

Lunch passed pleasantly, with the exception of Phoebe's reluctance to eat anything that was put in front of her, although her younger brother, Robbie, stuffed his face with enthusiasm. Calder liked Robbie. He seemed to view the hyperactive antics of his mother and sister with detached amusement. Calder hoped he would continue to find life so entertaining.

When the plates and the children had been cleared away and the adults were drinking coffee, the conversation turned to William's job. His firm, Orchestra Ventures, had just invested in a company that was growing human tissue from bone marrow that could somehow be used to replace heart pacemakers. Dr Calder was fascinated, and began asking William questions that he couldn't quite answer. William being William, he didn't admit to the fact that one of his colleagues was the medical expert and that he knew nothing, but instead made up his replies. Dr Calder caught him out, but did so politely.

The doctor sipped his coffee and eyed his son. 'It is good to see you money men doing something useful for a change, don't you think, Alex?'

'Yes,' said Calder, neutrally.

'Now what exactly did you do last week?'

It was a simple question, a father taking interest in his son's work. But Calder knew there was much more to it than that.

'I traded bonds, Father.'

'Traded bonds? What exactly does that mean?'

'Oh, you wouldn't be interested.'

'Ah. So you think it's a wee bit too complicated for us simple souls in the real world?'

'No. Not at all,' Calder said. He sipped his coffee. His father looked at him. 'All right. I bought some Italian government bonds. And then I sold them.'

'And you made money doing it?'

'Yes. Two million dollars. Or euros. It's more or less the same thing.'

'Two million!' Dr Calder stared at his son. 'So all you did was buy a few of these Italian bonds, do nothing and then sell them, and you made two million dollars. That's more than most people make in their whole lives.'

'I suppose that's right. Although it was a few hundred million bonds I bought.'

'I find that incredible. You made money out of money. Isn't that just gambling?'

'Not really,' said Calder. He tried to keep calm. 'It's investing. Allocating capital to wherever in the world it's most needed.'

'Adam Smith's invisible hand,' said William in support.

Dr Calder smiled at his son-in-law. 'I can see that you investing in a company that is going to improve the survival rates of people with heart disease is allocating capital to where it's most needed. But that's not what you're doing, is it, Alex?'

'The Italian government needs investment just as badly,' said Calder.

'But didn't you say that you sold the bonds last week? So they needed the investment two weeks ago, but they don't need it now?'

Calder thought of trying to argue about the role of price discovery in the financial markets, but he didn't have the heart.

'It's greed, isn't it?' said Dr Calder. 'Pure greed.'

'We are trying to make money. That is what we get paid for.'

'I really don't understand it,' said the doctor. 'There are thousands of you youngsters living in London passing all these bonds and shares and what have you around to each other and paying yourselves hundreds of thousands of pounds just for playing in your private little game. And what does the game produce? Nothing. Absolutely nothing. Or nothing that I can see, anyway. Whereas in the rest of the country, normal people do normal jobs, making things, helping each other, serving each other, and get paid a fair wage for it. I dread to think what your grandfather would have to say about it.'

Calder stared at his father, biting back the arguments. Calder's grandfather and great-grandfather had been ministers of the kirk, tough men with a hard line in religion.

'And what are you using to play your little gambling games, eh? The savings of these ordinary people. But you don't care. Win or lose, you still get paid.'

'The City brings in huge amounts of revenue for this country,' Calder said.

'So does betting tax. And duty on alcohol and cigarettes. That doesn't mean that booze and fags are a good thing for anybody.'

'Father, we've been through this before.' Calder was unable to keep the frustration from his voice. 'I like my job and I'm good at it. Taking risks is what I do best. Isn't that enough reason to do it?'

Dr Calder shook his head. 'I don't know where your mother

and I went wrong. There should be much more of a reason to be alive than gambling and greed, shouldn't there?'

Calder felt the old anger rising. At the age of sixteen, a year after his mother had died, he had decided not to study sciences at A level as his father had wanted. He had gone to an English university, not Edinburgh, where he had read history, not medicine. When he had become an RAF pilot, he had expected his father's disapproval and received it, but it was nothing to the contempt his father had heaped on him when he had joined Bloomfield Weiss.

Yet Calder had brought all this upon himself, driven by some deeply hidden but overpowering desire to do the opposite of what his father wanted. The doctor had a firm view of the world and the role that his son was to play in it. It was a view that Calder didn't necessarily disagree with, a view he admired even, but for Calder that wasn't what the struggle was about.

'Of course there's more to my life than gambling and greed,' Calder said, his voice rising in spite of himself.

'Really? What did . . . what was her name . . . Nicky think?' Calder thought he could trace the faintest of smiles on the old man's face, as though pleased he had once again managed to needle his son.

It was that smile that did it. Something inside Calder snapped. 'Besides,' he said, making no attempt now to repress the anger. 'It's *my* life. I'll do with it what I like. You've been trying to tell me what I should do for as long as I can remember. The thing is, I won't let you. I haven't in the past, and I won't in the future.'

'All I'm trying to do is to make sure that you don't waste your talents.'

'That's not what you're trying to do at all! You've got this fixed idea of the world, all very noble, I'm sure, and you want me to fit into it. Well, I won't. I *can* do a job I enjoy and I'm good at, even if it isn't up to your high moral standards. It's not illegal. It doesn't do anyone any harm.'

Dr Calder shook his head. 'It's up to you what kind of life you lead. You do what you feel you have to do.'

'I bloody well will, you interfering, sanctimonious . . .' Calder was shouting now, but he just managed to restrain himself before the words 'old bastard' flew from his mouth. There was silence around the dinner table as they all looked at him. Damn. He had sworn to himself that he wouldn't rise to his father's bait. He took a deep breath. 'I'm sorry, Anne. If you don't mind, I must be going. I have some stuff to do at home.'

'You can't run away from the truth that easily,' the doctor said.

'Father!' Anne protested.

'Don't worry, Anne. This was bound to happen,' Calder muttered, trying not to glare at his father. 'Thanks for the lunch. It was lovely to see you. And you, William.'

'I'll see you out,' said Anne.

They both withdrew from the dining room. Calder put his head into the playroom to say goodbye to the children, and Anne fetched his coat.

'I'm sorry about Father,' she said. 'He went way over the top there.'

'He always does,' said Calder. 'But so did I. I know I shouldn't let it bother me, but I wish he'd just accept who I am, what I do.'

'One day he might,' she said.

'Maybe,' said Calder without conviction.

Anne walked out of the house with him towards his car. 'I'm worried about him, Alex.'

Calder stared at his sister. 'Why? Is he ill?'

'No. But there's something wrong. We went up to Orchard House last month and there were things missing.'

'What sort of things?'

'Valuable things. Mum's bureau. The Cadell landscapes. The grandfather clock. The candlesticks. And most of Mum's jewellery.'

'No! Are you sure?'

'When I saw the other stuff had gone, I checked her jewellery box. It's almost empty.'

'Did you ask him why?'

'I asked him about the clock and the paintings. He said the clock kept on breaking. And that he never liked the Cadells.'

'That's just not true.' Francis Cadell was a Scottish colourist who had come into fashion over the last twenty years. The landscapes were scenes of the Tweed valley by the Eildon Hills, the doctor's favourite place in the world. They had been bought by his grandfather directly from the artist in the nineteen twenties. 'And Mum's jewellery?'

Anne nodded.

'He must be selling them to raise money.'

'That's what I thought. But he's not hard up, is he? I mean he's still got the surgery, and he's managed to survive on that for decades. He lives so frugally, as we know only too well.'

'How strange.'

'Could you ask him about it?'

'Come on, Anne. You saw what happened in there.'

'I know. But he won't tell me. Despite what you might think, he does respect you.'

'Oh, now that's ridiculous.'

'No, it's not. It's true. And I am still worried about him.'

'Well, as far as I'm concerned, the old bugger can go to hell,' Calder said. 'Sorry, Annie. I know you're a dutiful daughter and that's good. But there's only so much abuse I'm willing to take from him.'

But as Calder drove home he regretted his words. He was worried about the old bugger too. And the doctor had a point. Calder thought back over the last few weeks: his dabbling in the dysfunctional bond markets, Carr-Jones's abuse of Jen, Bloomfield Weiss's rigged investigation, Nicky's departure. Apart from Nicky, none of it was real. None of it was good.

But he was damned if he would let his father dictate what he did with his life.

With a pang, he thought of his mother. If she were alive, everything would still be fine. Of course, his father had always been a strict moralist, but before her death in a car accident this had been tempered with a strong seam of warmth and love that lay just beneath the surface. Anyway, his mother was a pushover, happy to collude with her children in undermining her husband's diktats, and the doctor could be relied upon to turn a blind eye. Then she had died. Twelve-year-old Anne had fallen apart in night after night of tears, but father and son had taken their loss bravely, no tears, no baring of the soul. The family froze over. The cold ran deep – permafrost.

Calder couldn't hide from the fact that, from one perspective, he was the cause of his mother's death. To be more precise, she had died because he had not done what she had asked him to do: if he had obeyed her, she would still be alive. He had been worrying over this question of cause and effect, responsibility and guilt, for nearly twenty years, and he still hadn't decided upon a satisfactory answer. She had asked him to get the bus back from the High School, but he had gone back to fetch some homework he'd forgotten and missed it by a minute. He'd called her from a phone box, and she had dropped everything to come and get him. She'd had to be quick to make sure that she would be in time to pick up Anne from her music practice. So she was driving too fast along the narrow lane. A farm worker who had had three pints at lunchtime was driving too fast in his lorry the other way. They met on a blind bend. Calder waited at school until eight o'clock that evening before a friend's mother picked him up.

Calder slammed his hand on the steering wheel of the Maserati, and muttered to himself for the thousandth time: *If only . . .*

7

Calder watched Jen weave her way through the debris of the trading room towards her desk. She was walking erect and proud, her face impassive.

He decided this was not good news.

'Well?' he said, as she took her seat.

'Siberia,' Jen muttered, not looking at him.

'What?'

'They're sending me to Siberia.'

'What do you mean?'

'I don't want to talk about it.'

Calder glanced across to the derivatives desk, where the traders were trying to look busy, but throwing surreptitious glances towards Jen. Carr-Jones had gone, presumably to hear the result of the investigation himself.

Calder stood up. 'Come on,' he said. 'Let's go.'

'Where?' she turned to him, her composure still intact. Just.

'Outside.'

She followed him. They didn't say a word as they left the building and crossed Broadgate Circle to Exchange Place, a square at the eastern end of Liverpool Street station. They sat on a marble block, next to a large bronze sculpture of a bulbous woman staring at the sky in blissful stupidity. It was cold, but shafts of watery sunshine sneaked in above the station roof and touched their faces. There were few people about, although they could hear the grinding and clanking of construction equipment nearby as yet more of London's buildings were dug up, hollowed out, remoulded.

'Tell me,' Calder said.

'Only Linda and Benton were there. Linda did the talking.

She said they'd be speaking to Carr-Jones after me. They've completed their investigation. Apparently, Carr-Jones's behaviour was inappropriate, but it wasn't harassment.'

'So they're not going to do anything?'

'They'll give him a "verbal warning", whatever that means.'

Calder sighed. 'I'm sorry, Jen. It isn't fair.'

'Absolutely, it isn't fair,' said Jen.

'So what's all that about Siberia?'

Jen turned to him, attempting a smile but not pulling it off. 'Oh, that's the best bit. Thanks to Carr-Jones's "inappropriate" behaviour, it's clear that we can't work close to each other any more. So one of us has to move. Guess who?'

'To Siberia?'

'Yes. Well, Moscow. Apparently there's an opening there. Linda wants to talk to me about filling it.'

'What! No one asked me about that.'

'I don't want to go to Moscow. I shouldn't *have* to go!' Jen said. A tear ran down her cheek. 'I'm sorry, I've been doing my best not to cry through all this, but I just can't help myself. The whole thing makes me so angry. Not just angry, it makes me feel like I'm totally worthless.'

The tears were flowing now. Calder reached out his arm to comfort her, but Jen shook him off.

'Ever since I came to London, everything has gone wrong. I thought I'd love it here, but instead I'm miserable. I used to think I was a smart woman, but now I think I'm just an airhead. I should have a good career here. I'm intelligent, I do well with clients, and no matter what Carr-Jones says, I was good with derivatives. But, basically, unless I agree to let pond scum like Carr-Jones abuse me whenever they feel like it, I don't have a future.'

'You do have a future,' Calder said. 'A good future.'

'Only if I ignore them, right?'

Calder didn't answer.

'Right?'

Calder nodded. 'You have to be realistic, Jen. That's what it's like being a woman in the City today. Look, other places are worse. Some of the money-brokers, the kind of places where they say, "Come on, love, show us your tits."'

'So that's supposed to make me feel better?'

'That's the way it is. There's nothing you or I can do about it.'

'Isn't there? It shouldn't be that way, you know. And we *should* do something about it.'

'I told you at the beginning of all this, there's no point in picking a fight with Carr-Jones.'

'Oh, yeah, you did. Course you did. But I have to. Someone has to stand up to pigs like that. And I'm disappointed that you're too much of a coward to do it yourself.'

Calder shrugged in feigned indifference. But her words stung him. He had been called many things before, but never a coward.

They sat for a minute, Jen getting control of her tears, Calder thinking about what she had said. A man and a woman sat down on the marble seat next to them, took out cigarettes with frenzied fingers, and lit up, drawing in mighty lungfuls of tobacco smoke.

Jen straightened up and sniffed in the cold air. 'Let's go back.'

They returned to the Bloomfield Weiss building in silence. Homer Simpson was sitting on Jen's chair, grinning inanely, a yellow sticker attached to his forehead. She picked up the doll. A slit had been cut into Homer's groin, and something white and tubular was shoved in there. She pulled it out. It was a tampon, one end scribbled red with a felt tip.

Jen glanced across to the derivatives desk. They were all watching her, grinning, sniggering. She flung Homer and the tampon into the bin, and her face crumpled in tears.

'Hey Jen,' said Calder, once again reaching out to comfort her.

'Leave me alone!' Jen sobbed, flinging his arm off her. She grabbed her bag and ran from the dealing room, pushing past Justin Carr-Jones on the way.

Calder picked up the yellow sticker that had fluttered to the floor and read it. Someone had scrawled in the red pen: 'Keep an eye on those hormones!'

He watched her leave. She was right. He was wrong. She was brave. He was a coward. He heard a whoop as Carr-Jones's team welcomed their leader's return.

And they were scum.

He picked the tampon out of the bin and made his way over to Carr-Jones.

'Someone left this on Jen Tan's chair.'

Carr-Jones removed the smile from his face. 'Now that *is* inappropriate,' he said. There was a titter from somewhere behind him at these words. 'Are you sure it's one of the Derivatives Group?'

'What do you think?'

Carr-Jones kept a straight face. 'I'll have a word with my people.'

'You do that. And if one of your people pulls a stunt like that again, I'll shove this up their arse.'

Carr-Jones looked as if he was about to make some clever comment, but he saw Calder's expression and changed his mind. 'Leave it with me,' he said in his most businesslike manner.

Calder stalked off and found Tarek. Tarek took one look at him and headed for his office. Calder followed.

'One of Carr-Jones's childish morons left this on Jen's chair, shoved into that stupid Homer Simpson doll.' He flung the tampon on to Tarek's desk.

Tarek looked at the article with distaste, but didn't touch it. 'Where's Jen?'

'She's gone home.'

'I'll have a word with Carr-Jones.'

'You do that. And did you know they want to move her to Moscow?'

Tarek nodded.

'Well, nobody asked me. And it's not happening.'

'Zero, sit,' Tarek said. Calder hesitated, and did as he was asked. 'Now slow down. Think about it. Actually, there's no way that those two can work closely together any more after what Jen has done –'

'What Jen has done? What Carr-Jones has done, more like.'

'OK. What Carr-Jones has done. But one of them has to go. And it has to be Jen. Carr-Jones is senior, and what's more to the point, he's the one who's bringing in the revenue. That's the way it is. That's the way it's always been.'

'Not this time.'

Tarek raised his eyebrows.

'Tarek. We can't let Carr-Jones get away with this. Jen is an intelligent woman, and she'll make a good trader, once she gets her self-confidence back. Leave her with me for six months. Then if she hasn't shaped up we can send her off to Moscow.'

Tarek rattled his beads. Waited a moment. 'I don't like the way Jen has been treated any more than you do,' he said. 'But she hasn't done herself any favours by taking on Carr-Jones. At this stage the best you and I can hope for is to save her job at Bloomfield Weiss. If she goes to another office, she can start over. If she's as good as you say she is, she'll do well, and she'll be back in New York in a couple of years, *inshallah*. But you can see that she can't stay here.'

'But Moscow?'

'Russia's getting its act together. Moscow's one of the fastest growing offices in the firm.'

'Come on, Tarek! This stinks. You and I have been friends for a long time. I'm asking you, as a friend, not to let them transfer Jen. Because it's wrong.'

Tarek assessed Calder. Thinking it over. Calder waited. He would wait all day for Tarek.

Then Tarek smiled, a rueful smile. 'All right. I'll see what I can do. But I'm not promising anything. Carr-Jones has friends in high places.'

Calder knew that was the best he could hope for. 'Thanks,' he said. 'And this time Homer had better be gone for good.'

Tarek managed a wry smile. But as he left his office Calder wondered why his normally unflappable friend looked so worried.

Jen came in late the next morning, carrying a canvas sports bag.

'Hi, Jen,' Calder greeted her.

She ignored him, unzipped the bag and proceeded to fill it with the personal belongings from the drawers in her desk.

'What are you doing?'

'Don't worry. I won't take any of the firm's records. And you're welcome to all the crap that's on my computer.'

'Don't do it, Jen,' Calder said.

'I saw a lawyer yesterday. I'm going to claim constructive dismissal and sexual discrimination. I've got a good case, apparently. Carr-Jones will pay. And if Bloomfield Weiss stand by him, then they'll have to pay as well.'

'Jen, Jen! Calm down. If you do this, there'll be no going back. You'll find it very hard to get another job in the City, certainly not one as good as this.'

'They're going to send me to Moscow, Zero.'

'They won't. I won't let them. Tarek will stop them.'

'Tarek! I didn't hear much from him yesterday.'

'I've worked on him.'

'I think he's been worked on already.'

She had almost finished. The bag was bulging. A single sheet of paper floated to the floor. Calder picked it up: it was a photocopy of a fax to Perumal in the Derivatives Group. Something about IGLOO notes.

'What's this?'

'I found it in the photocopier the other day,' Jen said, grabbing it from Calder, scrunching it into a ball and chucking it in the bin.

'Isn't it important?'

'I hope so,' Jen said.

Calder had one last try. 'Stay. If you can get through the next few months you can still make a good career here. In a couple of years this will all be forgotten.'

She zipped up the bag. 'You don't get it, do you, Zero? I don't want to work here if bastards like Carr-Jones are allowed to get away with that kind of thing. I don't care how much they pay me. I don't have to do it, and I won't do it. Now, goodbye. I'll see you at the Tribunal.'

8

The little man was irritating the hell out of Martel. He was keeping to his promise to stay quiet, and the sound of paint brushed on to canvas was virtually inaudible, but it was the way he would stop every minute or so and just stare. He was a dark, scrawny American with uncombed hair and a week's worth of stubble. And he had these bright little eyes that seemed at the same time to assess Martel as an object and also to see into his soul. Martel was beginning to fear that the artist, who had depicted Cheryl's innocent beauty so accurately, might identify some essential characteristic of his own personality that would be better left unexposed.

The idea had seemed like a good one when things were going well. But now things were not going well. Now he was tempted to give the man his money and tell him to go back to Tribeca on the next plane out of Jackson Hole.

The Italian bond market was still marching upwards. The truly frustrating thing was that all the news was panning out the way Martel had expected. The Italian economy was falling apart. The stock market had plummeted, factories were closing, unemployment was rising sharply. The government's finances were in a state of collapse. The budget deficit had overshot the level agreed with the other European finance ministers the previous autumn, and the Treasury had hit its borrowing limits. Public-sector workers were being put on shorter working weeks, and some weren't even being paid. The garbage collectors, the firemen, the auto workers and the nurses were all on strike, with the railroads and the airports due out the following week. There was a consensus in the press that interest rates had to come down, but the European Central Bank wouldn't listen. They were more worried about inflation in France and Germany, which had risen to five per cent, well above the ECB's statutory target. In fact, euro-zone short-term interest rates had just been raised for the seventh time in twelve months to eight and a half per cent, but the Italian bond market had taken no notice.

Massimo Tagliaferi and his ex-finance minister henchman Guido Gallotti were shouting loudly that the only way out of the mess was for Italy to ditch the euro. But with just over three weeks to go to the election, their Democratic National Party was still in third place in the polls. And the European Commission was fighting back, warning of the dire consequences to any member of the EU that tried to withdraw from the single currency. It was illegal, and if any country flouted the law there would be sanctions, cancellation of subsidies, even expulsion from the European Union itself.

Worst of all, urged on by their governments, French and German banks had begun to buy BTPs in an attempt to crush speculators like Martel. Following the *Wall Street Journal* piece there had been a rash of articles about him in the Continental press, most of them unfavourable. The message was that the EU would not let such irresponsible capitalists destroy their currency.

Martel was feeling crushed. His unrealized losses had now mushroomed to nearly a billion euros – he was almost wiped out. It was just like 1998 again, when he had desperately passed margin payments from broker to broker to support his yen position. Except this time the sums were much larger. This time, when the music stopped and he finally ran out of collateral to post, the collapse would be spectacular. There would be nothing left of the Teton Fund, it would be wiped out. As the market had moved against him, he had done what he had always done in the past, gambled more. Until there was nothing left in the kitty.

He studied the cash-flow forecasts on his desk. He had to

stay in the game for just another three weeks, until the election. It made no economic sense for Italy to stay in the euro. The election would prove it.

There was one problem staring out at him from the forecasts, a big problem, a massive problem. The IGLOO notes.

He swore to himself, grabbed the spreadsheet and walked out of his office, tripping up the easel on the way. The painter was sensible enough to keep quiet.

The Teton Fund's twenty or so traders and analysts worked together in a small dealing room expensively kitted out with all the latest technology, allowing them instant access to a digital torrent of information on any market in the world. Vikram was studying tiny blinking figures on one of his three flat screens.

'What's this number?' Martel jabbed his finger on the spreadsheet.

Vikram cut off his conversation and put down his phone. 'That's my estimate of what we will have to pay Bloomfield Weiss as collateral for the IGLOO notes at month end.'

The last business day of the month, the twenty-seventh of February, was only a week away.

'Surely that can't be right? You're showing that we'll have to find a hundred and fifty million euros. We haven't got that.'

Vikram looked at his boss and shrugged. 'The IGLOO notes are so damned complicated that they're revalued once a month, at month end. I've plugged in the numbers, and my estimate is that with the market where it is today we'll be a hundred and fifty million down. Bloomfield Weiss will want us to cover that loss.'

'Are you sure about that number?'

'No. It all depends what assumptions they use for volatilities. And of course the wrinkle that the redemption price is based on whatever currency replaces the euro in Italy, a currency that doesn't even exist yet, makes it even more difficult. But I've run the numbers the way I would if I were them. And that's the result.'

Martel blew air through his cheeks. 'You know we haven't got it. We could maybe scrape together twenty or even fifty million, but a hundred and fifty? No way. The whole thing would come tumbling down. Game over. Nothing left. *Rien. Nada.*' Martel expressed this eventuality through a series of rapid arm movements that threatened to decapitate Vikram's assistant. She ducked for safety.

Vikram nodded unhappily. He had his life savings in the Teton Fund too. 'I know. But there's no way around it.'

'There has to be!' Martel shouted, slamming his fist on Vikram's desk. A box of pens and pencils bounced off, spilling all over the floor. The other traders in the room stared.

Vikram met Martel's bulging eyes. 'I can't perform a miracle, Jean-Luc. Unless the market craps out again by next week, we're screwed.'

Martel glared at his subordinate. He was a clever man and ambitious, Martel knew, but he played by the rules. At times like this, you had to make your own rules. Martel tried to explain. 'I've told you many times before that the key to success is staying in the game. This is a classic martingale situation: as long as we can keep placing bets we *will* win eventually. That's where you have to be creative. If you can't do that, I'll have to.'

He began to pace up and down in front of Vikram's desk. 'All right. Let's think this through.'

'OK,' said Vikram wearily.

'Who does the revaluation? Bloomfield Weiss or someone else?'

'For deals as complicated as this the only place to get a price is Bloomfield Weiss.'

'OK. And they use their own model to come up with that price?'

'That's right.'

'And that model is totally dependent on what assumptions they plug into it?'

'Yes.'

'*Bon.* Then we need them to plug in the right assumptions.'

Vikram shook his head. 'We might have been able to fix that a few years ago, but not now. These investment banks have departments whose sole job is to make sure the prices in their systems are real prices, not made-up ones. Compliance units, risk-management units, credit control, multimillion-dollar computer systems. You can't get around them. And if you try and you get caught, you're in big trouble.'

Martel stopped his pacing and smiled. 'You know, Vikram. There's a way around any system. A human way. It's called greed. With the right incentives any system can be corrupted.'

Vikram closed his eyes. He knew what was coming next.

'I want you to get on a plane this afternoon and give the right person the right incentive.'

9

Perumal was early. No matter how hard he tried, he was always early. Especially when he was nervous.

He scanned the cavernous restaurant, which had once been a banking hall. Already the loud chatter of the diners was creating a wall of reverberating sound all around him. But it was cool. Cool black-clad waiters and waitresses serving cool Pacific/French cuisine on cool plates to bankers in cool suits. He guessed it was the kind of place that Vikram would appreciate.

Vikram Rana had gone from nowhere to become Perumal's best client in a matter of weeks. Although Bloomfield Weiss in New York dealt with the Teton Fund on the bond side, the Derivatives Group had never done any business with them. When Vikram had called up out of the blue, Perumal had been the lucky man on the end of the phone. After the IGLOO deal, Carr-Jones had tried to muscle in on the client, but Perumal had advised against it. It was an Indian mafia thing. A touchy-feely relationship that could easily be disturbed.

Of course, it was nothing of the kind. Vikram was to all intents and purposes American. Perumal guessed that originally he must have come from the north of India, from a high warrior caste. Perumal's family was lower caste, from the southern state of Kerala. When Vikram and Perumal met they ignored the shared sub-continent of their background completely.

The big question was, could Perumal conjure up another elephant like the IGLOO deal?

'Ah, Perumal, sorry I'm late.'

Vikram was elegantly dressed in Italian suit and silk tie. At six foot three, he towered over Perumal, and even under the suit it was obvious that Vikram's muscles were finely honed. Perumal instantly felt that spark of inferiority. I'm at least as bright as this guy, he told himself as he sat down with his menu. He had come in the top one tenth of one per cent in his country in the national exams. He had been granted a place at the Indian Institute of Technology in Madras. His parents hadn't bought him a good education, he'd earned it, in competition with tens of millions of others throughout India.

'Bit loud in here, isn't it?' said Vikram, looking round.

'Yes, I'm sorry. Shall we go and find somewhere else?' said Perumal, making as if to stand up.

Vikram smiled at him with just a trace of condescension. 'Don't worry. We're here now. I'm sure this will do fine.'

The waitress came. Somehow Perumal managed to order a starter, a heavy main course and a bottle of wine, while his guest stuck with a salad and a bottle of sparkling water.

Perumal tried to think of some small talk. 'Do you think that implied volatility is going to remain at these levels?' he began.

Vikram frowned. Perumal suddenly panicked that he should have said something about the weather or Vikram's flight. Then, to his relief, his guest replied. 'I think it will last into the summer. It's dollar volatility that's driving everything else. But I think actual vol will remain well below implied.'

Vikram and Perumal discussed the intricacies of option pricing through Perumal's first course. Things seemed to be going well.

There was a lull. Then Vikram asked the question Perumal had been praying for.

'I wonder if you would be able to construct something for us. Something a little unusual?'

'We can try,' said Perumal, pulse quickening.

'We've been studying the correlations between oil prices, the yen, gold and the weather. We think there's an arbitrage there. But we'd have to do something in really big size to take advantage of it.'

'What exactly were you thinking of?' asked Perumal, trying to restrain the eagerness in his voice.

Vikram then proceeded to describe what was probably the most complicated derivative Perumal had ever heard of. He listened closely, working out in his head how Bloomfield Weiss could lay off the risks involved one by one as Vikram enumerated them. For Bloomfield Weiss's Derivatives Group, complicated was good. Complicated meant plenty of opaque formulae where a few million could be filched from a deal without the customer noticing. Vikram's transaction was teeming with possibilities.

'Well? Can you do it?' Vikram asked when he had finished.

'I'm sure we can. When you said big size, what did you mean?'

'Up to a billion.'

'Dollars?'

'Dollars.'

A billion! Carr-Jones would love this. And he, Perumal, could do this deal. No doubt Risk Management, the department within Bloomfield Weiss responsible for monitoring these things, would need to be 'educated' to accept yet more risk on the Teton Fund, but Carr-Jones could handle that.

'I'm sure we would have that capacity.'

'Excellent,' said Vikram, his teeth flashing. 'I'll send you some written details of the kind of thing I'm thinking of as soon as I get back to Jackson Hole.'

'I look forward to them,' said Perumal. 'Are you talking to anyone else about the deal?' He tried to ask this casually, but it was key. It was always much easier to gouge big fees if Bloomfield Weiss wasn't in competition with another investment bank to come up with a keen price.

'I don't see the need,' said Vikram. 'You guys did so well on the IGLOO transactions that I'm sure we can trust you on this one.'

'Of course,' said Perumal.

'Speaking of the IGLOO notes. They must be tough to

revalue. What with redemption linked to a currency that doesn't even exist yet.'

'Not really,' said Perumal. 'It is hard to squeeze it into the back-office systems, but on the desk we've built a model that can do the job.'

'They're due to be revalued next week, aren't they?'

'Yes. You'll be showing a bit of a loss at this stage.'

'Do you think so?'

'Oh, yes. You've seen how strong the Italian government bond market has been. But it doesn't make sense. I'm sure the trade will come right in the end.'

Vikram picked at his salad. 'Hm. That's true. We are looking at this over a one-year horizon. It seems a pity to revalue it every month.'

'I'm afraid we have to,' said Perumal, blithely tucking into his meat. 'If nothing else, Risk Management will insist that we receive more collateral from you. If they had their way it would be revalued every day, but the IGLOOs are too exotic for that.'

'Hm.' Vikram nibbled a lettuce leaf. 'I think we'd rather they weren't revalued at all.'

Perumal stopped chewing. 'I'm sorry. I have to revalue them.'

'I understand. But can't you revalue them at par, or ninety-nine and a half or something?'

'But our model –'

'Your model will say what you want it to say.'

Perumal started chewing again. Now he knew what Vikram wanted. He wanted Perumal to plug a false number into the Bloomfield Weiss system. It was a simple request: only a question of typing three or four digits. But the consequences could be far-reaching. The Teton Fund wouldn't show a loss on their trades, and wouldn't have to provide collateral to Bloomfield Weiss to cover that loss. And if no one found out, that would be fine. But if they did find out . . .

People had lost their jobs and been drummed out of the City for mispricing derivatives.

'I don't think I can do that for you, Vikram,' said Perumal. 'We have strict internal controls.'

'Oh,' said Vikram, all friendliness evaporating. 'I was sure that you would be able to work around those . . .' he hesitated, '. . . formalities. It's only a revaluation, after all. When the notes mature we'll know whether we've made or lost money, and if we've lost, we'll pay.'

'I'm sorry,' said Perumal.

'So am I.' Vikram stood up, leaving his napkin on the table. 'And I thought Bloomfield Weiss wanted our business.'

'Will you call me about the yen–oil–gold deal?' Perumal asked.

Vikram didn't dignify the question with a response. He turned to leave the restaurant and then hesitated. 'Look, if you do think of a way to help me, call me at my hotel. I'm at the Strand Palace.'

'I'll do that,' said Perumal as he watched his best customer walk out of the restaurant, leaving him with his half-finished lunch, three-quarters of a bottle of wine and a whole bill. He sat down and refilled his glass to the brim.

What now? He couldn't possibly do what Vikram had asked. Could he?

Perhaps he should discuss it with his boss. That was what bosses were for, after all. But a moment's reflection told him that was a very bad idea. It would raise the stakes considerably if Carr-Jones became involved, changing a simple revaluation error into a full-blown conspiracy. Even Carr-Jones wouldn't go along with that. And what was worse, Carr-Jones would know that Perumal had let a billion-dollar deal walk out of the restaurant. A deal like that could make the derivatives desk ten million or more.

If only there was a way to swing it. Then the Teton Fund would become the most profitable client in the Derivatives

Group, probably in the whole London office. Although there would be no keeping Carr-Jones out of it, Perumal would receive a large chunk of the credit. And Bloomfield Weiss knew how to look after its revenue producers.

He still couldn't really believe that he was at Bloomfield Weiss. His family, his mother especially, had become so proud of him when he had been offered a job there a couple of years before. But even she had never expected him to do so well so quickly. Her elder brother, Uncle Achappan, had returned from ten years in Saudi Arabia a wealthy man. He had bought a big house with a swimming pool and several wide-screen TVs. Well, with a few Bloomfield Weiss bonuses, Perumal would be able to put him to shame. In fact, he would send some of the cash home to his family. A hundred thousand dollars would go a long long way in Kerala.

What would his mother advise? She was an honest lady, she had brought him up well, but he knew she'd find a way if she were in his place. His father, perhaps not, but his mother never ceased to point out that her husband, a civil servant with the Ministry of Education, hadn't the wit to make any serious money.

Could what Vikram asked be done? Possibly. There were all kinds of systems to be got round, credit geeks to be pacified, risk-management groups to be hoodwinked. But Perumal could do it. It had been impossible to cram the IGLOO structure into the system anyway, so the revaluation would have to come from Perumal himself. If Risk Management asked him to back it up, he'd blind them with science. Say he was using a jump diffusion model, that should do it. He looked honest. They'd trust him.

The only person who might find out was Justin Carr-Jones. He had an eagle eye and an intuitive feel for where the risks in his group were being run. That was a problem.

Then Perumal smiled. No. That wasn't the problem. That was the solution. Carr-Jones couldn't risk conspiring with one of his traders to corrupt the system. But he could turn a blind eye. For the fees from another elephant transaction, he could easily turn a blind eye.

Perumal took out his mobile phone and dialled Directory Enquiries for the number of the Strand Palace Hotel.

10

Much to Linda Stubbes's horror, Calder insisted on giving his statement to Jen's lawyer rather than Bloomfield Weiss's own solicitors. Stephanie Ward was a tall, thin woman who worked from an office near the Tower of London. She was meticulous, and it took them two hours before they had agreed on a statement. Calder wanted to make absolutely sure that his version of the events wasn't distorted in any way.

In the trading room, the subject of Jen was avoided. It was dangerous ground. Saying the wrong thing to the wrong person could get someone into all kinds of trouble. Keep your head down and your mouth shut seemed to be everyone's motto.

Calder tried to phone Jen at home several times. He didn't want her to think that he was like the others, pretending she had never existed. But she was using her answering machine to screen calls, and although he left a variety of messages, she never returned any of them.

He did get a call from someone else, though. Tessa Trew, the only woman remaining in Carr-Jones's Derivatives Group.

'I need to talk to you,' she said in an urgent whisper.

Calder looked over to where she was sitting, barely ten yards from his seat. She was looking away from him, towards the window on the other side of the trading room.

'What about?'

'I'll tell you when I see you.'

'All right. Where shall we meet?'

'Nowhere round here. I don't want to be seen. Let's go to the Midas Touch. It's in Soho. Nine o'clock this evening.'

'See you there.'

The Midas Touch was a hang-out for Soho's creative types in Golden Square. It was crowded at nine o'clock, but Calder spotted Tessa sitting by herself in a corner, smoking a cigarette and drinking what looked like a Bailey's.

'Can I get you another?' Calder asked.

She smiled, her lips red and wide. 'Love one,' she said. She was a big woman, tall, blonde and busty, but with no chin to speak of. She wasn't attractive, she wasn't even sexy, but she had something of the buxom barmaid about her, as though she was game for a spot of slap-and-tickle in the back room, should you feel the inclination.

She and Carr-Jones made an unlikely pair. She had worked for him in Tokyo and the two of them had made a successful team. Matt claimed to have known her vaguely at Oxford, and remembered her as an overweight mousy-haired mathematician from Somerville. He hadn't recognized her when she had transferred back to London. Calder guessed that the new Tessa fitted Carr-Jones's view of a woman's place in finance. She could use her charms and her brains to win business from a certain type of man. Calder had no idea whether she actually did sleep with her customers, but he suspected that all that was needed was the impression that she might.

Calder returned to the table with another Bailey's for her and a beer for him. 'Thanksh for coming,' she said.

'It looks like you got here a bit before me,' Calder said.

'It's been a hard week,' said Tessa, flicking her blonde hair back. 'You know what I mean?'

Calder drank some of his beer. 'Yes, I do know.'

She smiled unsteadily at him. 'You're cute, you know. I can see why Jen likes you.'

'She doesn't,' Calder said.

'Oh yes she does,' said Tessa with a sloppy grin. 'I've seen the way she looks at you. A girl can tell.' She placed her hand on his and leaned forward, giving him a full view of her cleavage.

Calder withdrew his own hand. Tessa shrugged and knocked back the Bailey's. 'Can I have another, please?'

'Are you sure?' said Calder.

'Ah, go on. I've got something to tell you. Something you need to know. But I'm taking a risk. Justin wouldn't like me talking to you, and you know what a bad idea it is to get on his wrong side. So get me another drink.'

Calder shrugged and returned to the bar. This had better be good, he thought.

She took a gulp. 'I want to talk to you about Jen. And about Justin. They never got on very well, you know.'

'I know,' Calder said in frustration.

Tessa shook her head. 'No, no, no, no. They didn't like each other.'

'Hi, Tess!'

A look of panic crossed Tessa's face. Calder turned to see two of the junior traders from the Derivatives Group at the bar.

'Shit,' Tessa hissed to Calder. 'What the hell are they doing here? They mustn't catch us. We must get out.'

'It's too late, they've seen us,' Calder said. 'Let's just be polite.'

'No!' With an effort, Tessa pulled herself to her feet and made for the exit of the bar. She took the Great Circle route, bumping into a group of drinkers. The two derivatives traders looked on in amusement. Calder followed her, giving the two men a friendly smile.

Tessa spilled out on to the pavement. She swayed. 'That's better,' she said. 'Let's find somewhere else.'

Calder looked at her doubtfully. He desperately wanted to know what she was planning to tell him, but she could scarcely stand up.

'Look, there's a pub,' she said, waving towards a side street. She stepped off the pavement and fell over. 'Oh, fuck,' she said, as Calder helped her to her feet.

'Hadn't you better go home?' Calder said.

'Yeah,' she said. 'Coffee. We'll have some coffee at my place.'

'I think you'd better go by yourself.'

'No, no,' Tessa said. 'You come with me. I want to talk to you.'

'No, really. Let me get you a cab.'

Tessa laughed. 'You're scared I'm going to jump on you, aren't you?'

'No,' said Calder.

'Yes you are.' Tessa seemed to make an effort to pull herself together. 'Don't worry, I'm perfectly safe. I know I'm a bit pissed, but I do want to explain what's been going on. Come back with me, have a cup of coffee and be on your way.'

'All right,' Calder sighed.

He hailed a cab, and directed the driver to the address in Pimlico that Tessa had given him. The cabbie glanced at Tessa, hesitated, and then let her in.

The journey passed in silence, with Tessa looking as if she was about to throw up at any second. But they made it to her flat, and Calder helped her with the keys and the stairs.

Tessa flopped into the sofa of the living room. 'Can you get the coffee?' she mumbled, pointing to the kitchen. 'Black, no sugar.'

Calder did as he was asked, eventually finding a jar of instant coffee amongst the debris of dirty plates and cups by the sink. As the kettle boiled, some music started up in the living room. Travis, he thought. It had been a mistake to come back with Tessa. He doubted very much that she would be able to say anything coherent to him. He was surprised by the state of her. Although she acted like a good-time girl, and he was sure she got pissed from time to time, he didn't have her pegged as a heavy drinker. How often had she made her way back to this flat completely smashed, he wondered.

He carried the two cups back into the living room, and stopped suddenly, spilling hot coffee on to his wrists. There was Tessa spread out on the sofa, naked apart from her G-string panties, her pale broad breasts flopping over her sternum. Her clothes were strewn around the floor. Her eyes were shut and her breath was coming in gentle, rhythmic whistles.

Calder swore to himself and put down the coffee. He found her bedroom, whipped the duvet off her bed and gently laid it on her body. She shifted and pulled the cover up to her chin. Then he let himself out of the flat.

Tessa waited a full minute after she heard the click of the latch. Then she sat up and clutched her head. She *was* drunk. But she knew exactly what she was doing. She had known all along. With the duvet still wrapped around her, she stumbled over to the phone and dialled a number.

'Justin? He's just left. It worked.'

11

Calder didn't see Tessa at her desk the next morning. He wasn't surprised: she must have taken the day off with a humdinger of a hangover.

Nils, Matt and he were busy. Nils Gunnarson's speciality was trading European corporate bonds. He was pretty good at it, too, but like many Bloomfield Weiss traders he had an inflated view of his own abilities. He was in his late twenties with close-cropped fair hair, a double chin, and a stomach that was thriving on the typical trader's fare of beer and takeaways. His accent was a bizarre mix of guttural Danish and money-broker cockney. He was an avid gambler, especially on football, and he and Matt would spend the lulls in the trading day discussing intricate spread-betting strategies.

There were whispers in the market that the finance director of United European Energy was about to resign. The prices of the bonds, which were trading at about ninety, were beginning to slide. Nils was talking to the Bloomfield Weiss analyst who covered the sector about UEE's accounts. There might be an opportunity brewing.

Calder was discussing the possibilities with Nils, when he could tell from his colleague's sudden tension that someone was hovering behind him. He turned. It was Carr-Jones.

'Got a minute, Zero?'

'Yeah. What's the matter? Have you decided to apologize after all?'

'I've just spoken to Tessa.'

'And she's got one hell of a hangover.'

'She has.' Carr-Jones flicked his eyes to Nils, who was listening intently. 'She told me something about last night which I found quite disturbing. I know she's upset about it.'

'If your staff drink themselves legless in the middle of the working week, then I'd say you've got a problem.'

'I think you've got the problem, Zero.'

'What's she saying?'

'She doesn't want to make an official complaint. At least not yet. She wants to think it over.'

'Complaint about what?'

Carr-Jones raised his eyebrows.

'That's ridiculous!' Calder protested. 'We went back to her place. I made her some coffee. She passed out. I covered her up and went home.'

Carr-Jones sat in Jen's empty seat next to Calder and lowered his voice so Nils couldn't hear. 'She says that when she woke up she had no clothes on.'

'Is this a set-up?' Calder said. 'Because if it is, it won't work. I did nothing to Tessa and she knows it.'

'John and Derek saw you two together. They say she was drunk and the two of you disappeared in a cab somewhere.'

'As I said, she was smashed out of her head. I helped her get home.'

'Very noble,' Carr-Jones said. 'I know Tessa is an attractive woman, and she has a reputation for . . . let's call it friendliness, but I think your judgement was poor.'

'Come on, Justin. I have no desire to become friendly with Tessa, believe me.'

'She isn't sure what she's going to do. She asked for my advice. I've told her to take a couple of days to think about it. She's sensible enough to know that making a formal complaint would lead to great difficulties for both you and her, but on the other hand she feels traumatized. Degraded.'

Calder looked Carr-Jones straight in the eye. 'If I'm called as a witness at Jen's Tribunal, I will tell the truth. I don't care what ludicrous claims Tessa makes.'

Carr-Jones stood up. 'Think about it, Zero. Just think about it.'

Calder glowered at Carr-Jones's back.

'What was that all about?' asked Nils, feigning only mild curiosity.

'You really don't want to know,' said Calder. 'Believe me.'

'Maybe you should listen to him.'

Calder and Jen were in a smart bar in Chelsea, not far from Jen's flat. Calder had insisted that they meet. He wanted to tell her what was happening at Bloomfield Weiss in her absence, and show her that he was on her side.

'What do you mean?' he said.

'Don't get me wrong,' Jen said. 'I appreciate what you're doing.' She gave him the hint of a smile, the first glimpse of warmth she had shown since they had met ten minutes earlier. Calder was shocked at how glum she looked. There was no life, no spark to her, whether of anger or of humour. The corners of her mouth pointed downwards and her eyes, normally so lively, were listless. Her black hair seemed lank and stringy. Even though she was no longer at work, she was wearing her habitual black trouser suit, but without her normal poise. 'Carr-Jones will screw you just like he screwed me.'

'I think I'll be OK,' Calder said. 'I mean, Tessa can't prove anything happened because nothing did. Plus, I make money. Bloomfield Weiss never forget that.'

'Whereas I don't?' said Jen.

Calder shrugged. 'You will,' he said.

Jen snorted. 'Come on. Do you think I'm ever going to work as a trader again?'

'You're good enough.'

'No need to give me a pep talk now. You're not my boss any more.'

Calder decided to ignore Jen's bitterness. She had every reason to feel that way, but he still didn't appreciate bearing the brunt of it. 'I've never understood corporate politics,' he said.

'Carr-Jones is the master.'

'I know. I just wish there was a way we could get back at him. Blackmail him like he's trying to blackmail me.'

'Blackmail him?'

'Yeah. That's what this stuff with Tessa is all about.'

Jen was silent. She seemed to be thinking.

'What is it?' Calder asked.

'Nothing.'

'Is there something we can use against Carr-Jones?'

Jen looked at him for a moment, a glimmer in her eyes. Then she shook her head. 'No, it's nothing.'

'Tell me.'

'There's nothing to tell.' Jen stared at him defiantly.

Calder sipped his bottle of beer. Jen sipped her wine.

'How's your case going?' he asked.

'Good. My lawyer knows what she's doing. She thinks we've got a chance, especially if you stick with your statement. Apparently very few cases actually go to the Employment Tribunal. It's expensive and something can go wrong for either side. But she thinks Bloomfield Weiss will come up with a deal. Several hundred thousand. She wants me to settle.'

'And you don't want to?'

'No. I want to take the bastard to the Tribunal and rub his nose in it.'

'Well, I'll tell anyone the truth who asks me.'

Jen looked down at her glass. 'Thanks,' she whispered.

'You don't look good,' Calder said.

'I don't feel good.' She took a deep breath. 'I feel lonely, I feel miserable, I hate London, I hate Bloomfield Weiss, I hate investment banking.'

'Why don't you go away for a few days?'

'I can't leave London until the case is over. Besides, when I come back things won't be any different.'

'Is there anyone you can talk to?'

'No. My parents haven't spoken to me since I told them what I was doing. They think I'm throwing away all the expensive education they gave me. I hardly know anyone here. There's one woman I know from high school, but she works so hard I hardly ever see her.'

'Who's that?'

'Sandy. She works for a US law firm here. Her life's not much better than mine. And mine sucks.'

'You can talk to me if you like.'

Jen didn't answer. She looked as if she didn't want to talk to anyone.

'What will you do afterwards? When the case is over?' Calder asked.

'I don't know,' said Jen. 'What can I do? No firm will employ me now, not here nor on Wall Street. There's nothing. Nothing.'

Calder wanted to comfort Jen, but he didn't know how. She was submerged in her own misery, without the willpower to fight her way to the surface for breath. He wasn't convinced that waging war against Carr-Jones would really make her feel any better.

'Why don't you settle with Bloomfield Weiss, take the money and go back to the States? You've got friends there. You're a smart woman. You'll find a job, probably a much better one than working for Bloomfield Weiss.'

'So you think I should give up?' said Jen, her voice tinged with anger.

'I think you should get out of London and start again. I'm just being realistic.'

'Realistic! You're always so goddamned realistic! Well, the reality is that Carr-Jones has ruined my life. And the reality is I'm not going to let him get away with it.' She drained her glass. 'Now I gotta go.'

'Jen . . .'

'I said, I gotta go.'

As expected, the UEE finance director resigned, admitting that there had been accounting irregularities relating to long-term contracts. But these amounted to a billion euros, more than anyone had expected. UEE bonds were now offered only, meaning no one anywhere would buy them. Some of Bloomfield Weiss's clients wanted to sell, but the Corporate Desk had no buyers. Would the Prop Desk step up?

Calder discussed it with Nils. Nils's view was that even with that big an accounting hole, UEE was pumping out enough cash to service its debt comfortably over the next three years.

'Shall we buy some?' Nils asked.

'What do you think?'

'If we can get them below sixty-five, I think they're a steal.' Nils's eyes were shining at the opportunity.

'OK. Let's bid sixty and see what happens.' Calder liked to back his people's judgement. It gave them confidence, and besides, he trusted them.

'How many shall we do?'

Calder put his face in his hands. Suddenly he felt weary. Normally he enjoyed this part of his job, putting his views on the line, risking millions for Bloomfield Weiss. Normally, he was careful. Normally, though he took risks, they were finely judged.

He didn't really know what was going on at UEE. They could have another five billion of bad contracts for all he knew. Nils's work wasn't bad, but there were still gaps. They should just tip their toe in the water. Buy a couple of million and see what happened.

But he was angry. Carr-Jones, Jen, Linda Stubbes, Tessa, they were all messing him around and he felt powerless to fight back. Nicky was gone. His trading P and L was lousy so far this year. He needed to do something to change this run of bad luck, shake things up a bit. So what if he lost Bloomfield Weiss a few million? If a billion euros was the extent of UEE's black hole, and if Nils's analysis was right, then the bonds would trade right back up to ninety and there was a fortune to be made. Time to take a risk.

Calder smiled at his colleague. 'Let's fill our boots.' So, they bought ten million at a price of sixty. Then ten million more. Then twenty-five. UEE had hundreds of millions of bonds outstanding. By lunchtime, Calder and Nils owned eighty million of them. The price had drifted up to sixty-five, but Bloomfield Weiss were the only buyers.

Tarek wandered over. 'What are you up to, Zero?'

'Buying UEE. It's good value at sixty.'

'Are you sure?'

'Yep.'

'You're really sticking your neck out on this one.'

'I've done it before, haven't I?' It was true, Calder had stuck his neck out on similar hunches many times before. And made good money out of them.

Tarek looked at his friend closely. 'OK. Just don't buy any more.'

So they stopped. Nils looked very nervous. Calder seemed unconcerned. At that moment he didn't care if he dropped the whole lot. Still the sellers came. The bonds gapped down to a price of fifty-five. Calder was sitting on a loss of nearly six million euros. He bought another twenty million.

Tarek hovered again. 'Can you come into my office, Zero?'

Calder followed him.

'What the fuck are you doing?' said Tarek, as Calder shut the door behind him. 'I told you not to buy any more.'

'I'm putting on a bloody good trade.'

'No you're not. You're winging it.'

'Nils has done the work.'

'Since when have you bought a hundred million euros of toxic waste without doing the work yourself?'

'It's OK. I feel good about this one. I'm backing Nils's judgement. What's the matter? Don't you trust me? I've taken risks this big before.'

'No, Zero, I don't trust you. Not today. I told you not to buy any more and you ignored me. You could lose forty points on this kind of trade if it goes wrong. That's forty million bucks. Now I'm telling you I want your exposure down to fifty million by tomorrow night.'

'Tarek? What is this? You've never second guessed me before.'

'Well, I'm second guessing you now.' Tarek held Calder's glare, his kind brown eyes looking almost sorrowful.

It was the sorrow that persuaded Calder. He was losing control and Tarek knew it. He took a deep breath. 'OK,' he said.

Tarek looked at Calder long and hard. 'It's Jen, isn't it?'

'No.'

'You're angry about what's happened to her.'

'You bet I'm angry,' said Calder.

'It's affecting your judgement.'

Calder shrugged and turned on his heel. He paused at the door. 'Why won't you stand up for her? You know she's being stitched up.'

'If I were you, Zero, I'd let her go.'

'I'm not going to.'

The look of sorrow remained in Tarek's eyes. 'You're a great trader,' he said. 'Usually. But you're a disaster at politics. You're way out of your depth on this one, and I'm not sure I can help you. Believe me, Jen's going down. Don't let her take you with her. Because she will, you know.'

12

The little girl squealed delightedly as Uncle Yuri reared up underneath her. She was a princess and he was a demented dragon who had saved her from the good but very boring Prince Vladimir. She loved the way her grandfather liked to turn the old fairy stories on their head.

She grabbed his short hair in her tiny fists and told him to lie down. Uncle Yuri immediately sunk to his knees and rolled over, tickling her in the process. She giggled uncontrollably.

'Stop all that noise in there!' came a cry from the kitchen. It was the little girl's grandmother, Uncle Yuri's wife. 'You're overexciting the child.'

Uncle Yuri got to his knees, and held his finger to his lips. The girl instantly became silent, dropping her guard, whereupon Uncle Yuri began tickling her again.

Uncle Yuri was not really an uncle. He couldn't be. He had no brothers and sisters, at least none that he knew of, for he had been brought up in an orphanage. People had begun to call him 'uncle' when he reached his thirties. He had a way with children. They instinctively warmed to him and he to them. He had a quiet calmness about him that made them feel safe with him. He was a little under middle height with unremarkable features, thinning hair, which was still dark, a small moustache and mild eyes. He lived with his wife of thirty years in the Crimean town of Yalta, in a smart but not ostentatious bungalow overlooking the Black Sea. So far they had three grandchildren. Uncle Yuri was hopeful that his own five children would produce many more.

His first memories had been of the orphanage, one of the hell-holes of the Soviet system, run by a sadist named Sergei

Tartarov. Little Yuri had no idea who his parents were. He and the other inmates had been bullied and abused since before he could remember. So he had developed his own method of survival. Merging into the background, avoiding trouble, but, if it came to him, being absolutely ruthless. In November 1964, at the age of fifteen, he left the orphanage. By Christmas, Sergei Tartarov was dead, his naked, mutilated body found in a nearby wood.

'Yuri! Sasha!' came the angry cry from the kitchen, but it was interrupted by the ringing of the telephone. Still panting, Uncle Yuri picked it up.

'Uncle? It's Myshko.'

'Myshko! How good to hear from you.' Uncle Yuri had known Mykhailo Bodinchuk since the latter was a sixteen-year-old spending summers at the family *dacha* on the Black Sea coast. They had struck up a friendship that had lasted seventeen years, and had been cemented when, at the age of twenty-three, young Mykhailo had decided it would further his interests if his wealthy ex-KGB father were to be permanently retired from the family business, and had turned to Uncle Yuri for help. Although still only thirty-three, Bodinchuk was now one of the wealthiest men in the Ukraine: he owned a couple of banks, and a number of privatized industries including a thriving arms-manufacturing business. He was also Uncle Yuri's favourite client. He, too, could be absolutely ruthless, but only when necessary. Uncle Yuri had grown heartily sick of the sadistic love of violence for violence's sake that characterized so many of his customers.

'I was just playing with Sasha,' Uncle Yuri said, explaining his breathlessness.

'And how's little Tatiana?'

'An angel. She smiled for the first time last week.'

'I'm sure she will be a beautiful girl, Uncle. I can't wait to see pictures of her.'

'She will, just like Katya, her mother.' Katya was Uncle Yuri's eldest and favourite daughter.

'I am sorry to take you away from your grandchildren, but I have a little job for you. It is a tricky one, but I am sure you will have no difficulty. You know how I keep only the most important assignments for you. This one will involve travelling to London . . .'

It was a perfect day for flying. There had been a hard frost overnight, and it had taken a while for Calder to remove the ice crystals from the red wings of his Pitts Special biplane. But now he was four thousand feet above the Suffolk countryside, he appreciated it. The sky was a deep clear blue, and from this altitude he could see at least thirty miles in each direction. London was marked by a brown murky haze far off to the south, to the north was Thetford Forest and the large US Air Force bases of Lakenheath and Mildenhall, and to the west the city of Cambridge, where he had first learned to fly in the University Air Squadron. Below, the farmland was still brushed with frost, and fingers of mist lingered in shallow valleys. In this sunshine all that would be burned off in a couple of hours, he reckoned.

He glanced around to make sure he was still alone in the sky. Then he lowered the nose, building up speed and energy for the manoeuvre. He pulled back on the stick, hauling the nose out of the dive and feeling the g-force pull him down into his seat. The aircraft soared to the vertical, speed decreasing, and when the top wing was in line with the horizon, he nudged the stick forward and to the right. The horizon revolved slowly, and with a touch of right rudder, the Pitts rolled off the top.

It wasn't quite perfect, but it was fun. Jerry, his occasional instructor, would have been impressed. Calder wasn't able to fly often enough to polish his aerobatic skills; he always seemed to be just a little rusty. But he could fly only at weekends, and then only when the weather obliged.

Since his days at Cambridge, Calder had been hooked on flying. He was a natural. He had joined the RAF eagerly, and then done his damnedest to make sure that he made it through the selection process to fly fast jets. He had trained on Hawks at RAF Valley on Anglesey, darting between the Welsh mountains making dummy runs on dams and bridges, learning to fly and to fight at high speed. Then, as a 'baby-budgie', he had been transferred to Cottesmore in Rutland for conversion training on the Tornado GR.1. A year at Marham flying Tornados at five hundred miles an hour a few hundred feet above the ground, and then it had all been brought to an end in that valley in Wales.

He closed the throttle, raised the nose of the Pitts, and as the wings buffeted with the first hint of a stall, pressed his left foot steadily all the way down to the floor. The nose fell and the world started to spin. After several rotations and a loss of a couple of thousand feet he recovered, now safely beneath the Stansted-controlled airspace for his route home.

'OK, Zero,'

Calder followed his boss through the trading room to his office. It was bonus day, the tensest day of the year, the day when life in the City was most removed from the real world. Although this time of year had always brought him good news, Calder hated it. For traders and salesmen at the big investment banks the monthly pay slip is only a part of their remuneration; their bonus can be several times their annual salary. For the last few years Calder's bonuses had been measured in hundreds of thousands of pounds. In the boom times of the late nineties top traders often pulled down millions, but that was rarer now, and Calder had been too junior to earn that much. Despite all this undeserved largesse, bonus time was traditionally a period of temper tantrums, whining, sulking and empty threats to quit and join the competition. The sound of one of his colleagues complaining that he had been 'ripped off' by a quarter of a million-pound bonus produced a queasy feeling in Calder's stomach. None of them was worth that much, he knew.

This was the first year he had been in charge of his own desk, and he would have to tell his troops what their pay was. Whatever the figure, he knew Matt would be pleased and Nils would complain. He was worried that they would give Jen zero, but she had worked hard for him and she deserved something.

'Sit down,' said Tarek, grabbing for his beads. He managed to take his own seat without allowing his eyes to move anywhere near Calder. This was going to be bad. Perhaps Tarek knew he'd be unhappy if they tried to stiff Jen.

Tarek took four white envelopes out of his drawer, hesitated and passed one of them over to Calder, still avoiding his eye.

Calder opened it, his eyes darting over the text and latching on to the figures in the centre of the one-paragraph letter.

£5,000.

Five thousand pounds! At first Calder couldn't understand it. He quickly checked the name at the top, and scanned the paragraph. There was no doubt about it. Bloomfield Weiss were pleased to provide him with an annual bonus of five thousand pounds.

Tarek's beads clacked noisily.

'What the hell's going on?'

Tarek sighed, and for the first time looked up. 'I'm sorry, Zero. Really sorry. Until yesterday, we had a much larger figure in mind. But, after extensive discussion, we've reduced it.'

'Discussion with who?'

Tarek shrugged.

'Bibby?'

Tarek remained motionless, his stillness assent.

'Why?' Calder asked. 'Last year the Prop Desk made forty-two million bucks, and for most of that time I was in charge.

I know we've had a bad start to this year, but that shouldn't matter.'

'Actually, there is a reason,' said Tarek. 'And I'm sure you know very well what it is.'

'Jen. But how can you take my bonus away over that?'

'The feeling is that Jen's actions reflect very badly on Bloomfield Weiss and that as her manager you could have done much more to prevent the situation getting out of hand.'

'That's total crap and you know it!'

Tarek stared at Calder, pain in his large brown eyes.

'So you want me to go back to my desk and call a head-hunter? Is that really what you want?'

'No,' said Tarek. 'Not at all. You're a very valuable member of the team and I desperately want to keep you. Which is why we will be prepared to grant you a guaranteed bonus of four hundred thousand pounds next year, in addition to whatever you earn as a result of this year's trading.'

Calder raised his eyebrows. 'Provided?'

Tarek nodded. 'Provided the situation with Jen is resolved satisfactorily.'

'So I get four hundred thousand if I drop Jen, and five thousand if I support her?'

Tarek nodded.

'That stinks.'

'It does,' Tarek said.

'So why did you stand for it?'

'I fought it,' Tarek said. 'But you've got a lot of powerful people against you. Benton Davis and, more importantly, Simon Bibby in New York.'

'And Justin Carr-Jones.'

Tarek shrugged.

'I can't believe you let that jerk run rings round you.'

Tarek said nothing as he fiddled with his beads. Then he looked up. 'Actually, this is all wrong. What happened to Jen, what's happening to you, your bonus. This isn't the kind of thing

I want to be involved with. Not the reason I'm doing this job.'

'Then why –'

Tarek lifted his hand. 'Listen to me, Zero. I thought long and hard about resigning last night. Not threatening to resign, really resigning. In the end I decided not to. I'll tell you why. Things like this happen at Bloomfield Weiss, and at every other investment bank. As you rise higher in the organization, you come across them more and more frequently. Now, people like you and me can try to stop them, we should try to stop them, but if we fail we shouldn't just quit – run away and leave the store to the likes of Carr-Jones. We should stay and try to make a difference next time.

'I want you here: I need you here. This will all blow over, and once it does you can do a vital job for us. If you have as good a year this year as I think you will, you've got a shot at a seven-figure bonus. Stick with it, Zero.'

Calder shook his head. 'What about the others?'

Tarek pushed the three other envelopes across his desk to Calder and handed over a slip of paper with two names written on it. Nils got two hundred thousand, Matt one hundred and fifty. That should satisfy them, although Nils would probably mount a token protest.

'And Jen?' he asked.

'What do you think?'

Calder turned the pages of the book in front of him, trying to concentrate. It was John Keegan's *The First World War*. He had been fascinated by military history since his days at university and still read it whenever he had the time, which was not nearly often enough. In every war, great generals were faced with the dilemma of which to choose: boldness or caution, opportunism or planning, seizing the initiative or careful preparation. Fortune favoured the brave and damned the foolhardy: it was only with hindsight that it was clear which was which. Normally he enjoyed reading Keegan and he had hoped that the horrors of

Flanders would take his mind away from the lesser horrors of Bloomfield Weiss. But they hadn't.

His first impulse after leaving Tarek's office was to storm out of the trading room, or at least to ring one of the many head-hunters who called him regularly. But he restrained himself. He had been at Bloomfield Weiss for seven years. Most of that time he had enjoyed himself, and he was very good at his job. So he had kept his cool, told Nils and Matt the news, deflected Nils's moaning, and even managed a stilted two-minute phone conversation with Jen. She wasn't surprised about the bonus, or lack of it. She sounded down, which didn't surprise him. She also sounded as if she wanted to get him off the phone as quickly as possible.

His anger had simmered gently during the day, and he had busied himself to try to take his mind off it. But now he was home he couldn't hide from it any longer.

He had always hated corporate politics, he had never been any good at it, and now he was getting shafted. The powers that be at Bloomfield Weiss had given him a simple choice: nearly half a million pounds if he went along with what they wanted, nothing if he didn't. It was a bribe, plain and simple. But Calder had no inclination to take it, even though Jen's case seemed to be a lost cause. He didn't need the money. How much money did a single male actually *need*? He already had a perfectly pleasant flat on which the mortgage was paid off, a car that he loved and the Pitts Special for tootling around in on sunny weekends. Nearly half of his bonuses he gave to the tax man and most of the rest he saved. He didn't need the four hundred thousand.

He was more worried about his job. He loved trading. After he had left the RAF, he had feared the years of desk-bound tedium that seemed to stretch before him, but actually he found life at Bloomfield Weiss almost as stimulating. He thrived on the feeling of managing a huge bond position, watching the market move against him and then move his way. With the adrenaline coursing through his veins, the total concentration, his mind racing through the possibilities, his mouth dry with the fear of what might go wrong, he felt alive again. Risking millions, he got almost the same buzz as he had felt hurling his body around the sky at five hundred miles an hour. Almost.

All traders were focused on their bonuses. It was their score card, a measure of how good or bad they were at their job. Most traders in his position would have felt honour-bound to quit. But he didn't. That would be to admit defeat, admit that he had been outmanoeuvred by Carr-Jones. Tarek hadn't been lying to him when he had said there were seven-figure bonuses in his future. He would stay, do his bit for Jen, take the political flak and come out fighting the other side.

He thought of what his father would say. Or Nicky. Nicky.

God, he missed her. She understood him, and although she didn't like part of what she understood – his love of betting millions on the whim of the market – she had always been on his side. Until two months ago.

He wanted to talk to her about all this. He trusted her instincts even where they were different from his own. She would be able to put things in some kind of perspective. With her, he could get through whatever Carr-Jones threw at him.

He glanced over to the phone. He wanted to call her, but was there any point? A brush-off, however polite, would just make him feel worse.

He had to try. He dialled her number. The phone rang. Four rings. Five. Six. Then there was a hiss as a recorded message kicked in. Calder dithered. Perhaps he should leave a message. What should he say?

Then he heard the voice. It was a voice he didn't recognize, a man's voice, deep, confident, happy. 'I'm sorry we can't come to the phone at the moment. But if you'd like to leave a message for Gavin or Nicky, please do so after the beep.'

Gavin! Who the hell was Gavin?

Calder threw the telephone at the wall.

13

Calder settled into his seat on the tube and opened the *Financial Times*. He still used the Underground, although many of his colleagues avoided it and took taxis or drove. At the early hour he travelled into work, there was never any problem getting a seat, even on the notorious Northern Line.

He spotted an article on Italy. Apparently the Italian press were howling for the blood of Jean-Luc Martel, the hedge-fund manager who was destroying their country's finances. With somewhat flawed reasoning, the newspapers were blaming him for the economic paralysis gripping the country. The Treasury reaffirmed its determination to see him off by encouraging local banks to support the government bond market. In a further leap of logic Guido Gallotti was saying that the only way to deal with speculators like these was for Italy to leave the euro. It looked as if people were finally listening to him. The DNP was moving ahead strongly in the polls with less than a week to go to the election.

Calder read the article with interest, but he was glad of his decision to stay well clear of Italy until things had calmed down. There was no way to tell which way this one was going to jump.

The train lurched into Camden Town and Calder turned to the Companies and Finance section. The front page grabbed his attention. There were rumours that the hidden losses on UEE's long-term contracts could be even greater than the billion euros mentioned earlier. The credit-rating agencies were considering downgrading the company's debt to junk status. He scoured the article for new facts, but couldn't find any. It didn't matter, he thought grimly. UEE's bonds would still be trashed. He was grateful to Tarek for getting him to off-load half his position, which he had managed to sell at only a small loss.

Nils was waiting for him, fear written all over his pasty face. He had not experienced a loss like this before. 'What do you think, Zero?'

'I think we're screwed. Any prices from the brokers yet?'

'There's a bid of forty-eight. But it's only good for a million euros.'

'What shall we do?' Calder asked.

'I think we should hold on,' said Nils. 'Even if there are bigger losses, UEE throws off so much cash I'm sure we'll get paid out at par eventually.'

'Sure?'

Nils glanced down at the scribbled calculations in front of him.

'Sure.'

Calder closed his eyes. Nils might well be right. And if he was, they would earn a handsome profit on the fifty million bonds they had bought at prices in the low sixties. But it might take years, and they would have to go through a lot of pain first. And they might be wrong. Since the Enron debacle several years before, when one of the biggest energy companies in America had turned out to be little more than a pile of fictitious contracts and lots of debt, the risks of hidden losses had become clear. UEE was no Enron, but still . . .

This was a bad trade. A really bad trade. Calder had made losses before, many times. But in each case he had taken a risk for all the right reasons. It was the nature of even good trades that you got them wrong sometimes. You took your losses and tried again.

But this was different. This was stupid. Dumb. He had filled his boots with bonds in the hope that everything would turn out well, ignoring the chance that it wouldn't. He deserved to lose money.

'Zero?'

He opened his eyes. Nils was looking at him expectantly.

'We sell.'

'But we'll take a hit of at least eight million euros!' Nils protested. 'And I'm positive we'll make it back if we hang on.'

'This was a crap trade,' said Calder. 'And I don't want to be staring at those bonds every day thinking what a moron I was to buy them. We were wrong. The eight million's already gone. We cut our losses and start again.'

'But –'

'We sell.'

Easy to say. Difficult to do. In the end, Calder was helped out by one of the most experienced bond salesmen at Bloomfield Weiss, Cash Callaghan. Cash persuaded one of his hedge-fund clients who specialized in 'distressed' bonds to buy the whole fifty million euros at a price of forty-five.

Calder walked over to Cash's desk to thank him. 'You got me out of a hole on that one,' he said. 'A deep hole.'

Cash was an overweight, fast-talking American, whose Bronx accent had barely softened during the fifteen years he had lived in London. He shook his head. 'As long as you guys keep digging those holes and jumping in them, we'll be right there to haul you out.'

Calder wasn't in the mood to fire another salvo in the age-old war between traders and salesmen. He smiled weakly and turned back to his desk.

'Hey, Zero!'

'Yes?' Calder paused.

Cash stood up and moved over to him, touching him on the arm. 'I hear you're getting crapped on by the assholes?'

'You could say that,' Calder replied cautiously.

'Well, hang in there. A lot of people here have a lot of time for you. They like you. If you can stick it out, you'll do real well. Believe me, I've seen traders come and go, and you're one of the best.'

These words jolted Calder. Cash Callaghan was not known for his lavish praise, except when he wanted something, and Calder couldn't think what he could possibly want that Calder had it in his power to give.

Cash noticed Calder's confusion. 'I'm serious. But if you do decide to quit, come talk to me. I know plenty of people out there who could use a good trader.' He smiled, clapped Calder on the shoulder and returned to his seat, leaving him momentarily stunned.

He recovered and returned to his own desk to tot up his losses, which came to slightly over eight million euros. It made a bad year worse. Two months in, and he was already six million dollars down. An unfamiliar pressure, a feeling he had never experienced before, gripped at his chest with slow, gentle, icy fingers. He remembered the time two years earlier, while he was still working in New York, when he had taken a huge position in the zero-coupon bonds of a major oil company with litigation problems. Zero-coupon bonds were bonds that paid no interest, and their prices were particularly volatile. At one point his unrealized losses on that trade had been up to twenty million dollars. But he had never wavered in his conviction that he was right, that he knew what he was doing, that he would make money in the end. And he had, thirty million dollars' worth, enough to make his reputation at Bloomfield Weiss. But not this time. This time he wasn't so sure. Not so sure at all.

Was he losing it? Was the pressure of the last few weeks getting to him? Could he still trade?

'Nice job getting out of that one, Zero.' Calder looked up to see Tarek hovering by his desk.

'Cash Callaghan bailed me out, thank God. I owe him one. I screwed up.'

'Don't worry about it,' said Tarek, patting him on the shoulder. 'It's history. Start thinking about tomorrow's trade.'

Calder smiled his thanks. But he didn't find the confidence

of Cash and Tarek in him as comforting as he should have.

Carr-Jones drifted by. 'Bad day?' he said, his voice laden with false concern.

'Very bad day.'

'I spoke to Tessa today. She still hasn't come into work. She's not coping well.'

'Poor girl.'

'Have you made up your mind about the Jen problem?'

Calder glared at Carr-Jones. 'You mean now that you've bribed me and blackmailed me at the same time?'

'I don't understand,' said Carr-Jones with a little puzzled frown.

Calder knew that if he weighed the pros and cons rationally, just as he should have done in his abortive UEE trade, he would go along with Carr-Jones. But he was not in the mood. He did not like being bribed and he did not like being blackmailed and he did not like Carr-Jones. The decision was easy, really.

'Justin, I believe Jen has been treated appallingly. I will do everything I can to support her.'

For a moment anger flashed across Carr-Jones's normally cool expression, betraying itself in a tightening of the lips and a touch of pink in his cheeks.

Then he got a grip on himself. 'Mistake, Zero. Big mistake.'

'We have decided to suspend both you and Tessa from work, pending this investigation.'

Calder stared at Linda Stubbes as she said these words, and then at the other people in her office: Benton Davis, Tarek and Carr-Jones. Benton and Tarek avoided his eyes, Carr-Jones met his gaze with a small smile.

'Is she saying I raped her?' he asked.

Linda took a deep breath. 'No, she's not. She's very upset. She knows that it would be her word against yours and she's ashamed of being so drunk, so she doesn't want to go to the police.'

'The reason she doesn't want to go to the police is that I did nothing, and she knows that. If she can't substantiate her accusation you should just ignore it.'

'It's not as simple as that.'

Calder glanced at Carr-Jones, who was watching the proceedings calmly. Of course it wasn't as simple as that. 'Why not?' he asked.

'This is the second claim of sexual harassment you have been involved in in a month,' Linda replied. 'We *have* to take it seriously.'

'Wait a minute,' Calder protested. 'Jen didn't accuse *me* of harassing her.'

'No. But there was the suggestion that you and she were carrying on some kind of intimate relationship –'

'That's just a figment of Justin's imagination!'

'Several other people have made the same comment.'

'Like who?'

'I can't say. Their statements were taken in confidence.'

'Jesus!' Calder looked round the assembled group. Tarek studied his worry beads. 'You know what's going on here, don't you, Linda?'

'We have decided to launch an investigation –'

'Justin is setting me up,' Calder said. 'He wants me to withdraw my statement about how he insulted Jennifer Tan. And all of you are going along with it.'

'Please, Alex, let's not get personal about this,' said Benton Davis in a deep authoritative voice. 'Linda is only doing her job.'

'And where's Tessa?' Calder went on. 'How come she isn't here to make these accusations? Jen had to sit here with Justin last time we went through this.'

'Tessa says she's still too upset to see you,' said Linda.

'And you let her get away with that?'

'I don't think you appreciate the seriousness of your situation,' Benton Davis said. 'Tessa could have gone to the police. You could be facing a rape charge.'

Calder slumped back in his chair. It hadn't taken long for Carr-Jones to come through with his threat. He was being stitched up and there was nothing he could do about it. Not for a rape charge – despite her claims, Tessa would never be able to prove that. But for a character assassination at the Employment Tribunal. Tessa would testify there that he had forced himself upon her. The other derivatives traders who just happened to be in the Midas Touch would back up part of her story. Others would testify that he and Jen were having an affair. Carr-Jones would say that his accusations against Calder were justified. Jen's case relied on Calder's credibility as a witness, credibility that had just been undermined. It would be Carr-Jones versus Calder and Carr-Jones would win.

Benton Davis coughed uncomfortably. 'You should leave immediately,' he said.

'Are you firing me?'

'No,' said Linda. 'That's not what I said at all. I will put this in writing so we can be quite clear about what is happening here.'

'Surely none of you believes a word Tessa says,' Calder said. 'Tarek? Look me in the face and tell me you think I raped her.'

For the first time Tarek raised his eyes to Calder. 'No, I don't believe you raped her. But these are serious allegations and the sooner they're investigated, the sooner you'll be cleared.'

'They're not serious. They're a joke.'

Benton Davis shook his head. 'We're not laughing.'

The taxi crept down the King's Road towards Jen's flat. She had been supposed to meet her friend Sandy for dinner at a little restaurant in Kensington, but once again Sandy had stood her up. Some crisis at the law firm she worked at. Except there was always a crisis at that firm. But Jen was patient with Sandy. She knew it wasn't Sandy's fault, her antisocial and unpredictable hours had made it virtually impossible for her to see anyone. And she was a good friend when they did manage to hook up.

As Jen reached for her purse to pay the driver, she debated again whether to ring Calder. She hadn't seen him since that evening in the bar when she had cold-shouldered him. She was beginning to regret that. He had given her an idea, an idea that looked as if it was about to bear fruit: for the first time in several weeks the immediate future was beginning to look brighter than the immediate past. Calder had stuck his neck out for her, behaved like a decent human being in an institution which seemed to be totally lacking in them. And it would be good to have an ally, someone she could trust.

She pulled out her phone and switched it on.

As it searched for a signal, she hesitated. Despite his boldness, despite his willingness to take risks, Calder was a Bloomfield Weiss man through and through. He was loyal, at a time when loyalty was as obsolete as the telex machine. A couple of months ago she had admired him for it. Now she thought he was just dumb.

The cab pulled up at the corner a few yards from the entrance to her building. She climbed out and paid the driver. As he pulled away, she was jolted by a blow from one side, she lost her balance and fell over, dropping her phone, her bag and her open purse, spilling coins in all directions.

'Oh, madam, I am so sorry. How clumsy of me. Are you all right?' It was a man's voice, soft, friendly, with a foreign accent. 'Are you hurt? Here, let me help you.'

A middle-aged man with brushed-back dark hair, a moustache and kind brown eyes took hold of one arm and helped her to her feet.

'Uh, I'm OK, I guess,' she said. Her initial instinct to yell at him was dispelled by his embarrassed smile.

'I was running to catch that bus, I did not see you,' the man went on. 'I left my glasses at my hotel. Are you sure you are not hurt?'

The man's effusiveness was a little too much. 'No, I'm fine, thank you,' Jen said curtly as she gathered up her bag, her purse and the loose change.

The man went down on his hands and knees to help her. 'Thank you,' she said, and hurried off, leaving the man in embarrassed confusion behind her. She passed Mrs Pinney in the entrance to her building, exchanged scowls, and took the lift up to the sixth floor. She unlocked her door and entered the flat, taking off her coat as she did so. She stared at the telephone in the living room.

Should she call Calder?

What the hell. She checked her watch – nine thirty, he'd definitely be home from work by now – looked up his home number and dialled it.

No answer, just the machine.

'Er, Zero, it's me. Jen.' Suddenly she got cold feet. Maybe it was lucky he hadn't answered. Maybe she shouldn't talk to him. 'Er . . .' Silence. 'That's OK. It's nothing. Bye.'

She put down the receiver, thinking how stupid she must have sounded. Never mind. If he called back, she wouldn't answer, she'd let her own machine screen him out. If only there was a way to erase messages on other people's machines.

Her phone! Where the hell was her cell phone!

She grabbed her bag and opened it. Not there. It must have fallen on to the sidewalk and bounced under a car, or something. Unless the man who bumped into her had it. Come to think of it, all that seemed a bit suspicious. But he was such a nice man, respectable, not her idea of a regular mugger or pickpocket. Except she didn't know what a regular pickpocket looked like.

There was a tap on her door. She hesitated, sliding the chain into its latch before opening it. There was the man. And in his hand was her phone!

Of course he wasn't a pickpocket. It was good of him to

follow her all the way up to her flat with it. Most people would either have ripped off the phone or left it there.

She smiled broadly.

'I'm so sorry, madam. I made you drop this.'

'That's OK. Thank you for bringing it back.'

'Not at all. It was the least I could do.'

There she was on one side of the door. There he was on the other. With the chain hooked, the door would only open a fraction, not quite enough for him to squeeze the phone through. The man smiled and shrugged.

'Oh, I'm sorry,' said Jen, unhooking the chain and opening the door wider.

The man handed her the phone, formally, with the tiniest of bows. It was sort of cute the way he did that, Jen thought. As she took the device from him, she noticed that he was wearing black leather gloves. She turned to put it on the little oak table in her entryway, the table she used for dumping the mail, leaving keys, that kind of thing. The trouble was, there was no space for it. The table was piled high with junk, unopened bills, a DVD overdue from the rental store, some tired lilies shedding their orange pollen left and right, a blown light bulb that she'd put out to remind herself to replace. There was also a photograph of her parents. It was her favourite picture of them: she had taken it on the day of her graduation from college, the love and pride they felt for the photographer radiating from their smiles.

The door shut behind her.

14

The hot water drummed on to his shoulders as he scrubbed himself vigorously. Calder was angry. And as the day had progressed, he just felt angrier. The shower wasn't helping.

He could not believe that Justin Carr-Jones had set him up so blatantly and got away with it. Calder had always thought that, provided he worked hard and made money, he would be treated decently at Bloomfield Weiss. And in his experience that had been the case. Until Carr-Jones had appeared on the scene.

OK, perhaps Jen was being overly sensitive to the kind of abuse regularly doled out to women, and to men for that matter, on a trading floor, but she was basically right. She shouldn't have to live with it if she didn't want to. And the way she had been made to suffer for telling the truth was appalling.

He also didn't like the way senior people at Bloomfield Weiss had allowed Carr-Jones to get away with it, even encouraged him. He wasn't surprised at Simon Bibby, the head of Global Fixed Income, who was notorious within the firm as a serial career killer. Several years before, while Calder was working in New York, Bibby had arranged for a young English trader to take the rap for a mammoth six-hundred-million dollar loss that had really been the responsibility of his boss. Now he was trying the same thing again. The spineless Benton Davis was going along with it, as was Linda Stubbes. Calder was disappointed in her; he thought she had more integrity. But the person who *really* disappointed him was Tarek. When Calder worked for him on the Prop Desk they had become friends and built up a strong mutual trust, cemented through the tribulations of the bond market. He knew Tarek could see what

Carr-Jones was up to, yet he hadn't lifted a finger to help either Jen or him. Too scared of exposing himself politically.

Well, some battles you had to fight, even if you ran the risk of losing.

Calder didn't like losing. Despite Jen's taunts, he wasn't going to give up and do the pragmatic thing: get another job. He knew exactly what his father would say. 'What did I tell you? The City is rotten and you'd be better off out of it.' Well, maybe he was right, but stuff him. And stuff Nicky as well, who would no doubt agree with him.

Carr-Jones was not going to win. Calder would make sure of that.

He turned off the shower. The phone was ringing. He swore to himself, grabbed a towel and padded out to the telephone in his bedroom. The answering machine cut in just as he was about to pick it up.

It was Jen. The message was hesitant. Confused. She mumbled some incoherent words and then rang off.

As the drips on his body cooled, Calder considered calling her back. She hadn't actually asked him to. But when he had last seen her, she seemed in a bad way. And the message was strange. There was something she wanted to tell him, he was sure.

Sod it. He was in too foul a mood to listen patiently to her woes and try to cheer her up. He'd call her tomorrow.

'Alex Calder? I'm Detective Constable Neville.'

The woman at the door waving an identity card was blonde, with rosy cheeks and wide innocent eyes. She was wearing a smart leather jacket and trousers. She had a slight northern accent. She didn't really look like Calder's idea of a tough policewoman.

Calder had just returned from an early morning session at the swimming pool, where he had thrashed up and down for an hour. He felt that oddly pleasant combination of fatigue and invigoration that strenuous exercise can induce in the deskbound.

He frowned. 'What is it?' His immediate thought was that Carr-Jones had set him up somehow. Maybe he had framed him in some way for the rape of Tessa Trew.

The woman looked grim. 'Can I come in?'

'OK,' Calder said. As he led her into the living room he resolved not to answer her questions and get a lawyer at the first sign of suspicion on her part.

The policewoman sat down. 'I have some bad news,' she said. 'It's about one of your colleagues from work. Jennifer Tan.'

'What is it?'

'She died last night.'

'No! How?'

'Her body was found in the courtyard of her building. It looks as if she jumped, but we're still keeping an open mind. She left a note. Or a text message, actually.'

'A text message?'

'Yes. From her mobile phone to her mother.'

'Oh, my God. The poor woman.' Calder struggled to take in what he had been told. Jen had killed herself. It seemed impossible. Too melodramatic for real life, or at least for office life. Occasionally men died in the RAF, where there were obvious physical risks even in peacetime, but at an investment bank where everyone sat around talking all day? One thought hit Calder straight away. Everything had changed. Everything.

'Was it . . . quick?' he said.

'She fell six floors.'

'Oh.' For a second he thought of the mess that would make. Then he tried to think of something else. 'I've never been there.'

'Do you mind if I ask you some questions?' the policewoman said kindly, taking out her notebook.

'No. No, not at all.'

'You worked with Miss Tan?'

Calder flinched at the use of the past tense. With Jen's death the present had become the past, ramming home his first reaction to the news. The world had changed, or at least his world had.

'Yes,' he said.

'I understand she had had some difficulties at work recently. She was bringing a case against Bloomfield Weiss for sexual harassment, and she had resigned.'

'That's correct.'

'Can you tell me a bit about it?'

Calder described the events of the last few weeks as they related to Jen. He tried to make his comments sound objective, but he was sure his anger shone through. The detective made notes.

'How did Jen feel about all this?' she asked.

'She was upset, naturally.'

'How upset?'

'Extremely. She was very angry – furious. But the last time I saw her she seemed depressed. Listless. Very negative. She talked about how lonely she was, how her parents no longer spoke to her, how she hated London, how hard it would be to find another job. She seemed obsessed with the case against Bloomfield Weiss.'

'Did she talk about taking her own life?'

'No, she didn't. And I can't imagine Jen killing herself. At least, not the Jen I used to work with. But on the other hand, she was definitely in a bad way last time I saw her. She called me last night. Left a message on my machine.'

The detective looked up sharply from her notes. 'Is it still there?'

'Yes.'

'Can I hear it?'

'Of course.' Calder went over to the phone and pressed Play. Jen's voice, the voice of a dead person, echoed round the room.

What Calder had thought sounded confused the night before now sounded desperate.

'Did you call her back, Mr Calder?'

'No,' said Calder, taking a deep breath, realizing that this was something he would have to live with for the rest of his life. 'No, I didn't.'

Calder's swipe card still opened the turnstile in the lobby of Bloomfield Weiss. He jabbed the button for the lift, and tapped his foot. From the moment the policewoman had left his flat he had known what he had to do. He had followed her out of the door, run down the hill to the main road and hailed a taxi. Only one thought had been in his head as the cab had fought its way through the traffic towards Broadgate.

The lift deposited him on the second floor. He marched through the swing doors into the trading room. There was an atmosphere of shock in the room, but Calder, normally so attuned to the level of activity around him, didn't notice it.

He crossed the floor to the Derivatives Group. Carr-Jones was talking intently to one of his people, Perumal, and so didn't see Calder approaching. But Perumal saw. His mouth dropped open. Carr-Jones turned.

Calder timed it just right. He lengthened the last two strides to position his left foot in the perfect spot to gain maximum momentum and swung fast and hard with his right fist. He caught Carr-Jones on the chin, before he even had time to register what was happening. His glasses flew off his nose, he slumped backwards and his knees buckled underneath him. He banged against a chair and slid to the floor.

Calder glared at his unconscious body for a second, then turned, moving rapidly towards the exit. Hands tried to grab him half-heartedly, but he shook them off.

'Zero!' He recognized Tarek's voice and paused.

Tarek ran towards him, panting.

'She's dead, Tarek.'

'I know,' Tarek said, holding up his hands in a calming gesture. 'But there's no need to get angry. Calm down.'

'There's every need,' said Calder. 'That's something you should have realized a long time ago. There's every need.'

'Here he comes!'

It was only six thirty in the morning, but all the employees of Teton Capital Management clustered round Vikram. A space had been cleared around the TV in the trading room, which was tuned to a business cable channel. Coverage had gone live to the Ministry of Finance in Rome. Martel slipped his way to the front of the crowd, his six foot seven inches ensuring that several people behind him couldn't see. They didn't complain, but jostled with each other for a better view.

Massimo Tagliaferi, Italy's new Prime Minister appeared with Guido Gallotti at his side. Tagliaferi was carrying a prepared statement.

Martel fidgeted as he waited. It was almost unbearable. He could feel the pride swelling inside him. Over the last few days he had become a changed man. Only a week ago he had felt at the far edge of despair, fighting for his very survival. But now the tide had turned: suddenly everything was going his way. He had even made love to Cheryl.

Thanks to the benign revaluation of the IGLOO notes, the Teton Fund had just scraped by until the election, juggling cash and bonds between accounts. As expected, there had been no clear winner, but Massimo Tagliaferi's DNP had joined up with the Northern League, the newly reconstituted Christian Democrats and a couple of minor parties to form a coalition. As leader of the largest party, Tagliaferi became Prime Minister and Gallotti was appointed Minister of Finance. Immediately there had been a clamour from the large countries in the European Union, especially France and Germany, that any attempt by Italy to leave the euro would be illegal, unconstitutional and might result in fines, cancelled subsidies and expulsion. But no one believed the threats, least of all the market. BTPs went into freefall. Martel's losses dissolved. He didn't close out his positions. He smelled profit. Huge profit.

Tagliaferi began reading from his text. Martel understood a little Italian, but a virtually simultaneous translation appeared in subtitles underneath. The room watched in dead silence.

At first Tagliaferi spoke of Italy's commitment to Europe, of its long history of trading constructively with its European partners, and of the new government's determination that this would continue. For a moment Martel was assailed by doubts again. Perhaps Tagliaferi didn't have the courage to go through with it. Perhaps French and German strong-arming had worked after all. Perhaps the Teton Fund's profits were once again going to slide into losses. He felt the familiar twist in his stomach. He could scarcely watch.

Tagliaferi turned the page and looked straight at the cameras, a barely suppressed smile on his face. He spoke and there was uproar. Martel had to wait a couple of seconds for the subtitles to catch up.

'It is in this spirit of friendship and cooperation that the Italian government announces the withdrawal from the euro and the creation of the "new lira" which will be allowed to float freely against international currencies.'

There it was! The room erupted in cheering. Martel's back was clapped by a dozen hands. Everyone was hugging each other, congratulating each other. Martel drew himself up to his full height and smiled.

'Look! They're redenominating the debt!' Vikram pointed at the screen, where Tagliaferi was continuing to outline how the transition would be accomplished. The redenomination was key. It meant that Italy's euro debt would be converted into new lire. Which meant that the Teton Fund would be able to buy back all the bonds it had sold in euros in the new currency, which would certainly weaken against the old, generating a sizeable profit. And the IGLOO notes would be worth a fortune.

The numbers flicked through Martel's brain. The Teton Fund would make hundreds of millions. No, more than a billion.

Tagliaferi had finished, and the camera switched to a reporter in Lisbon. The speculation that Portugal, Greece and Ireland would follow Italy in quitting the euro was intensifying by the second.

Then the screen changed again and Martel saw another reporter standing outside his own office building. It was barely light, yet a pack of journalists had gathered, hoping for that all important first interview.

'Here in Jackson Hole, Wyoming, we still have had no word from Jean-Luc Martel, the secretive hedge-fund manager who has been blamed by many for the financial crisis that caused the Italian government to take this drastic step. From this day on, Jean-Luc Martel will be known as "The Man Who Broke the Euro".'

There was another cheer in the trading room.

Martel grinned broadly. He liked that. He liked that very much. All George Soros had been able to break was the pound.

'What do you think, Vikram? Time to talk to the press?'

PART TWO

15

'You're too high . . . Steady . . . Don't lower the nose . . . Jesus!'

The Piper Warrior slammed into the grass runway and reared up into the air again, jarring the two occupants to their bones.

'I have control,' said Calder as he placed one hand on his own control column and smoothly opened the throttle to full power with the other. He pressed the mike button. 'Alpha Tango going around.'

'Alpha Tango. Would you like us to remove the trampoline from the runway?'

'No thanks, Angela.' Calder tried not to smile as he pointed the nose upwards. Angela was the most flirtatious radio operator in the east of England, with the sexiest voice. She didn't always stick to the rulebook, but she attracted visiting pilots from miles around. She did have a point, though. That was quite probably Ken's worst landing yet. Ken, Calder's student, was a fifty-year-old accountant from King's Lynn with a passion for flying that remained undimmed, despite the many hours he and Calder had spent bouncing around the circuit at Langthorpe aerodrome. Calder wondered whether Ken was actually getting worse with practice. He'd already done twenty-six hours, yet he was nowhere near his first solo. He was cowering in the left-hand seat, looking more like a timid schoolboy who had forgotten his homework than a successful businessman, or a competent pilot.

'I think that will be the last one for today,' Calder said. 'Once we've checked the landing gear we'll talk about what went wrong.'

Ken nodded, relieved that someone else would be responsible for getting the aircraft onto the ground.

Ken was a challenge, but Calder didn't want to give up. He had already taken three students all the way through to their private pilot's licence, and he had enjoyed teaching them. He had bought the airfield nine months earlier in partnership with Jerry Tyrell, an experienced flying instructor from Calder's old flying club who used to give him the occasional aerobatics lesson. It was situated not too far from his old stomping ground at RAF Marham, on a ridge above the tiny village of Langthorpe, with a beautiful view of the Norfolk coast seven miles away.

The airfield had come with a flying school, a maintenance hangar, eight aircraft, an enthusiastic band of local pilots and an unending supply of problems. But he and Jerry had enjoyed rolling up their sleeves and sorting them out. Jerry was in his late forties, recently divorced, and fed up with the family undertaker's business he had been running in a half-hearted way, so had been eager to sell up and move on to a job where he could fly full time. The initial division of labour had been obvious, with Jerry acting as chief flying instructor and Calder providing eighty per cent of the money. Since then Calder had been in the process of building up his own instructor qualifications.

The whole operation didn't actually make a profit yet, but Calder was optimistic that it would one day. More importantly, he was loving it.

He landed the aircraft carefully and taxied to the hangar, where Colin, the maintenance engineer, began to check over the landing gear. Then he and Ken made their way to the wooden hut which was the North Norfolk Flying School. A slight, dark-faced figure was standing by the door in jeans and a blue coat, watching him approach. Calder checked the car park and saw a BMW M3 he didn't recognize parked next to his own Maserati.

It was Perumal Thiagajaran. He was shifting anxiously from foot to foot.

Calder was not especially pleased to see a reminder of Bloomfield Weiss in the heart of his new world, but he gave a friendly smile and held out his hand. 'Want to learn to fly?' he said.

'Actually, no,' said Perumal, shaking it. 'Do you have a moment?'

'Go into the café and get a cup of tea,' Calder said. 'I'll be with you when I've finished with my student.'

A quarter of an hour later Calder joined him. The café was run by Paula, a hefty girl who also doubled as a fire officer. Every airfield licensed by the Civil Aviation Authority needed a fire truck, or in Langthorpe's case a fire Land-Rover, on duty at all times, and one of the many headaches of running the place was making sure that there were always two trained people available to operate it.

Calder and Perumal had hardly spoken at Bloomfield Weiss. Although Perumal was part of Carr-Jones's team, Calder had nothing against him personally and he remembered that he was about the only person in the Derivatives Group Jen would still speak to. Calder had him pegged as a harmless geek. 'So, if you don't want to learn to fly, what are you doing here?' he asked.

'Do you still stay in touch with Bloomfield Weiss?'

'No,' Calder replied. 'I keep well clear of the place.'

'So you don't do any work for them? Consultancy or anything?'

'No.'

'And do you speak to any of the bosses?'

'No.' In fact, Calder hadn't even spoken to his old friend Tarek since he had left. 'I'm quite pleased to be out of there.'

'After what happened to Jen?'

Calder nodded. 'That. And other things. The place has changed over the last few years. Or I've changed. Or something. I realized it wasn't fun any more. And it wasn't human.'

'I see.'

Perumal was silent. Calder sipped his tea. He had done his

best to think of Bloomfield Weiss as little as possible in the year since he had resigned. After Jen's death, the decision to leave had been easy. In that moment his determination to stand up to Carr-Jones had evaporated. He didn't want to play the game any more. He had briefly considered moving to another investment bank, but they all had their Carr-Jones equivalents. Like it or not, the bad guys were winning in the City.

He had felt a tremendous sense of relief when he had walked out of the Broadgate office that last time. It had been a clear, sunny day, and he had gone flying that afternoon. And the next day, and the day after that. The following week he had just returned from taking the Pitts out for a tumble through the skies when he fell into conversation with Jerry. They repaired to a local pub, and within an hour they had hatched the scheme of finding a flying school of their own to buy. Three months later and Langthorpe was theirs.

Perumal glanced at Calder anxiously and then stared deep into his cup. 'I'd like some advice.'

'OK,' said Calder. 'I'll do what I can. But, as I said, I'm a bit out of things.' Surely Perumal hadn't driven all this way for tips on how to climb the greasy pole at Bloomfield Weiss? If he had, he had definitely come to the wrong man.

'I know. It's because you are a bit out of things that I want to talk to you.' Perumal swallowed. 'Do you think there was anything suspicious about Jen's death?'

Now Calder's curiosity was aroused. 'Suspicious? What do you mean?'

'Just suspicious.'

'You mean, did she really kill herself?'

Perumal shrugged.

'No, I don't think there was anything suspicious,' Calder replied. 'The police looked into it and decided it was suicide. It was bloody obvious Carr-Jones drove her to it. We all know that. She sent some kind of suicide text message, didn't she? Why do you ask? What do you think?'

Perumal took a deep breath. 'I'm not so sure.'

'That it was suicide? Why not?'

'The timing of Jen's death was very convenient.'

'For who? Carr-Jones?'

'Maybe.'

'Because it got her sexual harassment suit off his back?'

'Not just that.'

'What, then?'

Perumal didn't answer.

'Are you saying Carr-Jones killed her?' Calder asked, his frustration building.

Another shrug.

'Have you told the police this?'

Perumal shook his head.

'Come on, Perumal, this is absurd,' Calder said. 'If you think Carr-Jones killed her, you should say so. If you have evidence, you should tell the police.'

Perumal sighed. 'It's not as easy as that.'

'Why not?'

'If I was sure, then I would know what to do. But I'm not sure. And I don't have anyone to talk to about it. Which is why I came up here.'

'OK, I understand.' Calder realized how nervous Perumal was and didn't want to scare him off. 'Why was Jen's death convenient to Carr-Jones?'

Perumal opened his mouth and then hesitated. 'If I tell you, will you promise to keep it to yourself?'

Now it was Calder's turn to pause. 'No, Perumal, I won't. If Carr-Jones did kill Jen, then I can't keep quiet. And neither should you.'

'I see,' said Perumal. Suddenly, fear touched his eyes.

'I take it you still work for him?'

'Yes.'

'And you're scared of him?'

Perumal refused to meet Calder's eyes. 'I'm doing well in

the group. I've brought in some big deals – massive deals. I'll get a big bonus this year. I'm a star. Like you were.'

'When you're talking about people dying, that kind of thing doesn't matter. You know that, or you wouldn't be here.'

Perumal shifted in his chair and turned to watch Paula wiping down the tables.

'Carr-Jones is not immune from the law, you know,' Calder went on. 'If he was involved in Jen's death, the police will arrest him and put him away. Where he belongs.'

'I'm not saying he was involved in Jen's death,' Perumal said.

'So what are you saying?'

'I'm saying that there are too many coincidences,' Perumal began.

'Go on.'

'Well, you see . . .' He hesitated. Calder waited, restraining his impatience to tell Perumal to spit it out. 'The thing is . . .' Perumal frowned and glanced at Calder. Then he panicked. He pushed his chair back from the table and scrambled to his feet. 'I'm sorry, I must be going now.'

'Wait!'

'No, I should never have come here. I thought you were someone I could trust, but I see I can't expect you to help me.'

'Perumal –'

'Forget I was here. Forget what I said. Please.' He rushed for the door. Calder followed him and watched him dart for his BMW and head for the airfield exit at speed.

Martel paced up and down in the hushed lobby of the Hotel Intercontinental in Geneva, eating up the distance from one end to the other in rapid giant strides. He knew he was making the reception staff nervous, but he didn't care. He had just come from a long session at Chalmet et Cie, the Swiss bank who had introduced him to many of his investors. He had only been waiting for this next meeting for five minutes, but he was already impatient.

It was hard to focus. Try as he might, he couldn't get his mind off his conversation with Cheryl the night before. As usual, the Teton Fund's troubles had kept him awake. He had tossed and turned for hours and then decided to call her. It was three o'clock in the morning in Geneva and nine p.m. in New York. She was staying at their one-bedroom apartment on Central Park West.

She had taken a while to answer.

'*Mon ange*, it's me.'

'Oh.' She sounded stunned. 'Oh, yeah. Honey. Gee. It's pretty late in Switzerland, isn't it?'

'Yes.' Martel glanced at the numbers on the hotel clock. 'Three-oh-six. I'm glad I caught you in. What are you doing?'

'Oh, nothing. Just reading in bed.'

'Is that where you are now?' Martel conjured up the image of his wife waiting for him, alone in the large bed. What was she wearing, he wondered.

'Yes,' she said, her voice strained.

Then Martel heard it. Quite distinctly. A cough. A man's cough.

'What was that?'

'What?'

'I heard a cough.'

'It was the TV.'

That didn't make sense. Martel strained. There was no background chatter. 'I can't hear it now.'

'That's because I've just turned it off.'

'But there isn't a TV in the bedroom.'

'What is this, Jean-Luc? Have you called me up just to give me a hard time?'

'No. It's just, I don't understand.'

'What's the matter? Don't you believe me?' Cheryl was beginning to sound angry. She was daring him to call her a liar, accuse her of having a man in her bedroom.

'No, *mon ange*. I just thought I heard someone else in there with you.'

'I don't believe this,' said Cheryl. 'I'm going back to my book.' And she hung up.

Martel called back, but the phone just rang six times and the answering machine cut in, his own voice asking him whether he wanted to leave a message.

He didn't.

It couldn't be true, could it? That Cheryl had a man in her apartment, *their* apartment? The concept of Cheryl cheating on him had never before occurred to Martel. He assumed that if anyone was going to cheat on anyone in his marriage, it would be him, and he congratulated himself on the fact that so far he had been strictly faithful.

Perhaps Cheryl was so unsatisfied with Martel's sexual performance that she had looked for fulfilment elsewhere? The very thought stung Martel's pride, stung it deeply. The return to normality in their sex life after the Italian triumph the year before had lasted for only a month. Now he was scared even to try to make love to his wife.

Was he, Jean-Luc Martel, a *cocu*? No. No, he just couldn't accept it.

When they both got back to Jackson Hole Martel would have it out with her. Force her to tell him the truth.

Martel paced even faster. Except he wouldn't. He knew he wouldn't. Cheryl wouldn't take kindly to that kind of inquisition. If she wasn't having an affair, she'd be justifiably furious, and if she was, she might walk out on him. He'd lose her. He hated the thought of that.

A pile of magazines rested on a coffee table in a corner of the lobby. Martel spotted *Fortune* among them. He picked it up, curious if the latest edition would include the interview the magazine had done with him a few weeks before.

It did. There was an article entitled 'The Man Who Broke the Euro?' Martel smiled, until he noticed the question mark. What was that doing there?

He flipped to the page. There was a photograph of him, a

good one. He was sitting in his office, leaning back in his chair with his hands behind his head, his tanned, handsome face displaying a mixture of quiet confidence and piercing intelligence. Behind him, through his office window, rose the magisterial Tetons in their white robes. The article was several pages long.

He speed read it. The first part outlined Martel's background, his previous triumphs and his thoughts on trading, including some of his more esoteric ideas linking Francis Galton, Charles Darwin and Richard Thaler, what he called 'The Evolution of the Crowd'. Martel's hypothesis was that the behaviour of the market was like an organism that evolved and changed according to the principles of natural selection and statistics. The *Fortune* journalist hadn't quite understood the subtleties of the theory but Martel was pleased. At last people were listening to him. Then followed a description of the events of the previous spring when Italy had left the euro. So far, so good. Then the tone of the article changed. Other people were interviewed, many of whom he'd never heard of. Two economists said that Martel's trades had actually had very little to do with Italy's decision to leave the euro. That in fact the press and politicians had been happy to use Martel as a scapegoat, whereas the real cause had been Italy's dismal economic performance. Martel's anger grew.

There were some quotes from Walter Lesser, the New York hedge-fund manager who had been unimpressed by Martel's arguments for shorting Italian government bonds. Rather than having the courage to admit that he was wrong, Lesser claimed that Martel had a reputation for taking imprudent risks, that the Teton Fund had nearly gone bust the year before, and that Martel had just been lucky.

There the article ended.

Martel was gripped by fury. He tugged at the pages in the magazine trying to pull them out. How dare Lesser? He, Jean-Luc Martel, had used his power and his genius to bring Italy to its knees. Everyone knew that.

The pages flew out of the magazine with a satisfying rip. One of the hotel staff scurried round the reception desk. 'May I take that, sir?' he said. Martel swore at him in French and the clerk scurried away again and picked up a phone.

Martel's stomach howled. That pain had come back with a vengeance. Because the Teton Fund was once again taking a big risk, a risk many times greater than that he had taken the year before.

Fortune might have doubts about Martel's massive Italian trade, but investors throughout the world had been impressed. The cash had flooded in until the Teton Fund's assets totalled more than three billion dollars. These investors had high expectations, which Martel felt under pressure to meet. For a year he had been dipping a toe into the water here and there, buying mortgages, Brazilian equities, gold, oil, searching in vain for the next big opportunity. Finally, he had found it.

Japan.

For decades, the Japanese stock market had gone nowhere. The economic miracle of the nineteen sixties and seventies was but a distant memory. But Martel had returned from a two-week tour of the Far East convinced that things were about to change. He detected a new confidence among Japanese manufacturers, and he had met a couple of highly placed businessmen and government ministers in Korea and Thailand who had intimated that the Japanese were soon to regain their position as the industrial powerhouse of Asia. So Jean-Luc Martel, The Man Who Broke the Euro, had decided that it was finally time for Japan to have its day in the sun again. He had begun buying Japanese shares. Billions of dollars' worth of them, using all the tricks in his book to maximize his exposure. This had included some enormous derivative trades Vikram had fixed up with Bloomfield Weiss.

The sheer weight of his buying had forced the market up for a few weeks. The Teton Fund was showing a nice profit, several hundred million dollars, but Martel had held out for more. He was greedy. He wanted to make the billions his investors expected.

Then had come the announcement that the biggest bank in Japan had discovered a pile of bad loans. In the following week three other major banks made similar discoveries. The market decided that Japan had not turned the corner after all. So prices slipped and slid, despite Martel's frantic buying in an attempt to single-handedly shore up Japan's industrial base. The Teton Fund's unrealized losses climbed over a billion dollars and were now nearing two. And once again Martel was forced into the agonizing business of passing collateral around between brokers in a desperate attempt to prevent them from shutting him down.

A hotel manager approached him with two burly porters. At the same time a slight, balding Arab with a thick moustache emerged from the bank of lifts.

'Monsieur –' began the manager.

'Fuck off,' muttered Martel in French and strode forward to meet the Arab.

'Monsieur Martel?' The Arab shook Martel's proffered hand limply. Martel was surprised by the piercing intelligence of the other man's large brown eyes. 'Tarek al-Seesi. I apologize for keeping you waiting.'

Perumal couldn't concentrate on the movie on the tiny screen in front of him, some trivial romantic comedy. It was mid-afternoon, and had been for the last several hours. Forty thousand feet beneath him was the Nebraska prairie, stretching four hundred miles on to the Rocky Mountains. The aeroplane would land in Denver in an hour or so, according to the captain. Then a two-hour wait and a smaller plane to Jackson Hole.

He had never actually visited his biggest client before. Carr-Jones had been nagging him for the last year, and in the end had ordered him to go. The New York office had been trying to steal the account, claiming it was ridiculous to cover someone in Wyoming out of London. Carr-Jones needed to prove that his team was in constant touch with the Teton Fund. That meant going there. It was all Perumal had been able to do to prevent his boss from coming with him. More talk of 'the Indian mafia'.

So here he was. Flying into the mouth of the tiger.

Perumal took a deep breath. Everything was spinning out of control. But it would all be resolved soon, one way or another. And when it was all over, he would be either dead or in jail.

He wasn't sure which was worse. If he went to jail, the shame would be impossible for his parents to bear. It would be impossible for *him* to bear. His mother was fiercely proud of her son. Perumal had earned a handsome bonus the year before and had been able to send seventy thousand dollars home. When he had gone back to Kerala in August his mother's delight in her son's achievements had been overwhelming. His wife, Radha, too, had been impressed. Theirs had been an arranged marriage, engineered by Perumal's mother, and Radha's family was richer than his. Now it was clear that Perumal's mother had been correct: her son would be able to look after Radha very well in the coming years.

His mother liked her comforts, but she wouldn't want her son to become a criminal. Neither would his father. A simply pious man, every morning he would do his *puja*, lighting incense and saying prayers before going to work. They would both feel that he had let down his family and betrayed them for all the effort they had put into his education. And they would be right. Almost better if he died.

And death was a real possibility. He had received the e-mail the week before. Three simple words: *Remember Jennifer Tan*. The sender's address was some gobbledygook; the message could have been from someone thousands of miles away or in the next office. Either way, its meaning was clear.

Calder had been his one hope. Although Perumal didn't

know him well, he knew he was honest and decisive and, most importantly, he was now outside Bloomfield Weiss. But Calder was too honest. As soon as Perumal had begun talking to him, he realized that Calder would insist on going straight to the authorities and blowing the whole thing open. And that was something Perumal wanted to avoid.

There was no way out.

He stared hard out of the window and thought he saw the indistinct shape of the Rocky Mountains far in the distance. Somewhere up there to the north-west lay Jackson Hole.

No, Perumal was not looking forward to this trip.

16

Calder slammed the door behind him and set out across the marshes. His cottage was isolated, a mile down the lane from the village of Hanham Staithe and half a mile from the sea. Or a mile and a half at low tide. The house was two hundred years old, constructed with a mixture of flint and ancient brick. It had once been at the end of a row of half a dozen similar buildings but the wind and the moisture and the isolation had worn the others away, so that nothing was left but barely traceable indentations in the pasture behind the house.

There would be no flying at Langthorpe aerodrome today. The clouds were low and grey, and there was a steady north wind blowing in from the sea. A north wind in Norfolk in January is bitingly cold, but Calder had dressed to withstand it. It meant he should be alone.

As he marched along the top of a dyke towards the sea, his steps rapid against the wind, he thought yet again about his conversation with Perumal the previous weekend. Each time Perumal's words and the expression of fear on his face came into Calder's consciousness he tried to ignore it. He had turned his back on the City and he wanted to keep it turned. The flying school and the airfield absorbed his energies: there was so much to do, so much to worry about, and he and Jerry really did seem to be making progress. He was spending a lot of time in the air, either teaching, or messing around in the Pitts. His aerobatic technique was improving and he thrilled every time he executed a near-perfect manoeuvre.

Yet he missed the City. He missed the camaraderie of the trading room. He missed the excitement of coming into work and never knowing what would happen from one day to the next. And he missed pitting himself against the market, taking those big risks, dancing on the edge of disaster.

He took the occasional risk flying, but it wasn't the same. Light-aircraft aviation was all about safety, and as the owner of a flying school he couldn't be seen to be flouting the rules.

A figure was silhouetted against the sky, bending over a tripod. A birdwatcher, that hardiest of Norfolk species. All around him the marsh was alive with the twitter and rustle of tiny birds, for whom these stretches of coarse grass and mud were staging posts in great global voyages. The small birds held no interest for Calder, but he was fascinated by the huge flocks of geese that gathered in complicated shifting formations in the wide Norfolk sky. Suddenly the peace of the marsh was interrupted by a roar as two Tornados passed low overhead and turned to follow the coastline eastwards. Calder thought he caught a glimpse of the lynx's head on the tail as the rear aircraft banked. His old squadron was still flying from Marham; he wondered how many of his former colleagues remained there. Within a few seconds the jets were gone and moments later the sound waves from those mighty engines dissipated into nothing.

He strode past the twitcher and exchanged a greeting and a smile. The birds twittered on, regardless.

What if Perumal was right? What if Jen hadn't committed suicide? Was it possible?

Jen had been found six floors below her flat. Presumably the police had asked themselves whether she was pushed or whether she jumped, and decided that she jumped.

But could they be fooled? By someone as cunning as Carr-Jones?

Possibly.

But why would Carr-Jones kill Jen? There was no doubt that he disliked her, but he had already ruined her life – why would he take the risk of ending it as well? Unless Perumal was right. He said Jen's death was too convenient. Too many coincidences. What the hell did that mean?

Perumal knew.

Calder arrived at the edge of the sand. It was low tide, the sea was over a mile away. He looked out over the wide expanse of sand and mud, criss-crossed with creeks and channels of seeping salt water, studded with millions of shells, a city of molluscs. Birds large and small scurried about, busily searching out the choicest neighbourhoods. The salt wind bit into his face from the northern horizon, where the dark grey of the sky merged with the slightly lighter grey of the sea. As he watched, a rip appeared in the folds of the darker fabric and a curtain of thin sunshine fell on to a patch of sea, barely a quarter of a mile long, which immediately sparkled white and yellow. In a moment it was gone, the slash repaired, the sea dark and shifting once more.

Calder turned. He looked back over the marshes to the low wooded hill behind his cottage, and the old windmill above it, its sails locked fast against the relentless wind. The birdwatcher was gone. There was no human to be seen.

A hundred odd miles beyond that low hill was the teeming metropolis, with its millions of workers getting and spending. Did he really want to go back to all that?

He headed home towards the cottage, the wind at his back now. He had known that when Jen had died his attitude to Bloomfield Weiss and the rest of the City had changed for ever. He had assumed that he could walk away from it, that he *should* walk away from it. But it wasn't that simple. Jen had stood up for what she had believed in. She had been intimidated, bullied, crushed to the point where she had lost her life. Calder remembered that last phone call to him she had made, just before she died. To his eternal regret he hadn't answered it.

Maybe he should answer it now.

Back at the cottage he dialled the Bloomfield Weiss switchboard and asked for Perumal. He tapped his fingers with impatience until the phone was picked up by a nameless colleague. Apparently Perumal was on a trip to the States but was expected back in the office the following morning.

Calder called the following day, to be told that Perumal had decided to take a couple of days' holiday, and would be in on Monday morning.

It rained on Monday. A succession of cold fronts had buffeted the aerodrome all weekend and there was no let-up forecast. Once again, nobody was flying. A flying school's finances were hostage to the weather. No flying, no students, no hirers, no income. In the long run, it should even itself out, but a bad summer could bankrupt an operation.

Calder was in his office, trying to find an avgas supplier who would give him a decent discount. Not easy. After the third brush-off he decided to try Perumal again. By this time, he had his direct line.

'Bloomfield Weiss.'

Calder didn't recognize the voice. 'Can I speak to Perumal, please?'

A pause. 'Who's speaking?'

'A friend,' Calder said.

Another pause. 'One tick.'

Silence. Then a different, familiar voice. 'Zero? It's Justin.'

Bloody hell. Calder might not have recognized the voice of the person answering the phone, but that person had identified his own mild Scottish accent. Calder considered hanging up, but that would just raise Carr-Jones's suspicions more.

'Hello, Justin,' he said, his mind scrambling for a plausible reason to be telephoning one of Carr-Jones's traders.

'You were asking for Perumal?'

'Yes. He called me last week about taking flying lessons.'

'Ah, I see.' Carr-Jones's usual quiet self-satisfaction seemed to have left him. He sounded subdued.

'What is it?' Calder said, suddenly knowing the answer.

Carr-Jones sighed. 'I'm afraid Perumal won't be taking up flying,' he said. 'He was involved in a snowmobile accident in America over the weekend. An avalanche. He didn't make it.'

'Jesus Christ,' said Calder. Although the news should have come as a total shock, Calder felt that somewhere deep down he had been expecting it. He searched for something suitable to say, but suspicion was flooding into his mind. 'I can't imagine Perumal on a snowmobile,' was all he could come up with.

'No,' said Carr-Jones. 'I can't imagine him flying, either.'

'Where did this happen?'

'Jackson Hole. Wyoming.'

'He was visiting the Teton Fund?'

'I'm sorry, Zero, I've got to go. There's a lot to deal with here, as you can imagine.'

The natural thing was to say how sorry he was for the loss of a treasured member of Carr-Jones's team, but already the suspicion was screaming at Calder that Carr-Jones was in some way responsible. 'Thanks for letting me know,' was all Calder said as he rang off.

Calder knew Perumal hadn't had an accident. He had looked too scared, he had raised too many questions. He knew too much.

But as he thought it through, he realized that no one else, with the possible exception of Carr-Jones himself, would be similarly suspicious. Calder knew things no one else did. He had a duty to tell the appropriate people. The police.

DC Neville looked even younger and fresher-faced than Calder remembered. But she had a file out on the table in front of her, and she was listening intently to what Calder had to say, taking notes and weighing him up as he spoke. They were in a featureless interview room inside the warren that was Kensington Police Station.

Calder told her everything, the background to Jen's 'suicide', her feud with Carr-Jones, Perumal's visit and his suspicion that

Jen's death had been convenient, and the news that he had died in an accident in Jackson Hole.

'Do you know what he was doing out there?' Neville asked.

'When I called last week, they said he was on business. There's a big hedge fund based there called the Teton Fund. You might have heard of them? It's run by Jean-Luc Martel. He's the guy who was blamed for forcing Italy to leave the euro last year.'

Neville's face was blank, but she was writing. She paused and looked up from her notebook. 'Have you mentioned your suspicions to anyone at Bloomfield Weiss?'

'No,' Calder said. 'I thought I'd leave all that to you.'

'Very wise,' Neville said. 'You can rest assured we'll be talking to them. And to the police in America. There may be a murder investigation under way there.'

'Was there any doubt about Jen's death?'

'The coroner recorded a verdict of suicide.'

'Was he correct?'

Neville picked up the file in front of her. 'I think so. Although in the light of what you've just told me, we should take another look.'

'Did you have any doubts at the time?'

Neville leafed through the file. 'Not really. The forensic medical examiner was a little concerned about the injuries to the victim's skull. He thought there was a possibility one of them might have been inflicted before the others.'

'You mean she was struck on the head before she hit the ground?'

'That would have been the implication had the FME been certain. But he wasn't. It was just a suspicion, barely hinted at in the report. He was sure she was still alive when she fell.'

'But she could have been hit on the head, perhaps knocked unconscious and pushed out of her window afterwards?'

'We did check that possibility. But we didn't find any signs of struggle in the apartment. No one saw anyone come in or go out. No sound of a fight. No unexplained fingerprints. No blood.'

'Nothing else?'

Neville scanned the file. 'The woman who lived opposite her passed her on her way in to the building that evening. She saw Miss Tan bump into someone on the street. Miss Tan dropped her handbag, he helped pick it up.'

'What sort of person?'

'White male, fifty or sixty, medium height, well dressed, dark hair, thin dark moustache. But after the collision he walked off.'

'So you were convinced it was suicide?'

'She was having a rough time, as you yourself told us. As did lots of other people. She had reason to be depressed, and to take her own life. And she sent a text message to her mother on her mobile.' Neville looked in her file. '"Sorry Mum". That's all. Sent right before she jumped.'

'I remember. But could that have been faked?'

'It could, but we have no evidence that it was.'

'It must have been a horrible message to receive.'

'Her mother saw it just before we had a chance to contact her. She called Miss Tan's mobile. I answered it. She was hysterical.'

'I bet.'

Neville grimaced at the memory and leafed through the file. 'There was a friend of hers . . . Sandy Waterhouse . . . know her?'

'Is she some kind of lawyer?'

'Yes. American. She said she was quite certain Jen wouldn't commit suicide. I interviewed her. She was quite credible.'

'But not credible enough to cast doubt on the coroner's verdict?'

'It's often difficult to be one hundred per cent sure in suicide cases. And we will follow up this new information you've given us. Can you let us know where we can get in touch with you?'

Calder handed her his North Norfolk Flying School card, which listed his mobile number. He had been worried that the police wouldn't take his concerns seriously. But now he had done his duty: DC Neville had heard him out and he could leave it to her and her colleagues to see if his suspicions were well founded.

Calder had planned to drive down to London and back in a day, but he decided to stop off at his sister's place in Highgate on his way home.

Anne was unloading the children from her Jeep as he pulled up outside her house. Phoebe was touchingly pleased to see him and leapt out of the car to give him a hug. Robbie grinned at him, and waved a half-eaten biscuit in his direction.

Anne prattled on at him and the children as she made tea. It was a long story about Phoebe and one of her friend's cats which Calder swiftly lost track of. He didn't mind, though. There was something comforting about his sister's chaotic existence.

Finally they were sitting down at the kitchen table with the children banished to the playroom. Calder explained why he had come down to London. Anne listened intently.

'I remember how upset you were when that girl died,' she said when he had finished. 'Almost more upset than I've ever seen you.'

Calder knew that the 'almost' referred to their mother's death. 'It's true. It shook me. It shook my faith in humanity. And I felt guilty. Perhaps I should have done more for her.'

'It seems to me that you did more than anyone else did,' said Anne with indignation. 'You put your neck on the line. And she didn't show any appreciation for that at all.'

'She was in no fit state to. I still beat myself up about not answering the phone that night she died.'

'Well, if it wasn't suicide, it probably wouldn't have made any difference.'

'Yes, but who knows what she wanted to say? What she wanted to tell me? About Carr-Jones, for instance.'

'Do you really think he could have killed her?'

Calder sighed. 'I don't know. Part of me almost wishes he had. In some ways it's not as bad as taking your own life. And if she did commit suicide, he drove her to it.'

'But murder? Cold-blooded murder?'

'Who knows? It's impossible for me to be objective about it. But I'm pretty sure the police took what I had to say seriously. I'll leave them to find out the truth.'

There was a sharp cry from the direction of the playroom and then a steady wail. Anne went off to sort it out.

She was back a moment later. 'There's something *I* wanted to tell you,' she said.

'Oh, yes?'

'Did you know Father has put Orchard House on the market?'

'No!' The news came as a complete surprise to Calder. An unwelcome surprise. The family had lived in that house since he was born. He hadn't been there for at least three years, but the knowledge that it was still there, that it was still the Calder family home, comforted him. It was a reminder of happy times, times when his mother was still alive, times when they were a family, when the whole was greater than the individual parts.

Anne was watching him, following the emotions in her brother's expression. 'I know. That's how I felt.'

'When did you find out?'

'I spoke to him last Sunday on the phone and he dropped into the conversation that someone was about to come and look at the house. He acted as though it was the most natural thing in the world. But you know Father. That was just his way of telling me.'

'Do you have any idea why?'

'I asked him. He said he wanted to live in a smaller place.'

'But he loves that house! It reminds him of Mum just as much as it reminds you and me.'

'I think he needs the cash. Remember last year I told you he sold Mum's jewellery.'

'And the Cadells. Did you ever ask him about that?'

'I tried to. He just changed the subject. You know what he's like.'

'But why would he need so much money?'

Anne stared at the dregs in her tea. 'Do you remember my friend Stacey McGregor from school?'

'Vaguely.'

'She lives in Hawick now.' Hawick was a small mill town about twenty miles from Kelso. 'She says she was in a newsagent's there and she saw Father. He was buying lottery tickets. A hundred quid's worth.'

'Lottery tickets! Father! He'd never be caught dead with those. Is she sure it was him?'

'Quite sure. She says he didn't recognize her. She's put on quite a bit of weight since he last saw her. But everyone knows what he looks like.'

'So are you saying he's spent thousands of pounds on lottery tickets?'

'I don't know. But I'm worried.'

'Yeah. You said that last year.'

'Aren't you?'

Calder wanted to say it didn't bother him because he didn't care. But it did. He knew how much it would pain the old man to sell Orchard House, how many memories it would hold for him. Something must be wrong. But he couldn't believe it was lottery tickets. 'Yes,' he said. 'Yes, I am worried.'

'I think you should go and talk to him.'

'Me! But at the best of times I'd only last half an hour in that house without having a row. No, you should talk to him.'

'I've tried and got nowhere. He won't listen to me. He avoids the subject, or worse, he lies. But I know he respects you. I think you can make him tell you the truth.'

Calder shook his head. 'This makes no sense.' But he knew that, despite appearances, it did.

'Alex?' His sister rarely asked him for anything. She was asking him now.

Calder sighed. 'All right. I'll do it.'

17

He flew up to Kelso the next morning, taking the flying school's Cessna 172, which was good for short-field operations. Several years before, he had come to an arrangement with the owner of a farm-strip a few miles from Kelso. For twenty pounds the farmer let him land and have the use of an old banger for a few hours. He hadn't told his father what he was doing. He didn't want to give him the chance to hide anything.

He arrived at Orchard House late morning. It was a long, low building of grey stone, with a pretty garden and an apple orchard to the side. His mother had loved the place; the apples reminded her of her native Somerset. It was a couple of miles out of town, in the tiny village of Cairnslaw. From Calder's old bedroom window you could see through the apple trees towards Kelso with its church spires, its ruined abbey, and its bridges over the broad River Tweed hurrying eastwards towards Berwick and the North Sea. By the gate stood a yellow and blue For Sale sign bearing the name of a local estate agent.

Calder parked the banger in the shade of a Chile pine, a monkey-puzzle tree. As a child he had been fascinated by its large pine cones and crazy branches. It was difficult to climb, but at the age of seven he had tried and succeeded. He had risen thirty feet, above the height of the eaves of the house, when he decided to come down. He couldn't. Too proud to shout for help, he stayed up there for two hours until his distraught mother found him. She called the fire brigade to get him down. His father was furious.

But Calder wanted to go higher. So he tried again, the following week, this time getting as close to the top as possible. Once again he couldn't get down. The fire brigade didn't seem to mind, but the doctor was very angry. He fetched his saw and began to lop off the lower branches. Only then had Calder started to cry.

But the tree was alive and well, and Calder found he now had no desire to scale it.

The garden was as tidy as he would expect, scarcely a dead leaf in sight. Snowdrops peeked out from the beds by the front door. Were they the same ones his mother had planted all those years ago, he wondered. Or did his father replenish them every year?

He went around to the back, eased the loose brick away from the top of the garden wall, and took out the key from its hiding place. He unlocked the back door and passed through into the kitchen. As spotless and tidy as an operating theatre. Although his father had done his best to leave the kitchen and indeed the whole house the same as it had been when his mother died, he had been unable to suppress his desire for order. Calder's mother, like his sister, liked to live in chaos. Dr Calder had indulged this while she was alive, but in the months after her death, he had tidied up. The place had remained tidy.

Calder wandered through the house. It was three years since he had been there. Its familiarity was comforting, bringing back a crowd of memories. It would be a shame to sell it.

Anne was right, there were gaps. The most obvious was in the dining room where the painting of the River Tweed by Francis Cadell used to hang. The other Cadell had hung in the drawing room, but that too had disappeared. The clock on the mantelpiece was gone, as was the bookcase. It must have been sold very recently: the books were still piled up on the floor. Calder opened the sideboard. The silver drawer was nearly empty.

He moved through to his father's study and the explanation was lying on his desk: the *Racing Post*, open to a meeting at York. There were notations on the page, with one horse, Mercator, ringed. There were two form guides on the desk, and an exercise book, filled with his father's neat handwriting: the doctor disapproved of the traditional GP's scrawl, believing in accuracy and clarity in all things. Calder had had qualms about going though his father's papers, but not now. He checked the desk drawers. The top one contained stationery and a collection of ancient pens and pencils. The second held a neat pile of lottery tickets bundled together with an elastic band. The third held bills. Calder riffled through them. On top was a statement from a bookmaker in Selkirk. Seven thousand pounds! That was serious money.

But it was the second bill that brought him up short. This bookmaker was based in Berwick. One hundred and forty-three thousand pounds.

Calder slumped into his father's chair, holding the bill in front of him.

His father was a gambler. A serious, hard-core, out-of-control gambler. He glanced at the scribbled notes, the form books. He was one of those deluded gamblers who thought they knew how the horses worked, but didn't. Like all those failed traders who thought they knew what made the bond markets tick, but didn't.

Calder considered how a bookmaker could let a family doctor run up bills of over a hundred thousand pounds. He must have believed his father's credit was good. The doctor must have been a long-standing customer who had paid off his debts over the years. Decades, even. Over time the stakes would have steadily risen until now he was over his head. He had probably made some desperate bets to win everything back. And lost.

Calder didn't know how long he sat there, staring. But he heard the sound of the front door slamming, and someone moving through to the kitchen. So his father still came back from the surgery for lunch. Calder kept quiet.

Five minutes later the doctor himself appeared at the study door, with a sandwich on a plate in one hand and three newspapers under his arm. It took him a second to notice Calder.

The newspapers slipped to the floor.

'Alex?'

'Hello, Father.'

The doctor looked at his son, and at the bookie's statement he was holding in his hand, and his face went white. Then the colour surged back. 'Alex! What the devil do you think you're doing breaking into my study and reading through my private papers?'

'Your gambling debts, you mean?'

'Whatever they are, they're no concern of yours!'

'How long?' Calder asked, quietly.

'I don't have to answer any questions from you about my affairs.'

'How long?' Calder repeated.

For a moment it looked as if the doctor was going to keep up the bluster, the righteous indignation. But then his shoulders sagged and he slumped into a chair by a bookcase, still holding his plate. He closed his eyes. There was only one explanation, and there was no point in trying to invent another. 'Since after your mother died.'

'How soon after?'

'Not long.'

'But how did you manage to lose that much?'

'It was just a run of bad luck,' the doctor said, searching for his son's eyes, his understanding. 'You know about bad luck in your line of work.'

'I do,' Calder said. 'And you can only lose as much as you risk.'

'It's not what it seems,' the doctor said. 'I'm good at this, you know. I know horses. Most years . . . many years, I come out ahead. But not last year. I think it was all the rain we had. Or maybe the jockeys are fixing races. Something's going on.'

'What's going on is you've lost control of your gambling.'

'I'll win the money back.'

'How? By putting the house on Mercator in the three-thirty?' Calder's voice was heavy with sarcasm. 'No you won't.'

'I'll wait for an odds-on banker.'

The racing slang sounded strange coming out of the mouth of his father. 'You've bet on a few bankers recently, haven't you, Father? And none of them have come off.'

'Aye.' Dr Calder nodded.

'How could you . . .' Calder suddenly found it difficult to speak, but he had to say it. 'How could you attack me for what I do when you were doing the same thing all the time?'

'This is just a hobby,' his father said.

'A hobby! You're ruining yourself.'

The old man sat up in his chair and faced his son. 'I'm sorry, Alex.'

'You can't just apologize!' Calder's voice had been calm and controlled, but now it was rising. 'It's not just the money, it's . . . I know I didn't act like it, but I've always respected you. Although I pretended never to listen, and I said I disagreed with you, underneath it all I was afraid you were right when you said I was just a gambler, that I was frittering away my life. That's why I got so angry. But now I find out you're even worse than me. How could you be such a hypocrite?'

'I knew what the horses were doing to me. I didn't want the same thing to happen to you. It's as simple as that.'

'Don't try to dress this all up as concern for me!' Calder was shouting now. 'If you were really so concerned for me, you wouldn't have lied to me! You wouldn't have criticized me all these years for doing honestly what you were always doing in secret. What would Mum think? And Anne?'

'Don't tell Annie.'

'I have to,' muttered Calder. 'I'm not hiding this from her.'

The doctor closed his eyes.

Calder took a deep breath, fighting to bring his anger under control. 'I want you to stop,' he said.

'But how am I going to win enough money back to pay that if I stop?' the doctor asked, pointing at the bill in Calder's hands.

Calder shook his head. 'You still don't get it, do you? You've been doing this for years, and you still think you can win. You can win one race, maybe two. But you can't beat the bookies in the long run. They have the odds on their side, and they have the information. They want you to win sometimes, because they know the more you win, the more you'll bet. But it *has* to stop.'

'Then what about that bill?'

'I'll pay it,' Calder said.

'But it's a hundred and thirty thousand pounds!'

'A hundred and forty-three thousand, actually.'

'Do you have that kind of money?'

'I can afford it,' Calder said. 'And I'll pay the other one. Are there any more?'

'One more,' said his father. 'It's for about ten thousand. In that bottom drawer.'

Calder opened the drawer and fished it out.

'OK. I'll pay these now. But I want you to take the house off the market. And I want you to promise me that you won't gamble again. Not even a lottery ticket.'

'I'm hardly likely to get myself into this kind of trouble again, am I?'

'Yes, you are. I also want you to promise me that you will go to Gamblers Anonymous. I'm sure you can find out where they meet.'

'That's not necessary.'

'Isn't it? You're the doctor. You make the diagnosis.'

They sat in silence, father and son, only feet apart.

'Father?'

Dr Calder once again looked his son directly in the eye. 'All right. I promise I won't make any more bets. And I will go to Gamblers Anonymous.'

'Thank you,' said Calder. Over the years he had watched

one or two of his colleagues succumb to serious gambling addiction, and he had seen how difficult, if not impossible, it was for them to give up. They ended up losing their jobs and often their families as well. He knew his father's promise was sincerely given. But would it be kept?

He used to think that his father was the most honest person he knew, but it had turned out he was just as deceitful as everyone else. This new knowledge shocked Calder to the core. The strict moral principles that had seemed like a granite foundation to the world as Calder knew it for as long as he could remember, had turned out to be sandstone. How could his father, whom he had believed to be the wisest and most moral man he knew, have been so weak? As he flew back to Norfolk that afternoon along the north-east coastline of England, he kept asking himself the same question. And he didn't come up with an answer.

Martel lurked in his office in Jackson Hole wondering why, for someone who had so much, he felt so miserable. The Japanese stock market had rallied sharply on the last two trading days of January, bailing him out. His losses were still huge, over a billion dollars down from nearly two billion the week before, but the market was finally coming back his way. The lower losses had meant that he had just been able to meet the demands for collateral from his brokers. And much to his relief, even with Perumal gone, the Bloomfield Weiss revaluation of the JUSTICE notes had been generous, several points above the level Vikram's own model had predicted.

JUSTICE was an acronym for the Japan US Trust International Capital Equity-linked note. It was a complicated beast, a power reverse dual currency bond with a Nikkei knock-in barrier and bells and whistles. The notes had been bought in dollars but were repayable in either yen or dollars at the investor's option. The Nikkei index was based on the prices of two hundred and twenty-five of the largest stocks on the Tokyo

Stock Exchange. If this index rose above ten thousand, then the investor would receive five times the gain. Under seven thousand and the investor lost five times the difference. At the time the deal was done the market was trading at about eight thousand five hundred. So it was a turbo-charged play on the Japanese stock market.

Martel had started with a five-hundred-million-dollar investment in these JUSTICE notes. This had grown to two billion, with Bloomfield Weiss once again agreeing to lend the Teton Fund eighty per cent of the price of the notes. At first Bloomfield Weiss had seemed reluctant to do the business, but in the end the sixty million dollars of fees that they would make out of the transaction had persuaded them. Martel and Vikram knew that the fortune the Teton Fund had made out of the IGLOO notes the year before had not been Bloomfield Weiss's loss. The investment bank would have been careful to lay off all the risk, probably with one of the big reinsurance companies, and they would no doubt do the same with the JUSTICE notes, leaving Bloomfield Weiss with nothing but a hefty fee. And the loan to the Teton Fund to buy the notes, of course.

But even though the market was looking better, Martel was still miserable. One reason was the *Fortune* article. Deep down he had always feared being exposed as a fake. It had finally happened. And in this case it seemed so unfair. Perhaps he had been lucky to survive the turmoil of the previous year, just as he had been lucky to survive the recent Japanese market turbulence. But you made your own luck. And it had been a stroke of genius to realize that there was a realistic possibility that Italy would leave the euro. *Fortune* might suggest that he hadn't been responsible for what happened, but little did they know that Martel had quietly granted a generous quantity of options in the Teton Fund to Guido Gallotti for his consultancy services. That showed Martel had influence.

He glanced at the portrait on the wall. It showed himself, in that very room, examining his screens in his moment of triumph. The painting had not turned out as badly as he had feared. The unkempt artist had captured Martel's rugged good looks, and the intense concentration with which he studied the markets in front of him. At times Martel thought he caught a hint of fear in those brown eyes. He had studied the brushwork minutely at close quarters to see if he could pinpoint exactly which strokes of paint had led to that perception, but he couldn't identify them. He was probably just imagining it: no one else would notice; certainly no one had made anything other than admiring comments about it. But his intensity was in complete contrast to the innocent confidence of his beautiful wife, a few feet further along the wall.

And it was Cheryl who was really bugging him. Had there been a man in the New York apartment? Suspicion was growing inside him like a canker. It had only been one cough, lasting all of two seconds, but it was enough. Of course he hadn't had the courage to confront Cheryl directly. But he had to know.

The obvious answer was a private investigator. The trouble was, he didn't know how to find one. He didn't want to contact the New York-based outfit his firm occasionally used for due diligence. Neither did he want anyone local. There was no one he could trust to ask for a personal recommendation. They might guess why he wanted to contact one, and he couldn't bear that. And of course he couldn't ask his secretary to do the research for him. He turned to his computer and opened up a search engine. It took him half an hour, but he finally found a likely looking individual in Denver, after Salt Lake City the nearest major city to Jackson Hole, but still over three hundred miles away. His name was Ray Pohek and he agreed to meet Martel in Jackson Hole in two days' time. He saw nothing strange in Martel's suggested rendezvous, a deserted road ten miles out of town.

As Martel put down the phone there was a knock at his

door. It was Andy and Vikram wanting to talk about hiring a new bond trader. Andy needed some support and Vikram had a suggestion. They discussed it for a few minutes, and then Andy returned to his trading desk. Vikram hesitated.

He seemed to be staring at Martel's monitor, still showing Pohek's website. Martel glared at him, and shut down his web browser. 'Well?'

Vikram snapped his eyes away from the screen. 'You saw the Nikkei was up three per cent again today?'

'Yes,' said Martel. 'Finally the market is behaving rationally.'

'Should we take the chance to reduce our exposure? I could call Bloomfield Weiss and ask for a bid on some of those JUSTICE notes. Now Perumal is no longer there, it might be a good idea.'

'They gave us a decent reval, didn't they?' said Martel.

'Yes. But who knows where the market will be next month?'

Martel leaped to his feet in frustration. 'Who knows? We know. I know.' Martel beat his own chest. 'That's the whole point. That's why we put ourselves through all this agony. The Nikkei is going to double over the next twelve months and we are going to be long. As long as possible. With all the leverage we've got, I'm looking for a two hundred per cent return on capital. Minimum. This is going to be the greatest hedge-fund trade ever. *Ever!*'

'But if the market drops again –'

'We'll survive. We always survive.' Martel shook his head. 'You're a smart guy, Vikram, but sometimes I wonder if you've got what it takes.'

Vikram's cheeks burned and he left the room without a word. Martel knew he'd hurt the man's pride. Perhaps it was too much for Martel to expect Vikram to share his own ability to see the big picture, but Martel was disappointed, none the less. He liked Vikram. He recognized his own emotional need for a protégé, an apprentice, an heir, and Vikram was the closest any of his people came to filling the role. He knew that

Vikram admired him, envied him even. The man wanted to be one of the hedge-fund greats, just like Martel. Martel shook his head.

He just didn't have the balls.

18

Calder left it to the end of the week before calling DC Neville to check on progress. He telephoned her from his tiny office in the flying school. It took him three tries before he got through. She sounded harried.

'I'm sorry I didn't get back to you, Mr Calder. Things have been hectic here.'

'Have you turned up anything on Perumal's disappearance?'

'I'm afraid not. I spoke to Bloomfield Weiss. They think there's no chance of a connection between the two deaths.'

'Who did you talk to?'

'A Mr Davis. Benton Davis.'

'Oh, yes. I'm not surprised you didn't get anywhere. He would be eager to make sure that anything swept under the carpet stays under the carpet.'

'Possibly.'

Calder caught the note of doubt in the detective's voice. 'What did Benton say about me?'

DC Neville hesitated before answering. 'He questioned your objectivity. He said you had become emotionally involved with Jennifer Tan, and you were unable to let her death go.'

'There's some truth to that,' Calder admitted. 'But that's because I'm sure there's something suspicious about it. Did you talk to the American police?'

'I spoke to the Teton County Sheriff's Office in Jackson Hole.'

'They have a real sheriff there?'

'Apparently. I spoke to one of his deputies. He didn't say howdy, though. And I didn't ask if he had a horse.'

'Do they suspect anything?'

'No. They think Perumal was just foolish. He had no experience on a snowmobile – he'd only been out on one for the first time the day before. Anyway, he went off by himself away from the trails and got lost. He ended up in a high-risk avalanche area. Sure enough, there was an avalanche. The man I spoke to seemed to think there was a good chance Perumal started it. They found the snowmobile, but not his body. They might have to wait till spring for that.'

'So they don't think anyone could have murdered him?'

'He was alone. Quite alone.'

'Oh.'

'So, I think we'll leave it there.'

'But it's too much of a coincidence! Perumal coming to me with his fears about Jen, and then getting killed himself a few days later. There must be something in it.'

'It was worth checking out. But we've done that now.'

'So that's it, then?'

'I'm afraid so.'

'That's not acceptable,' Calder protested. 'You can't just drop it.'

Neville's voice, which had been friendly, became firm. 'I'm afraid we can, sir. There are plenty of other things to be doing closer to home.'

'I want to speak to your superior.'

'Certainly, sir. His name is Detective Inspector Price. I'll tell him you'll be calling.' Then her voice changed again. 'Look, Mr Calder. I know how you feel. It seems to me that there are one or two loose ends as well. But it was all I could do to get the time to find out what I have. We've got two schoolgirls missing down here. You can call him if you want, but there's no chance my guv'nor will let me waste any more time on this. I'm sorry. But that's the way it is.'

Calder sighed. He realized there was no point in arguing. 'I understand. Thank you for doing what you've done.'

He put down the phone. The anger simmered inside him.

Once again Carr-Jones was going to get away with something. This time murder. Benton Davis and the other spineless cowards at Bloomfield Weiss would help protect him. Two people had died because of him. Two young, brilliant people. Calder slammed his fist hard on to the desk.

He had always believed that there were people of integrity in the City, people you could trust, people who would stand by you. He hoped that he was one of them. He had been helped out of scrapes in the past by friends in the market, many times. He would have counted Tarek as one of these friends, but Tarek had gone along with the others at Bloomfield Weiss in turning a blind eye to what was going on. Calder was sure that the likes of Linda Stubbes and Benton Davis had started their careers as decent people, but now look at them. A year ago he had decided he would have no more to do with any of them, and he didn't regret that decision for a moment. So why was all this bothering him? He should just stick with his plan and ignore it all, as he had done so successfully since moving to Norfolk. He had done his duty by telling the police. If they weren't interested, then neither should he be.

He thought again of his trip to Kelso the previous week. He still hadn't got over the shock and disappointment of his discovery that his father was not the man he believed he was. If anything he felt worse about it. Somehow his father continued to have a hold on him, even in his moment of shame. It had been bad enough to accept a year before that the institution he had worked for so loyally for so many years had become corrupted by the greedy, the sleazy and the ambitious. And now he had to face up to the fact that his father was just like those City traders he had fled from, abandoning their integrity in the quest for the big win.

Calder had just written out cheques to the three bookmakers totalling a hundred and sixty thousand pounds. He had plenty saved from his Bloomfield Weiss bonuses, but it was still a lot of money. If it solved the problem, that would be fine. As long as his father didn't just run up another hundred thousand in debts. Could he trust him? For Calder, that was the last question he thought he would have asked of his father.

He looked out of his window over the runway. An engine roared as a Piper Warrior started its takeoff roll. He glanced up. Where half an hour before there had been gloom and rain, there was now clear blue, with bright tufts of white scudding across the sky.

He couldn't just sit in his office stewing. He needed to get out.

He checked at the desk to confirm that his next student had cancelled, and decided to take the Pitts out for a whirl. In ten minutes he was airborne. He skipped through the puffs of cloud up to four thousand feet, found a patch of clear sky and did a couple of lazy-eights to warm up. Then he tried a slow roll, checking the altimeter to make sure he didn't lose height. Perfect: exactly four thousand feet going in and coming out. He did two more, both exact.

He was definitely improving with practice. He felt a powerful urge to stretch himself. Try something that was truly difficult, dangerous even. He had never done low-level aerobatics in the Pitts, not truly low level, and it was nine long years since he had flung a Tornado around two hundred and fifty feet above the Welsh mountains. Ever since he was a boy, he had wanted to do a low-level pass over an airfield with a slow roll. Just once. Just to show he had the guts.

He pointed the nose back towards the airfield.

It was against the rules. And Jerry would kill him. But he knew Jerry had taken a student on a cross-country navigation exercise to Ely. And none of the other instructors was working. There were no other aircraft in the circuit.

Damn it, it was his aeroplane and his airfield. And his life.

Just once.

Langthorpe was approaching. He radioed Angela and told

her what he was doing. Or part of what he was doing. He didn't tell her about the roll bit.

He descended on to the final approach at a hundred knots, and then at one hundred feet levelled out. As he passed over the runway threshold he pulled up on the stick and applied right aileron. He rolled round to inverted, pushed forward, and felt the familiar pressure of his weight on the shoulder straps. The ground rushed past only a hundred feet above his head. Then, as he completed the second half of the roll, he was a smidgen too quick in taking off the forward pressure on the stick and he felt he was losing height. Only a few feet, but at this altitude every foot was crucial. The wingtip swung around underneath him. For one dreadful instant he thought it would clip the ground, but it came up on the other side. Now that the horizon was in its usual place, he could see he was only twenty feet above the ground, if that. He slammed open the throttle and climbed rapidly.

The adrenaline exploded through his system and his heart raced. His palms were sweating on the control column. He had made it, but only just. Somehow he had lost eighty feet. If it had been a hundred and ten everything would have been over. As he turned downwind to land, he knew he had done something very stupid, something he wouldn't do again.

But he was very glad he had done it. Just once.

'Romeo Oscar, I thought the wheels were supposed to be pointing at the ground on landing, not the sky,' said Angela, her voice strained underneath the banter.

'I'll try that next time,' Calder replied.

He was taxiing the Pitts to its habitual parking spot when he saw a Warrior land behind him. It taxied rapidly over to the parking area, and Jerry hopped out. He was a short man with a thick dark moustache. He was usually a jolly fellow, patient with the dimmest student, but not this time. He marched straight over to Calder, who turned to face the retribution that he knew was coming.

'What the hell was that?' Jerry shouted when he was still twenty yards away.

'It was just a bit of practice while the airfield was quiet. There was no one else around.'

'Just a bit of practice! It was one of the stupidest stunts I've ever seen in my life! If you want to commit suicide take the pills, don't splatter a perfectly good aircraft all over the runway. Seriously, Alex, what were you thinking of?'

'I'm sorry, Jerry, I won't do it again.'

'What you did then goes against every rule in my book. Against all we're trying to do here. How can you teach a student to fly safely when you do that kind of thing yourself?'

'OK,' Calder said. He was feeling bad. 'I really won't do it again.'

'You're telling me you won't. I'm the CFI here, and I'm saying that you're not going up in that thing again until you can convince me you'll treat it with respect. I don't care if you do own the plane, or the bloody airfield.'

Calder's ears were burning. He didn't bother to argue. He knew Jerry was right. He went straight to his car and drove slowly home.

That evening he walked the mile or so from his cottage to the Admiral Nelson, in the village of Hanham Staithe. It was a bitter evening, but the pub was warm and welcoming, with a wood fire roaring in the grate. He exchanged a few words with Stuart and Jess, the local vet and his wife, and Archie, a wizened artist who lived on a decrepit boat laid up in the creek. Normally he would have chatted to them, but that night he wanted to be by himself, and they were perceptive enough to realize it. They were a friendly bunch and didn't seem to object to a recent immigrant from London, especially one who lived there all the year round.

He bought a pint of bitter and ordered a steak sandwich. He sat by the window and stared out at the raw darkness. He remembered the evening he and Jen had split that bottle of champagne in Corney and Barrow overlooking the ice rink, and her challenge to him to skate with her. He had genuinely believed that Jen had a future as a trader then. How wrong he had been. All that was just about a year ago and a hundred miles away and another life. But it was calling to him now.

He could try to ignore the past, but he wasn't a quitter – it just wasn't in his nature. He had tried half-heartedly to help Jen, but he hadn't done enough. If he continued to do nothing Bloomfield Weiss would cover up all trace of her death. The injustice of what had happened would always grate at him. He had almost killed himself that very day in a fit of angry bravado. It wasn't all going to disappear in the morning. He would have to face up to it. Now.

He didn't know whether Carr-Jones was responsible for the deaths of Jen and Perumal, but he knew that he had to find out. And when he had found out, do something about it.

19

He drove down to London the next day, to his sister's place in Highgate. Jerry was happy to let him go. Calder had explained what was worrying him, and how he felt he had to go down to London to sort it out. February was a quiet month for flying, with short days and bad weather, and Jerry was sure he could manage without him for two days.

'Don't come back till you've sorted yourself out,' Jerry said sternly. 'I don't want any more stunts like yesterday's.'

'There won't be any. I promise,' said Calder. 'And thanks, Jerry. I mean it.'

After the children were put to bed, or at least shut in their bedrooms, Anne opened a bottle of wine. It was nine o'clock.

'When's William back?' Calder asked.

'Any time between now and eleven. He's working on a deal, apparently.'

'I see.'

'He's always working on a deal.' Anne sounded more disappointed than bitter. She glanced around the large house. 'I suppose we have to pay for this place somehow. Are you hungry? I usually wait to eat until he comes home.'

'No, I'm fine,' Calder said, although he was starving. But he wanted to slip into their routine rather than disrupt it.

'Tell me about Father,' Anne said. 'I still can't believe it.'

Calder had spoken briefly to her on the phone, but he now went into all the details.

Anne was shocked. 'How could he hide it from us for so long?'

'He said he began after Mum died.'

'She'd have spotted it and stopped him. And he would have

been too proud to gamble in front of her. You must be angry, especially after the hard time he's given you over the years about your trading.'

'You can say that again. He promised me he'll go to Gamblers Anonymous. We'll see if he keeps *that* promise.'

'At least it shows he's human.'

'If being a hypocrite is human.'

'I'm afraid it probably is. You two are even more similar than I thought.'

'Oh, come on, Annie! Don't say that.'

'You're both gamblers. You both struggle to control it. And neither of you quite succeeds.'

'I'd never lose a hundred and fifty grand on the horses!'

Anne raised her eyebrows.

It was true that Calder had flirted with gambling at Cambridge. He had fallen in with a regular poker game in his first year. It had fascinated him, especially the idea that poker was actually a game of skill, and that by studying the probabilities you could place chance firmly on your side. Then a dissolute Wykehamist called Jonny had joined them one evening. Full of charm and whisky, he had bet heavily and lost, mostly to Calder, who walked away thirty quid up. The following week he was there again. Somehow, Calder managed to lose two hundred pounds to him, a significant sum for a student. As Calder left the game, cleaned out and having written all the IOUs his bank account could withstand, Jonny, who seemed three-quarters drunk, gave him the tiniest of winks.

At that moment Calder realized that poker was a mug's game. It *was* a game of skill, and there would always be a more skilful player to come along and take his money.

That's what he liked about trading: he could restrict his bets to those situations where the odds really were on his side.

'So, what are you doing in London?' Anne asked.

'The police don't have the time or inclination to follow up on Jen's and Perumal's deaths, so I thought I would. I found I couldn't just hide away in Norfolk and forget about it.'

'I'm glad you're doing something for the poor woman. Good luck.' Anne raised her glass and sipped from it. Then she frowned. 'Just one thing, though.'

'What's that?'

'If you're right and Perumal's death had something to do with him asking awkward questions about Jen, well . . .' She looked anxious.

'Well what?' Calder asked.

'It might be dangerous for you to run around asking the same kind of questions.'

It was something that had occurred to Calder. 'Don't worry,' he said. 'I'll be fine.'

'Be careful,' Anne said in her sternest tone of voice. 'I would hate it if something happened to you.'

The waiter listened attentively as Tarek gave him his complicated, but very precise, breakfast order. It involved mozzarella cheese, Italian bread, olive oil and black pepper. Tarek liked breakfast and he liked Claridge's, so Calder wasn't surprised when he had suggested meeting there at seven. At that time of morning the elegant dining room was almost empty, save for a scattering of extra-keen American tourists looking to get an early start. The businessmen would be in a bit later.

It was the first time Calder had seen Tarek since leaving Bloomfield Weiss. He thought he could spot the beginnings of a comfortable paunch above the belt of Tarek's trousers, looking incongruous on his thin frame. But his brown eyes were as large and as observant as ever. Despite the circumstances of their parting, Calder was pleased to see him.

'You must be getting used to being senior management now,' Calder said. 'Not having to be at the morning meeting.'

'Actually, I usually go to that still,' Tarek said. 'I try to keep in touch. Breakfast is a treat for special occasions. Like this.' He smiled.

'Don't you miss trading?'

'A bit,' said Tarek. 'And there's so much bullshit to deal with. But things are going well, *inshallah*, at least in Fixed Income. We're back on top of the league table for Eurobond issues, we made record profits last year, and I think I've finally got the salesmen and the traders to work well together.'

'That'll be the day,' Calder snorted. 'Speaking of salesmen, how's Cash Callaghan doing?'

'Still whippin' and drivin' those bonds.'

'And the Prop Desk?'

'Kevin Strumm from New York is running it now.'

'He's pretty good, isn't he?'

'Actually, he's very disciplined. But he doesn't have your flair. There were a couple of times in the last six months when I wanted to push him out of the way and load up on a big position myself, but he was taking profits, for God's sake.'

'What about Nils?'

'He's shaping into a competent trader. But he's frustrated with Strumm.'

'Well, I wish them both luck.'

Tarek took a bite out of his olive-oil soaked bread. 'You asked me if I missed trading. What about you?'

'No. Not at all.'

'Really?' Calder could see Tarek's brown eyes didn't believe him. 'Don't you miss the markets? Running positions? Taking risks?'

Calder smiled to himself, remembering his recent experience of being the wrong way up too close to the ground. 'No, no. I'm quite happy. The flying school I've bought is coming together. And I get to fly a lot.'

'You're welcome back, you know.' Tarek said. 'Any time. We need you.'

The waiter brought Calder's eggs and bacon, and he tucked into them. 'No, Tarek. Bloomfield Weiss has changed, and I haven't changed with it.'

'I disagree.'

'Oh, come on, Bloomfield Weiss belongs to the likes of Justin Carr-Jones these days. And Tessa Trew.'

'Actually she's left. Didn't you know?'

'No,' said Calder. 'Fired, I hope?'

'I'm afraid not. She left of her own accord last April. I'm not sure, but I think she fell out with Carr-Jones.'

'I thought those two were a team?'

'She probably got sick of him trying to rub his face in her tits,' Tarek said with a chuckle.

'I doubt any woman could stand working for him for very long,' Calder said. 'Even Tessa.'

'You're right that there have always been assholes like him around,' Tarek said. 'And there always will be. But the place is still being run by Sidney, and he's straight. He likes to make money, but he's straight.'

Sidney Stahl was the diminutive chairman of Bloomfield Weiss. He had little patience for bullshit and a reputation for straight talking. Everyone knew where they were with Stahl: if you made money you were in, if you didn't you were out.

'How long are you going to stay, Tarek?'

'Oh, I don't know. A while. Things are going quite well at the moment.'

'But there's a limit to how far you can get in an American investment bank, isn't there?'

'Why? Because I'm an Arab?'

Calder shrugged. 'Yes, frankly.'

Tarek smiled. 'Actually, I could leave Bloomfield Weiss and go into one of the family businesses any day. You know that. But I think I can run Bloomfield Weiss, or at least a big chunk of it. And I think people like Sidney will give me the chance. OK, he's Jewish and I'm a Saudi, but I'll make him money. I guess that's why I like the Bloomfield Weiss way of doing things.'

'Well, not me,' Calder said. 'I'm just glad I'm out of it.'

'Oh, well,' Tarek said. 'And I thought you were taking me to breakfast to ask for your old job back.'

''Fraid not. But I do have a favour to ask you.'

'Go on.'

Calder told Tarek about Perumal's visit, his subsequent disappearance, and the police's failure to find any connection between Jen's and Perumal's deaths. Tarek listened impassively.

'So what do you think?' Calder asked at the end.

'I think you should drop it.'

'Drop it? But I'm sure there's something going on!'

'No, you're not. You were obsessed with the whole Jen thing last year and it obviously hasn't left you since then. What happened to her was very sad, but it was a long time ago. You should forget about it. Perumal did something stupid on a mountain. That's sad too. But it has nothing to do with you.'

Calder frowned at him. 'Are you trying to put me off finding anything?'

'No. I'm trying to put you off looking. For your own sake. Sure, it's a bit of a coincidence, but in the real world coincidences happen all the time.'

'My gut tells me there's something in this.'

'And my gut tells me there isn't,' said Tarek.

'Can you at least ask some questions for me?'

'No. I'm sorry, Zero, I won't.'

Calder put down his knife and fork. A wave of disgust washed over him. Suddenly, he didn't want to eat. 'Just like you didn't want to have anything to do with Jen.'

'Carr-Jones shouldn't have said what he said to Jen. But she shouldn't have reacted in the way she did. Clearly she shouldn't or she would still be alive.'

Calder pushed back his chair, leaving bacon congealing in egg yolk on his plate and tossed a twenty-pound note on to the table. 'Not you, as well, Tarek?'

Tarek didn't respond.

Calder left the dining room in a mood of deep gloom, part anger, but mostly disappointment.

Tarek, too, was in a bad mood all morning. He found Calder's contempt hard to take. Tarek prided himself on his integrity; he needed it to combat the 'sleazy Arab' stereotype with which he was confronted every day. But he also prided himself on being realistic, and politically savvy. A year ago he had fought hard behind the scenes for Jen and for Calder, fought and lost. It was not the right battle to fight again. There was no percentage in digging up the Jen episode, none for him, none for Calder, none for her, none for Bloomfield Weiss. For all his intelligence, it was political realities like those that Calder failed to appreciate. He was a good trader, but he would never make it to any level of seniority in an investment bank. Whereas Tarek . . . Tarek thought he had a chance of going all the way.

Just before lunch, Carr-Jones popped his head into Tarek's office. 'Got a sec?'

Tarek nodded, and tried to banish his bad mood and put on his detached, implacable expression. That was always difficult with Carr-Jones.

'Sure, Justin. Come in.'

'Did you know Alex Calder has been stirring things up with the police? He's been to talk to them about Perumal's accident. And he still can't let go of Jennifer Tan.'

Tarek raised his eyebrows.

'Has he asked you anything?'

'Yes,' said Tarek. No point in lying.

Carr-Jones waited. Tarek waited. He was quite happy to leave Carr-Jones's fears unanswered.

In the end Carr-Jones continued. 'It can't help, raking over all this again. It's bad for the firm. It would be a good idea if you discouraged him.'

'Would it?' said Tarek, as enigmatically as he could manage.

'Yes, it would,' said Carr-Jones. And then, just as he was

about to leave the room. 'Oh, by the way. How's brother Omar?'

Tarek ignored him and looked at some papers on his desk. 'Go screw your sister,' he muttered in Arabic.

'Another prayer?' asked Carr-Jones. 'I never realized you were so pious.'

Tarek flicked the beads through his fingers, wondering what his misguided little brother was up to. No one in the family had heard from him for four years. But at some point Omar would make himself noticed. He always did. And Carr-Jones was right, of course. Once the powers that be at Bloomfield Weiss realized who his brother was, Tarek's career would be effectively over.

He repeated his earlier incantation to himself, louder this time. Then his phone rang. 'Yes?' he snapped.

'Tarek? This is Jean-Luc Martel.'

20

Calder stood outside the small terraced house in the quiet street in Ealing and rang the bell. It was opened by a woman in a white sari. She was an inch or two taller than Perumal, a shade or two paler, and surprisingly pretty, although her eyes seemed sunken. She was only in her early twenties.

'Mrs Thiagajaran?'

'Yes.'

'Hello. My name's Alex Calder. I was a colleague of Perumal's. I wonder if I can have a word with you?'

Radha Thiagajaran hesitated, but then let him into a cramped front room. His eyes were immediately drawn to two large photographs of Perumal on a small table strewn with chrysanthemums, a stick of incense on one side and a lamp on the other.

'Sit down, please. Can I make you some tea?' Radha asked with a strong accent. Much stronger than Perumal's.

'Yes, thank you,' Calder said. He decided to wait on the sofa while she made it. He thought it best to err on the side of formality with an Indian widow. He couldn't help looking at the photographs, the pleasant smell of the incense invoking the comfort of ritual.

She soon returned with a tray, and poured them both a cup.

'I was very sorry to hear what happened to Perumal,' Calder started. 'Please accept my condolences.'

'Thank you,' said Radha politely. But her face had that exhausted, washed-out sadness of the recently bereaved.

'Perumal came to see me up in Norfolk the weekend before he died. I'd like to talk to you about what he told me.'

'So that's where he went!' Radha said. 'He told me he was

off to play golf with someone from work. He was away all day, but he left his golf clubs here. Poor Perumal, for someone so clever he could be so stupid! Of course, I could have assumed he was seeing another woman,' she gave a half-hearted laugh, glancing at the photographs on the table. 'But not Perumal.'

'So he didn't tell you he was coming to see me?'

'No. Not at all.'

'You see, I think he might have been in some kind of trouble before he died.'

'Not Perumal,' Radha said firmly. Too firmly.

'It might have had something to do with a woman called Jennifer Tan. She used to work at Bloomfield Weiss with us. She killed herself about a year ago.'

'I do remember that. Perumal was quite upset. But he wasn't in any trouble. He was doing very well at work. Very successful, isn't it?'

Calder realized that it would be impossible to work around the widow's loyalty without alarming her. So he decided to alarm her.

'I think Perumal might have been murdered.'

'No!' Radha put her hand to her mouth.

'I'm not certain, but I think he had stumbled across something, something that got him into trouble. I think someone wanted him dead.'

'But it was an accident, was it not?'

'Maybe. That's what I'm trying to find out. Have you been out to Jackson Hole?'

'No,' Radha said, dazed. 'No. I was waiting until they found the body. They think he's still under tons of snow out there, what's left of him.' She paused, fighting successfully to stop the tears. Calder waited. 'We can't even have a proper funeral. Perumal has a sister who lives in Vancouver, and she's in Jackson Hole now. She's coming here next week. Perhaps she will be able to tell me something. Murdered?' She blinked, still confused by the thought. 'Why? Who would have done such a thing to my poor Perumal?'

'I don't know. I think it might have had something to do with Jean-Luc Martel and the Teton Fund.'

'I've heard of them. Perumal's client. His most important client. Perumal got a good bonus last year thanks to them, and he was hoping for an even better one this year. We were planning to move from this place. Buy somewhere in Fulham. We had even looked at a couple of houses. But now . . . I don't know now. Although Mr Carr-Jones has been very kind. He says there's a good pension for me. But what good is a pension without Perumal? A pension is for old people, isn't it? Perumal and I, we should have been old together.' Her lower lip shook. 'Murdered? No. It can't be.'

'Perhaps it isn't,' said Calder. He hated to upset her like this, but he had no choice. 'It's something I'd like to find out. Did Perumal mention any trouble with the Teton Fund?'

'No.' Radha bit her trembling lip and looked closely at Calder, trying to make up her mind.

Calder helped her. 'I know Perumal was an honest man. And he trusted me, which is why he came to see me a couple of weeks ago. He had second thoughts about telling me everything then, but given what's happened, I wish he had. I might have been able to help him. If he was in trouble, I'd like to find out why.'

The young widow smiled, a smile of tentative trust. 'He never admitted there was a problem with the Teton Fund, but I could see there was. He seemed to have conflicting feelings about it, about his whole job, in fact. On the one hand he would get very excited every time he closed a deal or Justin told him he had done a good job. On the other, he was constantly on edge, worried about something.'

'But you don't know what?'

'No,' she said. 'He was especially nervous before he went off to Jackson Hole. I knew there was something wrong. I asked him about it, but he just said it was a deal he was working on. There was more to it than that, I'm sure.'

'I tried to call him at Bloomfield Weiss, and they said he was taking an extra couple of days' vacation out there. Was that planned?'

'No, not at all. We had a very odd conversation about that. He said he wanted to try snowmobiling. I said it sounded dangerous and he should come home. He said not to worry. But he sounded tense, very tense, almost frightened. And he has hardly ever seen snow, Mr Calder, let alone gone skiing or anything.'

'Perhaps he just fell in love with it and wanted to stay on?'

'I know him. I don't think so. And why would he sound so scared? There was something else going on. Definitely.' She smiled at Calder again. He sensed that he was winning her trust – she wanted to tell him more. 'Perumal and I had an arranged marriage. I know that's hard for you to understand, but it's still quite common in my country. We didn't know each other at all when we married two years ago. But Perumal was a good man, an honest man and a good husband. And not just because he earned a good salary. He listened to his mother too much perhaps,' she smiled, 'but I'm not the only woman to have problems with her mother-in-law. I'm trying to keep her away, but she insists on coming over. Until they find him, it's so difficult.'

This time she couldn't fight back the tears. Calder waited while she dabbed her eyes with a handkerchief.

'Do you have anyone here to talk to?'

'Oh, yes. My own mother was here – she went back to India yesterday. I have younger sisters she needs to be with. There are many neighbours who have been very good. And Perumal's sister will be here soon.' She sighed and closed her eyes. 'I don't know what his mother will do if he has been murdered. She is so proud of him. She won't be able to cope with it.'

'Best not tell her, then,' Calder said. 'After all, we don't know what really happened. And I wouldn't mention it to any of the other people at Bloomfield Weiss. At least not yet. If I do turn anything up, I'll let you know right away.'

'Thank you, Mr Calder. I'm sure something was wrong. I hope you can find out what. And if you can discover where his body is . . .'

'I don't know if I can do that. But I'll try.'

'Please do.'

As Calder left the small house, he thought how lucky Perumal had been in his marriage. His mother had done a good job in finding him a wife. Perumal was becoming much more to Calder than just another derivatives geek, and his murder more than a key to explain Jen's death. He deserved justice as much as she did.

The bar near Covent Garden was crowded already. Calder had managed to nab a couple of seats with a view of one of the large screens suspended from the ceiling. Tottenham were playing Liverpool, kick-off was in twenty minutes, and he knew Nils would want to see the match.

Calder needed help from someone inside Bloomfield Weiss. After his conversation with Tarek he realized that this might be harder to arrange than he had first thought. There were still plenty of people who worked there that he would classify as friends, but they were mostly his contemporaries, or senior to him. They might well share Tarek's reluctance to ask difficult questions. What he needed was someone more junior, someone who could plug into the grapevine at a lower level, who could talk to Carr-Jones's minions, rather than Carr-Jones himself. The obvious choice was either Nils or Matt, both of whom had been through the Bloomfield Weiss training programme and had friends in the Derivatives Group. Of the two, Nils had the most initiative, and so Calder had called him. But Nils was ambitious and Calder had no idea whether he would agree to help.

He had been to see Stephanie Ward, Jen's lawyer, that morning. She confirmed that Jen would probably have won a large settlement from Bloomfield Weiss, although she was determined to take the case all the way to the Employment Tribunal. The chances of a win there were good, but the Tribunal was always a bit of a lottery. The lawyer explained with some bitterness that she wasn't surprised Jen had taken her own life. Suing a City employer was a stressful business: Jen was the third client who had killed herself.

Calder had asked for the phone number of Jen's American friend, Sandy Waterhouse. As she searched for it, the lawyer asked him whether he wanted to pursue Bloomfield Weiss himself for constructive dismissal. Calder had declined, politely. His eye was on bigger crimes.

His mobile phone rang. He pulled it out. 'Hello?'

'Alex? It's Benton Davis.' Calder had to strain to hear him above the noise of the bar.

'Hello, Benton.'

'I hear you've been asking about Perumal. And Jennifer Tan?'

'That's right.'

'The police have been to see me. I've set them right. You should know that this is not the kind of exposure Bloomfield Weiss needs.'

'Benton,' Calder said. 'I don't care what kind of exposure Bloomfield Weiss needs.'

'We've looked into the matter internally,' Benton said. 'There's nothing more to be done. And I don't want you discussing this with any Bloomfield Weiss employees, do you understand me?'

'I understand that you are trying to cover up a possible murder. And when I do find out what happened, Benton, I'll make sure everyone knows that.'

'I'm telling you to back off,' Benton said. Even with the background noise, his deep voice was authoritative.

'I don't work for you any more, thank God,' said Calder,

and cut him off, thinking how good it was no longer to be beholden to the likes of that man.

He saw Nils fighting through the crowd to get to him. Calder bought him a pint of lager, which Nils tucked into with practised ease. Nils's stomach now hung out in front of him in a definite beer belly, and his two chins had turned into three. But he was pleased to see Calder and drank his health greedily.

'I take it you chose this bar because of the match?' Calder asked.

'Dead right. I've got a lot riding on this one.'

'I thought you supported Man United?'

'I do. But you don't make money by just betting on the team you support, do you? Especially not if you're Danish.' He grinned.

'I suppose not.'

'Selling corners,' Nils said, taking another large gulp.

'What?'

'Selling corners. That's what you do. When the away team is stronger than the home team and they only play with one striker up front you sell corners. It always works. Well, nearly always.'

'Is that what you've done here?'

'Yep. Sold total corners at twelve.'

That meant that if the total number of corners in the match was fewer than twelve, Nils would make money. If it was greater, he would lose. It was a lot like trading bonds, which was no doubt why Nils liked it.

'Is twelve a good price?'

'Yeah. Should be eight. Do you want some action?' Nils took out his phone, ready to call his bookmaker.

Calder shook his head. 'No, thanks. But I'll get you another beer.' Nils had already sunk his first pint. There were heads on the TV talking football, but Calder was glad to see that Nils wasn't paying attention.

'So, how's it going?' Calder said, returning with another beer.

Nils grimaced.

'That bad?'

'It's not as good as it was when you were there. They brought Kevin Strumm over to head up the desk,' Nils said. 'And he's a wimp. He won't let me do anything without checking with him first, and the moment I build up a decent sized position he wants me to reduce it.'

'It's no bad thing to be careful.'

'You don't make money that way.' Nils smiled. '*You* knew when to go in large. That's something I learned from you.'

'Be patient. You'll get your break.'

'Maybe. But I've got to say, if the right job came along somewhere else, I'd take it.'

'Bloomfield Weiss are still the best in the bond business.'

'Perhaps. But it's not a God-given right. I'm keeping my options open. How about you? I heard you bought a flying school?'

'Yes. Langthorpe in Norfolk. It's going well.'

'Any money in it?'

Calder grinned. 'None. I'll be lucky if it ever turns a profit. But you should come up one Sunday.'

'Sounds a bit hairy for me,' Nils said. 'All right. You've bought me two beers. What's up?'

Calder told Nils all about Perumal's visit, his suspicions over Jen's death and the coincidence of his disappearance. Nils listened closely. 'Wow,' he said at the end.

'I want to find out why Jen's death was so convenient to Carr-Jones. And I want to find out whether she and Perumal were murdered. He was visiting the Teton Fund in Wyoming – I'd like to know what deals the Derivatives Group was doing with them, and whether Jen had any contact with them. Also, I understand Tessa Trew left Bloomfield Weiss just after Jen died. Apparently she fell out with Carr-Jones. I'd like to find out why, and where she's gone.'

'Wow,' said Nils again, taking a gulp of beer.

'Will you help me?'

Nils winced. 'I admit it does sound dodgy. Very dodgy. But I can't believe there's anything in it. And if there is, it's dangerous shit.'

Calder pressed on. 'You know some of the people in Carr-Jones's group, don't you?'

'Sure. I was on the same programme as Derek Grayling. And I know one or two others.'

'Can you ask them a couple of questions?'

Nils didn't answer, but glanced up at the screen. The players were coming out of the tunnel at White Hart Lane. Calder could see him begin to tense.

'Well?'

'It might piss some people off,' Nils said.

'It *will* piss some people off. Benton Davis for one. Carr-Jones for another.'

'What's in it for me?'

It was the standard investment banker's question and the question Calder had feared. 'Nothing. Nothing at all.'

Nils raised his eyebrows. 'Then why should I do it?'

'Two reasons,' Calder said. 'I'm asking you. And you worked with Jen. You know what happened to her was wrong. We both owe it to her to prove it.'

Nils didn't seem to react to this. Suddenly the noise level in the bar dropped a notch and Nils turned to the screen. The match had begun. Nils and Calder watched in silence. Within two minutes, Liverpool had won a corner. Then another. And another. A minute later and they conceded a corner at the other end.

'Shit,' said Nils. 'Four corners in five minutes! I've got to get out of this.' He pulled out his phone, hit a number and placed it to his ear. Calder didn't hear the conversation, but there was no mistaking Nils's reaction.

'Jesus Christ!' he said staring at his phone in disbelief. 'I'd have to cover at sixteen.'

He glanced at Calder in indecision. Calder could tell he had serious money riding on this. If he'd staked a hundred pounds a corner, he'd be set to lose four hundred quid. If he'd staked a thousand . . .

'Remember the UEE bonds,' Calder said.

Nils grinned ruefully. 'You're right.' He spoke rapidly into the phone and then slipped it back into his pocket. He glanced up at the screen in disgust. Another corner to Spurs. 'I'm outta here.'

Calder finished his beer and they made their way to the exit.

'Thanks, Zero,' Nils said.

'For the beer or the betting advice?'

'Both.'

'Well?'

They were standing on the pavement outside the bar. It was just beginning to rain.

'I'll do it,' Nils said.

21

'You're getting much better, Ken,' Calder said as he stood at the desk in the flying school and filled in paperwork. The weather forecast was good, and he had been forced to abandon his investigations in London for a few days to help out Jerry.

'Thank you,' said the accountant, grinning like a schoolboy. 'Those last couple of landings felt just right.'

'You must watch your speed on the approach, but if you keep this up next time, we could be looking at a solo.'

Ken almost jumped into the air, he was so excited. He shook Calder's hand warmly and headed out to his Mondeo in the car park. Calder smiled as he filled in the technical log for the aircraft they had just flown. A natural flyer Ken was not, but he certainly had perseverance. He would get to his first solo, although it would be a long haul from there to the licence.

Calder heard a cough behind him. A cough he recognized. He turned round. There, sitting in an armchair, was Justin Carr-Jones.

Calder felt an almost physical shudder of revulsion at seeing him here, in his territory, the world away from Bloomfield Weiss. He was wearing the investment-banker's uniform of suit and tie, but with his curly blond hair, glasses and pink cheeks he did look awfully young and powerless out of his own environment.

'Shouldn't you be at work? I take it you haven't come for a trial lesson?'

Carr-Jones stood up, smiled and held out his hand. Calder ignored it. 'Can we talk?' Carr-Jones said. 'Privately.'

'One moment.' Calder turned to his next student, a young man of twenty-two who had only seven hours' flying under his belt but was already making excellent progress. 'Sam, can you go out and check Alpha Tango? I'll be with you in a few minutes.' Calder led Carr-Jones to the little box that was the office he shared with Jerry, who was safely in the air.

Carr-Jones sat in the cheap chair opposite Calder's desk. 'I hear you've been asking questions about Jen Tan.'

'I have,' Calder said.

'I don't think it's a good idea.'

'I'm sure you don't.'

'It all happened a year ago. It's been thoroughly investigated by the firm and by the police. There really is nothing to be gained by going over that old ground again.'

'Perumal didn't disappear a year ago.'

'Perumal has nothing to do with Jen's death as you well know.'

'Doesn't he?' As usual in Carr-Jones's presence, Calder was finding it hard to maintain his composure. 'You know Perumal came up here to see me?'

'Benton said you told the police something like that.'

'He seemed agitated about something. Afraid.' Calder watched Carr-Jones for a reaction. There was none, so Calder went on. 'He asked whether I was suspicious about Jen's death.'

'That was sad,' Carr-Jones said coolly.

'Yes,' said Calder. 'It was.'

Carr-Jones glanced at him. 'Oh, I know what you must think. And I can understand why you slugged me, I suppose. But her suicide did explain a lot.'

'What do you mean?'

'How strangely she was behaving. Her response to what I said in that bar was way over the top. She was obviously unbalanced. Some people can take the pressures of the markets and some can't. She couldn't.'

Calder fought to control himself. 'Are you saying it wasn't because of you she killed herself?'

Carr-Jones smiled sadly. 'I've thought about it a lot since

then, as I'm sure you have. I think she got herself into a vicious downward spiral of depression. Her histrionics were a symptom of that. I only regret someone at Bloomfield Weiss hadn't insisted that she see a psychiatrist before it was too late.'

'Justin, that's crap.'

'No. It's what happened. I'm just sorry that you don't seem able to accept it.'

'Perumal suggested Jen hadn't taken her own life,' Calder said.

'Did he actually say someone murdered her?'

'That's what he implied.'

'Who?'

'He didn't say. But he did say he thought Jen's death was convenient for you.'

'Oh, I see,' Carr-Jones snorted. 'So I killed her? That's ludicrous.'

'Is it? Was Jen's death convenient?'

'Convenient? Of course it wasn't convenient! And anyway, that's a pretty revolting suggestion. I suppose he's talking about her lawsuit. But that was no big deal. She didn't have a leg to stand on. She was going to lose and she knew it, which is why she killed herself.'

'No, Perumal was talking about something else.'

'Something else? What else was there? Did he give you *any* idea what he meant?'

'No,' Calder said.

Carr-Jones relaxed slightly. Just very slightly. A tiny slump of the shoulders, a loosening of the jaw muscles, Calder couldn't put his finger on what it was exactly. But he was sure he had noticed it. And in that instant he knew that there *was* something else, something that Carr-Jones was anxious for Calder not to find.

'Bit of a coincidence, isn't it?' Calder said.

'What?'

'That within days of Perumal coming to see me, he should die.'

'Oh, come on, Zero, that was an avalanche. An act of God if ever there was one.'

'It's true. You'd have to be pretty smart to hide a murder with a ton of snow.'

'You're not suggesting I killed him too? He was in America and I was in London. I couldn't have. And believe me, I miss him. He brought us a lot of deals over the last year. This last week has been a nightmare on the desk without him. Our new risk-management system has fallen over and we've had to calculate the revals ourselves. They spend forty million bucks and end up with something worse than we had before. You remember how it is.'

'Actually, I'm trying to forget. These deals Perumal did. Were they with the Teton Fund?'

Carr-Jones didn't answer.

'He went on a business trip to Jackson Hole, Wyoming. What else could he be doing there?'

'Yes. With the Teton Fund. There was another Indian guy there who Perumal did lots of business with. Complex structures. Big size.'

'The kind of deal you make nice fees out of?'

Carr-Jones smiled. He picked up a white circular 'whizz-wheel' navigational calculator that was lying on Calder's desk. 'Is this some kind of slide-rule?'

'Kind of.'

Carr-Jones played with it for a moment, his mathematical mind swiftly assessing its dimensions, its possibilities, and then tossed it back on to the desk. 'You've told all this to the police, I take it?'

'Yes,' Calder replied.

'Did they find anything?'

'Not yet.'

'Not yet or not at all?' Now it was Carr-Jones's turn to examine Calder's reactions. 'I thought so. They found no evidence, so now you're fishing yourself.'

'I want to find out what happened,' Calder said.

'You know what happened. We all do. A year ago a disturbed young woman killed herself. A week ago one of my star traders lost his life in a mountain accident. There really is no point in asking more questions.'

'Isn't there?'

Carr-Jones looked out of the window as a Piper Warrior landed, applied full power and took off again in a 'touch and go'.

'I'd rather you didn't.'

Calder snorted. '*You'd* rather I didn't. You can't stop me, Justin. I don't work for Bloomfield Weiss any more. Your political manoeuvrings have no effect here.'

Carr-Jones picked up the whizz-wheel and fiddled with it again. 'Very neat,' he said, mostly to himself. Then he glanced around Calder's small office. 'You don't really own this airfield, do you?'

'We own the leasehold, yes.'

'But not the land itself?'

'No. It's owned by a local farmer.'

'And when is the lease coming up for renewal?'

The answer was in two months' time. The renewal should be automatic. The land was actually owned by Mrs Easterham, whose father had taken over the aerodrome when the RAF abandoned it in the seventies. Since his death she had retained a strong emotional attachment to it and she seemed to be pleased with the rejuvenating effect Calder and Jerry had had on the operation. No, there should be no problem.

But as Calder looked at Carr-Jones, he decided not to answer him. He suspected Carr-Jones knew already.

Carr-Jones noticed his hesitation and smiled. 'It would be such a shame if you had to close this place down after all the work you've put into it.' He got to his feet. 'You have someone waiting. Nice to talk to you, Zero.'

With that, he was gone, leaving Calder to gaze out over

the airfield which until a minute before he had considered his own.

'So you see, I thought it only fair that I should discuss this with you first. Give you a chance to match their offer.'

Mrs Easterham's voice cut like glass. Her clothes were from Chelsea and the highlights in her blonde hair were applied in Knightsbridge on her frequent trips to London, but she was a Norfolk woman through and through. Tall and thin, toughness fought with elegance in her demeanour and toughness won. This corner of Norfolk had been in her family for five centuries, and she felt it was her duty to ensure that it remained in her family for at least one generation more. Her husband had died many years earlier, and she had devoted her life to bringing up her two sons, now both at public school, and seeing to the farm, which was a large one, and well run.

Calder had not been surprised by Mrs Easterham's appearance so soon after Carr-Jones's visit. But he had been surprised by the offer she had received: two million pounds for five hundred and fifty acres of the Easterhams' farm, including the airfield.

'Have you no idea who this Brynteg Global Investments is?' he asked her.

'Not really. It's an investment company based in Guernsey. I've no idea who's behind it, I've just been dealing with a firm of lawyers in London. Brynteg is Welsh, isn't it?'

'Sounds it,' Calder said. Carr-Jones was Welsh. The bastard wasn't even trying to disguise the connection.

'Hardly a centre for international money-laundering, I'd have thought, but of course one never knows. Whoever they are, they're willing to put up a deposit of twenty per cent. And if they pay cash, who am I to quibble? The thing is, with agriculture in the desperate state it's in, I'm going to find it extremely hard to hold on to the farm. If I can sell half of it at this price, then the future of the rest is safe.'

'But they'll close down the airfield?'

'Sadly,' said Mrs Easterham. 'They were very firm about that. They want the land for growing experimental crops. Apparently it's the perfect location. I hate to do this to you, and I'm sure my father would have wanted me to keep it going if I possibly could, but I have no choice.' She watched Calder and Jerry's faces with concern. 'Which is why I would much rather sell it to you. You wouldn't even have to match the price. Just come somewhere close.'

Jerry glanced at Calder. 'I don't know, Mrs Easterham. We can see what we can do.'

Jerry was hoping that Calder would be able to come up with the money. Calder didn't want to dash his hopes directly. All the time he was thinking: was Carr-Jones so desperate that he was willing to spend two million pounds to keep Calder quiet?

'Well, that's good. But I need to get back to them by next week.'

After she had gone, Jerry raised his eyebrows at his partner. 'Well?'

Calder shook his head. 'Sorry, I can't do it.'

'Could you do part of it? Maybe we could borrow the rest from the bank. I have no idea, is two million quid a lot of money for that much land?'

'I think you'll find it's way over the market,' Calder said.

Jerry shook his head. 'I can't believe it. Just when things are going so well. And she assured us she would renew the lease when we bought this place last year. Greedy cow.'

'I can understand it,' Calder said. 'I suspect times are tougher for her than she lets on.'

'Maybe. But I'm screwed if this goes through. I know I've put less cash into this than you have, Alex, but it was everything I have. If I throw in the towel here, either I get a job somewhere else as a flying instructor for peanuts or go back to undertaking. And believe me, that's something I definitely don't want to do.'

Calder winced and put his head in his hands.

'Who are these people anyway?' Jerry said. 'What's the point of buying a big patch of farmland in the middle of nowhere at an over-the-market price? And why approach Mrs Easterham? It doesn't sound as if she had the place up for sale. There must be farmers going bust all over the country desperate to offload some land.'

Calder slumped back in his chair, studying Jerry. He was no dummy, which was one of the many reasons why he was such a good man to have as a partner.

Jerry's eyes narrowed. 'You know what's behind this, don't you, Alex?'

Calder nodded.

'Does it have something to do with your trips to London?'

Calder nodded again.

'Tell me.'

So Calder told him. Everything. Jerry listened, taking it all in.

'This Carr-Jones guy is a total bastard,' he said when Calder had finished.

'That's right.'

'Do you think he'd really pay two million quid to keep you quiet?'

Calder sighed. 'Anyone else, and I'd call his bluff. But Carr-Jones? I don't know whether it's his own money or someone else's, but I do know that if he makes a threat, he goes through with it.'

'So what are you going to do?'

Calder looked at his partner. 'This confirms Carr-Jones is hiding something. Something very big. If it was up to me, I'd still want to find out what. Two people have died.'

'But what about the airfield?'

Calder closed his eyes. Carr-Jones had foreseen this. It was all very well for Calder to risk his investment in the flying school. But he couldn't risk his partner's. At least, not without his consent.

'I'd like to carry on asking questions, Jerry.'

'Alex! I could lose everything here.'

'I know. But I'm more sure than ever that Carr-Jones is deeply involved in something very messy. I hate to run away from it. Let me go after him. If I can nail him he won't be able to go through with the purchase. We'll keep the airfield, he'll go to jail.'

'And if you fail?'

Calder shrugged. 'We lose.' He leaned forward. 'Look, I know this is an unfair thing to ask you, but unless we take the risk he'll get away with it. And that's something I couldn't live with.'

'Whereas I could?'

'Until today you'd never heard of him.'

'You like taking risks, don't you?' Jerry stood up and looked out over the airfield towards the North Sea. 'I wouldn't be here if it wasn't for you,' he said. 'I'd still be in the front seat of a hearse crawling around crematoriums at five miles an hour. I could never have bought this place by myself, or kept it going.'

'I needed you too,' Calder said.

'Sod it,' Jerry said. 'Nail the bastard.'

22

Calder drove down to London late that afternoon. It was seven thirty by the time he reached Highgate, but he decided to try Sandy Waterhouse's office anyway. He knew lawyers habitually worked late, and hc might be lucky.

She answered the phone. He introduced himself as a friend of Jen's who was in London for a couple of days and wanted to ask her a few questions about how Jen had died. After some prevarication, she suggested he meet her at her office at nine o'clock.

Calder arrived at the small marble lobby of the building that housed Trelawney Stewart, an American law firm he had vaguely heard of, at nine on the dot. He idly wondered about Sandy Waterhouse. She'd had a pleasant, quiet voice on the phone, with a soft American accent. She had sounded happy to meet him. Which was why he was a little surprised that she hadn't shown up by nine fifteen. Or nine thirty.

He took the opportunity to call Nils and find out how he was getting on. Nils was at home, watching a football match on TV – Chelsea, from what Calder could hear in the background. Nils had managed to speak to Derek Grayling, who said everything in the Derivatives Group was going brilliantly. It would be another record year. They kept finding new ways of ripping off their customers and the customers kept on coming back for more. Especially the Teton Fund, which was now the group's biggest account. But Jen had nothing to do with them, according to Grayling, and neither had Carr-Jones: Perumal handled them alone. Nor had Nils been able to find out any dirt on Tessa's departure. It was the old story – she left a top investment bank for a promotion and a guaranteed bonus at a lesser institution, in this case a bank in Stockholm. Calder thanked Nils and asked him to keep looking, although Nils wasn't optimistic about finding anything new.

As he slipped his phone back in his pocket, Calder was disappointed. If there was something going on in the Derivatives Group, and Calder was sure there was, it was too well hidden for Nils to find. It also seemed that Tarek was wrong in his suspicions about Tessa and Carr-Jones falling out.

It was nine fifty-five, and he had decided to call it quits at ten o'clock, when the lift opened and a tall, slim woman with short wispy blonde hair stepped out, looking around her. She smiled apologetically when she saw him.

'Alex? I'm sorry I'm so late. You shouldn't have waited for me.'

'That's OK,' Calder said. 'Working late?'

'I wish. This is about your average day, these days. I'm sorry, I thought I could get away earlier, but I was waiting for some comments back from Chicago. But you don't want to hear all about that.'

'Would you like a glass of wine or something?' Calder asked.

'Sure. There's a place around the corner. Come on, I'll show you.'

The place around the corner was small and almost empty. Calder bought two glasses of white wine. As he carried them back, he was struck by how attractive Sandy was. She was probably in her late twenties, with high cheekbones, clear blue eyes and a kind of poise that seemed completely unconscious, and all the more striking for it.

'I seem to remember Jen mentioning that you worked hard,' Calder said.

'All the time,' Sandy replied. 'I thought it was bad in New York, but it's even worse here. Still it's nearly over.'

'Are you going back soon?'

'I finish here next week, provided the deal I'm working on closes. Then a couple of weeks' vacation and I'm back to the grindstone in New York. I've done my two years.'

Calder felt a mild sense of disappointment. Silly, really.

'Jen was pretty good about it,' Sandy went on. 'I don't know how many times I must have stood her up. In fact, I was supposed to see her the night she . . .' Her voice trailed off.

'The night she died?'

'Yes. But Jen was understanding. Very understanding. I think we had the two worst jobs in London and it was kind of nice to trade moans.' Sandy's hair had fallen over her eyes, and she made no attempt to push it away.

'How did you know each other?'

'We went to high school together. In one of the 'burbs outside New York. We were in the same class, but we weren't exactly close. Then a classmate suggested I look her up when I was transferred to London. Jen became my only friend here. Outside of Trelawney Stewart, that is. We get to spend a lot of time with each other at that place.'

'She didn't have many friends in London, did she?'

'No. And she didn't understand why. I think Jen was quite a sociable person, or used to be. But that all changed when she came here. I don't know if it was the unfriendly people or her awful boss.'

'Justin Carr-Jones?'

'That's it. He crushed her confidence. I kept telling her that she should believe in herself. She was smart, bright, a fun person to be with. Sometimes I thought she was listening. But then work would get her down again. If I'd only shown up that night, maybe she wouldn't have . . . well, you know.'

'I'm not sure she did kill herself,' Calder said, quietly.

'What do you mean?'

'What do you think I mean?'

Sandy sighed. 'I don't know. At the time I didn't believe she had, either, but the police investigated, there was an inquest and I guess I've just accepted the result.'

'Why didn't you think it was suicide?'

'I saw her. The weekend before she died. We went to a

movie on Sunday afternoon. I do get the occasional Sunday off. She was pretty bitter, about Justin what's-his-name. She had some scheme for revenge, some way to really hurt him. She couldn't wait to get on to it. So I guess she didn't seem to me to be someone with no hope left.'

Calder's interest quickened. 'Do you know what this scheme for revenge was all about?'

'No. She didn't really tell me. It had something to do with that hedge-fund guy – you know, Frenchman. "The Man Who Broke the Euro".'

'Martel? Jean-Luc Martel?'

'Yeah. That's right.'

'Did she say *what* it had to do with him?'

'No. Not that I can remember.'

So Jen had a plan to hurt Carr-Jones? Calder recalled the last time he had seen her, in that bar in Chelsea, when he had remarked that it was a shame that they didn't have a lever to use against him. At the time he had thought his comment had sparked something. She had denied it, but what if his instinct had been correct? If she had found some way of putting pressure on Carr-Jones in the same way Carr-Jones had put pressure on Calder and Jen? Then her death could well have been 'convenient' for Carr-Jones, as Perumal had claimed.

But what pressure? Something connected with Jean-Luc Martel, Perumal's client. Except Nils had just told him that Jen had had nothing to do with the Teton Fund when she was working in the Derivatives Group.

Sandy interrupted his musing. 'I told the police all this. And they still seemed pretty certain it was suicide, didn't they? And the coroner.'

'That's right. And of course there was that text message to her mother. "Sorry Mum".'

'Imagine receiving a message like that,' said Sandy. 'When you're thousands of miles away. It must have been horrible for her mother.'

'It was. The policewoman I spoke to answered Jen's mobile. A straightforward note on a scrap of paper would have been kinder. What is it? What's the matter?'

Sandy was staring directly at him, her mouth half open. 'Mom,' she said.

'What?'

'"Sorry Mom". Jen would have said "Sorry Mom". Mum is English. And believe me, Jen was an American.' She frowned. 'If it was her who sent the message.'

Calder stared back, the implications of what Sandy was saying flooding into his brain. 'You mean if someone hit her over the head and pushed her out of the window, then that person might have texted a suicide message? Easier than forging a handwritten note.'

'They could have gotten her mother's number from the list in the phone.'

'Bloody hell,' said Calder. 'But perhaps the message did say "Mom", after all? Maybe I just misheard it.'

'No, it was "Mum". That's what they told me too. I remember thinking it odd at the time. But I didn't say anything, it didn't seem important.'

'Well, if that's correct, it proves that verdict was wrong,' Calder said. 'I'll call the police tomorrow to check it out.'

'Let me know what they say.' Sandy gave Calder a long appraising look. He found it uncomfortable, but also strangely thrilling. This woman was getting to him. 'I was trying to remember Jen talking about an Alex,' she said. She smiled. 'You weren't a secret boyfriend, were you?'

'I'm afraid not. We used to work together. You could say I was her boss, after Carr-Jones. She might have called me "Zero"?'

The smile disappeared instantly, to be replaced by a look of disappointment mixed with distaste. 'Oh, yeah. She did talk about you.'

Calder was shocked by the change in tone. Partly because

he had been enjoying Sandy's receptive mood, but mostly because of what it said about Jen's opinion of him.

'She can't have thought I was as bad as Carr-Jones, surely?'

'Not quite,' Sandy said. 'But you hurt her almost as much.'

'We got on well,' Calder protested. 'She said she was enjoying work for the first time in London.'

'Whatever.'

'Tell me what she said,' Calder persisted.

'She's gone now,' Sandy said. All traces of friendliness had disappeared. 'It's not worth dwelling on.'

But Calder wouldn't let it go. 'I don't understand. You said I hurt her. I thought we had a good relationship. I thought she liked me.'

'Oh, she thought you were wonderful,' Sandy said. 'Nice guy, good at your job, said encouraging things to her, let her have some responsibility. She thought you had just turned the world the right way round for her. And then that creep accused her of sleeping with you, and you dumped her in it.'

'Dumped her in it?'

'That's what she said,' Sandy's voice was bitter now. 'When she wanted to complain, you tried to stop her. When she wanted to take them to a Tribunal, you tried to talk her out of it. As soon as one of the boys was threatened, you all closed ranks against her. She thought she could rely on you and you let her down.'

'That's not true!'

'Whatever.'

'I was prepared to give a statement to the Tribunal.'

'Oh, big deal. You were prepared to say what happened. That must have taken real bravery. You didn't support her, though, did you? You didn't stand by her. You didn't resign yourself. You just let her carry the can.'

'That's not true. I did resign.'

'When?'

'After she killed herself,' Calder said quietly. 'Or was killed.'

Sandy gave him an I-told-you-so look. 'Is that why you want to prove she didn't commit suicide? So you don't have to feel so bad about it?'

'That's not fair.'

'Either way, she's dead.' Calder started to object, but Sandy cut him off. 'Hey. It's not me you have to convince. The person you have to convince isn't here.' Sandy took a large gulp of her wine. 'I'm sorry. I guess I'm still kind of angry about it.'

Calder was kind of angry about it, too. He wanted to prove to this woman that she was wrong, but he knew some of what she said was right.

She drained her glass. 'Can I go now?'

'Of course,' said Calder, but he was disappointed that his meeting with her had somehow gone so badly awry. 'Shall I help you find a cab?'

'I can do that myself, thanks,' she said, and gathered together her coat and bag.

Calder watched her get ready to leave. He couldn't let her go, just like that. 'Sandy,' he said.

She paused.

'Take this, and give me a ring if you think of anything else.' He handed her his card, which she took after a moment's hesitation. 'I know we've only just met, but I want you to believe me. What happened to Jen was wrong. I don't know exactly what it was that happened, but I do want to make sure whoever was responsible doesn't get away with it.'

Sandy looked at him coolly. 'Guilt,' she said. 'That's all it is. Guilt. We've all got it. We let her down, Alex, or Zero or whatever your name is. And there's nothing we can do to change that fact.'

Calder looked down upon the distinguished columns of one of the more venerable gentlemen's clubs on the other side of the street below. He was standing in a second-floor meeting room of Bloomfield Weiss's small but plush office in St James's. The chances of any of the club members dealing with Bloomfield Weiss were nil, but someone ten years ago had decided that this was the right location to establish a private-banking operation in London.

Bloomfield Weiss's international private-banking business was headquartered in Zurich and had offices in the major 'offshore' locations: Luxemburg, Jersey, Monte Carlo, Bermuda, Nassau and Miami, the gateway to Latin American money. Calder had only a vague idea of who their clients were: people who were too rich to share the same bank as the man in the street, the international money-nomads of no fixed abode who earned income in many jurisdictions and paid taxes in none, buyers of all kinds of esoteric products dreamed up and distributed by Bloomfield Weiss. Including hedge funds. Time to find out a little more about Jean-Luc Martel and his mysterious Teton Fund.

He had phoned DC Neville earlier that morning. It had only taken a little coaxing to get her to double-check the spelling of 'Mum'. It was with a 'u' not an 'o'. The policewoman had listened with interest as he had outlined the theory that Jen could not possibly have sent the text message to her mother spelled as it was. But when he urged her to reopen her investigation she was implacable. She'd make a note on file, but there wasn't enough evidence yet to take any further action. Jen had been in England a year, it was quite possible that the English usage was rubbing off on her.

Calder took a tiny bit of consolation from DC Neville's use of the word 'yet'. She was listening. In fact, Calder felt she was half-persuaded. From his earlier conversations with her he suspected the problem was convincing her to talk to her more sceptical boss.

'Alex! How are you?'

Calder turned to meet a tall, vigorous man with thinning blond hair brushed back and an immaculate double-breasted suit.

'I'm fine, Freddie.'

'It's very good to see you,' said Freddie Langhauser, pouring coffee from a pot on a sideboard into two cups. 'You were lucky to catch me here. I just got in from Zurich this morning, and I'm off to New York tomorrow.'

'Thanks for squeezing me in.'

Langhauser and Calder had been on the same Bloomfield Weiss training programme when they were both starting out in investment banking. They had not been close then, but the programme built up a level of camaraderie that survived the ups and downs of a career at Bloomfield Weiss. It was a kind of shared loyalty, a network of colleagues, friends even, who had suffered together and played together. Calder had phoned Langhauser the day before on the off-chance that he would be in town. If someone called you from your training programme asking for a favour, you at least listened.

'What is it, seven years now?' Freddie asked.

'More like eight.'

'Is it really? I hear you've jumped ship?'

'Last year. And I can report there is life after Bloomfield Weiss.'

'That is certainly good to know.' Freddie accompanied this comment with a combined bray and snort. Calder suddenly remembered how irritating this laugh was, and how it used to emerge at seemingly random moments.

Freddie swiftly dealt out the coffee cups and sat down. Busy.

'I won't take much of your time,' Calder said, taking his own chair. 'I believe you deal with hedge funds.'

'That's right,' the Swiss banker replied. 'Since the equity markets took such a pasting hedge funds have become much more popular with our clients. You could say I've developed some expertise in them over the last couple of years.' Another random bray.

'Do you know anything about the Teton Fund?'

Freddie smiled.

'I'll take that as a yes.'

'Until a year ago, I wouldn't touch it. Jean-Luc Martel's a smart guy, but I thought he took too much risk. He also has a couple of questionable investors. But then after he broke the euro everyone wanted a piece of him. And if people want to buy, who am I to stop them?'

'Have you placed any investors in his funds?'

'A couple. And I'm working on some others. Actually, I've a major client who's thinking of putting three hundred million in next month.'

'Three hundred million? Wow. Who are they?'

'You know I can't tell you that. Why these questions? Is there something wrong with the Teton Fund? Something I should know?'

'I'm not sure,' Calder replied. 'That's what I'm trying to find out.'

'Planning to invest?' Freddie said. 'Because they won't take direct approaches. I'm sure I can arrange something, although I believe they have a million dollar minimum.'

Typical of a Bloomfield Weiss man to try to turn the meeting into a sale, but Calder couldn't blame him. It made a useful cover story, though. 'Yes. I've got to put my ill-gotten gains somewhere.' Calder caught the hint of envy in Freddie's eyes that one of his training programme contemporaries might have a million bucks to fritter away on a hedge fund.

'You're the trader, you know the kind of risks Martel takes.'

'It's always hard to tell from the outside. You said something about questionable investors?'

'Yes. Originally Chalmet in Geneva sponsored the fund. Many hedge funds market themselves to investors outside the US. Much less regulatory hassle.'

'I see. And are Chalmet questionable?'

'Some of their clients are. They're big in Latin America. And they do well with Eastern European money. As you know, the Swiss banks have had to become much choosier about who they deal with over the last ten years. Somehow Chalmet seem not to have caught up with the rest of us.'

'So you think there's drug money in the Teton Fund?'

'It's impossible to know where it comes from. But I do know two of the biggest investors, both of whom are distinctly suspect. There's the Zeller-Montanez family from Mexico, and Mykhailo Bodinchuk.'

'Bodinchuk?'

'Ukrainian billionaire. Banks, oil, arms, brewing, aluminium. That's the legal stuff. Also trades in drugs and prostitutes, on a massive scale. Has a reputation for getting his way in business. We won't touch him.'

'Bloomfield Weiss won't touch him? He must be bad.'

Freddie didn't appreciate the dig. 'We won't deal with the Zeller-Montanez family either. They got caught up in a major money-laundering scandal a few years ago. You have to be careful these days, as I said.'

'Are any of these people active investors in the Teton Fund?'

'What do you mean?'

'I mean, do they have any influence on what happens?'

'I doubt it. For these guys, once the money reaches Switzerland it's supposed to be legitimate, invested conservatively.'

'I see. Well, thank you, Freddie,' Calder said, getting up to leave. 'It sounds an interesting opportunity. I'll give you a call.'

Freddie offered Calder his business card. 'Think about it. If you've got a million to spare, I'm sure we can squeeze you in.'

Calder left Langhauser's office and walked up St James's Street towards Green Park tube station. His phone chirped. It was Matt.

'Look, Zero, I've got to be quick.' Matt was whispering. Calder could hear trading-room noises in the background.

'All right.'

'Nils said you were curious about what was going on in the Derivatives Group.'

'Yes.'

'Something about Jen? And Tessa Trew?'

'That's right.'

'Well. I met some mates from Oxford in a pub a couple of months ago. I don't know if you remember, but I was there the same time as Tessa. I hardly knew her, but a couple of these guys did. We were talking about the amazing transformation to blonde bimbo she had undergone since she came to London. Then one of the blokes asked me what had happened to her at Bloomfield Weiss. I said I didn't know, all I knew was that she quit last year. He said he'd seen her just afterwards, and she was pretty angry. He'd asked her why she left Bloomfield Weiss for a two-bit Swedish outfit, and she said she couldn't get out of there fast enough. In fact, she couldn't get out of London fast enough. My mate tried to ask her why, but she wasn't saying.'

'Did she mention Carr-Jones?'

'No. My friend wouldn't know who Carr-Jones was, anyway. He said she just changed the subject. But he was pretty sure something had happened. Something pretty serious.'

'She quit just after Jen died, didn't she?'

'Yes. Around then.'

'Thanks, Matt.'

'No problem.'

As Calder took the tube back to Anne's place in Highgate, he thought through what Matt had said. Nils would never be able to find out what was going on within the Derivatives Group, but Tessa would know. And if she had really left Bloomfield Weiss that angry, she might tell him.

The very idea of talking to Tessa made his skin creep, but as soon as he got to Highgate he looked up all the major Swedish banks on the internet and phoned their head offices in Stockholm asking to speak to the derivatives department.

At the third try he struck lucky.

'Can I speak to Tessa Trew?' he asked the man who answered the phone in Swedish.

'One moment, please.'

Calder steeled himself. He knew this wasn't going to be easy.

'Tessa Trew.'

'Hello, Tessa. How are you?'

She recognized his voice instantly. 'Zero? Is that you?'

'Yes. It's me. How are you doing?'

'What do you care?'

Calder ignored her. 'I'm going to be in Stockholm tomorrow.'

Tessa snorted. 'Don't try to tell me you thought you'd look up an old friend.'

'I need to talk to you,' Calder said.

'Well, I don't need to talk to you, so goodbye.'

'Hold on! I need to talk to you before I talk to the police.'

Silence. But Calder knew he had just caught her before she hung up. 'What are you going to talk to the police about?'

'That's what I want to discuss with you.'

'I have nothing to discuss with you.'

'Meet me tomorrow evening. Seven o'clock. The bar of the Grand Hotel. OK?'

'No.'

'Suit yourself. I'll be there. And if I don't see you, I'll fly back to London and speak to the police. There is full extradition within the EU, you know.'

The phone went dead. Calder hit the internet again, this time looking for a ticket to Stockholm.

23

The view from the Grand Hotel over the harbour to the Old Town and the Royal Palace is glorious in summer, or even at midday in winter. At seven o'clock on a black February night, when the rain falls in giant drops of barely melted ice, it is non-existent. But inside, the bar was warm, sophisticated, murmuring with the elegant reticence of the Swedish establishment. Calder scanned the crowd. No sign of Tessa.

He wasn't surprised that she had no more desire to talk to him than he had to talk to her. But he hoped she would come, if only to discover what it was that he knew. Even with a cheap flight from Stansted airport, it was a long way to come for a drink. He finished his gin and tonic and caught the barman's eye for another one. A woman with mousy brown hair and glasses approached him.

'Can I have one of those?'

'Tessa? I didn't recognize you.'

She was soberly dressed in a blue business suit, which hid rather than emphasized her figure. The blonde hair had gone, as had the makeup and the contact lenses. The weak chin was still there, and once he looked at her properly it was obvious who she was, but he had been fooled.

'Don't worry,' she said. 'No one from the Bloomfield Weiss days ever does. I don't mind. That was the point.'

Calder asked the barman for another gin and tonic. They made their way to the only free table.

'So you left Bloomfield Weiss too?' Calder said.

'That's right.'

'More pay? Guaranteed bonus?'

Tessa leaned forward. 'You said you're going to the police. What about?'

'What do you think?'

'Don't play games with me,' Tessa said, steel in her voice. 'Say what you have to say and then I'll go.'

'I think Justin Carr-Jones killed Jen Tan a year ago. I think you were involved somehow. And I think he killed Perumal Thiagajaran this year, although I'm prepared to believe you had nothing to do with that.'

'Goodness, you have let your imagination run away with itself,' Tessa said. She seemed more relieved than alarmed by his suggestion.

'Did you think I was going to the police about something else?'

'One year later. You had no evidence. I didn't press charges. Nothing would have come of it.'

'Are you sure?'

Tessa held his eyes for a moment, and then the steel left them. She stared down into her drink and mumbled something.

'What was that?' Calder said.

'I said I'm sorry. For what I did.' She took a deep breath. 'It's probably the worst thing I've done in my life.'

Calder was surprised by the admission, but wasn't inclined to disagree with her. 'What about Carr-Jones? What went wrong between you and him?'

'That was all a year ago, too. It's in my past now. I've forgotten about it, or I'm trying to forget about it.'

'A year isn't that long ago.'

Tessa shook her head. 'I've got nothing to tell you.'

'Come on, Tessa. You've apologized for what you did to me. All right. I accept your apology. It's forgotten. It's not you I'm after, it's Carr-Jones. He must have done something a year ago to make you so upset. Why did you leave?'

Tessa bit her lip and glanced at Calder. Her self-confidence seemed to have gone with the hair dye. Then she answered him. 'I thought I could handle Justin. We'd worked together in Tokyo and I was doing well in London. He liked to treat me as a blonde bimbo, but I knew I was brighter than that. So did he, I think, although he'd never admit it. Justin doesn't understand women at all, or the relationship between men and women, and I took advantage of that. He thought he understood me; he assumed I was winning business by promising sexual favours. He didn't realize I was actually good at my job. But he gave me good bonuses and I thought, who's taking advantage of who?

'Justin sails pretty close to the wind, sometimes. He thinks you have to to succeed in this business and he's probably right. He knew he could rely on me to help get things done. Nothing illegal, but things that some people might call unethical.'

'Like claiming I raped you?' Calder said.

'As I said before, that's the worst thing I did, but yeah, I suppose, like that.'

'Go on.'

'Well, Jen hadn't a clue. She didn't understand Justin and thought the best way to deal with him was to fight him. For a girl so smart, and she *was* smart, she was dumb about that. Justin treated her horribly. He knew how to belittle her, crush her self-confidence. And she had no idea what to do about it.'

'Didn't you feel sorry for her?'

'To be honest, not at the time, no. She had this holier-than-thou attitude about how women should get on in work. I believed you could do very well as a woman provided you were willing to adapt to the environment. I think women like Jen believe the environment should adapt to the woman. The world doesn't work like that. It should, but it doesn't.'

'And then she died.'

'And then she died. Justin had made her so miserable, she killed herself.' Tessa fumbled for a cigarette in her bag and lit it. Calder thought he detected a slight shake of her hand. She took a couple of drags, giving herself time to regain her composure. 'It made me realize that I had got everything wrong. So what if I earned a half-million-dollar bonus that year? Jen hadn't played the game by Justin's rules, and her punishment? She had lost her life. That wasn't a game I wanted to play.'

'Did you feel responsible?'

'In a way, yes. I hadn't done anything to her directly, but I did set you up so that Justin could discredit her. But after Jen died I couldn't live with myself. I had to change my attitude to my work and that meant changing jobs. So I quit.'

'You expect me to believe that you're a different woman now?' Calder couldn't keep the cynicism out of his voice.

'You can believe what you like,' Tessa said. 'I don't really care. But I don't do things by Justin's rules any more. I might make a bit less money, but I'm still good at my job. And I can live with myself.'

'Hm.' Calder wasn't sure, although the hair and glasses suggested this change was genuine and not just something concocted for his benefit that evening. 'Why do people like Carr-Jones behave like that?' he said. 'I mean, he proved he could squash Jen, but why bother?'

'He hates women, especially smart women.'

'Do you know why?'

'Perhaps. He used to talk to me some nights, when he was pissed, especially when we were in Tokyo together. He hates his mother. She had affairs all the time when he was growing up. Still does. His father's a railway clerk in Wales, did you know that?'

'No,' Calder said.

'Anyway, she trampled all over him. Flaunted her affairs in front of her husband and her son. I think Justin got his ruthlessness from his mother. And probably his intelligence.'

'Sounds as if they deserved each other.'

'Probably.' Tessa nodded her agreement.

'Does he have any girlfriends?'

'Not that I know of. But he likes sex with women. I think he prefers to pay.' Tessa glanced at Calder. 'You're wondering why I stuck with him?'

'That thought had occurred to me,' said Calder.

'Simple. He's brilliant at his job, a rising star, and I thought he would take me up with him. I didn't realize then that the price was too high.'

Calder was beginning to feel some sympathy for Tessa. At least she had asked herself the difficult questions. There were too many people at Bloomfield Weiss who never even got to that stage.

'Did you hear about Perumal's accident?'

'Yes. Yes, I did.'

'I don't think it was an accident. I think it had something to do with Jen's death.'

'And how did you come to that conclusion?' Tessa asked, making no effort to conceal her scepticism.

Calder told her about Perumal's visit to him in Norfolk and Sandy Waterhouse's impression that Jen had a plan to get revenge on Carr-Jones, something to do with the Teton Fund. He explained that the suicide text message had probably not been sent by Jen, but by her murderer. A man who might have been paid for by Justin Carr-Jones.

Tessa listened closely. 'You have no proof of any of that.'

'No,' said Calder. 'But do *you* know of any problem Carr-Jones had with the Teton Fund?'

'Justin never dealt with the Teton Fund directly. It was always Perumal. Somehow he managed to keep his hands on that account.'

'OK. What about Perumal then? Was there some kind of dispute with the Teton Fund? Something dodgy?'

Tessa smoked her cigarette and stared at the crowd in the bar. The piano played a Sinatra tune. Calder gave her time.

'Yes,' she said at last. 'I think there was.'

'Tell me.'

Tessa glanced at him, hesitating. Then she seemed to come to a decision. 'Do you remember the Teton Fund shorted the hell out of Italian government bonds a year ago?'

'Of course I do. I was caught on the wrong side of that trade a couple of times before I gave up. The press blamed Martel for Italy quitting the euro.'

'Well, Martel and Bloomfield Weiss did some huge derivative trades. They were called IGLOO notes, massively risky, lots of upside if the Teton Fund got it right, disaster if they got it wrong. Perumal fixed them up.'

'How come I didn't know about this?' Calder said. 'I was busy trying to trade against him.'

'Come on, Zero. Since when have the Derivatives Group ever told the Prop Desk what they were doing?'

'I suppose you're right.'

'Anyway, as you no doubt remember, the trade went against Martel, at least initially. He just put on bigger size. We were making tens of millions in fees. But then it came to the month-end reval, and do you know what number was put in for the IGLOO notes?'

'No.'

'Ninety-eight and a half.' Ninety-eight and a half implied an unrealized loss for the Teton Fund of only one and a half per cent.

'And you think it should have been lower than that?'

'Yes. About thirty points lower.'

'Who did the reval?'

'Perumal.'

'What kind of loss did thirty points imply?'

'If my numbers are right, about three hundred million dollars,' Tessa replied.

'Three hundred million!' Calder digested the information. 'If anyone had found out the Derivatives Group were helping a client hide a loss that large, the shit would have hit the fan big time. It would have killed Carr-Jones's career stone dead. Do you think he knew what Perumal was up to?'

'Probably,' Tessa said. 'It wasn't obvious. The structure of the IGLOO notes was so damn complicated and I don't think any of the others on the desk thought much about it. I was curious, though, so I did my own back-of-the-envelope calculation, which is how I came to the thirty points. It was a big envelope, and I may be wrong, it's only an estimate. But I'm damn sure it was a hell of a lot more than the point and a half Perumal stuck in the system.'

'Would Carr-Jones have done the same calculation?'

Tessa nodded. 'Oh, yes.'

'Could he have told Perumal to input the wrong prices?'

Tessa considered the question. 'I've no way of knowing,' she said. 'Maybe he did. More likely he spotted the discrepancy afterwards and decided it was a question he just didn't want to ask. That would be typical of him.'

'Do you think Jen could have found out?' Calder asked. 'Used it to threaten him?'

'I don't see how.' Tessa frowned. 'She left the group before we did the deal. Unless . . .'

'Unless what?'

'Unless Perumal told her.'

'Why would he do that?'

'I don't know. But I do remember hearing something very odd a couple of days before Jen died. It was late, and there was hardly anyone else in the trading room. Perumal was at his desk talking to someone on his mobile. He seemed agitated, too agitated to notice me walking past. I heard him say something like: "Jen, please. Don't do it. I beg you not to do it. I wish I'd never told you anything." Then he saw me, hung up, and scurried off to finish the conversation.'

'What did you think he was begging her not to do?'

'As you can imagine, I was very curious at the time. When Jen jumped out of that window a couple of days later, I assumed he had been begging her not to kill herself. Or perhaps not to continue with the lawsuit. But it never really sounded right. Why was he even talking to her? Although Jen and Perumal were friendly enough when they worked together, they were hardly close. I couldn't imagine Perumal being the sort of person Jen would turn to when she was contemplating suicide. And the "I wish I'd never told you anything" made no sense.'

'Until now,' Calder said. 'If Jen had somehow got Perumal to tell her about the IGLOO reval and then decided to use it against Carr-Jones, Perumal would be in big trouble. Very big trouble. The kind of trouble that would put him in a panic and cause him to try to retract what he'd told her.'

'It would also put pressure on Justin. As you said, if the false revals came out, he'd be finished.'

'Maybe Jen tried to persuade him to back down on the lawsuit.'

'If she did, it was a stupid thing to do,' said Tessa.

'Because she's dead now.'

'Right.'

A waiter asked if they wanted some more drinks, but Calder ignored him. His brain was whirring. 'Perumal would have made the connection, of course,' he said. 'Which is why he was suspicious about how Jen died.'

'And why he came to see you.'

'But why did he wait a year? And why was he killed now?'

'Perhaps he decided to go to the police about Jen,' Tessa said.

'Or try to blackmail Carr-Jones himself.' No wonder Perumal had seemed nervous to his wife. Why hadn't he told him everything when he had come up to Norfolk? Stupid bastard. If he had, he might still be alive now.

Tessa shivered. 'God, I'm glad I'm out of there.'

'Have you ever heard of Mykhailo Bodinchuk?' Calder asked her. 'Or the Zeller-Montanez family?'

'No. Should I?'

'They're investors in the Teton Fund. They could be dodgy.'

She shook her head. 'Don't know them.' Then her brow furrowed. 'Maybe your imagination isn't quite as wild as I thought it was. This worries me.'

'Of course it does. Carr-Jones has killed two people and got away with it.'

'Yeah. What are you going to do?'

'Go to the police. Or the FSA.' The Financial Services Authority was the regulator for the financial markets in London.

'Oh.' Tessa shifted uncomfortably on her chair.

'You will talk to them, won't you?'

'I'm not sure, Zero.'

'But why not?' As Calder looked at her he could see the reason. There was fear in her eyes. 'Come on, Tessa. You have to talk.'

'Actually, I don't. You said yourself, two people have died. I don't want to make it three. Or four.' She looked pointedly at Calder. 'I managed to leave Bloomfield Weiss without making an enemy of Justin. I don't want to make an enemy of him now. Especially now.'

'What?'

'You heard me. I won't talk to the police. Or anyone else.' Tessa's voice was firm.

'But what was all that stuff about how you'd changed? This is your chance to make up for what you did to Jen.'

'Look. I'm glad I told you what I know. I owed it to you. And you can do with it what you like. Personally, I hope you screw the bastard. But I'm not going to risk everything by going against Justin. Jen did it. Perumal did it. I won't.'

'That's cowardice, Tessa.'

Tessa stubbed out her cigarette and got to her feet. 'You can get yourself killed, if you want to. But I'm not going to. Thanks for the drink, Zero.'

And she was gone.

24

'Can I get you something, honey?'

Martel stretched out his long legs towards the glowing embers of the fire, and smiled at his wife. 'An Armagnac, please, *mon ange*.'

He watched as she poured some of the expensive golden liquid from a decanter on the bar. Nismes-Delclou 1914, bought at auction. She poured herself a glass of mineral water and came over to curl up beside him.

She was dressed in a simple looking but desperately expensive black dress, silver and pearl earrings sparkling under her lustrous honey-coloured hair. God, she was beautiful. They had just returned from a party to raise money for the National Museum of Wildlife Art at one of the more spectacular ranches in Jackson Hole. Cheryl was the most stunning woman there, outshining two Hollywood starlets and three trophy blondes. What amazed Martel was that she never seemed to realize it.

'Golly, that was tedious,' she said as she snuggled up to him.

'Oh, I don't know,' said Martel. 'There were some pretty serious people there.'

'Yes. But all they ever talk about is money and what it can buy.'

'That's not necessarily true. They talk about travel. Culture. Charities. Their work, sometimes.'

'But it's always the smart places they've been to, the celebrities they've gone fishing with, their trip in a private jet to San Francisco just to see the opera, or the big deals they've done. Even the charity is a competition about who can give the most.'

'Oh, come on, *mon ange*. Those people are very generous. And so are we. Do you want me to stop giving money to the museum? I donated a million dollars last year.' He'd only done it because Cheryl was on the board. The least she could do was appreciate it.

'No, not at all, honey,' said Cheryl, kissing him on the cheek. 'I think it's wonderful that you do that. I just think that they shouldn't boast about it, that's all.'

Martel had actually enjoyed the evening. Everyone apart from Cheryl had been in 'elegant western' dress. Martel thought he looked good in his cowboy boots and Stetson: when in Jackson he liked to get into the cowboy thing. He had had a great time bragging to anyone who would listen about his Italian exploits and he had got a kick out of speaking for fifteen minutes to the one bona-fide film star present. He was convinced that the woman with the largest breasts at the table had made a play for him. He had ignored it, of course, but it was nice to be noticed.

'How was Denise's party?' he asked.

Cheryl had returned from her own little trip to New York that afternoon, having been to a friend's thirtieth birthday party the night before.

'It was fun. The people there were genuine. Real people.'

Martel didn't rise to it. Cheryl had taken a scheduled flight on principle, despite the fact that Martel had his own Falcon lined up with the others on the apron at Jackson Hole's airport. Even so, real people didn't just hop a thousand miles across the country to go to a party.

Cheryl leaned across and brushed his lips with hers. He sensed the gentle pressure of her chest on his, smelled her perfume, felt her tongue flicking and teasing its way into his mouth. For a moment he felt a surge of arousal and pulled her down towards him. Then the doubts flooded in. Who else had she been kissing that day? Who had she seen in New York? He pushed her away and sat up straight on the sofa. She slid on to his knee.

'Jean-Luc? Honey, what is it?' She touched his cheek.

Her face, the face that he loved, was so full of concern that for a moment he was tempted to ask her. Do you have a lover? Do you love me?

But he didn't. He feared he wouldn't get a straight answer, and it would only make her angry.

'I am sorry, *mon ange*,' he said. 'It is nothing.'

'But it must be something, honey. Is it more problems with the fund?'

Martel closed his eyes and nodded. It was the easy response.

'The stress is getting to you. You've got to take it easy. Take a few days off. Take a month off.'

'The markets never quit,' Martel said. 'And there is too much going on right now. There is always too much going on.'

Cheryl stood up and moved away from him, her expression a mixture of sadness and irritation. 'This isn't good, you know. It isn't good for you, it isn't good for us. You have to *do* something about it.'

Martel got up. 'I think I'm going to bed.'

'Don't walk away from me like that,' Cheryl said with sudden firmness.

Martel ignored her. She grabbed his arm.

'I said, don't walk away from me. We have to talk about this, Jean-Luc.'

Martel spun round to face her, unable to control his anger. 'You Americans have to talk about everything, don't you? Analyse everything. Well, talking won't fix this, Cheryl.'

'And what will, then?' Anger burned in Cheryl's eyes as she faced him.

'Loyalty, perhaps. Trust.'

'What do you mean by that?'

'Nothing,' said Martel, turning away from her, annoyed that he had been goaded into saying more than he had intended.

She grabbed his arm again. 'You have to tell me what you mean by that. Are you accusing me of something?'

Martel shook her arm off him roughly and marched up to bed.

'You can't just run away, Jean-Luc,' Cheryl called after him.

Much later, when they lay next to each other, back to back, a cold wall of silence running down the centre of the bed between them, Martel thought about what she had said. She was right, he couldn't run away. He had to know. He found himself torn between anger that she had probably deceived him, and a yearning to win her back. It was the uncertainty that was killing him. He didn't *know* that she was cheating on him. But he couldn't pretend that he hadn't heard that cough.

Pohek had followed Cheryl to New York, and Martel was meeting him early on Monday morning. He was counting on Pohek to put him out of his misery one way or the other.

And then there was that other matter. When he had blamed his tension on the Teton Fund, he hadn't been entirely untruthful. For once the markets were treating him kindly. The Nikkei was moving up slowly and steadily to the point where his unrealized losses were only a couple of hundred million. In a few days, he'd be in profit. And then the fun would begin.

But he had discovered something else, something that threatened to unravel everything, something that needed to be dealt with sooner rather than later. At least now Martel knew how.

It was a beautiful morning. The snow on the upper slopes of the Tetons shimmered in the early sunlight, warm and inviting, although the tree-clad base of the rocky wall was still in cold shadow. The sky was clear, except around the Grand Teton, where clouds came and went, descending and rising in varying shapes, sometimes forming a white mushroom, sometimes a cluster of greying cotton balls, sometimes a long flat wedge hovering above the mountain. The slopes would soon be crowded: already enthusiastic skiers were making their way across the valley floor to the lifts at Teton Village. It might be early in Wyoming, but it was late afternoon in Kiev. Martel took a deep breath and picked up his phone.

As he waited to be put through he felt his chest swell with a rush of power. He was becoming used to the power of billions, the power of being able to buy whatever he wanted, the power of bringing whole countries to their knees. But wielding the power to determine who lived and who died was a new experience. He found it intoxicating.

He remembered the first time, the first step, the first fix. It had been in Switzerland twelve months before.

They had been skiing all day, and Martel had done a good job of slowing to his guest's pace. But by the afternoon, his patience left him, and he whipped down a narrow black run leaving his companion far behind. He paused at a ridge overlooking the town of Saint Moritz far below and turned to watch the other man making his way down the slope slowly and gracefully, as if to demonstrate that he hadn't been competing with Martel. It was a mistake to show up his client like that, but Martel couldn't help it. With all that was going on, he sometimes just wanted to point his skis straight down the mountain and push off.

He took some deep breaths of the Alpine air, subtly different from that of the Rockies. He loved the skiing in Switzerland, even if Saint Moritz was not quite as challenging as Jackson Hole. It just had more class.

His companion joined him. Mykhailo Bodinchuk was a big man in a yellow ski suit with a chubby pink face. He was only in his early thirties, and he looked even younger, but he was one of the largest of the fifty or so investors in the Teton Fund. Like Martel he was successful. Like Martel he was unorthodox. But Bodinchuk required a different set of skills to succeed in the Ukrainian business world.

'There's a bar down there,' Martel said, pointing down a gentle slope to a small wooden hut. 'Shall we have a beer?'

'Why not?' said Bodinchuk.

They swept gracefully down the slope, took off their skis and unfastened their boots. Martel bought his guest the beer.

Two bulky skiers followed them in and propped up the bar, ordering a coffee between them. Bodinchuk was a careful traveller. Even on the ski slopes he didn't like to be alone. He and Martel usually met in Switzerland, the country Bodinchuk used as a base for his international investments. In fact, they had been introduced to each other through Chalmet in Geneva.

It was still mid-morning and there were few people in the bar. Martel's mouth was dry and he took a swig of beer before he spoke. 'The euro trade is looking good,' he said, lying with confidence.

'I'm glad to hear it,' Bodinchuk replied in passable American.

Martel hesitated. His heart was beating rapidly and his mouth was, if anything, drier. He was about to go a step further than he had ever gone before. He had tried everything to keep the Teton Fund afloat. Almost everything. But then had come the news from London that threatened to blow it all apart. He had thought long and hard about what he was about to ask his client, but there was no other way. No other way.

Another swig of beer. 'Actually, Mykhailo, I would like your assistance on a small matter.'

Bodinchuk rolled his eyes. 'Jean-Luc, when I invested in your fund three years ago it was supposed to be one of my legitimate businesses.'

'Which has given you a handsome return. Three times your money at the last valuation.' That was three times a hundred million dollars, serious money even to the Ukrainian.

'That's true,' said Bodinchuk with a smile. Martel knew Bodinchuk liked him. Martel's enthusiasm for turning one dollar into two by playing the markets intrigued Bodinchuk, whose own methods for making money were a little more direct.

'It's only a small thing,' said Martel. 'And for you it would be easy.' He glanced round the small bar. There was a couple in the far corner, the barman was cleaning glasses, only the Ukrainian minders were glowering at him. 'Let me explain.

There's a woman who works for an investment bank in London. Her name is Jennifer Tan . . .'

Bodinchuk listened, listened and acted. A year later there had been another meeting in Switzerland, Geneva this time, and Perumal Thiagajaran had been the subject of their conversation. Yes, Mykhailo Bodinchuk was proving himself the model of a proactive investor.

Now the Ukrainian's voice crackled down the line from Kiev. 'Hello, Jean-Luc. Is the market screwing you again?'

Bodinchuk sounded rushed. Martel was put on his guard. 'No, Mykhailo. The market is coming back our way. You will be glad to hear I haven't lost my nerve. We still have a massive position. I'm confident that in a couple of months we'll be sitting on the most profitable single trade in hedge-fund history. We're talking billions.'

'Excellent,' Bodinchuk said, warming a little. 'You have guts. You stick to your opinions. I like that.'

'It works,' said Martel.

'Yes, as long as it works.' Did Martel catch a hint of menace in that last comment? Martel knew that if the Teton Fund were to go under, he would lose more than his fortune, his ranch, his reputation and his self-respect. He would also lose the confidence of his investors. In Bodinchuk's case, that could be fatal.

'Mykhailo, there is one small thing you can help me with. I've heard someone is stirring up trouble at Bloomfield Weiss again. A man called Alex Calder who used to work there as a bond trader. He's asking questions about the death of the Chinese girl, and the Indian. Apparently he has discovered a link to the Teton Fund.'

'I see.'

'I wonder if it's time to . . . er . . . silence him?' Martel felt a delicious thrill as he said these words. He felt like one of those gangster bosses in the movies. Here he was deciding who lived and who died.

'No, leave it,' said Bodinchuk. 'The trail's gone cold. He won't find anything. Believe me, my man won't leave a trace. He never does.'

'But if he has linked the deaths with me then he has made some progress. I'm worried.'

'Don't worry.'

'I really think we should do something.'

'Listen, Martel.' Again, that hint of menace. 'I don't have the time or the desire to start a war with a major investment bank over what should be just a straightforward investment. The more dead bodies that appear, the more likely the authorities are to notice. I'm your client, not your hired gun. If you're worried, you sort it out. But be very careful how you do it. I don't want any of this coming back to me.'

'But, Mykhailo . . .'

'Your problem, Martel. And you had better be right about that trade.'

The phone went dead in Martel's hand.

Suddenly it was up to him. He *was* worried about this Alex Calder, no matter what Bodinchuk said. Should he try to do something about him himself? That seemed a lot more daunting than simply asking Bodinchuk to deal with it all. That had been death without responsibility.

No, he had to take action. He would need to find someone else to help him. Vikram perhaps? Perhaps not.

He checked his watch. Just about time to go to see Pohek.

He took his Range Rover and drove out of Jackson, fifteen miles to the north, to Antelope Flats, the rendezvous he had arranged with the detective. He had wanted to avoid meeting in Jackson: despite its transient population, the place was a small town, and someone of his height was easily recognized. As he drove, clouds descended as if from nowhere, pressing down on the mountains and the valley beneath them. Tiny snowflakes appeared, scurrying across the road, never seeming to actually touch the ground. The weather in Jackson Hole was fickle. A day could start out beautifully and change in a couple of minutes.

The meeting place was on a deserted road, just inside the Grand Teton National Park. He spotted Pohek's rented Buick pulled over in a small turn-off, next to a broken-down timber hut. There was nothing but sagebrush and snow in all directions; even the mountains had disappeared. No antelope, and certainly no sign of another human being. Martel drew up next to the Buick, bowling over a stray clump of tumbleweed as he did so. Keeping the engine running, he opened the door for Pohek to jump in.

Ray Pohek was in his late forties, thin with bad skin. According to his website he had been in the Denver Police Department before setting up his own detective agency. So far he had been businesslike in his dealings with Martel.

'Well?' Martel asked him.

'Nothing yet,' Pohek answered. Martel felt some of the tension release from his shoulders. 'She had lunch with a female friend, went to your apartment on Riverside Drive alone, went on to the party in Chelsea, came back home, also alone, and went to bed. Next morning she took a walk in Central Park, stopped in a couple of stores on Fifth Avenue, collected her bags from the apartment and went straight on to the airport.'

'So, you're sure she didn't see a man?'

'Quite sure. I had back-up from a New York associate, and of course we've bugged your apartment. She might have spoken to some guys at the party, she probably did, we have no way of knowing. But I guess that doesn't worry you?'

'No. Any phone calls?' Martel had had Pohek's associate bug the telephone in the apartment and the cell phone as well.

'She called her mother. She called you. She called a female friend – Bobbie Lawrenson. That's it.'

That was good news. If Cheryl was having an active affair it was highly likely that she would have called her lover, if not seen him, while she was in New York. But he still couldn't be sure.

'Here's my report.' Pohek handed Martel a brown envelope. Although he didn't say it, Martel was impressed that the detective had already written it all up. 'Do you want me to keep at it?'

'Yes,' said Martel. 'For another week, at least.'

'In that case I'll need more back-up here in Jackson,' Pohek said. 'I can't watch her twenty-four hours a day alone.'

'That's fine,' said Martel. He examined Pohek. He was clearly competent. He didn't look entirely trustworthy, but that was a good thing for what he had in mind. Martel took a deep breath. 'I might have something else for you.'

'Oh, yes?'

'Yes. I have a problem relating to a business matter over in London. There is someone there who is creating difficulties for me. Serious difficulties. I wonder if you know anyone who might be able to help me deal with him?'

Pohek's face remained impassive. 'I know what you're asking, Mr Martel. And the answer's no. I don't do that kind of work.'

'Ah, you misunderstand me,' Martel said, back-pedalling. 'I didn't mean that he should come to any harm.'

'Of course not, sir,' Pohek said.

'But you will be able to continue watching my wife?'

'Certainly, sir, I'll be glad to. Here's my invoice for what I've done so far.' Another envelope, white this time.

Martel opened it. His fee was steep, but Pohek was doing a good job. He wrote out a cheque for him there and then.

'Thank you, sir,' Pohek said, unable to suppress a grin. He stepped out of the Range Rover into the cold.

'Meet me here this time next week,' Martel said, and drove off.

Pohek watched him go. He examined the cheque Martel had given him. He knew there were wealthy people in Jackson Hole, but this guy was seriously loaded. And Pohek needed the money. Somehow since his divorce he had never been able to climb out from underneath the mountain of debt he had accumulated during his miserable marriage, no matter how hard he worked. He was way behind on his alimony, and his ex-wife was being a real bitch about it, not letting Ryan fly over from Miami to see him during the spring break. Pohek loved his son. He was a good kid, honest, hard-working, wanted to be a doctor when he graduated from high school, and it looked as if his grades were good enough for him to do it, too. That would need more money, of course. Somehow the boy's slut of a mother hadn't ruined him yet, but Pohek didn't know how long that would last. The kid was fourteen now, an impressionable age. If Pohek lost touch with him, God alone knew how he'd turn out.

He thought about Martel's request. Pohek hadn't shot anyone since he left the Denver Police Department, and he was sure he had been right to deflect Martel's enquiry. He had built up a good business over the last seven years and he didn't want to jeopardize it. He had been seriously tempted once, only six months before. A jealous wife had been so incensed with what she had discovered her husband had been up to, that she had offered Pohek twenty thousand dollars to deal with him. After thinking it over, Pohek had said no. Twenty thousand wasn't enough. But Martel would pay top dollar, there was no doubt about it. Pohek could catch up on the mortgage payments and the credit cards, and make sure he got to see Ryan this year. He could even start saving for college.

But killing someone? The two men he had shot while he was a cop had been no good low-lifes, both of whom would have happily killed him if he hadn't killed them first. But Martel's target could be a harmless innocent. Innocent? Innocent hell. All these money men were crooks anyway. The only difference between people like Martel and the junkies and small-time criminals he had dealt with on the streets of Denver was that the law left Martel to get on with it. If you stole five hundred bucks from a liquor store you ended up in prison. If you stole five hundred million, you ended up in a ten-million-dollar ranch in Jackson Hole. Martel didn't have to scramble about to meet mortgage payments or alimony; in fact he probably owned the bank that was putting the screws on honest, hard-working people like Pohek. If Martel had needed to fly his son out from Florida, he could fly him first class. Hell, he could use his own jet to do it. Pohek felt a surge of angry self-justification. People like Martel were screwing people like him.

A bluebird darted from the roof of the broken-down hut into the sagebrush, a tiny speck of colour in the grim landscape. As Pohek sat in his car looking out over the bleak plain, an idea formed in his mind.

Pohek decided to wait twenty-four hours before he made his move. He called Martel at the office from his motel in downtown Jackson. He used a new cell phone he had bought for the purpose. It took a little effort to get past Martel's secretary, but then he heard the man himself.

'Martel.'

'Good afternoon, Mr Martel. My name is Luigi.' Pohek had disguised his voice, it was deeper, rougher, and he hoped it would fool a non-native English speaker. The name Luigi was a bit corny, but it had the right connotations.

'Yes?' There was a note of interest in Martel's reply. He had picked up on those connotations.

'I understand you gotta problem in London you need taking care of.'

'Who is this?'

'I told you. Name's Luigi. I'm a freelance.'

'Freelance what?'

'Well, that depends on what you're looking for, Mr Martel.'

'How did you know to call me?'

'A little bird.'

'Have you been speaking to Ray Pohek?'

'I don't know no Ray Pohek,' said Ray Pohek.

There was silence. Martel was thinking. Pohek didn't want to rush him. 'I'll call you back in five minutes, Mr Martel.'

Pohek smiled to himself as he lay back on his bed in the motel room. He was pretty sure Martel would go for it. He dialled again. This time he was put straight through.

'Well?' he said.

'I might have something for you,' Martel said. 'Can we meet?'

'No way. That's not how I work. You tell me the target, I deal with it, you pay me.'

'How much?'

Pohek took a deep breath. 'A hundred thousand bucks.' He knew the figure was way over the market price. But he doubted Martel knew it too. He also suspected Martel could afford it. Besides, Pohek was taking a big risk here. He wanted to be paid enough not just to keep his debts at bay, but to get rid of them. Maybe put something aside for Ryan's college education.

'That's a lot of money, Luigi.'

'I'm good,' said Pohek. 'It's like anything else, you pay for what you get.'

'But I don't know anything about you,' said Martel.

'And that's the way it's gonna stay.'

'Then how do I know I can trust you?'

'You can't trust guys like me. But you don't have to. You pay me when the job's done. If I don't take care of your problem, you don't pay nothin'.'

Martel was thinking. 'OK, but how can you trust me?'

'I know you're an honest guy. Also, I know where you live. Guys owe me, they pay, don't worry about it.' There was a pause. 'Do you want more time to think it over?'

'No,' came the reply. 'I'll give you the details. But I need the job done quickly. Like in the next few days.'

Pohek smiled and took out his notebook. 'That's no problem. Fire away.'

25

It was fucking freezing. The wind blew in from the North Sea and bit into his body, slicing through his clothes. Although in theory the temperature was above thirty-two degrees, it felt colder than the damn Rocky Mountains at ten thousand feet. Ray Pohek wished he'd brought his thermal underwear. England just wasn't supposed to be like this.

He was standing in a thicket a few yards from the old windmill, looking down on the cottage. He had followed Calder from his home to the airfield that morning and back again in the afternoon. His plan was to watch him for a day or so, and figure out the best time and place to strike. He wanted to avoid the cottage if possible. It was nicely isolated, but it might be locked at night, and there was too much chance of something going wrong as he broke in. There was also more chance of leaving forensic evidence in a building: outside somewhere was best.

Pohek had been confident he could carry out the task Martel had set 'Luigi'. After all, he had been trained to kill in the police department, and he had several years' practice in tailing people. Doing the job in England had brought added cost and complications that he wouldn't have faced in the States. The biggest difficulty had been a weapon. He didn't feel comfortable using a knife, he obviously couldn't take a firearm on the plane or even in his checked luggage with all the security at airports, so he had had to figure out where to buy one in the UK. A search of press reports had suggested Harlesden in north London. After two false starts, he had succeeded in acquiring a Smith and Wesson .38 and some ammunition from a Jamaican for five hundred pounds. He was sure he had been ripped off, but he didn't care. Frankly, he was just pleased to get out of there alive.

Hiring a car had been easier. He had a credit card and driver's licence under a false name, and they didn't ask for his passport. So, suitably equipped with weapon and wheels, he had driven up to Norfolk and found himself a hotel in Cromer, a town about twenty miles from Hanham Staithe.

Now here he was, freezing in the gathering darkness, keeping an eye on the cottage through infra-red glasses.

Suddenly he saw a figure emerge from the building. He could recognize Calder now by the way he moved, quick and efficient. The man was clearly fit. Calder walked straight past the garage that housed his Maserati and strode out on to the lane towards the village. Pohek's pulse quickened. He decided to leave his car, and jogged along the parallel road on the ridge, keeping Calder in view. After about a mile Calder came to the village and a pub.

Pohek smiled. Perfect.

Calder stood at the edge of the small group of drinkers as Stuart, the vet, told an involved story about the vicar's dog swallowing his teenage son's condom. Calder wasn't listening. His thoughts were on Jen and Perumal. It was now clear to him that Carr-Jones had arranged for both of them to be killed. It was also clear that he didn't have the evidence to prove it. Without Tessa's support he didn't have nearly enough to go back to the police.

He had to find that evidence. Jen and Perumal had been killed, but he was the only person in the world who knew that fact and cared about it. If he didn't do anything, no one else would. He had spent a year trying to escape from the memory of Jen's death, but he realized that he had succeeded only in suppressing it, not eradicating it. Now, with what he had learned, he had to face up to the fact that she had been murdered. He could walk away, or he could do something about it. If he was going to be able to live with himself, there was no choice.

There seemed to him to be two options. Go to Jackson Hole, or confront Carr-Jones directly.

Confronting Carr-Jones would achieve little. He would smoothly deny everything, and continue with his plans to buy the airfield. Calder had managed to get Mrs Easterham to agree to delay her response for another ten days. And Calder had spoken to some lawyers about the situation if Brynteg Global Investments did buy the land. It wouldn't be easy for them to refuse to renew the lease, but it would be possible for a landowner to make life extremely difficult for an airfield operator. The Civil Aviation Authority was very strict about airfields: it would only take a fence or two erected in the wrong place for them to revoke the licence. Aircraft could land and take off from an unlicensed aerodrome, but training wasn't permitted there, and training was at the core of the flying school, and indeed the whole operation. If Brynteg Global Investments did buy the airfield, Calder would fight them. Calder just had an unpleasant feeling that he would lose.

So that left travelling to Jackson Hole to see if he could find out more about Perumal's death and the Teton Fund's shenanigans with derivatives. But how would the flying school cope without him for two weeks? He'd have to cancel lessons, losing valuable income for the school. There were countless things on his to-do list, from trying to recruit an assistant for Colin, the maintenance engineer, to dealing with the Civil Aviation Authority's latest directive on emergency planning. And he would be absent when Mrs Easterham accepted Carr-Jones's bid for the airfield. Then there were the innumerable minor crises that popped up from day to day. It seemed unfair to dump all that on Jerry.

But if there was to continue to be an airfield to worry about, he had to prove that Carr-Jones was a criminal. And do it quickly.

He felt a touch on his elbow.

'Are you OK?' It was Jess, the vet's wife and a teacher at

the local primary school. 'I know Stuart's stories are pretty boring, but you seem more than usually distracted.'

'Yeah, sorry.' He returned her concerned smile. 'Problems at the airfield.'

'They must be serious.'

'They are.' Calder drained his glass. 'Sorry, Jess, I think I'll be off.'

'Good luck,' she said. 'With the problems.'

'Thanks,' said Calder as he slipped out into the night and the walk back to his house.

The wind had died down, but not before blowing away the scraps of cloud from the night sky. The stars were emerging and there was half a moon hanging over the parish church. Calder usually walked to the pub. Spending all day at the airfield, he didn't get as much exercise as he would like and the two-mile stroll there and back refreshed him. He enjoyed the isolation of the darkness, the marsh illuminated in the moonlight, and beyond that the blackness of the sea. Although he frequently met walkers along the lane in the summer, he scarcely ever did so in winter, especially after dark. But in front of him were a woman and a dog, both of whom he recognized.

'Evening, Mrs Mander. Hello, Curly,' he said, bending down to pat the young fox-terrier who had trotted up to greet him.

'Ooh, it's raw out tonight,' said Mrs Mander, pausing to urge on her dog. 'I went into Norwich this morning, and poor Curly hasn't been out yet today.'

'He doesn't seem to care about the cold. Or the dark,' Calder said.

'He'd be out here all night if I'd let him.'

They parted and Calder continued on his way. Half a minute later he heard a commotion behind him. He turned to see the fox-terrier yelping around the legs of a man walking alone. They were about fifty yards away. Mrs Mander scolded the dog and dragged him away, apologizing as she did so.

Calder turned back towards his cottage, still half a mile

distant and quickened his pace. Odd for someone else to be out at this time, especially heading away from the village. He looked over his shoulder. The man behind was gaining on him and Mrs Mander had disappeared round a bend. Every nerve in Calder's body screamed danger. He had to move now before the man caught up. Of course, there might be a completely innocent explanation for the presence of the man in the lane, in which case what Calder was about to do would seem very odd. But after Jen and Perumal he wasn't willing to take any chances.

Without warning, Calder took off at a sprint up the lane. He heard a crack, and turned to see the man pointing something in his direction. A gun.

Jesus! He jinked to the right and leapt a gate into a field. He landed on his feet and felt a sharp pain in his ankle. He cursed, and started running into the darkness, trying to take up a zigzag pattern, doing his best to ignore the pain. He remembered from his Initial Officer Training days at Cranwell how difficult it was to hit a running target with a handgun at even thirty metres, although his pursuer was closer than that. He looked back and saw the man vaulting the gate behind him.

His left ankle was weakened, and he could only move at half speed. The field was a large one, with no cover, just pasture and the occasional streak of groundwater glimmering dimly in the moonlight. There was a copse just beneath the ridge on the other side, but it was a long way, at least two hundred yards. Over to his right stood a group of twenty or so cows. Bullocks, actually; Friesians, if he remembered correctly. He darted towards them and heard another shot. He looked back into the darkness. The man was gaining on him.

The bullocks looked up as if dazed by the darkness and he plunged into the middle of them. They skittered to either side of him, but they were big beasts, not easily frightened. A couple of them lumbered towards his pursuer.

Calder realized that with his bad ankle he wasn't going to

make it to the far hedge before the man with the gun caught up with him. And once that happened he was dead. So he spun round, trying to keep one of the bullocks between himself and the gun. The animals were jumping in all directions. He heard another sharp report and a sound more like a roar than a moo. One of the beasts next to Calder bucked and bolted into the darkness. The other animals began to follow at a rumbling canter. In the gap between two of them, Calder saw his pursuer.

He sprang, hitting the man in the middle and sending them both to the ground in front of the stampeding bullocks. Miraculously, none of the hooves flying over their bodies hit either of them. Calder lunged for the hand holding the gun. The man writhed and bucked. He was strong and quick – they were evenly matched. The two bodies rolled over into one of the broad pools of standing water left by the recent heavy rain. The cattle had thundered off into the distance.

Calder concentrated on trying to prise the gun from the other man's grip. A mistake. His adversary twisted round, jerked his arm and let go of the weapon, causing it to fly in an arc through the air. It came down with a splash several yards away. Calder, unbalanced, found himself face down in the water. The man slipped himself on to Calder's back, grabbed his head and ground his face into the mud.

With his eyes and mouth shut and cold water about his ears, Calder bucked and kicked, but he couldn't dislodge his attacker. He tried to twist his head to one side to breathe, but it was impossible. The pressure on the back of his head was firm, ramming him into the mud.

His lungs felt about to burst. In a few seconds he was going to drown in three inches of water and a couple of inches of mud.

He went limp, trying to give himself a moment to think, and perhaps confuse his attacker. But the downward pressure on his head didn't ease off. He only had seconds now before he either opened his mouth to take in a lungful of mud and water, or passed out through lack of oxygen.

The weight of the man on his back seemed to be growing heavier. Calder couldn't move.

He had only the time and the strength for one last attempt. He squeezed his elbows closer in to his body, and then with one heave, pushed upwards and at the same time drew his knees up under his waist. Then he straightened his legs, sending his backside into the air and the man tumbling over his shoulders. He ripped his head out of the water, and took a deep breath.

The man turned and scrabbled for the gun, which lay somewhere under the water. But he was looking in what Calder was sure was the wrong place. Still gasping for air, Calder threw himself over to a spot five yards from his attacker, where he had seen the gun fall. He plunged his hands into the water and within a couple of seconds felt hard metal. He lifted the revolver out of the water and pointed it at the other man, who was still frantically splashing about.

'Stop,' he called, fighting for breath.

The man looked at him, rose to his feet, turned and ran.

'Stop!' Calder shouted again aiming the gun with two hands at the retreating figure. But the man wasn't going to stop.

Above the gun sight at the end of the barrel Calder could see the man's back, presenting a steady target as he ran at a constant speed and direction away from him. All Calder had to do was press the trigger. But he hesitated. Calder had never killed anyone before and he didn't want to start now, even if seconds before his target had shown no similar qualms.

He lowered the revolver to point it at the rapidly moving legs, now twenty yards away. There was still a risk he might miss the limbs and cause a fatal injury higher up.

He pressed the trigger.

Nothing. Water or mud had jammed up the firing mechanism.

Calder let the gun fall to his side as he watched the man sprint back to the gate and the lane. Then he limped home across the field, wet, cold, covered in mud and cow dung, out of breath, his heart racing. But still alive.

26

The rain was falling hard on the Isle of Dogs, the stretch of godforsaken land surrounded on three sides by the River Thames that now acted as a platform for the giant office buildings containing the densest gathering of financiers in Europe.

Calder stood in the partial shelter of a young leafless tree, the Canary Wharf Tower behind him, in front of him another building, almost as big, into which he had seen Justin Carr-Jones hurry an hour and a half earlier, accompanied by Derek Grayling and a man he vaguely recognized from Capital Markets. Somewhere in there lurked a rating agency, which was the likely venue for Carr-Jones's meeting.

After he had been attacked and nearly killed on the way back from the pub Calder had abandoned his reticence about confronting Carr-Jones. He was angry, and he was impatient, and he was sick to death of being pushed around by that scumbag.

He had waited outside the entrance to Bloomfield Weiss's building, with the idea of following Carr-Jones and bundling him into a suitably isolated corner. His plans had been partially foiled when he had seen him leave the building with the two others. Calder had followed their taxi from the City to Canary Wharf. He knew that he should really wait until Carr-Jones was alone, but he couldn't face the idea of tamely following the three of them back to Broadgate and watching Carr-Jones go back to work.

So, when he saw the group of three men dressed in raincoats step out of the building and look for a cab, he moved forward.

'Justin, how are you?'

Carr-Jones turned to face Calder. The first thing that Calder noticed was a black eye and a grazed cheek. The second thing was the expression of fear on his face. Real fear.

'Do you have a moment?' Calder's words were polite, but there was menace in his voice. Menace that the other two men picked up on.

Derek Grayling instinctively moved nearer his boss.

'Alone,' Calder said.

Carr-Jones looked panicked. Calder himself must have appeared desperate from the expression on Derek Grayling's face. 'Shall I call the police, Justin?' he asked, pulling out his phone.

'Should he?' Calder asked Carr-Jones.

Carr-Jones swallowed and shook his head.

'You two take a taxi back to the office,' Calder commanded. 'Justin will be with you shortly.'

Carr-Jones nodded. 'I'll catch you up,' he said.

Glancing doubtfully at his boss, Grayling hailed a cab. Once he and the other investment banker were safely inside, Calder grabbed Carr-Jones's arm. 'Let's go somewhere a bit more private, shall we?'

'I can't talk to you,' Carr-Jones said, but he allowed himself to be dragged down some steps and on to a lower pathway along the old dockside. Above them the Canary Wharf Tower stretched eight hundred feet up into the air, but they were invisible from ground level, and in this rain there was no one to watch.

Calder propelled Carr-Jones into a secluded passageway leading underneath a building and backed him up against a wall. By this time they were both soaking wet, Carr-Jones's glasses were covered in water, with drips running off the frames. Their faces were inches apart.

'Nasty bruise,' said Calder, touching Carr-Jones's cheek. The other man flinched as he did so. 'How did that happen?'

'Slipped on the steps outside my apartment on the way to work,' he said. 'In the rain.'

'Uh-huh. Did you know someone tried to kill me? In Norfolk? Someone you paid, no doubt. Perhaps the same man you paid to kill Jen and Perumal.'

'No,' Carr-Jones said, shaking his head vigorously. 'I didn't pay anyone.'

'You see, I know you killed those two,' Calder said. 'Or arranged for them to die.'

'I didn't.' Carr-Jones's voice was hoarse.

'Of course you did. You and Perumal covered up the revaluation losses on the IGLOO notes last year. Jen found out from Perumal what you'd done. She threatened to expose you. Didn't she?' Calder gripped Carr-Jones's lapel and pushed him up against the wall. 'Didn't she?'

'I'm not telling you anything,' he said. But he was breathing hard.

'So then you had her killed.'

'I didn't. I swear I didn't.'

'Why should I listen to you?' Calder slammed Carr-Jones into the wall. 'Why shouldn't I just beat the shit out of you and toss you into that dock there? Seems like it's either you or me.'

'You wouldn't dare hit me,' Carr-Jones said, trying to regain his old bravado. 'I'd bring charges of assault.'

Calder hit Carr-Jones once in the stomach. Carr-Jones doubled up and groaned. 'I don't think you're going to the police, Justin.' As Carr-Jones straightened up, Calder hit him again.

Carr-Jones closed his eyes. 'All right, all right. Let me go. Let me go, and we'll talk.'

'You'll tell me what you did?'

'I can't.'

Calder shoved Carr-Jones towards the dockside.

'Listen to me!' Carr-Jones pleaded. 'Listen to me. I'll explain.'

Calder stopped just short of the edge, with the black rain-spattered water of the Thames lapping ten feet below. He hesitated, and then shoved Carr-Jones towards a solitary wooden bench. Carr-Jones slumped on to it.

Calder leaned over him. 'Talk to me.'

Carr-Jones hunched in the rain, his tan raincoat now sodden dark brown. He bent down, breathing deeply. For a moment Calder thought he was hyperventilating. Carr-Jones might be cool under the fiercest fire in the political jungle, but it was becoming clear that he was a physical coward. 'You need to back off,' he said.

'Hey, now's not the time to threaten me,' Calder said.

'It's not me. See these marks?' Carr-Jones pointed to his face.

'You didn't get them slipping down some steps?'

'I was attacked. This morning, outside my flat. It was still dark and this guy pushed me into a mews and pulled a gun. American guy. He said he'd blow my head off unless I kept quiet and stopped you asking questions. Then he hit me a couple of times. The thing is, I believe him. I'm sure he will kill me.' He glanced at Calder.

'I'm sure he will too,' said Calder.

'You've figured out a lot,' Carr-Jones said. 'I won't tell you how much of it is accurate. But I will tell you that I didn't kill Jen and I didn't kill Perumal.'

'If you're so innocent, how come you threatened to buy the airfield?'

'I wanted you to stop digging. Needed you to stop digging. Because if you stumbled across what had really happened and went to the police with it, we'd both be dead. Simple as that. That's why you have to back off.'

'Tell me about the IGLOO reval last year. Did you know Perumal was faking it?'

Carr-Jones shook his head. He was beginning to regain his composure. 'I'm not telling you anything. You said you'll kill me now, but I know you. You won't. If I talk to you, then I'm dead. Just like Jen and Perumal.'

For a moment Calder considered beating the shit out of him anyway, and even tossing him into the dock. But looking at the small, bruised, rain-sodden man next to him, he couldn't bring himself to do it.

He joined Carr-Jones on the bench, watching the rain pummel the water in the disused dock in thousands of tiny eruptions. The thing was, he believed him. Carr-Jones would happily destroy someone's self-esteem, or their career, but he wouldn't murder them. A smart political operator like him didn't have to. Death and physical danger were anathema to him.

He hadn't killed Jen. He hadn't killed Perumal.

'OK. So if you didn't kill them, who did?' Calder asked.

'I don't know for sure, and I'm not about to speculate.'

'Jean-Luc Martel?'

Carr-Jones didn't reply.

'All right. But I want you to assure me that Brynteg Global Investments are going to withdraw their offer for the airfield tomorrow.'

'Will you stop asking questions?'

Calder turned and grabbed the other man. 'I'll do what I damn well like. But if you go through with that offer, I will come and find you and I will destroy you. Do you understand?'

'Yes, yes,' said Carr-Jones. 'I'll see the offer is withdrawn.'

Calder let him go.

Carr-Jones slumped back on to the bench, relieved to be released. 'What are you going to do now?'

Calder stood up. 'You're convinced that if I ask more questions you're going to die?'

Carr-Jones nodded.

'In that case I'm going to fly to Wyoming and ask Jean-Luc Martel some more questions. See you.'

Calder smiled at the expression of dismay on Carr-Jones's face, and walked away.

Calder's next move was obvious. The key to Jen and Perumal's deaths lay in Jackson Hole. He had felt contempt for Carr-Jones's fear, but the man wasn't a fool. Until Calder managed to bring the people responsible to justice, he was in danger. So the sooner he acted, the better.

He drove back up to Norfolk to pack for a week or more in the Rocky Mountains in winter. And to tell Jerry that the threat to the airfield was lifted, even if the threat to one of its owners was still very much present. Jerry promised to mind the shop while Calder was away. Jerry was clearly relieved about the airfield, but Calder found his partner's concern for his well-being touching. Once again he felt he had picked the right man to go into business with.

Calder intended to spend the night before his departure at his sister's house, but when he called her, she said their father would be staying for a couple of days. He tried to back out, but his sister wouldn't have it, and he supposed she had a point. He just didn't have the strength for a fight with the old curmudgeon. He decided he would ignore any criticism and try to be polite. The same intentions he held every time he met his father.

He was making his way southwards through the fens, the Maserati loitering behind a lorry laden with sugar beet, when his mobile rang. He didn't recognize the number. 'Hello?'

'Alex Calder?'

'Yeah.'

'It's Sandy. Sandy Waterhouse. Jen's friend.'

'Oh, yes.' Calder recognized the soft American accent.

'Look. If you're in London I wonder if we could meet up. I'd kind of like to talk to you.'

'Oh, OK,' said Calder, surprised. 'I'm on my way down there now, actually. I'm flying to America tomorrow morning, but I might be able to meet you for a quick drink this evening.'

'Can you do later? Say nine o'clock in that wine bar we went to before? And this time I won't keep you hanging around, I promise.'

'When did you say your flight was?' Anne asked. The children were upstairs being read to by their grandfather, William was still at work, and Calder and his sister were cracking through a bottle of New Zealand sauvignon in her kitchen.

'Nine-oh-five from Heathrow. Change planes in Denver and wait for several hours.'

'Are you sure you have to go?'

'You said yourself it would be good for me to do something about Jen's death. And I feel the same way about Perumal. These people should still be alive, Anne.'

'And so should you,' said his sister. 'What about that man in Norfolk? He'll be back, you know. It sounds like he's already scared the hell out of that Carr-Jones chap.'

'I know. But there's not much I can do about that. If someone's after me, they're after me. If I just potter about my normal business I'll be a sitting duck. I've got to get them before they get me. That means I have to go to Jackson Hole.'

'What about the police? Someone tried to kill you, for God's sake! It's their job to catch whoever it was, not yours.'

'I thought about that, but who would I go to? The nearest police station to Hanham Staithe is ten miles away. By the time they got to my house, the guy would be long gone. I'd answer lots of questions and stir things up a bit, but without Tessa or Carr-Jones being willing to talk to the police, I have no evidence linking Jen to Perumal and the Teton Fund. No, I've got to go straight to the enemy.'

Anne drank her wine. She looked angry. And upset.

'What is it?' Calder asked.

'You know you could get yourself killed?' she said, her voice shaking.

'I'll be careful. I'll be all right.'

'You might say that, you might even believe it, but it's not true. How can it be true when two people have already died?'

'I'm still alive, aren't I?'

'You were lucky, Alex. You seem to live your life assuming that you always will be lucky, but one day your luck's going to run out.' A tear ran down her cheek.

'Don't worry, Annie.' Calder stood up and put his hand on her shoulder.

She brushed it with her fingers. 'I couldn't bear it if you went. After Mum. It would kill Father. It would leave me in a pretty bad way, too.'

Calder kissed her on the top of her head. 'I'll be fine,' he said firmly, willing it to be true.

Anne got up from the kitchen table, grabbed a tissue from a box on the window-sill and blew her nose with it. 'Why do you always have to take such stupid risks? I couldn't stand it when you were flying those jets. And then you had your accident. At least when you were trading it was only money you might lose, but now you're back at it, aren't you? Playing games with your life. I wish you were like Father and put it all on the horses.'

'I'm not sure that would be such a good idea, now, would it, Annie?' Brother and sister turned to see their father standing in the doorway. 'What's all this about?'

'Tell him not to be such an idiot, Father,' Anne said.

Calder bristled. It was a flagrant breach of sibling rules for Anne to draw their father into an argument on her side. 'OK, I admit I'm in some danger,' he said to her. 'But don't you see, someone has to stop Martel and others like him from getting away with killing innocent people? It's just like someone has to fly aeroplanes or join the army to keep the rest of us safe. It just happens that in this case it's me who has to do it.'

'You love it, don't you?' Anne said. 'Admit it. You love it.'

'I was scared yesterday,' Calder said.

'Oh, yeah, I'm sure you were scared. But that's just part of the thrill.'

'You don't know what you're talking about,' Calder growled angrily. But he knew that she did. That she was right. The prospect of going to America, facing up to and getting through some as yet unknown danger did excite him. But he couldn't admit that to her. He could barely admit it to himself.

'What's all this about innocent people getting killed?' their father asked.

'It's nothing,' said Calder. 'You wouldn't understand.'

Dr Calder sat at the kitchen table, poured himself a glass of wine and looked at his son levelly. 'Try me.'

With a sigh, Calder briefly explained about Jen and Perumal, Carr-Jones and Martel.

'See?' Anne said, appealing to her father. 'He's crazy, isn't he?'

The doctor stared into his glass of wine, his very stillness giving him authority. It was the pause before the diagnosis. 'You have to let him do it, Annie,' he said at last in a voice that was soft and rich, barely above a whisper. 'It is dangerous, but it's the right thing to do.'

She shot him an angry glance. 'He's going to go, whatever I say.'

'Aye, and so he should.'

Anne wiped a tear from her cheek. 'Perhaps you're right. I do find it difficult though. And, Father, I'm sorry about that crack about the horses.'

'That's all right. It was the truth, after all.' Then the doctor answered the question he knew his children wanted to ask. 'I have been to a session of Gamblers Anonymous, as Alex suggested. The first thing you have to do is admit you are a compulsive gambler. That's harder than I expected.'

Calder smiled at his father. For once, he felt pride in the proud man. 'Are you going again?'

'Aye. In three weeks' time. And of course, thanks to your help, I've taken Orchard House off the market.'

Anne reached over and squeezed her father's hand. He looked as if he were about to withdraw it, recoiling from the sign of affection, but then he let it rest and smiled at her.

Calder checked his watch. 'Oh, Christ, I'm sorry, I've got to go. I agreed to have a drink with the lawyer friend of Jen's. I shouldn't be back very late, but don't wait up for me.'

'But we've hardly had a chance to talk,' protested the doctor.

'No,' said Calder, for once with regret.

'I'll see you out.'

They walked out into the night. The sky was clear and it was just possible to see the stars through the orange glow of London.

'Thank you for supporting me, Father.'

'Och, Annie gets herself too worried. Especially about you. She always has.' They stood in companionable silence for a moment.

'Alex?'

'Yes.'

'Thank you for paying off those debts.'

'It was nothing.'

'It was a lot of money. An awful lot of money.'

'I can afford it. As you have pointed out many times in the past, I was paid too much in the City. I put by a bit. Quite a bit.'

'I'd like to pay you back.'

'Don't worry about it,' Calder said.

'No, seriously. I could maybe pay you back a few hundred a month. Perhaps a bit more when I could.'

'Where would you get the money for that, Father?' Calder said. Then he knew the answer. 'No, Father. Definitely not. I don't want you gambling to repay me. That's not why I wrote those cheques in the first place.'

'Oh, I wouldn't do that,' said his father. 'Who knows where I might turn up a bob or two?'

Calder stared at the doctor, the pride he had felt in him ebbing away. Then, afraid his father would notice his disappointment, he turned quickly on his heel into the night.

Calder was in a bad mood as he walked past the Trelawney Stewart building. Why couldn't his father just forget the bloody money and the horses? Plus he was not looking forward to another lecture from Sandy on his failure to support Jen, especially after what he had just been through. He had assumed he would have to hang around for another hour, but Sandy was waiting for him in the bar near her office, nursing a glass of fizzy water. She smiled tentatively when she saw him.

'They let you out early tonight, then?' Calder said.

Sandy shook her head. 'Nine o'clock isn't really early, is it? And after this I'm going back up there. I can see this becoming an all-nighter.'

Calder winced. 'I thought you'd have finished here by now?'

'I should be skiing in Austria with a friend as we speak. But the deal didn't close and I'm still here.'

'Bad luck.'

Sandy shrugged. 'I'm used to it. Let me get you a drink.'

'I'll get it.'

'No. Let me.' She smiled. Calder let her get him a glass of white wine to add to the half bottle he had already drunk. The wine bar was quiet; she returned a moment later.

'Why do you do it?' Calder asked.

'Be a lawyer?'

'Work so hard.'

'I've got no choice. The client gives Trelawney Stewart the deadline and Trelawney Stewart agrees to meet it, no matter how ridiculous it is. That's what we do. That's why we charge such exorbitant fees.'

'You could quit. Do some other kind of law.'

Sandy glanced at Calder. 'You're right. It's very strange. I mean I worked really hard to get to this situation. You might have guessed it already,' she smiled, 'but I'm pretty competitive. I went to Harvard Law School. During my second year I tried out for the summer associate programme at one of the top firms. Out of hundreds of applicants, Trelawney Stewart took me on, and they are one of the best corporate law firms in New York. They wined and dined me and told me I was wonderful, so when I graduated I went to work for them full time. And now I'm here they just make me work harder and harder. The better you are as an associate the more work you get to do. I suppose eventually I'll make partner and earn godzillions of bucks, but until then all I do is read hundreds of pages of legal documents and make corrections.' She glanced again at Calder. 'It's just not logical when I put it like that, is it?'

Calder smiled and shook his head. 'But you're going to stick with it?'

Sandy sighed. 'I guess so. I'm just not a quitter. And I suppose I've got something to prove.'

'To whom?'

'Myself. My dad, maybe. He's a hotshot banker. He's never told me he wants me to be a hotshot lawyer, but I guess at some level I'm just trying to please him. It's infuriating.'

'I know the feeling,' said Calder. 'A hotshot banker? He's not –'

'Arthur Waterhouse? Yes, yes he is. Sorry, I try not to let that slip out in conversation.'

Arthur Waterhouse was chairman of Stanhope Moore, a blue-blooded American bank that had just been swallowed up by the gigantic US Commerce Bank. He had a reputation for old-fashioned integrity. Which in today's world of investment banking meant he was a dinosaur.

'It's nothing to be ashamed of, is it?'

'No but . . . I wouldn't want you to think I'm just some privileged rich kid. Even if I am.' She smiled nervously.

'I'll forgive you,' Calder said, returning her smile.

'Speaking of which,' Sandy said, clearly glad to be changing the subject. 'I owe you an apology.'

'What for?' Calder asked.

'I shouldn't have said some of the things I said last time I saw you.'

Calder shrugged. But he was more inclined to accept Sandy's apology than Tessa's.

'I've been thinking about our conversation since then,' Sandy went on. 'And if you're right and Jen was murdered, I'm very glad you at least are trying to do something about it. Everyone else has given up.'

'That's certainly true,' Calder said.

'Jen wouldn't have quit.'

'I know.'

Sandy smiled. 'I told you we went to high school together? I remember one time in our senior year Jen kicked up such a fuss. She twisted the school board into knots.'

'Now, why am I not surprised?'

'You may not think it to look at her, but she was brilliant at soccer. So brilliant she decided the girls' team wasn't good enough for her, she wanted to play for the boys. The Athletics Director wouldn't let her; he didn't see why she couldn't just play with the rest of us. But Jen was having none of that. When she didn't get what she wanted out of him, she teamed up with a local lawyer and laid into the school board. It was a big deal: it was all over the letters-to-the-editor pages in the local paper. Her parents were mortified, but she didn't care. In the end the school board caved in, and they let her on the boys' squad.'

'How did she do?'

'She only started once. They said she wasn't good enough to be a regular first-team player.'

'Ooh. I bet she wasn't happy with that.'

Sandy shrugged. 'She seemed to accept it. She spent the rest of the season on the bench and we lost our best player. But I guess she'd made her point.'

They were silent for a moment, thinking of Jen.

'So, what have you found out?' Sandy asked. 'Do you mind telling me about it? I am interested.'

'All right,' Calder said. So he told Sandy all he had discovered about Jen's and Perumal's deaths, about Carr-Jones's protestations of innocence and the faking of the Teton Fund revaluations.

'Do you really think two people have been murdered?' Sandy said, her eyes widening.

Calder nodded.

'And no one's doing anything?'

Calder shook his head. 'Just me. The American police are convinced Perumal died in an accident, and the British police think Jen's death was suicide. I did talk to them about the "Sorry Mum" message, but they weren't convinced. It was definitely "Mum", though, we were right about that.'

'So you're going to the States tomorrow?' Sandy asked.

'Yes. Jackson Hole. I want to find out more about Perumal's death and I want to see this Teton Fund at close quarters.'

'Good.' Sandy fiddled with her wine glass, now almost empty. 'Um. I've been thinking.' She looked at him nervously, strands of hair falling over her eyes. 'I know I was pretty horrible to you before, but I'd like to help you on this. Once this deal does close, I'll have some time before I'm expected back in New York.'

'What about your skiing holiday? Can't you rebook it?'

'I thought of that,' said Sandy. 'But the woman I was going with from work can't get the time off next week. I've screwed up her vacation too.' She smiled, to herself rather than to Calder. 'I would have asked Jen. It would have been fun. And that made me think. I'm still angry about what happened to her, even angrier now I've heard what you have to say. I owe it to her to help you.'

Calder smiled politely. 'Good. Well, if I think of anything, I'll let you know.'

'Wait a minute,' Sandy said. 'I'm serious. While you're in the States perhaps I can do some stuff here. I can be pretty persistent if necessary. I'm sure I can help.'

Calder looked at her. It would be good to have an ally, and useful possibly. Nils was there to help at Bloomfield Weiss, but there was a limit to how much Calder could ask him. Sandy did seem a capable woman, and the idea of spending more time with her appealed. Appealed quite a lot. 'Will you have the time?'

'I'll make the time.'

'All right, then,' Calder said. 'Thanks. There is something you could do. There are a couple of suspect investors in the Teton Fund: the Zeller-Montanez family from Mexico and a Ukrainian called Mykhailo Bodinchuk. It might be worth trying to find out something about them.'

'OK,' she said, pulling a Palm out of her bag and jotting the names down on its tiny screen. 'I'll see what I can dig up. How can I get in touch with you? Does your mobile work in the States?'

'It should do.'

'And you will let me know if there's anything else I can check out?'

'I will, don't worry.'

Sandy drained her glass, ready to go back to work.

'Oh, Sandy?'

'Yes?'

'You should be careful. Remember Jen and Perumal were probably both murdered. And someone tried to kill me a couple of nights ago.' Calder briefly explained his struggle in the dark field with the anonymous man. 'So if you sense any danger, any danger at all, just drop it. Do you understand?'

Sandy gave Calder a broad smile. 'You drop it. I'm going back to work. Have a nice trip.'

Pohek watched the tatty car draw up to the house in Highgate and an Asian man get out and ring the bell. A cab. Calder answered the door, and handed the man a bag. A moment later he was inside the cab. It turned in the road and passed Pohek's car. He waited and followed. He had been lucky to catch it. He had decided to start staking out the house that morning at six-thirty, and it was barely six forty-five.

He had checked in with Martel as Luigi the night before to report his success in the supplemental job, scaring the wits out of the runt with the glasses. He hadn't mentioned the disastrous scramble around the Norfolk cow field, but just said that he was waiting for the right time to deal with Calder. Martel had been apoplectic in his impatience and Pohek had rung off. He would finish the job, cash the cheque, and then Luigi would disappear for good.

The cab wound its way through some small streets and then on to a major highway. The traffic was building, and Pohek found it relatively easy to hang back three or four cars. This was something he was good at: following without being seen. Cab and bag could mean only one thing, and his suspicion was justified as he began to notice signs for Heathrow airport. He followed the cab to Terminal Three and parked his own car in the short-term car park. He soon picked out Calder at the United Airlines check-in. From that desk there were flights to a number of destinations in the US: Los Angeles, Dallas, Chicago and Denver. Denver. Flights to Jackson Hole connected at Denver.

Pohek smiled. It looked like he was going to get another crack at the hundred grand. And on his own territory he was much more confident of success.

27

The Teton County Sheriff's Office was at the back of the courthouse in the centre of Jackson. It was a bright morning and the town was bustling under the watchful gaze of the ever-present mountains. Skiers and snowboarders hauled their unwieldy equipment to bus stops. Tourists took pictures of each other in front of the Million Dollar Cowboy Bar or underneath the arches made of elk antlers on the four corners of Town Square. Locals passed each other with a friendly wave or a 'howdy'.

As he waited in the hallway Calder's attention was caught by a sign advertising a Firearms and Home Defense course. Above it was a montage of the mug shots of the sheriff and his loyal deputies. Most of the men had moustaches, but the sheriff had the biggest of the lot, an enormous white walrus that established his dominance over the town. His office had a comfortable, friendly feeling about it: not the kind of place you would expect to see a real criminal.

Calder was met by not a sheriff, nor even a deputy, but a sergeant, and a detective at that. He wore shirt, tie, neat jeans and cowboy boots. Sergeant Dave Twiler was in his early fifties with close-cropped grey hair, a medium-sized moustache and eyes that had spent a lifetime squinting at the sun. He acted as if Jackson was still the sleepy western town it must once have been.

He led Calder to a small office and indicated to a chair by his desk. 'Take a load off,' he drawled. People really did drawl in Jackson.

'Thank you for seeing me,' Calder began.

'You've come a long way. You want to ask about

Perumal . . .' he leaned forward to examine the name on the folder lying on the desk in front of him '. . . Perumal Thiagajaran?'

'That's right. I was a friend of his from work in London. His widow asked me to try to find out some details about what happened.'

'Oh, yes. I spoke to Mrs . . . er . . . his widow on the phone. I'm really not sure there's much I can tell you that I haven't told her. It was a tragedy. Fortunately,' he paused and tapped the wooden surface of his desk, 'it's our first mountain death so far this winter in Teton County. But with all the skiers we get here and the hikers, let alone the snowmobilers, there will be more. We dug someone out of an avalanche only last week. It was a miracle we got to him in time.'

'So what happened to Perumal?'

'He was riding a snowmobile up on Twogatee Pass. There's a whole mess of trails up there, hundreds of miles of them, but he decided to go off into the snow by himself. For a guy who's only been out on a sled once before, that's just plain dumb. It always makes sense to have a buddy with you. We'd had a lot of snow, the avalanche risk was extreme and he got caught in one. Or started it most likely. In ninety per cent of cases it's the victim who starts the slide.'

'So who raised the alarm?'

'The snowmobile rental place. Of course, the trouble was it was dark by then. So a lot of people spent a lot of time searching the trails. It was only the following morning when we could get a chopper up that we spotted his sled. We got some rescuers up there as quick as we could, and a dog, but they couldn't find him. We looked for four days.'

'So he's still under the snow somewhere?'

'I guess so. Usually we do find the bodies, but the avalanche slid into a ravine, and the snow's pretty deep there. Sometimes the snowmobile kind of floats on top of the slide and the body is pulled down. Our poles are about nine feet long, but the snow's a lot deeper than that. We'll find him in the spring. When it thaws.'

'His wife will be relieved.'

'Yeah. It's always tough when we can't find the body.' Sergeant Twiler's face betrayed genuine sympathy.

'No one saw the avalanche?'

'No. We did find a pair of snowmobilers who rode right by there that morning. But they didn't see anything.'

'Did they see anyone else?'

'Matter of fact, they did. They saw a couple on a snowmobile riding off the trail about a half-mile from the avalanche site. We've been trying to contact them but without success.'

'A couple? A man and a woman?'

'That's what it looked like. But the snowmobilers didn't get close enough to make an ID.'

'Do you have any doubts this was an accident?'

Twiler hesitated before answering. 'Whenever we can't find the body, we assign a detective to the case, just to ask questions. I took a look at this one myself. We keep it low-key: as you said, there's a lot of distress around these situations. Of course, in this case it was harder because the victim came from overseas. But we got a call from a British police officer a couple of weeks back. You must have been talking to her?'

Calder nodded. 'I have.'

'Well, I'll tell you what I told her. This looks like a classic accident. You have to treat the mountains with respect. And the snow; especially the snow. This guy had no respect. He did something very stupid and paid the price. We see it all the time.' Twiler smiled faintly, a crinkling of the eyes rather than a movement of the lips. 'I don't want to sound too harsh. I feel sorry for the man. At home he was probably a sensible, cautious guy. There's something about these mountains that makes people feel invincible.' He sighed. 'And we have to pick up the pieces. There are always wives, or girlfriends, or parents, or children. All we can do is educate people to be careful.'

'So no suspicious tracks? No signs of a struggle?'

Twiler shook his head. 'Of course, I can't guarantee that he wasn't murdered. Especially since we haven't found the body. But there is no evidence that he was. And when I checked back with the police officer in London, she said she'd talked to his work place and they told her there were no problems.'

'What about the couple on the snowmobile? You said you couldn't contact them.'

'This is a tourist town, people come and go all the time. They were probably back at work in LA or Chicago or wherever by the time we were looking for them.' Twiler looked closely at Calder. 'Do you think the victim was in some kind of trouble back in London?'

'I think he might have been,' said Calder. 'Did you speak to the people he was visiting in Jackson Hole?'

'The Teton Fund? Yes I did. They say his behaviour was natural. Nothing unusual or suspicious.'

'He didn't appear worried or frightened?'

'Not according to the man I spoke to. Vikram Rana. Another Indian guy. About the only one in Jackson. Why all these questions? Have you got something I should know about? Until we find the body, this is still an active case.'

'I saw Perumal just before he came out here,' Calder said. 'He looked nervous. Frightened. But he wouldn't tell me what it was about. Then when I heard he'd had an accident, I was suspicious. That's why I talked to the police in London, and why I'm here.'

'And you have no idea why he was frightened?'

Twiler's interest was genuine, a diligent policeman doing his job. But trying to explain the machinations of Martel, Carr-Jones and Perumal to this man seemed a waste of time, especially since Calder had no firm evidence. 'I'm working on it,' he said.

'Well, let me know if you turn up anything,' said Twiler. 'And when we do recover the body, I'll make sure the coroner takes a close look for you. But that probably won't be for a couple of months yet, maybe longer.'

'Thanks. Oh, can you give me the address of the place Perumal rented the snowmobile from?'

'Sure. The Double D Ranch. Up by Twogatee Pass. It's about forty miles north of here.'

Calder smiled. 'Thanks again for your time. Perumal's widow wanted me to ask you to do all you can to recover the body as soon as possible.'

'You tell her we'll be sure to keep her informed.'

'I suppose you saw Perumal's sister last week?'

Twiler frowned. 'No. Matter of fact no one has come here from the family. It's kind of strange. I guess it's a long way from London.'

'Mrs Thiagajaran was waiting until you recovered the body. But she did mention that his sister would be here.'

'Well, if she was, I sure haven't seen her. You take care, now.'

The Double D Ranch was about a mile off the main road heading east over Twogatee Pass. It overlooked a half-frozen river that wound through a valley of snow and willow bushes flaming crimson and gold. The ranch had the traditional gate, buck-rail fencing and log buildings, but there the similarity to the Ponderosa ended. There were snowmobiles everywhere, bright purple and green, revving up, filling up with fuel, shuttling from spot to spot. The noise shattered the peace of the valley, and petrol fumes stained the cold air.

Outside a hut labelled 'Rentals', a man was working on one of the machines, nodding to some rhythm in his head.

'Hi,' said Calder, aiming for the informal.

The man stopped what he was doing and stood up, arching his back as he did so. He slowly turned. 'Howdy,' he said.

He was tall and skinny, with long lank fair hair receding off a high dome of a forehead. There was a tuft of hair on his chin that looked more like an oversight with the razor than an actual beard. His face was lined and weather-beaten, making his age hard to determine. He could have been anywhere from thirty to fifty.

'Can I hire a snowmobile?' Calder asked.

'Ever done it before?' the man asked.

'No,' Calder said.

'Well, I'm sorry. If you're a beginner, you need a guide, and the tours for the day already left,' the man said, nodding towards the group of snowmobiles which were now roaring off along a trail up towards the Pass.

'Oh,' Calder said, looking disappointed. Then he smiled. 'Perhaps you can take me?'

The man looked at the injured machine at his feet and smiled, showing two lines of America's finest dentistry, looking pristine against the brown wrinkles of his face. 'Sure. It's a great day for it.' He held out his hand. 'Name's Nate.'

'Alex.' Nate's handshake was firm.

'Anyplace in particular you wanna go?'

'Yes, there is, actually. I'm a friend of Perumal Thiagajaran's. The Indian guy who got caught in an avalanche a few weeks ago?'

The smile disappeared.

'Anything wrong?'

'We shouldn't of let him go out like that alone. I'd taken him out the day before and he was just a beginner. Truth is, he didn't even really take to it. Then the next day he managed to persuade one of the other guys that I said he was OK to rent a machine. He told them he was hookin' up with some guys from one of the other outfits. They let him do it. And then the crazy sonofabitch goes off-trail by himself.'

'Do you know where he went?'

'Sure. I'd taken him there the day before. He said then he wanted to go just with me, not on a tour. It's more expensive, but hell, if the customer's payin', who am I to argue? He said he wanted to go someplace isolated. A lot of people want that, you know? Come out here lookin' for isolation in the mountains and find themselves surrounded by a hundred thousand tourists when they arrive.' A note of anger crept into Nate's voice as he said this. 'So I took him out to Gough's Creek. It's real quiet there, and it's not on any tour route.'

'And that's where he returned the next day?'

'That's right. I guess he liked it.'

'Can we go there now?'

Nate frowned, and then shrugged. 'I guess so. Let me get you kitted out.'

Nate got Calder a helmet, gloves, a suit and, of course, a snowmobile. Nate put on his own helmet, a shiny high-tech piece of equipment which came to a point across his chin and made him look like an extra in a *Star Wars* movie. Calder had never ridden a snowmobile, but it didn't take Nate long to explain how. It was like a simplified motorbike on caterpillar tracks and skis. Within a few minutes Nate and Calder were on their way.

They followed a trail for about ten miles through meadows and trees, with the mountains surrounding Twogatee Pass looming above them. For once, the Tetons were out of view. The scenery was breathtaking, but the noise of the snowmobiles, something between a whine and a howl, shattered the peace of the place, removing any sense of isolation. The trail was obviously heavily used, and twice they passed groups of snowmobilers playing in the snow, sweeping up and down slopes, leaping over bumps, or just powering over pristine meadows.

Nate turned off on to one of these, and Calder followed. They were now off the trail, although there were tracks where other snowmobiles had passed that way. After a mile or so they entered some trees, twisted down a hill and found themselves in a small secluded valley. They continued for about a quarter of a mile, the ground rising, as the streambed at the bottom of the valley became a kind of ravine. Eventually, Nate stopped.

It was a relief to turn off the engines and listen to the silence. Or almost silence. The wind whispered in the trees, a bird chattered a few yards away, and somewhere down below a stream trickled on its thousand-mile journey to the sea.

Nate took off his alien-warrior helmet and pointed down towards the ravine. 'This is the place.'

A clearly defined line ran along the ridge close to where they were standing. Beneath it the surface of the slope was disturbed, throwing up what looked like giant snowballs. Down at the bottom of the ravine the snow was piled high.

A beautiful place. A lonely place. But the wrong place to die.

Calder walked towards the edge, gingerly. 'Was he riding down there?' he asked, trying to work out how Perumal could have manoeuvred his snowmobile down into the ravine. It looked possible, but difficult for a beginner.

'No, he was up here, right where we're standin'. Most slides are a result of the weight the victim puts on the snow himself, not on snow fallin' down on top of him from above. This here is prime slidin' area. 'Bout a forty-five degree angle, little less maybe. And look at the snow.' He led Calder a few yards back down the valley, where they could see the fault line close up. 'See, the snow's in layers. That there is sugar snow.' He showed Calder a layer of fine smooth crystals. 'Above that is harder crust. And then, after a snowfall, you can get a foot or so of powder. Now, you drive a snowmobile on there and the weight creates a fault line. This crust gets detached and just slides off the sugar snow. Slides real fast. These granules act kinda like tiny ball-bearings. You don't got much time to get off of that.'

Calder looked down to the snow in the ravine. 'So he's under there somewhere?'

'Yup. They found the snowmobile but no sign of the body. The snow there's pretty deep. Twenty feet, maybe. Poles only go down nine feet or so. I came up here to help them look the second day. Didn't find nothin'. They gave up after the fourth day.'

'When will this thaw?'

'Could be quite a while,' Nate said. He looked up at the sky and then at the ravine, which was in shadow. 'Don't get much sun down here. June, maybe.'

Calder winced. 'So you were part of the rescue party?'

'Not right away. I'd bin over to Utah, seein' some friends. When I came back there was all kinds of trouble. We really shouldn't of let him out by hisself.'

Calder surveyed the scene and then climbed down the slope. Snow had fallen since the avalanche and it was difficult to see more than the general shape of what had happened. With so many people combing the area for days, Calder knew it was highly unlikely he would find anything. He did see some animal tracks along the bottom. 'What are those?'

Nate glanced at them. 'Coyote.'

Calder shivered. But if the rescuers' sniffer dogs had been unable to find Perumal, it was unlikely a coyote would.

He looked back up to the ridge. 'This may sound an odd question,' he said, 'but is there any way that this avalanche could have been started on purpose? By someone else. While Perumal was travelling below the ridge.'

Nate looked at Calder doubtfully. 'It is possible to start an avalanche with a snowmobile if you know what you're doin'. You kinda kick the sled over on to one ski, and that acts like a knife. It cuts into the snow, creates a fault line, and if the conditions is right, you can get a slide. But the other guy would have to be ridin' above the victim. And your friend was ridin' by hisself.'

'We don't know that for sure.'

Nate shrugged. 'There was only one set of sled marks. If there was two of 'em and one above the other, then you'd see two sets of tracks goin' into the avalanche.'

'Perhaps Perumal was murdered and then thrown into the avalanche afterwards,' Calder said.

Nate shook his head. 'Doesn't look like that to me. Looks

like he went too close to the edge, started a slide, and went with it. Simple as that.'

'But isn't it odd that he was out here anyway?'

'I guess he must have liked his trip with me and wanted to come by again.'

'Did he seem that enthusiastic?'

'Not really. He wasn't what you'd call a natural. He could barely handle the snowmobile. He did say he liked the scenery, but they all say that.'

'Was he tense?'

'Yeah. Kinda.'

'And you came past here the day before?'

'Yeah,' Nate said. 'We came through here. Like I said, he wanted to go someplace quiet.'

Calder shook his head. 'It doesn't make sense. Does it?'

Nate held Calder's gaze. 'You know,' he said. 'I've been thinkin' about that myself. What if he did this on purpose?'

'You mean killed himself?'

'It's possible. He was askin' 'bout avalanches and I told him the kind of places to stay clear of. There had been a big snow the day before we went out, and the avalanche risk was extreme. Maybe he went out lookin' for trouble and found it.'

'Maybe he did.' Calder looked at Nate admiringly. He might talk real slow, but he wasn't dumb. That was the only explanation he had heard so far that made any kind of sense.

Jen and Perumal. Two suicides?

Too convenient.

'You know what you are, Vikram? An asshole. A one hundred per cent dumbfuck. Did you know that?'

Vikram didn't respond. His face was stony and his lips tight.

'What kind of stupid deal is it that we end up having to find eight hundred million bucks just because the market's gone down a little?'

The truth was, the Japanese stock market had gone down a

lot. It had crashed through the seven thousand knock-in barrier on the JUSTICE notes and was now trading at six thousand five hundred. At that level it would be impossible to hide the fact that the JUSTICE notes were underwater at the next revaluation, now only a week away. Vikram had just pointed this out to Martel, whose response was to pulverize the messenger.

'If you want to make money on the upside, you've got to accept losing money on the downside,' Vikram replied calmly. 'You know that, Jean-Luc. If the market goes above ten thousand, we make out big time. Now, you can't get that kind of return profile without accepting the risk that you might lose if you're wrong. That would be a free lunch, and we all know those don't exist.'

'That's why I employ you. You're supposed to come up with profiles where we make money, not lose it. You never told me we could be in this kind of situation.'

'We discussed exactly this,' Vikram replied, his voice icy. 'I pointed out we'd be in trouble if the Nikkei ever got down below seven thousand. You said it wasn't going to happen, so it wasn't worth wasting time thinking about. Well, it's happened.'

'So, you're blaming me now, are you?' Martel's eyes were bulging. 'I want you to get on a plane to London today and sort this out with Bloomfield Weiss.'

'And how am I to do that exactly? Don't forget Perumal is no longer there. And even if he were, it would be impossible for him to fake a reval with the market so low.'

'Then do some more. Double up. Roll it over. Come on, use your ingenuity. If you offer these guys a big enough fee, they'll do anything.'

'But Jean-Luc . . .'

'Go. I want you on a plane this afternoon. Take the jet if you need it.'

Vikram left the room.

Martel swore to himself and glanced at his screen. The Nikkei had closed one and a half per cent down that day.

Because of the time zones, the Japanese market was shut for most of the working day in Jackson Hole. He still checked the closing number several times a day, even though it never budged.

He called Phil Spears, the senior Harrison Brothers equity salesman he spoke to in Tokyo, on his home number. It was four o'clock in the morning there, but Martel didn't care.

'Yeah?' Spears sounded groggy.

'What's taking this market down?'

'Er . . . ?'

'Come on, Phil. Are you seeing much volume over there? Who's selling? And why are they doing it?'

'Is this Jean-Luc?'

'Of course it's Jean-Luc. Give me some colour, will you?'

'Well.' There was a pause. 'Er, there's some selling from overseas and the domestic accounts are net sellers as well. Not many buyers out there. I think a lot of the selling is momentum driven. On the downside. If you know what I mean.'

Martel listened to the information carefully, without really taking it in. 'Do you see the market bouncing over the next few days?'

'Er, yeah. It could. Or it could go down.'

'But a rally's a real possibility?'

'Possible, I guess. But I wouldn't count on it. This market's hard to read.'

Martel snorted. All these salesmen were useless. He didn't know why he listened to any of them. 'Call me when you get in to your office,' he said.

He stood up and began pacing. One week. That's all he had until Bloomfield Weiss revalued the JUSTICE notes and demanded cash. Cash he didn't have. He winced as the pain bit into his stomach. He really should see a doctor about it. There was something physical going on, it wasn't just nerves. Things were looking tough, but there was still some hope. The market might bounce. It would have to bounce a long way, but it was possible. He was still convinced that at some time in the future the market would climb above ten thousand. The difficulty was to make sure that the Teton Fund was still around when it did. Perhaps Vikram would put together some new scheme with Bloomfield Weiss that would buy them some time. That was what derivatives were supposed to do, after all, shift risk around. Well, he wanted one that would shift the risk from this month to next month. Was that too much to ask?

There was still a chance he could get more cash into the fund. The Artsdalen Foundation had promised him three hundred million bucks. If the market rallied a bit that could make all the difference. Where was that money? They were probably still pissing about with due diligence or documentation or something. He dialled a number in Switzerland.

'Langhauser.' It was eight o'clock in Zurich. The man was working late like a good investment banker should.

'Freddie, Jean-Luc Martel.' Martel managed to suppress the anger in his voice. He was enough of a salesman not to antagonize a new client.

'Ah, Monsieur Martel, how are things with you?' Langhauser said, switching to French.

But Martel stuck to English. He hated the way the Swiss-Germans massacred the French language anyway. 'Very good, Freddie. In fact, that's why I was calling you. How are the Artsdalen Foundation coming along?'

'Pretty well. I know they're taking their time, but they are careful people, and three hundred million dollars is a serious commitment for them.'

'And for us as well.'

Langhauser laughed pointlessly. Martel winced. God, this man was irritating. 'There are just one or two tax details they need to look into and then they'll be ready to sign,' the Swiss banker said.

'I understand,' said Martel. It was all very well locating hedge funds offshore, and in fact the Teton Fund was technically domiciled in Bermuda, but it did lead to all kinds of tax-related complications any time anyone wanted to invest some money. 'Just a tip-off. We're expecting some big gains next month, and if the Artsdalen Foundation can invest by month end they might get a piece of that. There's nothing like being twenty per cent up on a new investment one month in, is there?'

'It's going to be tough to make that deadline, but I'll see what I can do,' said Langhauser with enthusiasm. If Martel was telling the truth and the Teton Fund did do twenty per cent in the first month, he, as their adviser, would look a genius to the Artsdalen Foundation.

Martel put the phone down. There was still hope.

If Alex Calder didn't blow the whole thing open, anyway. Martel knew he was now in Jackson Hole and he was expecting to hear from him soon. When would this man Luigi do his stuff? Who the hell was he, anyway? Probably just a time-waster. He wished that he could somehow get Bodinchuk involved. Then he would be able to rest easy: Alex Calder was just the kind of problem Bodinchuk could deal with.

He checked his watch. Time to see Pohek and find out what Cheryl had been up to. His stomach flipped again.

They met in the usual place, the isolated turn-off in the Antelope Flats. A low grey cloud had settled over the plain, shrouding the upper reaches of the Tetons. This time they were not quite alone, a solitary moose stood munching something a quarter of a mile away. It paid no attention to them.

Pohek had good news: he had found no sign that Cheryl was seeing anyone. Martel was relieved. He told him to remove the bugs from the ranch in Jackson Hole and the apartment in New York. He hated the idea of Pohek listening to his private conversations anyway, especially his arguments with Cheryl. He also told him to stop following her to New York: she was going there again the following morning for a couple of days. But he should keep an occasional watch on her in Jackson Hole, just in case.

As Martel drove back to his office he was in a slightly lighter mood. Perhaps the man in Cheryl's apartment was a one-off. That he could live with. All marriages had their indiscretions and this was one he would be happy to forgive and forget. Who knows? Perhaps he had imagined the whole thing all along.

28

It was nine o'clock in the evening and Sandy's eyes were beginning to hurt. There was something about internet searches as opposed to other forms of computer activity that always gave her a headache. She was wrestling with a report in Spanish about the conviction of three of the leading members of the Zeller-Montanez family. At least they weren't called García or Martinez: then the search really would have been a nightmare.

Sandy's deal was dragging on, much to her frustration. It was supposed to be an agreed takeover by a giant American pharmaceutical company of a small British biotechnology outfit, but there were major disagreements over the details and neither side would back down. Sandy's vacation was suffering.

But she had refused, with some success, to get roped in to other transactions, which meant that she had the occasional chunk of free time as draft agreements were being considered in Hampshire and New Jersey before zipping their way back to her for further processing. She was using this time to help Calder. The internet link in her office was very fast and no one raised an eyebrow that she should be plugged into a computer for hours on end.

She paused, rubbed her eyes and wandered over to the water cooler. That was enough on the Mexicans. Although not impossible, they looked unlikely conspirators with Martel. The Mexican authorities, acting with the US Drug Enforcement Agency, had rounded up fifteen members of the Zeller-Montanez family and their henchmen eighteen months before. Most of them had been convicted. It was clear that there were still many millions of dollars belonging to the family slopping around the offshore banking centres of the world, but there was nothing to suggest that they were still a force in the world of organized crime, or that they had any particular link with Jean-Luc Martel apart from a three-million-dollar investment in the Teton Fund, arranged by Chalmet on a discretionary basis.

Refreshed, she sat down at her computer again, and started on Bodinchuk. This turned out to be much more productive. Bodinchuk had many interests in the Ukraine, and some outside. He was linked to a spate of assassinations in Moscow and Kiev in the late nineteen nineties, when bankers were being shot at the rate of one a week. It was at this time that Bodinchuk, still in his twenties, had risen to prominence. His own father, a former senior officer in the KGB with substantial interests in the Ukraine, had been murdered, probably by a business rival. In the vicious battles that had been fought over the carcass of the Soviet Union, Bodinchuk had emerged a winner.

Sandy stared at a large picture of him in *Euromoney*. Blond with blue eyes, thick yellow hair, broad smile and a puppy-face he looked more like a friendly Labrador than an international businessman. But as she looked more closely at her screen, blowing up the picture and enhancing the resolution, those eyes gave her the creeps. Deeply set amid puffs of skin above and below, the smile lines that you would expect to see on either side were absent. She shuddered.

There was a limit to how much she could get from the internet or the press reports that were referred to there. How to find out more? Did she know anyone who knew Russia? It was an area of the world with which Trelawney Stewart had very little to do. There was a two-man office in Moscow, but Sandy knew neither of the two men. And Sandy knew very few men outside Trelawney Stewart.

Then she remembered a Russian investment banker she had met when she had first moved over to London. They had been introduced at a party given by one of her Trelawney Stewart colleagues and he had asked her out to dinner. They had gone to a trendy restaurant in Mayfair and had had a good evening. He had called a week or so later for a follow-up. After a month and three cancellations later, he stopped calling. What was his name? Oleg something.

Sandy checked her Palm. There he was! Oleg Kalachev. Harrison Brothers. She was just about to dial his home number when she checked the time. A quarter past midnight. Another late night, but for once she felt she was doing something useful. She'd call him the following morning.

They met in a small French restaurant in a narrow street in Soho. A less flashy location than their previous encounter and more intimate. She soon remembered why she had made the effort to see Oleg Kalachev two years before. He was in his early thirties, well-dressed, tall, fair-haired, good-looking without being vain, and had impeccable manners. His accent was American, with only a trace of Russian, but he affected a diffidence and relaxed charm that were more British. A wealthy young banker at ease with himself.

'I've been dying to ask this ever since you called me,' he said. 'Why did I hear from you all of a sudden? I must confess I'd given up on you ages ago.'

'I'm really sorry about that,' Sandy said. 'It was nothing personal. You should know that I've managed to stand up every man I've tried to go out with since I've been in London. After a while I called it quits.'

'Ah. So I'm very privileged to see you here now?'

Sandy smiled. 'For once, no. I'm going back to the States in a week or so, which means that for the first time in two years I actually have some free time. So I thought I'd call some of my friends here to see them before I left.'

'What a good idea,' said Oleg.

Sandy smiled shyly. 'And you're still at Harrison Brothers two years on?'

'Yes. Miraculously I've survived all the downsizing and

reorganizing. In my world there is no substitute for local knowledge and contacts. And I understand the American investment bankers quite well. I know how to do things their way.' Oleg's long fingers were fiddling with a tiny salt cellar as he said this, sending it on a little dance around his wine glass.

'Do you cover the Ukraine as well as Russia?'

'Oh, yes. The Ukraine is a bit of a basket case, but there are still some privatizations to go for.'

'So you know the people there?'

'Some.'

'What about Mykhailo Bodinchuk?'

The salt-cellar stopped dead. 'Not well.'

Sandy smiled. 'That bad, is he?'

'Let's just say that he's not someone a nice girl like you would want to get to know.'

'Is he part of the Russian mafia?'

'He's his own mafia. He's got to be one of the richest men in the Ukraine by now. But he arrived there the tough way. Starting with his father, who was a mean sonofabitch himself.'

'I read that he was murdered.'

'That's right. By his own son.'

'By Mykhailo Bodinchuk? How do you know?'

'Everyone knows. You don't find out what's going on in Russia, or the Ukraine, by reading the press. Everybody knows Bodinchuk got his father killed. And that anyone who ever competed against him in any business deal wound up dead too.'

'I read about the spate of bankers murdered in Moscow a few years ago. Was Bodinchuk involved?'

'He was. He won that war. And a similar war in Kiev in two thousand and two. You don't mess with Bodinchuk. No one wants to be his enemy. In fact, no one wants to be his friend, either. That's almost as dangerous. He's not a client, is he?'

'No,' said Sandy, shaking her head vigorously. 'Nor is he ever likely to be.'

'That's good to hear,' said Oleg, cutting into his fish.

'Do you know if he has anything to do with Jean-Luc Martel? The hedge-fund manager.'

'I know Martel. Or know of him,' Oleg said. 'And to answer your question, there is some connection. The rumour is that Bodinchuk is a major investor in the Teton Fund, a fifty- to a hundred-million slug. Also, I've seen them together, and they looked like good buddies.'

'Where was this?'

'Saint Moritz. Last year. A lot of the big guys from the former Soviet Union like to ski there, so I end up going to the place at least twice a season.'

'It must be tough.'

'Oh, it is. It is.'

'When *exactly* was it you saw them?'

'About a year ago. Let me think. Early March, I'd guess?'

'Just before Italy quit the euro?'

'About then.' Oleg sipped his wine. 'Why, may I ask?'

'I'm sorry,' Sandy said. 'It's hard for me to say.'

'You mean it's for a client?'

'Oh, no. It's for me. Or a friend of mine.' Sandy thought of Jen, and the warm glow brought on by the wine, the atmosphere and Oleg's company left her. 'Yeah, a friend.'

Oleg reached across the table to touch her hand. 'Well, if it's personal, this is a personal message from me to you. Stay well clear of Mykhailo Bodinchuk. You understand?'

Sandy smiled quickly, pleased but a little confused by his concern. 'I understand.'

Later, as they left the restaurant and were making their way up a narrow lane towards a larger road and taxis, Oleg spoke. 'I'm glad you called me up. Even if it was only to pump me about Bodinchuk.'

'So am I,' said Sandy. 'And it wasn't just that. I did enjoy myself tonight.'

'Look,' Oleg paused on the kerb. 'I wouldn't normally ask

this so early, but since it looks as if this might be my last chance before you leave for the States, would you like to come back to my place tonight?'

Sandy smiled. 'No. I'm sorry Oleg. Not tonight.'

'All right. But if you ever need to ask anyone about some other Russian thugs, you know who to call. Seriously. It would be nice to see you again.'

A taxi pulled up beside them, and Sandy kissed him on the cheek and jumped in. As the cab navigated through the late-evening Soho crowds she smiled to herself. Maybe she should have gone back to his place. She did like him. And it had been a long long time since she had spent the night with a man.

Vikram looked down upon the city of Boston and beyond that the bent arm that was Cape Cod. Only an hour until they landed at JFK. As he had expected, his day in London had been a waste of time. Justin Carr-Jones had been nervous but firm. Bloomfield Weiss were up to their limit for the amount of business they could do with the Teton Fund. He had politely dismissed the transaction that Vikram proposed, which would have provided Bloomfield Weiss with a fee of thirty million dollars. When it was clear that Carr-Jones would not be tempted, Vikram beat a retreat. He was in no doubt that there would be a disastrous revaluation of the JUSTICE notes at month end, less than a week away now. He didn't want to bring that problem forward.

If only Martel had sold out a chunk of his position the week before, as Vikram had suggested. At the time, Vikram had smarted under Martel's ridicule: he had been made to feel like a wimp. But now it looked as if he was right after all.

But was he? There had been several moments in Vikram's career at the Teton Fund when he had been convinced that he was right and Martel was wrong. Sometimes it had been a question of pure mathematical brainpower. Although Martel was good at the math, he wasn't as good as Vikram. Very few people were. At high school in California, college and graduate school, Vikram had always been the first to find the solution to a complicated problem. Which was what had attracted him to finance. In the world of derivatives, the guy who found the solution made the money.

He had honed his skills at an investment bank on Wall Street, but had leapt at the opportunity to join Martel. Vikram truly believed that he was smarter than everyone else. In a hedge fund, he could prove it. And that meant he would make millions.

That, at least, had been his plan. But working for Martel, he had learned something he hadn't expected. You needed more than simply being smarter than everyone else to succeed. Martel's success wasn't a function of the size of his brain. It wasn't even a result of a rational weighing of risks and rewards, which at least was something Vikram could aspire to. Martel had something else, a talent that was missing in Vikram's make-up, but that he desperately wanted. Martel seemed to know when to take the big bets and when to stick with them. There had been so many times when Vikram would have flinched: the failure of the technology bubble to burst in late 1999, the resilience of the Italian bond market the year before, and now the continued weakness of the Japanese stock market.

Vikram could see only disaster looming. But perhaps Martel could see something else. Perhaps Martel would come through, yet again.

The idea that Martel would once more make Vikram look a fool both angered and thrilled him. One day Vikram would learn. One day he would have his own fund and put Martel in the shade.

The plane was approaching New York. Vikram had a meeting with some derivatives guys at US Commerce on Wall Street, for which he held out little hope, and then he was supposed to hop on to Martel's jet and fly straight on to Jackson Hole. But what if he stayed, just for a few more hours? He had promised himself he wouldn't, but what the hell? In dangerous times, live dangerously.

Cheryl was getting ready to leave the apartment. She was planning to check out a new ceramics gallery which had opened in the Village. It was wonderful to get out of Jackson Hole and to experience the freedom of New York again. With stress taking an increasing toll on Jean-Luc and the deterioration of their relationship, the snowbound ranch was feeling more and more like a prison. Her trips were becoming more regular.

She felt bad about Jean-Luc. His vulnerability, his many weaknesses, had been what had first attracted her to him. Where others either admired a wealthy playboy or sneered at an arrogant speculator, she had seen a small insecure boy in a six-foot-seven-inch body. His obvious need for her, the fact that she alone seemed to understand his insecurities, had pulled her to him, despite herself. When this giant of a man lay in her arms, totally surrendering himself to her, she couldn't fail to respond. And although she affected to despise all the trappings of excessive wealth, she had to admit that she had been curious to see how the other half a per cent lived.

But there had been a cost to marrying Martel, as she had always known there would be. Some might view the life of an accountant as dull, but she was stimulated by it. She liked turning numerical chaos into order and truth. The wife of Jean-Luc Martel could never again become a simple accountant. Even at the wildlife museum there were countless billionaires who were reluctant to leave the finances in her hands without adding their million dollars' worth of advice.

And now there was no sex. And without sex, no children. Cheryl was a healthy young woman with strong natural appetites, still decades away from the society wives with facelifts, boob jobs and HRT she saw around her. She was in the wrong place with the wrong man. But she had chosen that path, she had taken the vows, and now she should keep to them.

The buzzer rang. She opened the door.

'Vikram!'

'Hi, Cheryl.'

He was carrying a small bunch of orchids. He was smiling, but nervously. Not knowing how she would react. And she didn't know how to react.

'But I thought we agreed . . .'

'I couldn't help it,' he said, stepping into the room.

'But Jean-Luc will find out. He probably has a private detective tailing you right now.'

'I don't care.'

'Yes, but I do. I don't want to get caught. I don't want him to find out. I really think –'

She couldn't finish the sentence. Vikram dropped the flowers and slid his arms around her waist and pulled her towards him. He kissed her deeply, passionately. She tried to resist, she placed a hand against his broad chest and began to push him away, but something in her began to respond.

Half an hour later she was lying on her bed, naked, Vikram's pale brown body next to her. And what a body. Strong muscles, perfectly honed, full of vigour. She stroked his short black hair. He murmured something; she couldn't quite hear what.

Perhaps she had just made a dreadful mistake. There was a good chance that Jean-Luc would find out, and then she would be in all kinds of trouble. But it wasn't just that. He would be hurt, dreadfully hurt. And while she didn't love him – she wasn't sure if she ever really had – she was fond of him, and she didn't want to cause him pain.

What she had just done was wrong. She had never been unfaithful to Jean-Luc before Vikram. Vikram and she had cut off their brief affair the moment Vikram had spotted the private investigator's website on her husband's computer. Jean-Luc must have suspected something when he had heard Vikram coughing in her bedroom, this bedroom. She had intended never to be unfaithful to him again, she truly had. And now here she was.

She, Cheryl Dillon of Kington, Wisconsin, was a bad, bad girl.

She smiled. And it felt wonderful. She rolled over and planted small kisses on Vikram's chest, and then on his flat, hard stomach. She worked her way down. He chuckled. So did she.

Boy, did it feel wonderful.

29

Calder woke very early. There was a seven-hour time difference between Wyoming and London and it would take him several days to adjust. It was still dark in Jackson Hole when he called Sandy in London from his hotel room.

She sounded pleased to hear from him.

'Any luck?' he asked.

'I'd say so.' Sandy told him all about her researches on the Mexicans and Mykhailo Bodinchuk. There was a note of pride in her voice. Calder couldn't blame her; she had done well.

'Excellent,' he said, when he had heard her out. 'With a stake that big in the Teton Fund, Bodinchuk might well have decided to help Martel. A man like that would have no qualms about killing Jen.'

'Yes, but did he?'

'You're right. That's just a guess. I need to find out more.'

'What about Perumal? Any sign he was murdered?'

'None yet. But the idea that he would take it into his head to ride off into the wilderness is difficult to believe. The guide who took him out the day before suggested he might have intended to kill himself. There could be something in that, I suppose.'

'Another suicide?'

'I don't know. I'm planning to check out where he was staying, and then go and see Martel himself.'

'Is that a good idea? That guy sounds scary.'

'I need to get him talking. Find out about Perumal's visit. Maybe provoke him into saying something he doesn't mean to.'

'Well, be careful.'

'I will.' Usually Calder was irritated by people telling him to be careful. But this time he was pleased to detect the note of concern in Sandy's voice.

'I wonder how the awful Justin Carr-Jones fits into all of this,' she said.

'The more I think about it, the more I think he was telling me the truth. He's a nasty piece of work, but he didn't kill anyone. He was more scared than I was. The answer's over here, in Jackson. How's your deal going?'

'Nearly there. I have what I hope is the final draft in front of me as we speak. I might even be out of here tomorrow.'

'Will you go straight to New York?'

'I should be able to take a few days' vacation. I might even get to go skiing after all. But is there anything else I can do to help you?'

'I don't think so now. Thanks for all you've done. You've been a great help.'

'No problem. Let me know what happens. And if I can help, just call.'

Calder felt a tinge of disappointment as he put down the phone. It had been nice to know that Sandy was working with him, even if she was several thousand miles away. She would disappear to New York soon, never to be seen again.

A shame, that.

He checked in with Jerry at the airfield. Everything was under control. Mrs Easterham had called to say that Brynteg Global Investments had pulled their offer; Jerry said she was clearly disappointed about the money, but she sounded relieved not to be losing the airfield. Britain had been besieged by a series of cold fronts so there had been very little flying. That was bad for business, but at least it meant that Jerry could cope without Calder for a few more days. As Calder put the phone down, he hoped that his absence would only be for a few more days and not permanent.

He brought his mind back to the matter in hand. Next call was to Nils. Calder explained what Sandy had discovered about

Bodinchuk, and asked Nils to see if he could find any signs of a link between the Ukrainian and the Derivatives Group. Nils sounded pretty doubtful – the Derivatives Group had clammed up as far as he was concerned – but he promised he would try.

Finally, Calder called Radha Thiagajaran. He needed to find out where Perumal had stayed while he was in Jackson.

'Oh, hello, Mr Calder, how are you?' Radha said politely when she answered the phone.

'I'm in Jackson Hole, seeing what I can find out about Perumal.'

'Goodness. And have you discovered anything?'

'Nothing yet. I'm afraid they still haven't found the body.'

'Oh dear, I feared as much.'

'I'm not entirely happy about the explanation of Perumal's death. I'd like to ask a few more questions. Do you have the name of the hotel Perumal was staying in?'

'Oh, don't worry about that, Mr Calder. Don't ask any more questions on my account. I have resigned myself to waiting until the snow thaws. They will find Perumal's body in a month or two, isn't it?'

'But since I'm here, I may as well do what I can.'

'It's really not necessary.'

'Do you know the name of the hotel?' Calder persisted.

There was silence at the other end of the phone. Calder didn't know whether Radha was looking for the name or just thinking. Finally, she answered. 'The Wort Hotel. I don't have the address.'

'I'll find it. Did Perumal's sister visit you?'

'Yes she did. But she's returned to Canada now.'

'Did she say whether she had discovered anything?'

'She did ask around. But no, nothing. I think there is nothing to find out, Mr Calder. We are better to let sleeping dogs lie.'

'Have you got her address as well? I might want to exchange notes.'

'OK,' Radha sighed and read out an address and phone

number in British Columbia. 'But I really don't think she can tell you anything.'

As Calder hung up he pondered Radha's change of attitude. It was as if she didn't want to know anything more about Perumal's death. Grief was a strange thing. Perhaps she had found comfort in reconciling herself to an accident, and she didn't want to disturb that presumption. Calder felt a pang of guilt: what right had he to intrude upon a widow's grief, especially when he had no proof that her presumption was false?

The Wort Hotel was only four blocks away. Calder decided to take an indirect route along a quiet side street. He paused to tie his shoelace, glancing behind him as he did so. Fifty yards back, a man in a blue jacket turned on to a cross street. He was too far away for Calder to make out his features clearly. Calder paused twice more, but didn't see the man again.

The Wort was the oldest hotel in town and one of the smartest, more substantial than the place Calder had picked at random for his own lodgings. Unlike most of the other buildings in town, it was made of brick, but inside it was warm and comfortable and all wood – wood-panelled walls, a grand wooden staircase and a wood fire burning in the grate. It was still early and guests were checking out.

Calder waited for a lull before approaching the woman at the front desk. 'Can I help you?' she asked.

'Yes. Can I speak to the manager?'

'One moment please.' Calder waited while the woman shuffled papers into files. She was probably in her twenties, tall, gaunt with short purple-dyed hair, and small oval glasses. Calder thought he detected a Germanic accent. He saw her name tag read 'Ilse'.

He waited. She filed. He coughed. She ignored him. Eventually he repeated himself. 'The manager?'

Without acknowledging him, she picked up the phone and spoke a quick couple of words. In an instant a tall, clean-cut man with an open, friendly face appeared from an office behind the reception. There seemed to be a lot of open, friendly faces in Jackson.

When he began to enquire about Perumal, the man, who said his name was Bill, ushered Calder back into his office, which was cramped with a surfeit of computer equipment. He left the door open.

'It's one of the least pleasant parts of this job, dealing with guests who have passed away. We had two last year, one in a car accident and one from a heart attack. Mr Thiagajaran is the only one so far this year, but we're only in February.'

'I was a colleague of Perumal's,' Calder said. 'His widow has asked me to try to find out a bit more about what happened to him.' A lie. Oh, well.

Bill shook his head. 'I spoke to her a couple of times right after the accident. Poor woman.'

'And you probably saw Perumal's sister?'

'No.' Bill thought about it for a moment. 'No, I don't believe I did.'

'Never mind,' said Calder. 'Unfortunately, Perumal was in some trouble at home. Related to work. Did he act strangely while he was here?'

'No. Not that I can remember. He wore a suit, so you could tell he was here on business. He kind of stuck out. We do get the odd banker swings by, but they usually try to blend in a bit. You get more stares wearing a coat and tie than a cowboy hat in this town.'

'I can see that. I understand Perumal extended his stay by a couple of days. Do you have any record of when he decided to do that?'

Bill frowned. 'I don't think there was any extension. But let me look.' He swung on his seat and turned to his computer with obvious enthusiasm. 'Everything's on here. It's a little tricky to tell when exactly a reservation was made, but I might be able to figure something out.' He tapped and squinted for a couple of minutes. 'You're right. He did ask to extend his reservation. When he checked in.'

'*When he checked in?* Are you sure?'

'Yes. Here, let me show you.' Bill pointed to his screen.

'No, that's OK.' But this information didn't tally with the idea that Perumal had suddenly changed his mind during his trip, as he had suggested to Bloomfield Weiss. And to his wife. When Perumal had arrived in Jackson Hole, he had known he would take those extra days to go snowmobiling. Odd.

'You didn't happen to see anyone following Perumal? Perhaps asking questions about him?'

'No, sorry. The cops have already asked me.'

'Did you have any Ukrainian nationals staying here?'

'Ukrainian? Is that a country?'

'It is now.'

'Let me check.' With alacrity Bill interrogated his computer. 'No, nothing. We had three from the UK, but that's no good to you. Turkey? France? Argentina? Nothing from the Ukraine.'

Calder let him stare at his computer screen a little more for inspiration, but when it was clear none was coming, he got up to leave. Bill ushered him past the reception desk and its guardian.

'I think I know who you mean.'

Both men turned towards the purple-haired receptionist. 'Yes?' said Calder.

Ilse flashed a smile so quick Calder wasn't sure he had seen it. 'The Turk. Or he said he was Turkish. I don't believe he was.' She spoke fast in good English.

'How do you know?'

'You work in hotels in Germany, you meet a lot of Turks. Half the workers there are Turkish. And I don't think he was one. I think he might have been Russian. Or possibly Ukrainian.'

Bill and Calder exchanged glances. 'And how do you know that?' Calder asked.

'I heard him talking on his mobile phone once. It was in the parking lot – I was just leaving work. He was speaking some kind of Slav language. I thought it was Russian, I studied a little at school and I recognized some words. But it could have been Polish, or Bulgarian. Or Ukrainian. I thought it was very strange for a Turk to be speaking Russian.'

'Do you know what he said?'

'No. As I said, I only understood one or two words and I can't remember what they were.'

'Do you remember what this man did while he was here? Did he act strangely? Did you see him follow Perumal?'

'If he did, I didn't notice him. But he did hang around in the lobby a lot, trying to look inconspicuous. I only noticed him because I'd heard him speak Russian or whatever it was and I was curious. That's what people do when they're following someone, don't they, hang around?'

'I suppose so,' said Calder. 'What did he look like? Do you remember that?'

'Certainly. About fifty, maybe older. Well-dressed. White, or Caucasian, don't they call it? Black hair brushed back. And a thin moustache.' Calder felt a surge of excitement. The description was too much like that of the man Jen had bumped into in Chelsea to be a coincidence.

'You don't remember his name, do you?'

'No, but we can look it up.' Ilse beat Bill to the computer in his office, and within seconds had brought up the relevant booking.

'She's smart, that girl,' Bill murmured into Calder's ear. 'Scary but smart. We keep her away from the guests if we can, but we were short staffed today.'

'Here we are,' Ilse said. 'Esat Olgaç. Or at least that's what he said his name was. Arrived January twenty-sixth. Checked out Friday the twenty-eighth.'

'The twenty-eighth?' On the twenty-eighth Perumal was out on a snowmobile with Nate. It was the next day, the twenty-ninth, that he was killed. What had Mr Olgaç been doing checking out then? 'Do you know where he went?'

'The airport,' Ilse said.

'That's not on the computer,' Bill protested.

'I remember,' Ilse said, giving him a withering look. 'He got the airport shuttle for the last flight to Salt Lake. He was concerned whether he would make it. Also I remember he was carrying an Indian doll.'

'Native American,' Bill corrected her.

Ilse ignored her boss. 'A squaw. I asked him about it. He said it was for his granddaughter.'

Calder left the Wort Hotel in good spirits. It seemed highly likely that Bodinchuk had had a man in Jackson Hole following Perumal. But it looked as if the man had left Jackson Hole the day before Perumal disappeared, which didn't quite make sense. Perhaps they changed their plans. Or perhaps it was some kind of ruse. When the Sheriff's Office eventually recovered Perumal's body Calder was willing to bet that they would find evidence that he had been murdered.

It also seemed likely this Olgaç had murdered Jen. Bumped into her on the street, followed her up to her apartment on some pretext or other, hit her over the head, sent a text message to her mother from her mobile phone, pushed her unconscious body out of the window and run off. And he'd done it at the behest of Mykhailo Bodinchuk.

But it wasn't the Ukrainian who had tried to kill Calder in Norfolk. Calder hadn't seen enough of the man to recognize him again. But he had definitely been younger than fifty: he was still able to run pretty fast. And Calder had caught a glimpse of his face: no moustache, bad skin. Old acne scars or some kind of skin disease. Definitely not the Ukrainian, but possibly the same man who had followed him that morning. He would have to keep his eyes open.

*

Ray Pohek watched Calder step out of the Wort Hotel from quite a distance. He was concerned that Calder might have spotted him earlier. Pohek was experienced, but it was tricky keeping someone under surveillance in a small town when there was only one of you and the target was suspicious. The cold helped. Pohek had three jackets and a couple of hats which he could switch, and a selection of scarves that were useful for keeping the lower part of his face hidden. This watching was all very well, but he needed to act. It was difficult to do anything in town, but next time Calder left Jackson Pohek would strike. He hoped that at some point Calder would make his way to Martel's ranch just outside the town. Pohek had scoped the route and he knew what he would do and where he would do it. But until then he would just have to watch and wait for the opportunity.

Calder paused, looked up and down the street and then strode rapidly towards his hotel. Pohek didn't follow him directly, but scooted around the block, switching his jacket as he did so. He saw Calder hurry into the parking lot behind the hotel. Pohek rushed back to where his own car was parked, started up and just made it in time to catch Calder's rented black Bronco as it pulled out on to the street. There was quite a bit of traffic, and so Pohek was able to tag along a few cars behind.

It soon became clear that Calder was heading north, out of town. Not to Martel's office as he had expected, but up towards the Grand Teton National Park and Yellowstone. Pohek tensed. His opportunity was approaching. He had a hunting rifle in the trunk and a Smith and Wesson in a holster under his arm. He was concerned that Calder's four-wheel-drive SUV would be better able to deal with the back roads than his own Buick. But there hadn't been a snowfall for a couple of days, and as long as Calder kept to the ploughed roads it ought to be possible to keep up with him.

The Bronco continued for several miles along the straight highway, past the wildlife art museum and the airport. There was little traffic now, so Pohek had to hang well back. To his left, the Tetons loomed out of the cloud. Those damn mountains gave him the heebie-jeebies. There was something intimidating about them, like they were giant boulders that were going to roll over the river and crush him or something. Nothing like the mountains they'd got back in Colorado.

Up ahead, he saw the Bronco turn suddenly off the highway. He accelerated to catch up. The side road was ploughed but they were now into low hills and it was difficult keeping the Bronco in sight. Pohek fumbled with his map to try to gauge where he was. He rounded a bend, just in time to see the Bronco come to a T-junction and turn left. Pohek slowed at the junction and turned that way himself.

The road ahead twisted downhill through some aspen to a river bed. No Bronco. Puzzled, Pohek slowed for a moment so that he could glance quickly at his map to check if there was a track heading off to left or right. Then he heard the roar of an engine and the blare of a horn and through his peripheral vision the Bronco leapt out of the trees straight towards him. Before he had time to react, it rammed into his car just above the rear wheels, sending it into a spin. For two seconds trees, road, sky and Bronco swirled round in a complete revolution and then his car hit the trunk of an aspen. Instantaneously the airbag exploded, striking him in the face and pressing him back into his seat. He sat there, stunned, as the airbag deflated in front of him. He heard the hiss of his engine wheezing a complaint, and then the sound of the car door being opened and the click of his safety belt being released. A moment later strong arms pulled him outwards, towards the cold air. He didn't resist, and he was soon slumped on the hard cold road. Hands frisked his jacket and he felt warm steel against his temple.

He heard a click as his pistol was cocked.

'Keep still,' growled a voice in some kind of British accent. Scottish, he guessed.

He kept still.

'Who are you?'

Pohek said nothing. Just swallowed. Lying with his cheek pressed against the tarmac facing the tyre of his own car, he couldn't see his interrogator.

'Wallet.' Pohek did nothing. The barrel of the gun jabbed into his temple. 'Pass me your wallet.'

He reached with his right hand to his pants pocket and pulled it out, holding it away from his body and to the side. It was snatched from his fingers. 'Well, well. Ray Pohek. Or is it Ron Daly? Two identities. Three credit cards to one plus a firearms licence says it's Ray Pohek of Denver. Occupation: private investigator. Very interesting. Don't I recognize you, Ray?'

Pohek kept quiet.

'Haven't you been on vacation to England recently? I'd recognize that lovely complexion anywhere. I should shoot you now, just like you tried to shoot me then, shouldn't I? But first, a couple of questions. Will you answer a couple of questions?'

Pohek tried to keep his silence, but he could feel the sweat breaking out all over his body, despite the cold.

'Talk to me, Ray Pohek. Are you going to answer some questions? Or do I just press the trigger now?'

'OK, OK,' Pohek said.

'That's better. Now. Who are you working for?'

'John-Luke Martel,' Pohek mumbled.

'Speak up! I can't hear you.'

'John-Luke Martel,' Pohek repeated, louder.

'And Mr Martel wanted you to kill me?'

'Indirectly.'

'What do you mean, indirectly?'

'Yeah. Yeah he wanted you killed.'

'I see. Ever heard of someone called Mykhailo Bodinchuk?'

'No.'

'Are you sure?'

'Yes. Yes!'

'What about Esat Olgaç?'

'No.'

'Perumal Thiagajaran?'

'No.'

'Jennifer Tan?'

'What is this? I don't know none of these people. Just John-Luke Martel. That's all.'

'OK.' He could feel the pressure of the gun relaxing slightly against his temple. 'I've got a problem,' said Calder.

Pohek decided not to interrupt the other man's train of thought.

'See, I can't turn you in to the sheriff because you haven't done anything illegal here yet. I can't let you go because you'll just try to kill me again. So all I can do is pull the trigger now.' Again the pressure of the barrel on his temple.

Pohek lost it. He felt a warm wet patch spread across the front of his pants, pressed against the surface of the road. His bowels would go next. 'Please, no. Don't do it, Mr Calder! I won't go nowhere near you. I won't touch you, I swear to it. Don't kill me. Just don't kill me!' He felt the sobs come. What a way to die, weeping in a pool of your own piss, but he couldn't help himself.

He closed his eyes.

Nothing.

Then Calder spoke. 'OK, here's what we do. I've got your details, I know who you are. I'll lodge them somewhere safe. If I'm killed, the police here and in the UK will be informed that you were responsible. You'll end up in jail or the chair. Unless you leave the country, change your identity . . . How much is Martel paying you?'

'A hundred grand.'

'That's not enough to give up everything and risk the death penalty, is it? You stay well clear of me. I'll take the gun, by the way. And your mobile phone. Just stay lying there face down until you hear my car leave. OK?'

'OK,' Pohek replied. With a surge of relief, he felt the pressure removed from his temple. He lay there trembling for five whole minutes after he had heard Calder drive off, the damp patch around his groin becoming noticeably colder. As he pulled himself to his feet and began the long trek back to the main highway to call for a tow truck, he decided Calder was right. It wasn't worth it. He had had enough of being Luigi. From now on it was back to snooping on cheating spouses.

30

Calder drove straight back to his hotel, hoping he had done enough to put off Ray Pohek. Rationally, it would have made sense to shoot him. There was some justification after all: Pohek had tried before to kill Calder and might well try again. While in the RAF, Calder had accepted that he might be called upon to kill other people for his country. He had been trained to do it. But in this case he just hadn't been able to pull the trigger. He was a civilian now, and he couldn't end someone else's life unless his own was directly under threat. That was all there was to it.

He scribbled out some hasty notes about Pohek and Martel, looked up the address of a law office in Jackson in the Yellow Pages in his hotel room, and walked the three blocks. For a suitable fee, a lawyer agreed to keep one copy of the notes safe and show them to the Sheriff's Office if anything happened to Calder. Calder asked the lawyer to Fed Ex another copy to his sister, sealed, with a note that this was a kind of will, only to be opened in the event of his death. He didn't want to scare her unnecessarily.

The evidence was building against Martel, but it was all circumstantial or unverifiable. Tessa wouldn't testify to the police and neither would Carr-Jones, he was sure. There was no proof that the Ukrainian at the Wort Hotel had been following Perumal or that he was, in fact, Ukrainian. Even Perumal's body was somewhere deep down under the snow, away from the authorities' scrutiny. Calder had to shake things up a bit. He needed to talk to Martel. Whether Martel would say anything of any use, he didn't know. The only way to find out was to ask him.

The Teton Fund offices were perched on a hill just outside town, facing the mountain range. The building was made of logs, but there was nothing primitive about it. In the lobby, a stream ran down inside a glass-encased wall of rocks. A red-haired woman with a pretty smile asked him to wait in one of the sturdy log and leather armchairs beneath a large photograph of the Grand Teton itself. Calder was beginning to realize that not only did the majestic mountain dominate Jackson Hole from the outside, its image reached into the interior of nearly every building in the town. He waited. And waited.

After an hour and a half, he heard the thump of heavy footsteps on the wooden staircase behind him. He turned to see a giant of a man bounding towards him. Calder scrambled to his feet and looked up at Jean-Luc Martel, who smiled and pumped his hand, his free arm waving a dramatic gesture of welcome.

'Ah, Alex Calder, the great bond trader of Bloomfield Weiss. Your reputation precedes you. I apologize for keeping you waiting, it's frantic back there.' He nodded to the mysterious domain up the stairs.

Calder examined Martel. Tanned, assured, self-confident, enthusiastic, he looked every inch the successful hedge-fund manager. But was he a murderer? Calder realized he didn't know what a murderer looked like. But he did know this man had employed someone to kill him.

'Not at all,' Calder said, summoning a polite smile. 'Thank you for taking the time to see me. And I don't work for Bloomfield Weiss any more. I've given up on the markets.'

'Oh really? Well, we're always on the lookout for new talent. You might find the quality of life in Jackson Hole suits you better than London. Or New York.'

'I might well.' Calder smiled again. 'Do you have time for a quick word?'

Martel looked at his watch. 'Actually, I am very busy right now. The markets, you understand. But I would like to speak with you very much. What shall we do?' Martel tapped his chin as if lost in thought. 'I know. I am taking the afternoon off to go skiing tomorrow. Why don't you come to my ranch for lunch and then we can spend a couple of hours on the slopes together? It is rare that another aficionado of the markets comes to Jackson Hole, and it would be a pleasure for me to have the chance to discuss things with you. Have you been skiing in Jackson Hole yet?'

'No,' said Calder.

'We have the best snow in the world. It will be an honour for me to show it to you. Get hold of some boots and skis and I'll see you at my ranch at one o'clock tomorrow.'

'I shall look forward to it,' said Calder, and before he knew it he was ushered out on to the street.

He had expected Martel to be evasive. He wasn't sure whether to be pleased or suspicious that Martel wanted to spend so much time with him. On balance, he felt suspicious.

Martel stood by an upstairs window in the corridor and watched Calder get into his car. He smiled. He had known Calder would seek him out eventually. Calder was a trader and Martel understood traders. They took risks. Well, Calder had just taken one risk too many. Martel had given up on Luigi, and Bodinchuk didn't want to know, so he would have to deal with this problem himself. If all went according to plan, Calder wouldn't be a problem for much longer.

Martel strode into his dealing room. If only Calder were his only problem. The atmosphere in the room was painful. There was virtually no activity and there hadn't been for about a week. All the Teton Fund's resources were concentrated on the one trade: Japan. They were up to their limits with every broker they dealt with, they had sold every liquid security to raise cash to cover their losses, there was nothing to do but watch and wait. Martel had no idea what his traders discussed when he wasn't in the room. When he was there, they kept quiet, staring ahead at their screens or making pointless phone calls. Anything to avoid meeting his eye and his anger.

The Nikkei had ticked up two hundred points during the previous couple of days to six thousand seven hundred. This was still well short of the average level of eight thousand at which Martel had put on his bet. The two hundred points had released a little cash, which was welcome. But not nearly enough to meet the almost inevitable demands that were coming.

Today was Wednesday. The last day of the month was the following Monday. On that day Bloomfield Weiss would revalue the JUSTICE notes. Unless the market was much higher, the revaluation would show a massive loss. Since Bloomfield Weiss had lent money to the Teton Fund to buy the notes in the first place, they would demand extra cash to make up for the fall in the value of their collateral. Five hundred million dollars' worth, at least. Unless Martel had that cash ready, the Teton Fund would unravel within days. The consequences would be catastrophic for Martel. And not just for him; his positions were big enough that they could rock the whole financial system. The Japanese stock market would be hammered as Martel's brokers scrambled to sell his positions to raise cash. This would only make the situation worse, the markets would panic and the Teton Fund's losses would soon far exceed its capital. The brokers would lose hundreds of millions too. A bloodbath.

Martel smiled wryly to himself. Maybe he would be remembered in history as the man who broke more than the euro. He could put a serious dent in the whole financial system.

Five days. Vikram was on his way back from London and New York, but from what he had told Martel over the phone, there was no chance of doing any more derivatives with Bloomfield Weiss or anyone else. Two things could still happen to bail Martel out. Firstly, the Nikkei could rally a thousand points or so. Unlikely, but just possible. Or he could get enough money in the fund to meet Bloomfield Weiss's demands for cash. That meant the Artsdalen Foundation had to come through with their promised three hundred million investment. If the market moved up a bit further, that might just cover it.

Martel took a deep breath and called Freddie Langhauser in Zurich.

'Jean-Luc. How's it going?' Langhauser had abandoned French and decided to treat Martel in the more informal American manner.

'Great, Freddie, great. We're winding up for a huge month next month. If you can get your guy in now, it would be perfect timing.'

'I'm trying,' said Freddie. 'But as you know, they like to take their time.'

'I really think we can hit twenty per cent next month,' said Martel. 'And that would be a terrific start.'

'I know, I know,' said Langhauser. 'I do have one concern, though.' He sounded hesitant. Martel closed his eyes. He knew what was coming. 'There are some rumours going round the market.'

'Rumours?'

'Yes. That the Teton Fund has a massive position in Japanese equities. And that you are sitting on large losses.'

Martel forced a laugh. 'There are always rumours about us, you know that. People are jealous.'

'So there's nothing in these rumours, then?'

'Well, I don't deny we have a big position. That's how we're going to make the big returns next month. And it's true that the Japanese market has gone down. But it's becoming more volatile by the day, and high volatility is good for us. Many of our trades involve options and, as you know, when volatility goes up the price of options goes up. That's exactly where the hidden value in the fund is.'

'I see,' said Langhauser.

Freddie Langhauser wasn't an options trader, but a private banker. Options theory scared the hell out of most bankers, with its Greek alphabet, its calculus and its impenetrable jargon. Martel was confident that the fact that high volatility was bad for the JUSTICE notes would escape him.

'There's still time,' said Martel. 'If your client can commit to the funds by Monday, we'll let them in at the month-end price.'

It would be tight, but it should be just possible to get the Artsdalen money to Bloomfield Weiss in time.

'Thanks,' said Langhauser. 'I'll see what I can do.'

Martel put the phone down and stared at the Tetons across the valley. How he admired their solidity, their strength, their permanence.

He was still in with a chance.

Martel's ranch wasn't quite as large as Calder had expected, but it nestled in a staggeringly beautiful location. The sunlight sparkled on the rushing water of the Snake River and on the flanks of the Tetons soaring high above. He was met at the door by a Hispanic maid who showed him through to a large room, with ceilings rising up thirty feet to the timbered roof. At one end was a seating area and at the other a sturdy dining table, with places set for three in the middle, and a vast bronze chandelier suspended above it. There were two fireplaces constructed of what looked like stones from a river bed, with fires blazing in each one. And then there was the view from the windows of the river and the mountains.

He felt the first twinges of fear creep up on him. His neck and shoulders were tense and he felt a dull pain in his lower back. The day before it had seemed a good idea to confront Martel directly, to shake things up a bit, but now he was in Martel's house, alone, at his mercy, the idea didn't seem quite so brilliant. He took a deep breath. As long as he kept his wits about him, he'd be OK. But he was looking forward to reaching the relative safety of the public slopes.

He was left alone for barely a moment before a door banged open and Martel appeared, accompanied by a not-quite-so-tall, square-shouldered man with light-brown skin, and a woman.

'I am so glad you could come, Alex. This is Vikram Rana, who does my derivatives business for me. He will eat lunch with us, but sadly he has to work this afternoon. And this is my wife, Cheryl, just back from New York. She will join us just for a drink. She finds all this talk about the markets tedious, don't you, *mon ange*?'

Mrs Martel was wearing jeans and a white sweatshirt. Her blonde hair was tied back in a pony tail. Her cheeks glowed pink. She had a simple, guileless beauty that was surprising to see in the wife of a budding billionaire. She gave Calder a broad all-American smile and shook his hand. Calder felt safer with a woman around, especially this woman. She didn't look like the type to be an accessory to murder.

'Now, has Rita got you a drink?' Martel said.

Calder asked for a tomato juice, Vikram a Diet Coke, Cheryl a glass of white wine and Martel himself a whisky and ginger ale.

'Did you find some skis, Alex?' Martel asked.

'I rented some from a shop in town this morning.'

'Excellent. Are you a good skier?'

'Reasonable,' said Calder. He actually thought himself quite good, but he knew that Martel was probably an expert. Somehow he suspected that Martel would want to show off that fact, and Calder was determined not to rise to the challenge.

'There's glorious powder up there at the moment,' said Martel, moving Calder towards the window. 'The snowfall is so heavy here and the atmosphere so dry that you get much more powder than in the Alps, for example.'

'It's a beautiful view,' said Calder.

'I love the Tetons,' said Martel. 'Do you know where the word comes from?'

'No.'

'When some French trappers saw the mountains from the Idaho side, they called them "Les Trois Tétons". "Tétons" means “tits” in French, in case you didn’t know.’ Martel laughed. ‘Chalmet raised a couple of eyebrows when I told them my fund would be called the Teton Fund. I love to annoy these Swiss bankers; they take themselves so seriously. But how could I call it anything else? Anyway, I think of them more as Titans. They have so much strength, so much power. Especially the Grand Teton. You know, after nine eleven a lot of people came here looking for strength and comfort. A lot of people.’

Calder examined the tallest mountain, silent, overbearing. Its edges were rough, folds and wrinkles and crags, sharp broken shards of rock slashing through the snow.

‘And then there’s the river. The fishing in the Snake River is some of the best in the country and we have a creek that runs through the property just on the other side of the house. Do you fly-fish?’

‘I don’t have the patience for it,’ said Calder. The idea of the hyperactive Martel quietly watching a fly drift down a stream was difficult to imagine.

‘Patience? You don’t need patience,’ said Martel. ‘It is totally absorbing. It is like you are hunting the fish. Did you know there is a species of cutthroat that exists only in this river?’

As they were admiring the view, a flash of movement in the reflection of the window pane caught Calder’s eye. Behind him, inside the room, Vikram stepped behind Cheryl to fetch some ice for his drink from a side table. As he did so he seemed to let his hand drift over her behind. Cheryl flicked it away and gave him an admonishing glance, but it was a glance tinged with something else, something unmistakable.

Vikram and Cheryl were lovers.

Calder glanced quickly towards Martel, but he seemed oblivious to what was happening behind him, in fact he probably couldn’t see the interior of the room reflected from where he was standing.

Calder turned, slowly. ‘You must like it here, Mrs Martel.’

‘Oh, I do,’ she said. ‘I’m from Wisconsin. We’ve got the cold and the snow but we don't have the mountains. Mind you, I have to get out of here every now and then or I'd go crazy.'

'Cheryl spends a lot of the time in her studio,' said Martel, with a note of pride. 'You see all the ceramics in this room? All her work. I keep telling her she should open a gallery in town, but she won't listen.'

Calder examined a tall multicoloured vase standing on a plinth by his elbow. It reminded him a little of a Henry Moore sculpture in clay, except more sensuous. 'I like this one.'

'Do you want it?' Cheryl asked him.

'No, I couldn't possibly take it,' said Calder, surprised.

'*Mon ange*, that is one of your best pieces!' Martel protested.

'Oh, don't worry, honey. I can always make another.' Cheryl picked it up off its plinth. 'I'll just go put it in bubble wrap for you. You don't want to break it carrying it around.'

'But Cheryl!' Martel's brows were knitted in anger.

Calder realized that Cheryl was playing some kind of game with her husband. He didn't know whether she knew of the enmity between himself and Martel, or she just sensed it. Either way, he couldn't resist playing along.

'Thank you, Mrs Martel. I shall treasure it.'

'Cheryl, please,' she said in a manner that was all friendliness and no flirtation. 'I know you will. I could tell by the way you were looking at it. To an artist, that look is the greatest kind of praise.' With that, she took the vase and left the room.

'Let's sit down,' said Martel, unable to hide the irritation in his voice.

Although he was happy to needle Martel, Calder wanted to get him talking. So he changed the subject. 'Tell me about the Italian trade last year. You caught me on the wrong side of that a couple of times. In the end, I just gave up.'

Martel recovered from his anger instantly, and launched into a lengthy discourse about the Teton Fund and the euro. Calder encouraged him, gently stroking his ego at the correct points. But he wasn't faking his interest. Martel's stories brought back some of the excitement of the markets that he had tried not to think about over the preceding year, but that he so sorely missed.

Eventually, after the soup and a *salade Niçoise*, Martel ran out of steam. 'But how can I help you? What brings you to Jackson Hole?'

This too was a game. Both he and Martel knew exactly why he was there, but Calder still wasn't sure why Martel wanted to play. Calder knew what he was looking for, but what was in it for Martel? Why didn't he just refuse to talk to him and send him packing? It worried him.

Still, best to keep playing. 'I was a colleague of Perumal Thiagajaran's. I've been in touch with his widow in London, and I'm trying to find out a bit more about how he died.'

'That was a tragic accident, wasn't it, Vikram?' Martel said. 'He and Vikram did a lot of business together.'

'So I understand,' Calder said. 'Presumably that's why Perumal was here?'

'Yes,' said Vikram. 'He and I discussed some ideas for new trades. I enjoyed working with him. He was a smart man: one of those people you can share ideas with and generate something that's new to both of you.'

'How long did he spend at your offices?'

'Oh, we had dinner, and then we spent a morning together. It was scarcely worth him coming all this way, but I appreciated the effort. I think his boss had put him up to it. I guess we must be one of Bloomfield Weiss's top derivatives accounts.'

'What kind of derivatives business do you do? As you can guess, the bond guys and the derivatives guys don't talk much.'

'With Bloomfield Weiss it's mostly structured notes – deals that can express a view on a range of different markets at once. And we do them in large size.'

'You mean, they allow you to take on bigger positions when the credit lines from your brokers are full?'

Martel laughed. 'I can assure you the Teton Fund has access to all the credit it needs. We are one of the most sophisticated investors in the world. Sometimes we need something a little more complex than a simple government bond to achieve what we want. For example, Bloomfield Weiss came up with the IGLOO notes when we had a view that Italy would drop out of the euro. They were responsible for a large part of our profit on that trade.'

'Why do you trade with London and not New York?'

'The IGLOO notes were a European deal,' Vikram answered. 'Bloomfield Weiss's European derivatives business is run out of London. Once we'd done a few big trades, and they worked, we decided to stick with the London office. We do get the odd call from salesmen in New York fishing for business, but we tell them where to get off.'

Typical Bloomfield Weiss, Calder thought. Starting a turf war over a big client. 'And you did all these trades with Perumal?'

'Yes. Just him.'

'And did Perumal revalue the trades?'

'What do you mean?' asked Vikram.

'I mean, didn't Bloomfield Weiss have to revalue the trades on a regular basis, if only to determine how much the notes were worth as collateral?'

'I guess so,' said Vikram. 'I really don't remember.'

'What about now? Do you have any of these notes outstanding at the moment?'

'Come now, Alex,' Martel interrupted. 'You can't expect us to talk about our current trading positions.'

'No, of course not,' Calder said. 'But I wonder whether Perumal's death caused you any difficulty. Or whether there was someone else at Bloomfield Weiss willing to take a lenient attitude towards revaluations. Justin Carr-Jones, perhaps?'

'I don't know what you're talking about. Do you, Vikram? I don't know this Justin Carr-Jones.'

'He's the head of the Derivatives Group at Bloomfield Weiss

in London,' Vikram said. 'And to answer your question, I do miss Perumal. He was a smart guy and a good person to deal with. But I'm not aware of any difficulties in revaluing our portfolio of structured notes, either now or in the past.'

'I see,' said Calder. 'Have you ever heard of Jennifer Tan?' Both Martel's and Vikram's faces were blank. 'She used to work for me at Bloomfield Weiss, and before that for the Derivatives Group. She fell out of a window last year. The police think she killed herself. I think she was pushed.'

'And you think this might have something to do with Perumal's death?' Martel asked, with what seemed like genuine curiosity.

'I do.'

'But surely that was an accident?'

'Was it?'

Vikram and Martel exchanged glances. 'We think so,' said Vikram.

'Do you know why he decided to stay on in Jackson Hole a couple of days?'

'No,' said Vikram. 'I thought he was travelling back to London on the Friday; at least, that's what he told me he was doing.'

'So he didn't mention going snowmobiling?'

'No. He didn't really look like a snowmobiling kind of guy to me.'

'I hate those things,' Martel interrupted. 'Noisy, filthy, disgusting, driven by idiots. You know they let them into the National Parks now? They ruin the peace for everyone else. There's nothing you can't see on a good pair of cross-country skis.'

'What do you think, Vikram?' Calder asked.

'I've never been on one.'

'Vikram doesn't even ski,' said Martel. 'He comes to a mountain paradise like this and he won't even put on a pair of skis.'

'I work out,' said Vikram defensively. 'And in the summer I take out my mountain bike. I like the mountains.'

Calder decided to continue the dance. He now realized what they were doing: letting him talk to see how much he knew. He was willing to play that game, in the hope that one of them might make some tiny slip that he could pick up on. 'Do you know Mykhailo Bodinchuk?' he asked.

Martel looked at him with interest. 'Yes. Yes, I do. He's an investor in the Teton Fund. A large investor.'

'How large?'

Martel smiled. 'You know I can't answer that.'

'I think that someone who works for Mykhailo Bodinchuk killed Jennifer Tan and Perumal. Someone who pretends to be a Turkish citizen named Esat Olgaç, but who is actually Ukrainian. Middle-aged, dark hair brushed back, thin moustache.'

Martel looked surprised, and rather pleased, Calder thought, a reaction Calder wasn't expecting. If Martel was involved in Jen's death, then he should be concerned about Calder discovering a link to Bodinchuk.

'That can't be true,' Martel said, maintaining his composure. 'I know Mykhailo has a reputation as a tough customer, but he wouldn't kill people in cold blood, would he? Besides, why would he want to kill Perumal and the woman you mentioned?'

'I hoped you might be able to tell me. I thought it might have something to do with the derivative trades you do with Bloomfield Weiss.'

Martel laughed. 'I can assure you that isn't the case.'

Calder gave him a small smile. 'That's good to know. Now what about Ray Pohek? Do you know him?'

This time Martel was genuinely surprised. He looked over his shoulder, and then glanced quickly at Vikram. 'What's he got to do with any of this?' he said in a whisper.

'That's what I was wondering. But he does work for you, doesn't he?'

Martel recovered and sat up straight. 'That's really something I'd rather not discuss. It's personal.'

'Personal?'

'Yes. It has nothing to do with Perumal, or Bloomfield Weiss, or you.'

'Nothing to do with me? Then why has Pohek been following me since I arrived in Jackson Hole? And why did he try to kill me back in England last week?'

'*What?*'

'I caught Mr Pohek following me yesterday. I think I scared him pretty badly. I've lodged some papers somewhere safe which suggest that if something happens to me, the police should look very closely at Ray Pohek. And at his employer. You.'

'Oh, no, no, you don't understand. I am employing Pohek in another capacity altogether.'

Calder glanced at Martel: the Frenchman's concern seemed to be sincere. Vikram didn't seem to know what was going on either, but he looked very interested in finding out.

'I do understand,' Calder said. 'I understand that a week ago he chased after me waving a gun and firing real bullets.'

Martel was stumped. No denial. No explanation.

They were interrupted by the approaching whump-whump of a helicopter. Calder turned to see a Bell 407 landing on the lawn in front of the ranch. Martel seemed relieved by the interruption. 'Ah. Time to get your skis, Alex. We will be off in a moment.'

'In that?'

'Absolutely. It's much quicker than driving. I'll see you outside in five minutes.'

Lunch broke up and Calder made his way out of the house to the driveway where he had parked his Bronco, still sporting a dent from Pohek's car.

He was nervous about joining Martel in a helicopter. The prudent thing would be to cry off, get in the Bronco and drive away. For a moment Calder was tempted. But as long as Martel remained free, Calder's life was in danger, unless of course he gave up entirely and went back to Norfolk. He had come too far to do that: he would never forgive himself if he quit now. And anyway, once he got on to the crowded slopes he would be safe.

He stopped by the car, hesitating. He looked from the helicopter, rotors still turning, to the mountains. He took a deep breath. What the hell. He'd stick with Martel.

He did fish out the gun he had taken from Pohek and zipped it into an inside pocket of his coat, which would have to double as a skiing jacket. Then he put on the hired boots, gathered his skis and clomped round the house to the chopper on the lawn. Martel was waiting for him in his own flash equipment: red high-tech boots, orange jacket and fat yellow skis bearing the name of a manufacturer Calder didn't recognize. Vikram was still in street clothes, happy to miss the mountain and go back to the office. Martel folded himself into the helicopter, Calder squeezed into a back seat and the pilot stowed the skis and hopped in.

As the pilot went through his pre-take-off checks, Martel turned to Calder and grinned. Calder didn't smile back.

31

The helicopter lifted off, watched by Vikram, a diminishing figure on the snow-covered lawn. To Calder's surprise, it turned south, following the Snake River downstream for a few miles, and then gained altitude. It soared high over a ranch and was soon above the mountains. Calder looked down on a wilderness of trees, snow and rock. Quite a lot of rock. Teton Village and the Jackson Hole skiing area were now several miles behind them.

He tapped Martel on the shoulder. 'Where are we going?'

'You don't want to mess around with the lifts, do you? Unfortunately they don't let helicopters into the Tetons, but there are some nice runs I know in the Snake River Range. The only way to get to them is by helicopter. It's not far.'

Calder had assumed skiing would involve lifts and busy slopes packed with skiers where he would be safe. But he was going to be dropped in the middle of nowhere with Martel, whom he knew, or thought he knew, had been trying to kill him. Perhaps he should have been more careful and driven away when he still had the chance. But there was no way out of it now.

He looked down. This was going to be difficult skiing, Calder thought, very difficult skiing. For a Briton who took the occasional holiday to the Alps, Calder considered himself competent. He had skied down many black runs in France and Switzerland at high speed. But he knew he would be nowhere near as skilled as Martel. The important thing was not to allow Martel to tempt him into overreaching himself. He felt the awkward bulk of the pistol under his jacket. If this was some kind of trap he would not be afraid to use it.

After twenty minutes or so, the helicopter hovered over a narrow ridge before lowering itself on to a flat plateau no more than twenty yards square. Calder admired the skill of the pilot. Mountain flying was treacherous even at the best of times, with unexpected downdraughts and turbulence threatening to surprise the unwary, but this man clearly knew what he was doing.

Martel and he climbed out and put on skis and goggles. The view was breathtaking. Every way he looked, there were mountains, and to the north the forbidding peak of the Grand Teton itself. The valley of the Snake River was out of sight and there was no sign of habitation anywhere. He was alone in the wilderness, alone with Jean-Luc Martel. He patted his pocket and felt the comforting shape of Pohek's gun.

The Bell rose into the air and powered off over the ridge just above them.

'Normally the helicopter would stay with us and take us back up when we finished the run,' Martel said. 'But it's already nearly four o'clock. We don't have that much time until it gets dark. So we'll ski down the whole mountain from here, and a car will meet us at the bottom. Believe it or not, there is a road down there.'

He surveyed the gentle bowl beneath them. 'Don't worry, I know this mountain very well. But you must be careful to stick with me. There are some, how do you say, dead ends, where you go down and come to a cliff with no way back up. Also there are avalanche risks here. You see this bowl?' He pointed to the smooth, pristine snow beneath them, lined on three sides by ridges like the one they were standing on. 'If you go to the left, you start an avalanche. If you go to the right, it is not so steep, no avalanche. I know that. For you, it is not so obvious. So you stay with me, OK?'

'OK,' Calder nodded. He thought of Perumal who had blundered in his ignorance into an avalanche. Calder had no intention of making the same mistake.

Martel set off down the ridge. He skied fast but with terrific grace, especially for a man so large. Calder followed, and managed to keep up, although his turns were not as tight or as graceful. The snow was the purest powder, a delight to cut through. Calder felt a sense of intense elation as he carved his way through the bowl, sun and wind on his face, the swish of snow beneath his feet, and all around the beautiful emptiness of the Rockies.

Martel led him down to the bottom of the bowl and gathered enough speed to make it most of the way up the slope on the other side. Calder didn't quite have Martel's momentum on the downward run and so had to walk up the slope crab fashion on his skis. Martel was fast uphill as well as down and Calder found it impossible to keep up with him. But fortunately he saw Martel wait for him at the crest of the ridge.

The tall man turned and grinned. 'How do you like it?'

'It's wonderful,' said Calder, his suspicion almost gone. 'Truly wonderful.'

'Ready for some more?'

Calder nodded, and Martel set off down another bowl. This one was slightly steeper and Martel picked up the pace, but Calder kept up. The slope seemed to flatten off before a steep edge, but Martel didn't slow up and so neither did Calder. He was keeping his eye on Martel, copying his every move, knowing that Martel would take the best line down the slope.

Suddenly Martel seemed to soar into the air over the edge. Calder had a split-second to decide whether to try to stop or to follow him. Stopping might be more dangerous, he thought, and a second later he too was in mid-air. He landed on a slope that seemed to be little more than a cliff pointing straight down. Martel in front was somehow weaving from side to side in the powder, putting some brake on his downward speed, dodging patches of bare rock. Calder realized he would have to do the same thing or he would simply hurtle down the slope in little more than a glorified fall. Somehow he managed to control his skis, jumping from side to side in an unsteady rhythm.

At the bottom there seemed to be a brief run-out, too narrow to stop on, and then another drop. Martel reached the run-out and sped on over the next precipice. Through his peripheral vision, Calder noticed that Martel seemed to twist in the air to the left.

As he hit the edge, he leaned to the left as he had seen Martel do. Once more his skis abandoned the snow. Beneath him was a sight that filled him with panic. Twenty feet below was an even narrower run-out, little more than a ledge, and far too narrow to stop or even slow down on. Beyond that was sky. Wide open blue sky. As he had been trained to do in the RAF, he channelled the instant surge of energy released by the panic into a reaction, tucking up his skis, which were still pointing to the left, and bracing for impact. He hit the snow, slid and one ski dangled over the edge. Fortunately his weight was sufficiently far back on the other ski to maintain some grip, and he shot off to the left along the ledge. It became a chute down between a boulder and the cliff face and then he hurtled out into a wide expanse of gently sloping snow.

Half-way down was the gangling figure of Martel, looking back up at him.

Calder drifted down to him, breathing heavily.

'You are a good skier,' Martel said with grudging admiration.

Calder gasped for air. He was shaking. He looked back at the cliff he had just avoided. There was a fall of at least two hundred feet to a field of boulders. If he hadn't twisted to the left, as he had seen Martel do, he would surely be down there now. Dead.

It was clear that was exactly what Martel had hoped would happen.

Martel turned and sped off down the slope. Calder followed. His only hope was to keep up with him. He was sure Martel wasn't bluffing when he said there were many dead-ends on the route down. He suspected that Martel had counted on him missing the last turn and hurtling off into space, so he hoped there would be nothing quite as difficult to come.

He was right. But his muscles were tiring and the concentration was taking its toll. He did fall eventually, at a relatively easy traverse, which he took too fast. One ski caught in thick powder and spun him around. He went over the edge and fell perhaps twenty feet, snow, rock and sky spinning, before landing in a deep drift. The impact of the snow knocked the breath out of him, but he neither felt nor heard anything breaking.

He lay there motionless for a minute or so, and then struggled to clamber into an upright position, which was very difficult. One ski remained attached to his boot. The other had spun off somewhere. He looked around and couldn't see it. Above him was some snow, then ten feet of rock face and the traverse. Below was twenty feet of snow and then air. Another cliff face. The ski must have gone that way.

He looked around for Martel and couldn't see him.

He took off the one ski and struggled up the slope trying to carry it. The snow was deep and fine, his poles plunging far down into it at every step, and it was hard work making progress. At one point he sank to his chest, and he had to swim to keep himself above the snow. It took him ten minutes of struggling just to reach the rock face. His back hurt around the base of the spine where he had damaged it ejecting. That was worrying: his doctors had warned him that any further injury to his spine could do permanent damage to his nervous system. That was why they had forbidden him to ski. Naturally, he had taken no notice.

It was only ten feet up to the traverse, and the rock was cracked and broken with plenty of handholds, but try as he might, he couldn't climb up in his ski boots. He slumped, defeated, against the rock face.

In normal circumstances, the thing to do would be to wait

for help. Perhaps Martel was already down by the car that was meeting them at the bottom of the mountain, raising the alarm. Or perhaps he wasn't. Calder glanced at the sun, slipping ominously down towards the mountains to the west. He only had an hour or so until it was dark. Already the patch of snow he was stuck in was in shadow, a shadow stretching twenty miles from a mountain ridge far off to the southwest. Without the sun, it was cold. It would only get colder.

He pulled out his mobile phone and switched it on. No signal. No surprise.

He was going to have to get himself down the mountain. No one else would do it for him.

He took off his gloves and boots and plunged his stockinged feet into the snow. Instantly his socks were wet. It would be impossible to carry poles, boots and skis while climbing the rock face, so he flung the boots in a high arc up on to the ledge above. That was relatively easy. The single ski was much more difficult, because every time it reached the snow above, it just slid down again, and Calder had to catch it before it continued on its way down the mountain to join its partner an unknown number of feet beneath him.

Finally, on about the tenth attempt, he threw it up and it stayed up, probably wedged against the boots.

By now his hands were cold and his feet were wet and freezing. He began to scale the cliff face. The bare rock bit into his hands, and especially his feet. He found his toes were tougher than the soles of his feet and so he climbed on tip toe. He had to arch his back to stretch upwards for handholds, and his spine complained loudly. He quickly reached a point about two feet from the top, but those last two feet seemed almost impossible. He tried to propel himself upwards in a kind of leap. His right hand reached a hold at the top, but as he swung round his wrist twisted and he let go. He fell, cracking his head on a stone.

The impact of hitting the snow beneath didn't register on

his consciousness. When he opened his eyes he found himself lying on his side in the snow. It was cold, very cold, and his head hurt. Despite the cold, the mattress of snow around him felt soft and comforting. He closed his eyes again.

A weak but urgent voice somewhere deep inside his brain called to him, at first in an undistinguishable whisper, then louder. 'Get up, you lazy sod! Get up! If you don't get up in the next few minutes you never will!'

With a supreme effort of will, Calder opened his eyes again. Moved his arms and legs. Wriggled and writhed and pushed and heaved until he was once more at the bottom of the rock face.

His hearing registered a sound that had been in the background for a while. The thud-thud of a helicopter. He looked up. The sun had now completely disappeared behind the mountains to the west, but it was still light enough to see a yellow helicopter circling higher up the mountain back the way he had come. He stood up and waved, but the machine was circling too far away to see him.

He waved again and shouted.

Suddenly the helicopter quit hovering, pointed its nose northwards and sped over a ridge. Calder could still hear it, but he couldn't see it. And it couldn't see him.

He set about the rock face again. Perhaps when he was back on the snow, he could ski down to a more open area where he would be able to see the chopper.

He reached the same stretch of rock that had confounded him before. Once again he propelled himself upwards. This time as his cold fingers reached the handhold he pulled upwards, preventing the swing that had broken his grip the last time. He clutched at another hold with his left hand and pulled with both arms. Somehow he dragged himself up on to the ledge.

He lay there panting, his feet numb, his arms exhausted and his head aching. But he could still hear the helicopter, just over a shoulder of the mountain. The gloom was deepening and it would be difficult for them to see him, but there was still a chance. He fixed the ski to his right boot, and gingerly slid along the traverse, following Martel's tracks in the snow in front of him.

The traverse curved around the shoulder of the mountainside and Calder saw the helicopter diminish into the distance. Giving up. Going home. Calder pushed off through the snowfield after it, waving as he did so, moving faster and faster, but not as fast as the helicopter. Eventually he fell over, in a tumbling, head-over-heels wipeout.

He pulled himself to his feet. The helicopter was gone. Just as worrying, so were Martel's tracks. Calder had no way of knowing the way down the mountain. He looked back. It was at least half a mile and several hundred feet higher to where he had taken off down the slope after the helicopter. He was exhausted. He couldn't face trudging all the way back up there in his heavy ski boots.

Below him, there seemed to be a benign snowfield down to some fir trees, silhouetted against the blue glimmer of the flanks of the Tetons on the other side of the valley. Calder skied down. He went slowly and carefully, pausing frequently to check the best line. He remembered Martel's words about the risk of an avalanche. This bowl looked to be about forty-five degrees, similar to the one Nate had pointed out as being 'prime slidin''. Tough. There was nothing he could do about that. He carried on gingerly, listening out for a tell-tale creak of snow beneath his ski.

It would be wrong to describe his feet, still wet in his boots, as numb, because they hurt. It was an urgent pain, but it was impossible to locate specifically where it came from. He couldn't feel his toes, or any part of his foot below the ankle. It just hurt. Skiing slowly on one leg in his condition was tiring and his lower back shouted its own message of pain to add to the general assault on his nervous system.

The light had gone by the time he entered the trees. He wasn't really skiing, just sliding from tree to tree. It was dark in the wood and he felt very alone. The silence enveloped the mountain, smothering him with its dead hand. When he paused, all he could hear was the rasp of his breathing; when he held his breath, his blood thundered in his ears. The temperature was falling rapidly. He remembered that the high for the day had been forecast as twenty degrees. That was Fahrenheit, twelve degrees below freezing. He dreaded to think what the low for the night would be. He had to keep going. He didn't like the idea of spending the night up on the mountain.

Then, what he knew was bound to happen, happened. The trees came to an end. Another precipice. No way down. He could see descent was impossible to the left, so he slid along to the right for a hundred yards or so. Still no way down.

He slumped against a tree. He wasn't going to get down that night. He was going to spend the night on the mountain.

He felt like sinking to the ground then and there. But he knew that his best hope was to be spotted in the morning by a helicopter. To do that he needed to be in the open. And the open was back up the hill through the trees.

Somehow he struggled upwards, back to the upper limit of the tree line. Somehow he managed to pile up enough snow to make a rough shelter next to a couple of tree trunks. Somehow he managed to break off some branches to make a kind of a mattress. He pulled his hat over his ears, took off his wet socks and shoved his feet into the damp padded ski-boots and curled up into a ball.

It was cold. So very, very cold. He shivered. He looked up at the stars. There were thousands more than there ever were over London and they were much closer. The peak of the Grand Teton glimmered against the starlit sky, watching over him. In his shelter the edge came off the cold, and his shivering ceased. He was tired, exhausted, beyond exhaustion. Worried about hypothermia, he fought to keep himself awake, fought and lost. At some point during the night he fell asleep.

He was wakened by the sound of a helicopter. He was cold and dog-tired. He tried to stand up but his legs, or more accurately his feet, wouldn't let him. So he crawled out of his ramshackle shelter and into the open snow. He stopped on all fours, craning his neck upwards, watching the helicopter circling half a mile away. The Tetons were ablaze with the glory of the dawn. Without his goggles, which he had left back in the shelter, the glare overcame his raw eyes. But he heard the thud of the helicopter coming closer. He could feel the downwash of the blades. And then the glare disappeared as the shadow of the machine hovered overhead and the great blades whipped up the powdered snow like a tornado.

32

'Merde!'

Martel slammed down the phone. Cheryl had just relayed the message to him that Calder had been found on the mountain, exhausted and suffering from exposure, but alive. Martel scanned the floor of his office, still strewn with papers, found the tallest pile, took a run up, and gave it a blistering kick. Prospectuses, spreadsheets and research reports went everywhere. One booklet hit the opposite wall a satisfying six feet off the ground. Perhaps he should have played rugby after all.

It had been such a good plan, a work of genius, and he had been so sure that it would succeed. No matter what notes Calder had left about Pohek, Martel could not have been blamed, at least for murder. It was a skiing accident, plain and simple. Certainly Martel would have had to apologize to Calder's family, whoever they were, for his irresponsibility in leading a poor skier down a difficult hill; he would have to show public anguish and guilt. But a murder charge? No chance.

Once he had realized that Calder was no longer following him down the mountain, Martel had dawdled. He delayed reaching the road where the car was supposed to meet them for as long as possible, thus giving the rescue effort little time before darkness closed in to find Calder. That, combined with some misleading information about where he thought Calder fell, had ensured that the helicopter hadn't spotted him. But the bastard had survived, and Martel would now have to answer a further battery of tedious questions from the Sheriff's Office.

Still, at least Calder had divulged his knowledge of a link between Bodinchuk and Jennifer Tan's death. That was just what Martel needed to get the Ukrainian involved. He picked up the phone and dialled the number.

'Good evening, Mykhailo.'

'Martel? I thought I told you to sort out your problems yourself from now on.'

Martel winced at the irritation in Bodinchuk's voice. 'I have been trying,' he said soothingly. 'Believe me, I have been trying. But I think I need some professional help.'

'I've told you, I don't want to get involved in a war against an investment bank. They're expensive. You sort it out.'

'But you are involved.'

'What do you mean?'

'Calder knows that a Ukrainian killed Jennifer Tan and was following Perumal. He knows that Ukrainian was connected to you. He told me so yesterday. He doesn't have hard evidence yet, but I think it's only a matter of days before he goes to the police.'

'I see.'

'So, what I suggest is –'

'Quiet! I'm thinking.'

Martel stayed quiet for about a minute. It seemed like an eternity.

'All right, Martel. I'll call my man now. This problem will be sorted out once and for all, I guarantee it.'

'Excellent. I knew you'd –'

But the phone went dead.

In Kiev, Bodinchuk dialled Uncle Yuri's number in the Crimea. They spoke for several minutes. Bodinchuk liked to chat with Uncle Yuri: it calmed him, made him feel less insecure, less vulnerable. He would prefer not to use the old man as often as he had recently, but this was turning into one of those instances where Uncle's superior skills and one hundred per cent success rate were required. Uncle Yuri said he had been dozing after a strenuous afternoon playing with the grand-children. He assured Bodinchuk that an excuse not to spend the weekend clearing out the garage under the watchful eye of his wife would be welcome. Bodinchuk told him that a jet would meet him at Simferopol and take him on to Salt Lake City. From there, Uncle Yuri would take a scheduled flight to Jackson Hole under whatever name he chose.

There. That was that dealt with. Bodinchuk turned his attention to the evening's task. He was taking out an important government minister, softening him up to make sure that certain key contracts went to the right people. He wasn't quite sure yet where the minister's tastes lay: sex, drugs, booze, or just simple dollar bills. But it would not take him long to find out.

Vikram sat slumped in front of his computer screen. He was trying to calculate what price Bloomfield Weiss might come up with for the revaluation of the JUSTICE notes. The notes were so damned complicated there were at least four different ways of going about revaluing them, each highly dependent on the assumptions plugged into the model. But whichever method was used under whatever assumptions, the result was always a big loss. It was just a question of how big.

Vikram glanced around the room. A couple of the traders were laughing – gallows humour. No one had done a trade for days. Any confidence they might have had that Martel might pull something out of a hat had long since gone. The Teton Fund was history.

What would that mean for Vikram? He would have to leave Jackson Hole. That was probably a good thing. Although he loved the mountains, especially in the summer, when he could easily spend a whole day on his mountain bike losing himself in their embrace, he had never felt at home. He was one of only two Indians in the town – the other was a waitress. The native whites were not openly hostile to him, in fact they were unfailingly polite, but in Jackson Hole he felt like he was an exotic Asian, whereas in California he had felt like he was a Californian.

When the Teton Fund blew, it would take his savings with it. He would have no money, but at least he would have his brain. He was still young – there was still time to make his millions.

He would miss Cheryl. Man, would he miss Cheryl. Since that afternoon in New York only two days before, they had met three times. They were getting careless: they would soon get caught. He didn't care. It was more than just sex, it was more than just the delicious thrill of screwing the boss's wife, although both of those factors were still important.

He was beginning to realize that he loved her.

Would she leave her husband and follow him? Probably not. Vikram knew that although the passion had left their marriage, she was still fond of Martel. But then she didn't know very much about him, did she? Not as much as Vikram.

It was suddenly clear to Vikram that the great, intuitive trader he had so admired was a monster. Vikram no longer wanted to be like this man; in fact, he wanted nothing to do with him. The signs had always been there, but Vikram had ignored them, or assumed that they were a necessary part of genius. Jennifer Tan's 'suicide' so soon after she had begun causing so much trouble. Martel's boasting about his friendship with Bodinchuk. Bodinchuk's Ukrainian trailing after Perumal. And now Martel's attempt to lead Alex Calder to his death.

Vikram had stood by and let it all happen. He was a smart guy, he could have figured out what was going on if he'd wanted to, he just hadn't been prepared to admit it to himself.

He was sorry about Perumal. Although he had initially dismissed him as the Indian equivalent of a country bumpkin, the man had had a good brain. They had done some good work together. And now he was under twenty feet of snow.

Was it too late? Was Vikram already so complicit in all this death that there was no hope of going back? He wasn't sure of the legal position. But he had his dignity to think about, self-esteem, honour, call it what you will. Vikram had done his best to ignore his Indian heritage. But his father had come from a high caste, a warrior caste, and the Rana name was one that he had been very proud of, something that his ancestors had fought and died for many times over the centuries. Try as he might to deny it, this family pride was embedded somewhere deep inside Vikram the Californian. He knew that if he was to leave Jackson Hole with his belief in himself intact he would have to do something. And do something soon.

At two o'clock in the afternoon Vikram left the office. On most Fridays this wouldn't be too much of a problem. On the penultimate working day of this particular month it might be. But if Martel came looking for him, asking him to go over the possible revaluation numbers for the JUSTICE notes yet again, tough. He might come in to the office on Saturday. Or he might not.

The moment he was out of the office parking lot he reached for his cell phone.

'Hello?'

He smiled at the sound of her voice. 'Hi. It's me.'

'Where are you?'

'I left work early. I'm on my way home. Can you meet me?'

'I'm supposed to be going to the museum.'

'Please.'

A pause. Then a chuckle. 'OK. See you soon.'

Vikram drove through the small town of Wilson, about five miles from Jackson, and turned on to a steep winding road. His house was at the very end, away from the people, surrounded by nothing but lodgepole pines and magnificent views. He parked his car outside, lit a fire, and opened a bottle of Californian wine, Insignia from the Joseph Phelps vineyard. It was Cheryl's favourite, she said. Martel always insisted that they drink French.

He heard the sound of her Mercedes SUV drawing up outside, and his heart beat fast with anticipation as he went to the door to meet her. She stepped in, her face flushed, and put her arms around his neck. She kissed him long and deep.

He pushed her away. 'Not yet, my darling.'

'Why not?' she frowned.

'I'm worried about something.'

'Not the darned Teton Fund.' Cheryl's frown deepened.

'Yes, partly.'

'Vikram! I've heard that too many times before. You take your clothes off right now, or I'm walking out of here.' Her tone was half-mocking, half-serious.

The wine was open. The fire was burning. Cheryl was standing right before him. The enormous burden of the day's worries suddenly seemed lighter. Vikram smiled. He pulled Cheryl towards him and ran his hands under her top, stroking the bare skin of her back. She shivered. 'You first,' he said.

Half an hour later they were lying naked in front of the fire, wine bottle half empty.

'You're tense, darling,' Cheryl said.

'I need to talk to you,' Vikram replied.

Cheryl pulled herself up on to one elbow. 'Oh, oh. Sounds serious. What about?'

'The Teton Fund.'

'The Teton Fund! No one ever talks to me about the Teton Fund. I'm too stupid to understand the Teton Fund, even though it was me who helped set it up.'

'You know I don't think of you like that,' Vikram said.

Cheryl smiled and kissed his cheek. 'Yes. I know. Tell me. I'm curious.'

'It's not good,' Vikram said. 'I think the reason Jean-Luc has never told you about the fund is he knew you wouldn't like what you heard.'

'So, tell me now.'

Vikram told her. He told her slowly, gently. He told her about the enormous risks that Martel ran. About how the fund had been very close to disaster the year before when Martel had taken the huge bet against the euro, and how even greater disaster was now imminent. He told her about Jennifer Tan's convenient death, about Perumal, about Martel's relationship with Bodinchuk and about the real reason why Martel had taken Calder up the mountain.

She listened, her knees hunched up against her chin, her eyes never leaving Vikram as he spoke.

When he had finished, he waited for a reaction. For a long time there was none. Then she blinked.

'Are you saying that Jean-Luc is a murderer?'

Vikram nodded.

'Do you expect me to believe you?'

Vikram nodded again.

Cheryl pulled her knees tightly towards her chest and bit her lip. A touch of pink appeared in her cheeks. The pink of anger. She rocked back and forward.

Vikram stretched forward a hand to touch her thigh. She pushed it away. 'It must be difficult to take all this in,' he said.

'You bet it's difficult,' she muttered. She looked straight at him, tears forming in her eyes. 'You know what's the worst part of all this?'

'What?'

'That you went along with him.'

Vikram sighed. 'I know. I'm not proud of that. I'm not proud of that at all.'

'You shouldn't be!' A tear ran down her cheek. 'Oh, Vikram.' Cheryl's voice was laden with contempt. But not just contempt. Pain.

'I need to know something, Cheryl. If I do go to the police, if the Teton Fund blows up, I'm going to be in severe trouble. I'll lose all my savings. Everything's in the Teton Fund, more than everything. I've borrowed as much as I can to invest, this house is mortgaged to the limit. But it's not just money. I'm sure I will have broken some laws along the way. When the Teton Fund goes it's going to take a lot of people with it. One of them's bound to be me.'

Cheryl was listening. Vikram touched her cheek. 'I can do all that. But only if I know you're with me. It's a ridiculous thing to ask. If you get yourself a good lawyer, you might still come out of all this OK. So why should you stick with me? You're right, I've stood by for too long. There's a price for not standing by any longer. I don't mind paying that price as long as it doesn't include you. That's something I couldn't bear.'

Cheryl threw her arms around him. 'My darling, you won't lose me. Do what you have to do, you'll never lose me. I'm just as guilty as you. I've lived off the fruits of Jean-Luc's ego for the past eight years. I don't need the money, I really don't. I just need you.'

Vikram smiled. For the first time in a long time, perhaps in his whole life, he knew who he was and what he wanted. And she was right there in front of him.

The hospital bed felt wonderful. When Calder had arrived a doctor had examined his head and then his feet, and there had been some discussion about frostbite and hypothermia. Someone else had talked about insurance and filling in forms. He had told them about his back and they had taken an X-ray. Then they had let him sleep. Wonderful sleep.

He woke up to see a woman smiling at him. An attractive woman, a woman it took him a moment to recognize.

'Sandy!'

The smile broadened and her blue eyes twinkled.

'What the hell are you doing here?'

'I told you I was planning to go skiing. They say Jackson Hole has the best skiing in the US, so I thought I'd give it a try.'

'This is a great choice for a holiday, I can tell you. The perfect place to relax.'

'I arrived last night and checked into your hotel. They said you were missing on the mountain. I was worried. Then they found you and I came here. You'd just gone to sleep when I arrived.'

'Sorry about that,' Calder said. 'But I'm glad you came.'

'You told me you didn't need any help. It looks to me like you do. How did you manage to get stuck up a mountain anyway?'

'You should ask Monsieur Martel that. Actually, on second thoughts, you'd better not.'

'Speaking of the Martels, his wife came along an hour or so ago. She left you this.' Sandy held up the vase Calder had admired at the Martels' ranch, carefully swathed in bubble wrap. 'She seemed pretty angry with her husband for abandoning you on the mountain.'

'As well she should be.'

The door opened and a woman appeared whom Calder dimly recognized as the doctor from the morning. 'Ah, you're awake. How are you feeling?'

'Better, I suppose,' Calder said. 'I'm still tired. And my back's a bit painful. But my feet feel better.'

'How's your head?'

'Fine.' Calder reached up to touch the side of his skull. There was a bump under his hair. A pretty sizeable bump. 'What about my spine?'

'I've examined the X-ray. It looks good. We can see the earlier fracture and where it's healed, but there doesn't seem to be any additional damage. So there's a good chance you'll be OK. You should see your own doctor as soon as you get home. In the meantime, take it easy.'

Calder nodded politely. Somehow he thought there was little chance of that.

'In fact, you can go now, if you want. You should stay in bed for a couple of days; your body's been through a lot. Your friend Sandy says she'll look after you.'

Calder glanced at Sandy. She shrugged. 'Someone's got to. You're clearly not capable of keeping yourself out of trouble.'

*

It was ten o'clock at night in London and Justin Carr-Jones was still at his desk. He had another three hours to go before he would call it quits. He would be in over the weekend, but then so would some of his team, and the work he really wanted to do had to be done out of the view of any of them.

It was over a week since he had been beaten up and threatened on his way to work and then been accosted by Calder. Since that day he had received no more threats. He assumed Calder was in Wyoming, and he hoped that it was becoming clear to whoever it was had threatened him that it was Calder, not himself, who was making trouble.

But there were still the JUSTICE notes to deal with. He had known they would be a problem for over a month now. However complicated the structure, Carr-Jones had a feel for the profitability or otherwise of any trade. Before the last month-end, at the end of January, he had expected that the notes would be under water, but it hadn't bothered him unduly. He had assumed that the Teton Fund was big enough to cover any losses. It was one of the most powerful hedge funds in the world, for God's sake. When Perumal had had his accident, Carr-Jones had had to revalue the position himself. Given what he suspected had really happened to Perumal, it seemed wise to come up with a high number. The new computer system was still riddled with bugs, so it had been perfectly possible to revalue the notes generously without anyone noticing.

The market was lower now, and Carr-Jones had heard rumours that the Teton Fund had gambled all on its Japan trade. Vikram's visit had spooked him, but he had held his nerve. It really would have been impossible to arrange any more JUSTICE deals, given what the market was doing, and fortunately Vikram had seemed to understand that. Carr-Jones ran the numbers every day on Perumal's model – a spreadsheet on his computer. As of Friday's close the JUSTICE notes were down six hundred and thirty million. That was better than earlier on in the week, the market was rallying strongly, but the chances of the notes being anywhere near break-even on Monday were zero.

If the Teton Fund blew up, the losses on the notes would soon come to light. The hundreds of millions Bloomfield Weiss had lent them to buy the notes would be at risk; much of it wouldn't be repaid. Bloomfield Weiss would have a big problem. Carr-Jones's challenge, the challenge of his career, was to make sure that the blame for this lay everywhere but with him.

He had a plan. The first stage of that plan was to line up the fall guys. There were four of them. First was Perumal. Certain changes needed to be made to spreadsheets he had written and notes he had made to suggest that he had deliberately misled Carr-Jones and Risk Management about the risks he was running. Second fall guy was the computer system. This was easier. It cost forty million dollars and it still didn't work. Third was Risk Management. That was no problem: Carr-Jones was an expert at intimidating, browbeating and blaming back-office departments. If they couldn't work out that Bloomfield Weiss was so heavily exposed to such a dodgy credit risk as the Teton Fund, they weren't doing their job properly. And the fourth was Derek Grayling, who hadn't yet done any work on the Teton Fund, but, although he didn't know it, was about to on Monday.

This led in to the second stage of the plan. Carr-Jones couldn't escape the fact that he was ultimately responsible for the derivatives Bloomfield Weiss had done with the Teton Fund. What he had to do somehow was to be seen to be responsible for the solution and not the problem. This needed careful preparation.

Carr-Jones tapped out an e-mail to Risk Management complaining loudly about the state of their computer system and how he was worried that it was producing erroneous figures. He pointed out that some of the more complicated derivatives still had to be revalued on a monthly and not a daily basis. This was quite unacceptable. He was concerned that the potential risk exposure on some of these structures had been seriously underestimated. He demanded immediate action before the revaluation exercise on Monday. The e-mail was copied to Simon Bibby and Benton Davis. It was dated Friday, 25 February. Proof that Carr-Jones had been the first to spot the problem.

Carr-Jones hit Send and went back to Perumal's computer models. He smiled. Poor Derek Grayling. By Monday lunch-time the guy wouldn't know what had hit him.

Sandy drove Calder back to the hotel in her rented car. He flopped straight on to his bed. He was still tired. 'It's nice of you to bring me back here,' he said. 'But do you want to get some skiing in today? There's still time. I'll be OK here by myself.'

'Don't be silly. I promised the doctor I'd look after you. Besides, you've got a lot to tell me. Here. Have one of these.' She opened two bottles of beer and handed one to Calder. He examined the bottle.

'"Moose Drool"? What the hell's this?'

'It's the local tipple. What's wrong with it?'

'It sounds disgusting.'

'I thought the moose looked kinda cute.'

Calder tried it. 'Not bad,' he said. In fact, the cold beer tasted wonderful. He was glad Sandy was staying. He could feel his spirits lifting in her presence. And she was right: he needed someone to talk to. He told her what he'd been doing over the previous few days. She was a good listener and she brought a fresh enthusiasm which invigorated Calder, exhausted as he was. She paid close attention and her lawyer's mind picked up on blind spots or inconsistencies, of which there were many.

But it took a while before either of them noticed the message light flashing dimly on the phone by the bed.

There were two of them, one from his father and one from

Nils. Calder called his father first. The doctor seemed pleased to hear from him. 'How are your investigations going?'

'I'm making some progress,' Calder said.

'And you're still in one piece?'

'More or less.'

'Well, I won't ask what that means, I don't want to scare Annie. Are you getting a chance to ski at all?'

'Er . . . yes. I went skiing yesterday, actually. It was . . . let's say it was exhilarating.'

Dr Calder chuckled. 'You never do things the easy way, do you? Listen, I've got some good news. I'm going to be able to pay you some of your loan back.'

Calder's heart sank. 'I thought I told you I didn't want to be repaid.'

'I know. But I'm uncomfortable owing you so much money.'

'You don't owe it to me, Father!'

'Well, there's a cheque waiting for you when you get home.'

'How much?'

'Sixteen thousand pounds.' His father was trying to sound matter of fact, but he couldn't keep the note of pleasure out of his voice. 'It's just a start. I'll pay the rest back over time.'

Pleasure Calder didn't share. 'Sixteen thousand! Where the hell did you get sixteen thousand from?'

'Uncle Richard. You remember Uncle Richard, don't you?'

'But you haven't spoken to Uncle Richard for twenty years.'

Uncle Richard was Dr Calder's younger brother. A black sheep. Calder had never been entirely sure what his sins were. He knew that he had been involved in property speculation in the early nineteen seventies, and had had to leave the country in a hurry in nineteen seventy-four when the boom turned to bust. He had ended up in Hong Kong, where he was involved in some kind of export–import business. Calder had apparently last met him when he was three, but he couldn't remember the man at all. Dr Calder never spoke about him.

'Aye, well. He was good enough to lend me the money.'

'Why would you want to borrow money from him rather than me?'

No answer.

'Father, I know where that money came from.'

'Uncle Richard.'

'No. It came from a bet. The odds-on banker you were talking about. You said you'd stop, Father! You promised me. And Anne.'

'I told you I've given up and I have. You'll find the cheque when you get home. Goodbye.'

The phone went dead. Calder put his head in his hands. Already his father was back at it, less than a month later.

'Gambling?' Sandy said gently.

Calder nodded. 'Yes. I only found out a few weeks ago. I thought he'd kicked it, but . . .'

'He won?'

'He won big. It's only going to encourage him to bet more.' Calder glanced at her to see if she understood him. She did. 'He lied to me. Blatantly. He never would have done that before. It's so unlike him.'

'I'm sorry.'

Calder shook his head. 'I don't know when it will end. If it will end.' He took a deep breath. 'Anyway. Better call Nils.' He looked up his home number in the vain hope that he would be in.

'Yeah?' Nils answered before the second ring.

'I thought you'd be out. Friday night and everything?'

'No. Got to research tomorrow's matches.'

Nils was getting the spread-betting bug badly, Calder thought. A year ago he would never have missed a Friday night on the town. The irony was that he probably thought he was being conscientious preparing so thoroughly, whereas what he was actually doing was turning a bit of fun into something much more serious. But Calder could only worry about one gambler at a time. 'I'm glad I caught you. What's up?'

'Good news,' Nils said. 'I've got some interesting stuff on Perumal.'

'Tell me.'

'I worked late last night. And I mean very late; you've got to hang around till after nine to outlast those derivatives guys. When everyone had gone home, I checked Carr-Jones's computer. You know how people are always leaving computers on all night? Well, I didn't even have to log in to his.'

'Excellent.'

'I went through his e-mail archive looking for any mention of Bodinchuk. Nothing. So then I tried Perumal's machine. They haven't got a replacement for him yet, and his computer still has all his stuff on it. Anyway, there was an e-mail to Mykhailo Bodinchuk. A couple of e-mails, actually. From last year.'

'Really? What did they say?'

'The first said Perumal was worried about Jen, and she needed to be taken care of urgently. The second was dated a few days later. It said Perumal would show Bodinchuk's man where Jen lived.'

'I can't believe it,' said Calder. Could Perumal really have set Jen up like that? 'Did you print out a copy?'

'Well, that's the thing. I tried to, but the printer jammed. You know what a useless piece of crap it is. I was trying to unjam it when Carr-Jones came back on to the trading floor. I have no idea where he'd been. I didn't know what to do: once he got to his desk he would see that I had been snooping in Perumal's e-mails, they were right there on his screen. So I just grabbed my jacket and walked straight out of there.'

'And the e-mails?'

'Still jammed in the printer. Of course when I came in this morning there was no sign of them.'

'Carr-Jones must have found them.'

'I can try to check Perumal's machine tonight.'

'You could try,' Calder said. 'You'll be unlikely to find

anything. Carr-Jones will have deleted them: he wouldn't want them coming out. He wants all this firmly swept under the carpet.'

'But at least we know Perumal and Bodinchuk were working together,' Nils said.

Calder thought it over. 'I ran into Martel's private thug a couple of days ago. This suggests Bodinchuk's man was working with Perumal, not Martel. I still can't believe it. But well done, Nils. Very well done.'

'Thanks. It was sort of fun.'

Sandy had opened two more bottles of Moose Drool and handed one to Calder. She sipped from her bottle. 'What was all that about Perumal?'

'Nils says he set up Jen.'

'No?' Sandy's brows knotted. 'Bastard.'

'When he realized Jen was threatening to expose the dodgy revals, he must have got scared and persuaded Bodinchuk to kill her.'

'How would he know Bodinchuk?' Sandy asked.

'Hmm.' Calder thought for a minute. 'He might well have known that Bodinchuk was an investor in the Teton Fund. Perhaps Perumal called him up out of the blue and told him his investment was in trouble unless he did something about it. Or maybe Vikram put Perumal on to him. Then this year when Perumal was having second thoughts, Bodinchuk had him dealt with. He knew too much.'

'Well, at least we know who killed Jen,' said Sandy. 'And the bastard's where he deserves to be, under a pile of snow.'

'I suppose so,' said Calder.

'What's up?' Sandy asked. 'You look doubtful.'

'It's just hard to believe of someone like Perumal. I mean, I can understand him faking a reval. An ambitious investment banker who overstepped the line: there have been plenty of those before. But killing someone? Or arranging for someone to be killed? If anyone looked harmless, it was Perumal.'

'If Jen really was going to expose him, he was in big trouble,' Sandy said. 'People do desperate things under pressure.'

'I suppose that's it,' said Calder. 'I just wish I could have got him to talk when he came to see me in Norfolk.'

'Well, you never will now.'

They pondered that thought.

'I still don't understand how he died,' Calder said. 'The receptionist in the hotel said the Ukrainian thug checked out the day before the avalanche and went to the airport. So who killed Perumal?'

'Carr-Jones?'

Calder shook his head. 'I really don't think so. Perhaps it was Martel or Vikram or Ray Pohek. Whoever it was, how did they do it? Maybe they engineered the accident somehow, just like Martel did with me on the mountain yesterday. The really annoying thing is we still don't have any hard evidence to prove anything. I bet those e-mails Nils found will disappear into a digital hole.'

'Perhaps that guide's right,' said Sandy. 'Perhaps Perumal did kill himself. I mean, it sounds as if he was in serious trouble whatever happened.' She sighed. 'Once they find his body, we'll know.'

Calder stared at her.

'What?' she said. 'What is it? You're looking all weird!'

Calder smiled. 'I think I know what happened to Perumal.'

33

Saturday morning. Sandy and Calder got up early to drive the forty miles to Twogatee Pass. Sandy was wide awake on Greenwich Mean Time, but Calder found it hard to drag himself out of bed. His body was definitely mending, though.

They arrived at the Double D Ranch at eight o'clock. Already it was active, with snowmobiles buzzing about, preparing for the morning's customers. They approached the rental office, which was manned by a scrawny kid of eighteen or so. Nate wasn't there.

'How're you doin'?' the kid asked.

'Good,' said Calder.

'You guys come for a tour?'

'I'm afraid not. I'm enquiring about a friend of ours, Perumal Thiagajaran. He was involved in that accident last month.'

'Oh, yeah, the Indian guy.' The kid sucked through his teeth.

'I wonder if you could check the day he rented the snowmobile? We'd like to see what time he checked it out and when he was due back.'

The kid paused a moment to think the request over. Then he shrugged and pulled out a large black book, more like a ledger than an exercise book. He opened it in front of Calder. Each double page represented a day, split up between snowmobiles, all numbered, guides and customers. He found the correct day and ran his finger down until he found Perumal. 'It's right here, see? He checked the sled out at ten a.m. He was due back by four thirty.'

Calder bent over the ledger.

'My, this is a busy place,' said Sandy brightly. 'How many snowmobiles do you have here?'

As the kid answered Sandy's questions, Calder carried on looking at the book. The pages were upside down and the writing was none too clear, but in a few seconds he had found what he was looking for.

He straightened up. 'Thanks. By the way, where can I find Nate?'

'Out by the pumps.'

Calder and Sandy strolled over to Nate, who was filling up a snowmobile. Nate frowned as he saw them coming.

'Got a minute?' Calder said.

'I'm kinda busy right now,' Nate replied.

'No. I think you've got a minute,' Calder said firmly. 'Can we go somewhere private?'

Nate finished filling up the snowmobile, pulled out the nozzle and replaced the hose. 'C'mon.'

They followed him to the main building of the ranch. Inside was a small restaurant. It was three-quarters full with customers eating breakfast, fuelling themselves for the day's snowmobiling. A group of four men were crowded round a deer-hunting video game, noisily cheering each other on.

Nate found a table in the corner. 'I got a lot to do, and I'm takin' a group out later.'

'The day our friend Perumal died, you said you were seeing friends in Utah,' Calder began.

'That's right.'

'How did you get there?'

'I drove.'

'In a car?'

'My truck. It's out back. Wanna see it?'

'No. You sure you didn't go by snowmobile?'

Nate froze.

'Because, you see, you booked a snowmobile out that day.'

For several seconds Nate said nothing. Then he spoke. 'Sure, I booked one out. But my plans changed. I didn't actually take it.'

'Yes, you did. And when Sergeant Twiler of the Sheriff's Office comes asking, he'll be able to prove you did.'

Nate didn't say anything.

'On the day Perumal died, you were out there somewhere,' Calder nodded to the door and the hundreds of square miles of mountain range beyond. 'My guess is you were out there with him.'

No answer.

'Nate. Did you kill him?' Nothing. 'Did you kill Perumal?'

Calder stared hard at Nate. He could see the man was tense, struggling with himself, trying to make up his mind. Calder gave him time. Finally Nate exhaled. His shoulders slumped. 'I didn't kill him,' he said.

'I know,' said Calder. 'So tell me what you did do.'

Nate took a deep breath and then started his story.

Forty thousand feet above the Arctic Circle, Uncle Yuri was scribbling furiously in his notebook. He should have been asleep; it always made sense to be well rested before an assignment. But as he had tried to drop off in the luxury of one of the leather seats in Bodinchuk's Gulfstream, he had been struck by an idea. What if he made some balsa-wood figures for little Sasha? Models of the dragon and the prince and the princess in that game they always played. He used to be good at carving when he was a boy: he was sure he could still do it. And he could paint them. Or better yet, they could paint them together!

What he really wanted was to get right down to work, but although the Gulfstream was equipped with champagne and caviar and pornographic DVDs, it didn't have balsa wood. So he amused himself making sketches.

The job ahead didn't worry him. He would meet someone in Jackson Hole with the equipment he would need. Myshko had insisted that he act quickly: he wouldn't have time for his usual careful preparation. But the target was neither guarded nor a professional: a fat westerner rather than a wary Russian. No problem.

He smiled to himself as he thought of the expression on little Sasha's face when she saw his models.

Martel stared out over Antelope Flats. There had been a snowfall overnight and the sagebrush was coated with a dusting of white sugar. The wind had picked up and wisps of clouds were scudding across the broad sky, before gathering around the mountain tops. Martel was in a foul mood. Not only had Cheryl refused to talk to him the night before, but she had kicked him out of the bedroom. *His* bedroom. Something was seriously wrong with her, and he had no idea what. He had gone off to find a bed in one of the guest rooms, which was comfortable enough, but he hadn't been able to sleep. Cheryl's attitude irritated the hell out of him. Here he was, facing the biggest challenges of his career, and she ignored him. He needed her love and support and she kicked him in the balls. That woman managed to screw everything up.

Martel saw a dot travelling fast over the sagebrush two miles away. As the dot drew nearer it grew into Pohek's red Buick. Martel was looking forward to this meeting.

The Buick pulled up next to the Range Rover. Martel noticed a large dent in the driver's door and some severely scratched paintwork above the front wheel. He clicked open his own door and Pohek climbed in, clutching a large manila envelope.

'Morning, Mr Martel.'

'Morning, Luigi.'

Pohek shot Martel a look of panic.

'Oh, I know who you are,' Martel said. 'Or rather, who Luigi is. What are you trying to do? Make a fool out of me? Betray me to Alex Calder?'

'No, Mr Martel, nothing like that,' Pohek gabbled. 'It was for security.'

'Security, eh? In France we know how to deal with people

like you. We built a machine specially for the purpose. The guillotine!' Martel leaned over and clapped one hand with a chopping motion into the other, a couple of inches from Pohek's face. Pohek pressed himself back into his seat. 'What were you thinking of? You had no idea what you were doing, did you? You tried to kill Calder twice and failed each time. Pathetic. Now get out of my sight! I don't want to see you again.'

Martel sat still, waiting for Pohek to leave the car. But the other man didn't move.

'I said, get out!' Martel yelled.

'I've got something for you,' said Pohek quietly, touching the envelope resting on his lap.

'Let me see.' Martel reached across to grab it.

'Not unless you pay me,' Pohek said, snatching it away.

'What is it?' Martel growled.

'Your wife. And another man.'

'Who?'

'The money,' Pohek said.

Martel was tempted to beat the man to pulp and just take the envelope, but reason prevailed. Pohek's knowledge could do Martel serious damage. Pay him and he'd keep quiet. It was the easiest way.

Martel sighed and scribbled out a cheque. 'There.'

Pohek smiled, examined the cheque, folded it and put it in his pocket. He handed Martel the envelope.

Martel grabbed it and began to slit it open with his finger. Then he stopped. His heart was racing. Inside was what he had most feared: evidence of Cheryl's infidelity. He felt an urge to stuff the envelope back into Pohek's hands and send him off to Denver. What he didn't know couldn't destroy him. Couldn't destroy his marriage.

Except he did know. The cough he had heard over the phone had been real. Cheryl was really seeing another man. These things had happened, were still happening, and he knew about them. He couldn't simply chase that knowledge away.

He took a deep breath and opened the envelope. There were at least a dozen prints of Cheryl with someone else. Someone he knew only too well.

Vikram.

'When were these taken?'

'Twice. The day you went off skiing in the helicopter. And yesterday afternoon at Vikram's house.'

Martel flicked through the pictures. In none of them was there any actual physical contact, beyond the holding of hands. They certainly weren't caught *in flagrante*. But even in black and white in two dimensions there was no mistaking the looks they were exchanging.

That was the worst, the most painful kind of infidelity.

Martel closed his eyes. 'Go,' he said. 'You've got your money, just go.'

'Do you want me to carry on following them? I'm sure I can get some better evidence. Give me a couple of days.'

'I said, go!'

Pohek went. In a few seconds his car was speeding across the flats back towards Jackson. Martel was glad to see the back of him. That last comment with its implication that in the next forty-eight hours his wife would commit enough adultery for Pohek to be sure of snapping her at it particularly angered him.

He sat there for half an hour, the envelope on the seat beside him, staring over the flats towards the Tetons, looming up into the clouds. They had betrayed him, those mountains, his giant friends. They had let his wife and his protégé turn him into a cuckold right beneath their gaze.

Martel was angry. It wasn't the sudden flash of anger that he might have expected to feel after what he had just seen. It was a slow, steady burn, building up the pressure inside him, a fist twisting his guts tighter and tighter, half a turn at a time. He had to fight back. Fight against Vikram, against Cheryl, against Japan, against Bloomfield Weiss, against Calder, against Pohek, against the whole damn lot of them. Most men, he knew, would collapse under the enormous burden that the world was placing on him. But not Martel. He was one of the most powerful investors on earth, no, *the* most powerful. Nations had crumbled before him. He wasn't like most men. He could stand up against the world, fight it and overcome it.

Martel pulled out his cell phone, checked for a signal and called Kiev.

Vikram would get what he deserved.

34

The taxi dropped Calder and Sandy off outside a small cream-painted clapboard house in a tree-lined street of small cream-painted clapboard houses. Calder asked the driver to wait. They were in New Westminster, a suburb of Vancouver. The temperature was well above freezing, but the sky was grey and it had just rained. The flight from Jackson Hole had taken them four hours, including a connection in Salt Lake City, and they had taken a cab from the airport.

Calder thought it a little odd that Sandy had come all the way to Canada with him, but he was growing to like her company more and more and he didn't want to put her off by asking her to justify herself. It was clear that a year after the event she was still angry at Jen's death and wanted to do something about it. She was a determined woman and needed to see justice done as much as Calder did. But did she like being with him as much as he liked being with her? It was impossible to tell. She seemed at the same time both cool and friendly, straightforward and detached.

Calder glanced at her. She gave him an encouraging smile. He rang the doorbell.

It was answered by a small woman wearing a sari. Her skin was dark, almost black. 'Yes?'

'Can I speak to your brother?' Calder asked. The woman frowned in indecision. 'Tell him it's Alex Calder. I'm a friend of his.'

'It's all right, Sita,' said a voice from inside the hallway. In a moment Perumal appeared next to his sister. 'Come in, Zero.'

They followed him into a formal sitting room. It reminded Calder a little of Perumal's own sitting room in Ealing, but of course it lacked the photographs, the flowers and the incense.

'You found me, then,' said Perumal, indicating that Calder and Sandy should sit down. Even though he had been hiding in safety for a month, he looked wary. 'Does anyone else know about me?'

'Just us,' said Calder. 'This is Sandy Waterhouse. She's a friend of mine. And a lawyer. Very discreet.'

Perumal smiled at Sandy. Sandy glared back. The look of wariness returned to Perumal. 'How did you find out?' he asked Calder.

'Sandy and I were talking. We thought maybe you'd killed yourself. It would be understandable. We knew you were in deep trouble. It seemed totally out of character to take a couple of days' holiday to go snowmobiling by yourself. Then I realized that as long as everyone *thought* you were dead the pressure was off you. You didn't actually have to *be* dead. Perhaps the reason the rescuers couldn't find your body was because it wasn't there. So we went back to see Nate. He told us how you and he had ridden out to the ravine. He left your snowmobile part way down the slope and started an avalanche with his own machine. Then the two of you rode off on his snowmobile and he drove you up to Canada in his truck.'

'Just as far as Calgary. I took a bus from there to Vancouver. I still can't believe we got away with it.'

'Some other snowmobilers did see you that day, but they thought you were a couple – man and woman. The police were looking for the two of you as witnesses, but weren't surprised they couldn't find you.'

'Nate hasn't told anyone else, has he?'

'Not yet.'

'It's fair enough he told you, I suppose. I said I'd pay him ten thousand bucks up front and then an extra five thousand every three months if he kept quiet. But he said he'd have to talk if he was ever accused of murdering me.'

'I'm beginning to see how you got yourself out of all this

trouble,' said Calder. 'But how did you get yourself into it?'

Perumal sighed and rubbed his face. 'It all started with that massive Italian trade the Teton Fund did last year.'

'I thought so,' said Calder. 'Was Jen involved?'

'Oh, yes. Very much so, yes.'

'Tell me.'

So Perumal told them.

First he explained how Vikram had persuaded him to fake the revaluation of the IGLOO notes with the promise of bigger deals to come. To his great regret, Perumal had gone along with the suggestion. No one had noticed. Perumal was getting plenty of credit and a big bonus for all the business he was doing with the Teton Fund, but he felt very unhappy about it.

Then Jen had resigned and brought the sexual harassment action against Bloomfield Weiss. Perumal had always liked Jen when she had worked with him in the Derivatives Group, and admired her. She wasn't stupid, and it had been unfair of Carr-Jones to treat her as such. Perumal had hated the way his boss had insulted her, bullied her really, and felt ashamed of himself for not standing up for her. Not that it would have made any difference. So when Jen had suggested going out for a drink with him after she had resigned, he agreed, provided it was somewhere well away from the City.

They had met in a bar somewhere in South Kensington. Jen had been charming, and they both had quite a lot to drink, much more than Perumal was used to. As Jen explained what had happened to her, Perumal became sympathetic and indignant in equal measure. Then Jen mentioned the IGLOO notes. She had found a copy of the term sheet in the photocopier and had worked out that the Teton Fund must be sitting on a large loss. She laughed and asked whether the Derivatives Group were fudging the reval, or whether they would force the Teton Fund to admit to the loss. She talked about how she had been involved in faking revaluations for clients when she was in the group. He had felt an urge to help her, support her, confide in her. So he told her what he had done.

A couple of days later, Carr-Jones had pulled Perumal to one side. He looked very worried. He said that the Derivatives Group should do no more deals with the Teton Fund. He said he was concerned that someone might check up on how the IGLOO notes had been priced, and asked Perumal if there was a problem with them. Perumal denied that there was, but inside he was panicking. He realized that when he had had that drink with Jen, she had been looking not for sympathy, but dirt. He doubted that she had ever faked a reval herself: she was just fishing. And he had swallowed the bait. He was convinced that Jen had told Carr-Jones that she knew about the mispricing of the IGLOO notes. He assumed she would try to use this knowledge to force Carr-Jones to back down in her legal action. Perumal called her and begged her not to expose him, but she wouldn't listen. She was determined to make Carr-Jones apologize or suffer or both. So Perumal phoned Vikram and told him he was in danger of being discovered and would have to admit to what he had done.

A few days later Jen was found dead. Perumal didn't know exactly what had happened to her, but he knew it wasn't suicide. And he was pretty sure that either Vikram or Carr-Jones was responsible for it.

Italy quit the euro, the Teton Fund redeemed the IGLOO notes for a massive profit, and it was business as usual. Neither Carr-Jones nor Perumal mentioned their earlier conversation about dubious revaluations, nor did they mention Jen. Perumal tried to blank her death from his mind.

A year later along came the JUSTICE notes, and the whole nightmare started again. At first the trade had begun to go the Teton Fund's way. Then the Japanese banking system had wobbled and everything had gone pear shaped. The Nikkei share index had been hovering just above the knock-in barrier of seven thousand, and volatility was sky high, both of which implied a disastrous price for the JUSTICE notes. In the middle of January Perumal had received the call he had expected from Vikram asking him to arrange a favourable month-end revaluation.

He had refused. He regretted what he had done the year before. It was now clear that the mispricing of the IGLOO notes had been more than just an administrative sleight of hand, soon forgotten. He knew he would be asked to do it again and again. So he said no.

Then he received the anonymous e-mail: *Remember Jennifer Tan.* The meaning was obvious: the subject line was *JUSTICE notes.* Unless he went along with Vikram's request, he would suffer the same fate as Jen. He didn't know what to do. He considered speaking to Radha, but he was frightened of what her response would be: say no and take the consequences. It was impossible to talk about any of this with Carr-Jones without reopening the whole mess with the IGLOO notes. Besides which he was now highly suspicious of his boss's role in Jen's death. When he drove up to Norfolk to discuss his problem with Calder he became nervous that Calder would insist on revealing everything to Bloomfield Weiss and so he left without telling him anything. He became desperate. There seemed no way out, until he'd had the idea of appearing to go along with whatever Vikram wanted and then arranging his own death.

So when he had met Vikram at the Teton Fund's offices in Jackson Hole he agreed to fake the revaluation. Three days later he disappeared. The disappearance itself had gone surprisingly well; the problem had been his family. There were a few days when Radha hadn't known what had happened to him. And, even worse, there was his mother. He had known it was essential that his family appear to be genuinely grief stricken right after his 'fatal accident' was reported. His sister, Sita, had flown from Vancouver to London to tell Radha the truth in person, and had then flown on to India. After an initial reaction of anger, Radha had forgiven him. She was pleased that he was still alive and glad that he had decided not to continue with the fraud. But his mother was still furious and refused to speak to him. He hadn't had a chance to get past her to talk to his father.

Calder remembered when he had called Radha from Jackson Hole and she had been so eager to put him off his investigations. He also realized why no one in Jackson Hole seemed to have met Perumal's sister: she hadn't even been there.

'You're lucky to be alive,' Calder said. 'There was someone watching you in Jackson Hole. He probably would have killed you; we think he killed Jen. But he left town. Presumably he was called off when you assured Vikram you would do what he wanted.'

'That seemed the easiest way of keeping myself out of trouble until I could arrange the avalanche.'

'Aren't you missing out something?' Sandy said coolly.

'What?' asked Perumal.

'About Jen's murder?'

'What about Jen's murder?'

'You see, we know you fixed it.' Sandy's voice was full of contempt.

Perumal looked genuinely shocked. 'Fixed it? Fixed Jen's death. How?'

'We know you got in touch with Mykhailo Bodinchuk and suggested he "take care of" Jen. And then you met the man Bodinchuk had hired to kill her and showed him where she lived.'

'I don't know what you're talking about. Who's this Bonchuk man?'

'Mykhailo Bodinchuk?' Calder said. 'Ukrainian businessman? Lead investor in the Teton Fund?'

'I don't know any investors in the Teton Fund. Why should I?'

'The e-mails to Bodinchuk were found on your computer,' Sandy said.

'When?'

'Last week.'

'Have you got copies?'

'No. But someone's seen it.'

'Someone? Who?'

Calder raised his hand to prevent Sandy answering. If Perumal was involved with Bodinchuk, he didn't want to put Nils in danger. 'Someone reliable,' he said.

Perumal seemed very agitated. He put his head in his hands. Then he looked up and stared directly at Calder. 'I know nothing about this. I don't know who killed Jen, but it certainly wasn't me. Maybe someone's trying to frame me. It's easy to frame a dead man, isn't it?'

Calder glanced at Sandy, who was still scowling at Perumal. 'Did Carr-Jones have anything to do with this, do you know?'

'I've been thinking a lot about Carr-Jones,' Perumal said. 'He must have known what was going on, but he did a good job of keeping a blind eye. I mean, he could easily blame the fake revaluations on me: all he had to do was not ask difficult questions. But the more I think about it, the more I believe it was Vikram or Martel who arranged for Jen to die, not Carr-Jones.'

'Will you tell other people what you've just told us?' asked Calder.

'And get myself killed?' said Perumal. He glared at Sandy. 'Or get myself thrown in jail for a murder I didn't commit?'

'If you really didn't get Jen killed, this will be your chance to prove it,' Calder said.

Perumal looked at the two of them and waggled his head. An Indian 'yes' Calder realized after a moment. 'All right. I'll talk.'

'Thank you,' said Calder, smiling for the first time. 'Thank you very much.'

'You know, everything is over for the Teton Fund on Monday, isn't it?' Perumal said.

'Monday? The last day of the month?'

'That's right. The twenty-eighth of February. I copied the

model I used to revalue the JUSTICE notes onto a floppy disk. I've been tracking the Japanese stock market. And with the Nikkei where it is, the valuation will be low.'

'How low?'

'I estimate it'll show a loss of about thirty points.'

'On how much?'

'Two billion dollars'

'Jesus. That's six hundred million!'

'That's right. And Bloomfield Weiss lent the Teton Fund the money to buy the notes. So if the collateral value goes down by six hundred million, Bloomfield Weiss will need eighty per cent of that amount to secure their loan.' Perumal paused to let it sink in. 'That's four hundred and eighty million bucks.'

'And you don't think the Teton Fund has that much cash available?'

'I'm sure they don't. The Nikkei has rallied a little this last week and that will have released some cash, but not five hundred million dollars.'

'So the Teton Fund's finished,' said Sandy.

'It's not just that,' said Perumal. 'Once people realize Martel's going down, they'll be falling over themselves to sell Japanese equities ahead of him. The Teton Fund has a huge position that will have to be unwound. The Nikkei will be trashed. It will be a bloodbath. The brokers will lose serious money. It will spill over into other markets. You could be looking at a full-scale global panic.'

Sandy glanced at Calder doubtfully. 'Is he making any sense?'

'Yes,' said Calder, frowning. 'He is.'

The cab was still waiting outside, and they asked the driver to take them to an airport hotel. Their flight back to Jackson Hole wasn't leaving until first thing the following morning.

'He's lying,' said Sandy, sinking into the back seat.

'Perhaps.'

'What do you mean, perhaps? Of course he knows who

Bodinchuk is, he sent him an e-mail, for God's sake! He was the one who got Jen killed.'

'Perhaps he's right,' said Calder. 'Perhaps it was a set-up. Perhaps his e-mails were tampered with.'

'Oh, yeah. Just on the off-chance that someone might break into his computer and start snooping?'

'I just can't believe Perumal would have anything to do with murdering anyone.'

'He's a clever man. And devious. Look how he fooled everyone about his accident. And he didn't even tell his wife.'

'If he's so clever, why would he leave such an incriminating e-mail on his computer?'

'We all make mistakes,' said Sandy in frustration.

'At least he'll testify.'

'If we can find him. He'll be off to another sister in Australia by tomorrow.'

'I think he'll talk.'

Sandy stared out of the window. Calder realized that she was angry. Angry at him, but mostly angry at the man who she believed had killed her friend.

'So what do we do now?' she said. 'I guess we can't just find ourselves a Mountie and tell him to arrest Perumal. Not without that e-mail.'

'I'm afraid not. Nor can we go to the Teton County Sheriff and get him to call out the posse.'

'They'd probably lynch Perumal anyway,' said Sandy. 'They'll be pretty upset when they find out he's alive and they've spent days poking around in snowdrifts for nothing.'

'Maybe I should speak to DC Neville again,' said Calder. 'That's where the one murder is still outstanding. I could get Perumal to fly over to London and talk to her.'

'He'll be gone,' said Sandy. 'Besides, on Monday everything blows.'

'That will be spectacular.'

'You don't think you should call someone at Bloomfield Weiss?'

'And warn them?'

'They could use it.'

Calder sighed. 'I thought about it. But I'm not sure I owe them anything.'

'It's going to put a nice big hole in the financial system.'

'Nothing the financial system doesn't deserve. I'm doing this to find out who killed Jen and to make them pay for it. I'm not trying to save Bloomfield Weiss's arse.'

Sandy raised her eyebrows. 'OK.'

'What?' said Calder, irritated.

'I said, OK,' Sandy repeated in a studiedly neutral tone.

They got to the airport hotel and checked into separate rooms. Calder was surprised at how irritated he felt. Sandy had got under his skin. He had become used to her as helpful collaborator, and her criticism stung. He dialled her room.

'Fancy a beer in the bar?'

'I don't know,' said Sandy. 'I'm a bit tired. I think I'll rest here.'

'Oh, come on. What if I find one with a cute picture on it? A Mountie or something.'

There was a pause. 'All right,' said Sandy. 'See you down there in ten minutes.'

The bar was empty. It was also poorly stocked with beer, but Calder did his best.

Sandy joined him. 'What's this?' she said, picking up her bottle. 'A maple leaf? The moose was cuter.'

'Can't get more Canadian than a maple leaf.'

'Huh,' said Sandy. But she drank anyway. It was still afternoon outside, although it was dark and timeless in the bowels of the hotel. She glanced at him. 'Sorry,' she said.

'That's OK,' said Calder.

'But I don't trust Perumal.'

'I know.'

'And I do think you should talk to Bloomfield Weiss.'

Calder shook his head.

'They have the clout to make the authorities take notice,' Sandy continued. 'If Perumal's right, it's not just the Teton Fund that's in trouble. It's Bloomfield Weiss. And the Japanese stock market.'

'Probably.'

'There's going to be one hell of a panic.'

'Good,' said Calder.

'Come on, Alex. You don't really mean that. Those kind of financial crises are bad for everyone. Companies, governments, workers, the developing world. Everybody suffers.'

'So you think we can do anything about that?'

'I think we should try.'

Calder glanced at Sandy sitting next to him. She was in earnest. And he knew how she was feeling. He had been a good Bloomfield Weiss employee for many years. He had sweated and struggled to make them money over the years, and more particularly, not to lose it. Shouldn't he at least try to help them?

But look what they'd done to Jen. To him.

'I tried talking to Bloomfield Weiss before. They don't want to know. And the last thing I want to do is bail out Carr-Jones.'

'Carr-Jones is history. He'll never survive this. You could try again. Isn't there anyone there you can trust?'

Calder thought about it. Bloomfield Weiss wasn't all bad. There were still some good guys there. Guys he didn't want to let down. 'I don't know. Maybe.' He glanced at her and smiled. 'There's only one way to find out.'

It was quiet in the bar and there was no chance of being overheard, so he pulled out his phone and made the call.

'Yes?'

'Tarek? It's Alex.'

'Zero? What the hell are you doing ringing at this time? Where are you?'

'I'm in Canada. And I'm sorry if I woke you.' It was midnight in London.

'No, that's OK. What is it?'

'Bloomfield Weiss is in big trouble.'

'Tell me,' said Tarek.

So Calder told him. Everything. And Tarek listened. As he told the story, Calder could hear how convincing he sounded, how it all hung together. Some parts were still uncertain, but the essential points were clear: Vikram and Martel had worked with Perumal in falsifying the revaluation of their security holdings, Jen had discovered this and had been murdered as a result, and now the Teton Fund was about to blow up, doing severe damage to Bloomfield Weiss and much of the financial system as it went.

When he had finished, Tarek muttered something in Arabic about Allah.

'Do you believe me now?' Calder asked.

'Yes,' said Tarek. 'Yes, I do believe you. And actually Perumal is right about the Teton Fund. It's up to its credit limits with us, and probably with everyone else on the street. If it goes, it will take a lot of people with it.' There was silence down the phone line, but Calder sensed Tarek wanted to say more. 'I'm sorry, Zero. Sorry I didn't listen to you before. Thanks for coming to me with this. I'd have understood if you'd decided just to let us screw ourselves.'

'It was tempting,' said Calder. 'But what do we do now? If you talk to Benton Davis or Carr-Jones, or even Simon Bibby, they'll deny it. You don't have much time.'

'You're right. There's only one person who can sort this out.'

'Who's that?'

'Sidney Stahl. I'll talk to him now.'

'Will he listen to you?'

'With what I'm going to tell him, he'll listen. Believe me. Give me your number and I'll call you back when I've spoken to him.'

Calder put the phone down and turned to Sandy.

'I think you did the right thing,' she said. 'However badly Bloomfield Weiss treated you and Jen, a financial meltdown isn't good for anyone.'

'I suppose so. Tarek took me seriously enough to go straight to the chairman. We used to be good friends.' Calder smiled. 'Maybe we still are.'

'The chairman? That's Sidney Stahl, isn't it? Do you think he'll bury it?'

'Not Sidney,' said Calder. 'At least you can rely on him to act. I just want to be sure that that action leads to Martel's arrest and doesn't just cover Bloomfield Weiss's arse.'

'What about Perumal?'

'If he's guilty, they'll nail him. But I still don't think he is.'

'And those e-mails to Bodinchuk?'

'Perhaps he's right. Perhaps they were planted by somebody. Someone trying to distract our attention from Martel.'

'Like who?'

Calder thought. 'It must have been someone in London. Not Carr-Jones, because we know he got rid of the e-mail jammed in the printer. If he had wanted Nils to have the information he would have left it for him to find the next morning.'

'Who, then?'

Calder shook his head. 'Beats me.'

Sandy gave him a look that said I told you so.

They waited in the bar for Tarek's phone call. Half an hour later it came. 'I spoke to Sidney,' Tarek said. 'He wants you to call him in New York at nine o'clock tomorrow morning.'

35

It was six o'clock on a Sunday morning in Vancouver when Calder called Sidney Stahl in New York. Sandy had pulled on a T-shirt and jeans and joined him from her room just down the corridor. Her hair was still tousled from sleep and she looked delectable. She sat on the bed next to Calder, her head close to his as she tried to hear what was said on the receiver of the hotel-room phone. Calder forced himself to concentrate. Even though he didn't work at Bloomfield Weiss any more, he was still nervous of speaking to its chairman. Sidney Stahl had a reputation for not suffering fools gladly; in fact, he massacred them.

Calder dialled the number Tarek had given him, and a moment later heard Stahl booming down a speaker phone. He was a small man with a big voice. 'Zero! Great to hear from you. Tarek tells me we've got you to thank for pointing out what deep shit we're in.'

'You're welcome,' said Calder. 'Who's there with you?'

'I got Arnie Robach, our general counsel. Don Machin, head of Global Equities. And Simon Bibby. Remember him?'

'Hello, Simon,' said Calder.

'How are you, Zero?' Bibby replied, with transatlantic bonhomie. The very sound of his voice reminded Calder of the duplicity and political knife-wielding that he had fled from the year before.

'I hope no one has spoken to Justin Carr-Jones about any of this?' Calder said. 'I don't trust him. I made that very clear to Tarek yesterday.'

'No one's spoken to him,' Stahl said. 'Yet. But before we get into that, tell us what you know.'

Calder repeated to Stahl what he had told Tarek the night before.

'We've done some checking this end,' said Stahl. '*Without* talking to London. We got big exposure on the equity side to the Teton Fund. It's all secured, but against Japanese stocks, so if the market craps out some more, we got a bigger problem. And for some reason, these JUSTICE notes don't show up as credit exposure on our system.'

The accusation was left hanging. Bibby picked it up. 'I received an e-mail from Justin Carr-Jones on Friday night. He says he's worried about the way Risk Management are accounting for some of our risk exposure on the more complex derivatives. I think they have some important questions to answer.'

Calder closed his eyes. Bibby was already starting the finger-pointing exercise that followed any cock-up at Bloomfield Weiss. 'If it's any help, Perumal reckons the notes will show a loss of about six hundred million dollars tomorrow,' he said. 'When you ask the Teton Fund to cover that, they won't be able to and the whole thing will unravel.'

'We gotta get in there right now,' said Stahl. 'I've met this guy Martel. He's got the biggest ego I've ever seen, and I've seen some big ones. He's not about to give up without a fight.'

'I'm sure if we talk to Justin he can straighten all this out,' Bibby said. 'We need these JUSTICE notes revalued. And I think it would be useful to hear his side of the story.'

'No,' said Calder.

'I really think –' Bibby began.

Stahl interrupted. 'Why no?'

'Because, for the last year, whenever I've tried to get Bloomfield Weiss to do the right thing Carr-Jones has stopped me. He'll do it again now.'

'You're taking this too personally,' Bibby said.

'You bet I'm taking it personally.' Calder was doing his best to control his anger, but he wanted to reach out over the two thousand miles that separated them and strangle Bibby's disembodied voice. 'For me this is entirely personal. Jen Tan should not have been insulted the way she was. She should have been treated fairly. She should not have been murdered.'

'But we're talking about business here,' Bibby protested. 'How we're going to get Bloomfield Weiss out of this mess.'

'That's personal too,' Calder said. 'Look, Sidney. I didn't have to call Tarek. I didn't have to warn you about what's happening. I did it because I felt it was the right thing to do, and because, although I hate to admit it, I still feel some loyalty to Bloomfield Weiss. I can help you if you like. But you have to do it on my terms.'

'Which are?' Stahl's voice was gruff.

'I want Martel.'

'You can have him when all this is over,' said Stahl.

'Oh, no,' said Calder. 'I'm not going to give him the chance to get away. I can get him arrested this afternoon. Then you really will have a mess on your hands tomorrow.'

'Don't worry about it, Zero. If this guy Martel is responsible for the murder of one of my people, he'll pay. I'll make damned sure of that.'

Unlike many of the people who worked for him, Stahl had a reputation for straight talking, for following through on what he said. Calder was inclined to believe him.

'All right,' he said. 'I think I've got a way we can nail Martel *and* get him to hand over the Teton Fund to Bloomfield Weiss control.'

'How the hell do we do that?' Stahl asked.

'As you say, Martel doesn't like to give up. He still thinks he's in with a chance. He believes Freddie Langhauser has a client who is going to put up three hundred million. We say we have that client. We have a meeting. Then we tell him everything we know. We say there's no new client, the Teton Fund is history. We show him Perumal. And then we get him to give you control and tell us how exactly Jen was murdered and on who's say-so. We have a plane full of lawyers, accountants and traders waiting to move in on the Teton Fund and the cops ready to take Martel away. And we have people on hand in London to deal with Carr-Jones if necessary.'

There was a disconcerting silence at the other end of the phone.

It was broken by Bibby's voice. 'Sidney. I really don't think there's any need –'

'We do it,' Stahl interrupted. 'Who goes to Jackson Hole?'

'We need a trader in charge,' said Calder. 'Tarek?'

'Yeah, Tarek. And me. I'll go.'

Calder smiled. 'Good.'

'I'll make the call. We'll talk again later on today.'

Calder heard Bibby's voice raised in protest, and then the click as Stahl hung up.

Calder glanced at Sandy. 'Did you hear that?'

'I heard it all. Let's just hope it works.'

Three hours later Uncle Yuri's scheduled flight from Salt Lake City landed in Jackson Hole. He was met like an old friend by a man he didn't know, who took him out to a parking lot. He led him to an old pick-up truck with Wyoming plates, a gun rack carrying a powerful hunting rifle and a handgun, and in the back various other pieces of equipment that Uncle Yuri might need. There was also a folder containing information he might find useful, and a brief message from Mykhailo Bodinchuk himself.

Two targets.

That wouldn't be a problem. But first Uncle Yuri would need to find a quiet spot somewhere to zero in the sights on the .270 Winchester. He looked at the hundreds of square miles of wilderness all around him. That wouldn't be a problem either.

He also wanted to stop off at one of those enormous American DIY stores and buy some balsa wood and a knife.

*

Calder and Sandy flew back to Jackson Hole later on that day. Calder called Tarek, who had himself just arrived in New York. Everything was in hand. Stahl had called Martel and fixed up a meeting with him for the following afternoon at two o'clock, ostensibly to thrash out the final points before the Artsdalen Foundation would sign the investment agreement and transfer three hundred million dollars to the Teton Fund. Stahl had made no mention of credit problems or revaluation losses. Apparently Martel had tried to hide the relief in his voice but failed.

Don Machin had arranged for some of his best equity traders to fly from Tokyo to Jackson Hole. Although he traded bonds, not equities, Tarek would be the man on the spot responsible for overseeing the Teton Fund's position once Bloomfield Weiss took over. Under muted protest, Simon Bibby was flying to London that evening with a group of internal auditors and a couple of derivatives traders from the New York office. They would ensure a proper valuation of the JUSTICE notes the following day. Stahl had called Freddie Langhauser and told him under no circumstances to let the Artsdalen Foundation make a real investment in the Teton Fund.

Bloomfield Weiss's general counsel, Arnie Robach, had been in touch with a whole array of lawyers and agencies, including the SEC, the New York District Attorney's office, the FBI, Scotland Yard, and the Teton County Sheriff. There were all kinds of problems with jurisdictions and evidence, but the preferred strategy was to question Martel about securities fraud and then take it from there.

Stahl planned to call the president of the Federal Reserve Bank of New York. Although he had no jurisdiction over the Teton Fund, he did have responsibility for the Wall Street brokers who had dealt with it, and for the liquidity of the financial system. Also, Bloomfield Weiss would need political help in dealing with the Japanese, whose stock market and brokers were about to be severely damaged by the maverick hedge fund. But Stahl wanted to delay that call until the next morning, when he was installed in Wyoming. If the Teton Fund's troubles were to be sorted out without disrupting the market, it would need coordination from all the brokers the fund had done business with. Stahl wanted to make sure that Bloomfield Weiss and not one of his competitors were in prime position to act as the coordinator.

Calder tried to get hold of Nils to ask him more about Perumal's e-mails. But Nils was out. Perhaps he had taken Calder's advice and gone on holiday or a business trip to keep himself out of trouble.

At about five o'clock, Sandy knocked on the door of his hotel room. 'Come on,' she said.

'Where are we going?'

'Outside. There's nothing more you can do now.'

'What if Stahl wants to get hold of me?' Calder said.

'OK, take your mobile. But let's go.'

Sandy was right. It was a relief to get outside and to feel the fresh air. It was still light, although Jackson was draped in grey. The hills and mountains surrounding the town were out of sight, and the streets and rows of houses merged into the nothingness. Sure enough, they had only walked a few yards when it began to snow. Large soft flakes drifting slowly to the ground. Soon it was impossible to see more than twenty yards around them. They walked on regardless, following a random route through the little grid of streets that was Jackson.

'Shall we go back?' Calder asked.

'No,' said Sandy, sliding her arm through his. 'I love the snow.'

Calder smiled. 'I'm sorry,' he said. 'This isn't much of a ski holiday, is it?'

'Oh, I don't know. Action. Adventure. I got to see Vancouver airport. It's everyone's dream vacation.'

'I'm very glad you're here,' said Calder.

'I saw you doing your bit for Jen when no one else cared. I admired that. I thought you deserved some help.'

'Well, one more day and then you can be up on the slopes. Looks like the snow will be great. When do you start in New York?'

'A week tomorrow. But I've got a ton of stuff to organize. I haven't even gotten an apartment yet – I'm planning to stay with a friend until I find one.'

'It's a shame,' Calder said.

'What is?'

'That you're going to New York. I mean it would have been nice to see more of you, if you were staying in London.'

'I thought you spent all your time flying around in little airplanes?'

'That's true,' Calder smiled. 'Much as I love the airfield, it does screw up my social life.'

'I don't suppose the little airplanes would fly as far as New York?'

'No, they wouldn't,' Calder said. 'But big aeroplanes do.'

He glanced at her. She looked down at her feet, embarrassed. A particularly large snowflake landed on her nose. She brushed it off with her gloved hand.

They walked on in silence, not sure if they had just said something important, or nothing. Calder was intensely aware of the pressure of Sandy's arm through his.

'Is that a restaurant?' Sandy said, pointing to a squat log cabin emerging from the gloom.

'I think it is.'

'Can we go in? I'm starving, and it would be nice to have some real food.'

The restaurant was warm and cosy and shrouded in snow. It was also almost empty. As she shed her winter garments, Sandy seemed to glow in the warmth. They sat at a corner table and ate and drank and talked and watched the snowflakes pile up on the window-sill outside. Calder's mobile phone didn't ring once.

When they left the restaurant, several inches of snow had

settled on the sidewalk, and the street surface was white. It wasn't much after nine o'clock, but in Jackson on a Sunday night, that was late. They struggled back towards their hotel through the snow. On the small ski-mountain on the edge of town piste-bashers were already crawling up and down the steep incline, headlights on, taming the night's wild flakes into the domestic surface of tomorrow's nursery slopes.

Calder felt Sandy stop. 'Alex?'

He turned. Her lips touched his for an instant. She smiled, her eyes shining in the light from a streetlamp, wisps of hair and snow brushing her face. For the first time, he noticed a faint smattering of tiny freckles on her nose. At that moment, to him, she was the most beautiful woman he had ever seen.

He kissed her.

She was tender with him that night, at first, almost shy, careful not to hurt his wounded body. And he was careful with her, sensing that it had been a long time. But once he had entered her, their hunger for each other overcame their inhibitions, and their bodies writhed and thrusted in a breathless tumult of lovemaking.

36

In Japan it was already the next day: Monday, 28 February. Unfortunately for Martel, it was not a leap year. But the Japanese stock market was doing well and the Nikkei moved up another two hundred points to six thousand nine hundred.

In London, Carr-Jones scanned the screens as soon as he arrived at his desk just before seven. The market rise boded well for the Teton Fund revaluation. As did the fall in implied volatility on the options exchanges. Implied volatility is an esoteric number derived from options prices that roughly equates to the market's view of how volatile the market will be in the future. A high number was bad for derivatives like the JUSTICE notes, a low number was good.

Despite the good news, Carr-Jones knew that the JUSTICE notes would still be showing a whacking great loss. So he put his plan into action.

At seven thirty Derek Grayling wandered in. At seven thirty-five Carr-Jones told him to revalue the JUSTICE notes using the computer model he would find on Perumal's machine. The model that Carr-Jones had doctored.

At eight ten he received a call from the head of Risk Management, responding to his e-mail of the previous Friday. Carr-Jones gave the man a bollocking. Risk Management's failure to implement the new computer system adequately meant that there were serious market risks going unreported. The head of Risk Management, who was used to Carr-Jones arguing passionately that he was overestimating the risk attached to derivatives deals, tried to argue back, saying that his department had relied on information from Carr-Jones's traders to evaluate the risk exposure on the JUSTICE notes and others.

Carr-Jones cajoled the man into insisting that it was Perumal who had given them the relevant information. Once he had hung up, Carr-Jones made a note of that for the record.

At eight thirty-five Derek Grayling presented Carr-Jones with a revaluation of the JUSTICE notes showing a loss of only four points.

Carr-Jones glanced at the paper. 'This makes no sense.' His voice was full of derision. 'Where did you get that number?'

'From Perumal's model.'

'And you think the loss is only four points?'

'That's what the model says. John double-checked it.'

Carr-Jones ostentatiously scanned his screens. 'With the Nikkei at where it is today, the loss is going to be more like twenty or thirty points. We could have a real problem on our hands. John! I want you and Derek to work on a revaluation of the JUSTICE notes. I want it accurate and I want it by ten o'clock.'

Carr-Jones sat back and left them to it. At ten o'clock he would have the true number for all to see. Then all hell would break loose. A demand would go through to the Teton Fund to provide more collateral in either cash or government bonds. And he would call Bibby in New York to explain how his knowledge and experience had helped him uncover the most appalling systems cock-up and to warn him that there was a big problem brewing with the Teton Fund.

Then, at nine thirty on the dot, Carr-Jones saw a group of men in suits approaching his desk. One of them was Simon Bibby. There were two derivatives traders he recognized from the New York office and, scariest of all, some New York internal auditors.

'Got any results on the JUSTICE reval?' he barked to Derek Grayling.

'Not yet. But it's looking bad,' came the plaintive reply.

Carr-Jones leapt to his feet and crossed the trading floor to meet Bibby, a deep frown on his face. It was vital that he spoke before Bibby could say anything. No time for small talk, market talk or any other talk. 'We've got a big problem, Simon.'

Bibby glanced quickly at Carr-Jones. Bibby was a sharp political operator, the sharpest. In that moment, Carr-Jones knew that his career was being decided.

Bibby paused for a second to make up his mind. He gave Carr-Jones the tiniest of smiles, and then he turned to the people accompanying him to make sure they were listening. 'What's the problem, Justin?'

If it hadn't been so vital to maintain his frown, Carr-Jones would have let out a whoop. Bibby was going to let him get away with it!

'I'm worried about a big trade Perumal Thiagajaran did a couple of months ago. I think the Teton Fund's going to blow. And none of our systems have picked it up.'

'That's what we're here to sort out,' said Bibby. 'Have you done the reval yet?'

'We've done a first run through using Perumal's model, but it didn't make sense to me. The model's misleading – I don't know why, but frankly I'm suspicious. John and Derek are rechecking the numbers now. They say it looks bad, but we don't know how bad yet.'

'OK, fellas, get to work,' said Bibby to the two New York derivatives traders. John and Derek watched in panic as the men descended upon them.

And so Simon Bibby and his loyal lieutenant, Justin Carr-Jones, began to sort out the Teton Fund mess.

Calder was woken by the insistent ring of the telephone next to his bed. He rolled over and bumped into a warm naked body. Sandy. He smiled and reached over her to pick up the phone.

'Zero?'

It was Nils. 'Hang on.' Calder put down the phone and walked around the bed so that he could talk without squashing

Sandy. She stirred and reached out an arm to touch his naked thigh. 'I tried to get hold of you yesterday.'

'I got your message,' said Nils.

'Where are you?' Calder could hear the sound of construction equipment in the background.

'In Broadgate Circle. It's safer than talking in the office.'

'I understand. I just wanted to tell you we found Perumal.'

'Found him? You mean the snow melted?'

'No. In fact, it's still snowing out here now. We found him in Vancouver.'

'Alive?'

'Very much alive. And we asked him about the e-mails. He says he's never heard of Bodinchuk.'

'Well, of course he says that.'

'The thing is, I believe him. Is there any way we can get hold of a hard copy of the e-mail?'

'Tricky. The Derivatives Group is buzzing around like a wasps' nest. Bibby's over here with a couple of heavies from New York. I'll try and stay late tonight and see if I can get back into Perumal's computer, but I wouldn't be surprised if these guys work till midnight. They have that look about them.'

'Do what you can. But don't worry, it will all be over today.'

'What do you mean?'

'The deal Perumal did with the Teton Fund is going to blow up.'

'So that's what Bibby's doing here.'

Calder told Nils briefly about his plans to confront Martel that afternoon with Sidney Stahl and Perumal. 'I've put in a good word for you with Stahl. That can't do you any harm.'

'Says you,' muttered Nils. And he was gone.

Uncle Yuri rested his rifle on a rock and kept his eyes on the house below. Snow had been falling steadily for most of the night, although it had eased off in the last couple of hours. Snow was good: it would quickly hide his tracks. It also meant that Vikram would have to do some shovelling to get his car out. Here, at the end of the small road, it would be a while before the plough made its visit. It was also nicely isolated, out of the sight of neighbours.

Inside the radio erupted into life a few inches from Vikram's ear. He opened his eyes, his head muzzy. He had lain in bed wide awake for most of the night worrying about Cheryl and Martel and the Teton Fund, and then fallen into a deep sleep an hour before the alarm went off. As he woke his worries came crowding in again. He was convinced the Teton Fund wouldn't survive the day, in which case it would be better to go to the authorities immediately. He'd need a good criminal lawyer: perhaps he should fix that up before turning himself in. Where did you find a good criminal lawyer in Wyoming? In any case, that would take time, and it was important to be sure that he had offered his cooperation *before* the Teton Fund blew.

He hauled himself out of bed and into the shower. The water cleared his head. He decided he would go to the Teton County Sheriff first, and then get in touch with Ed Forder, a lawyer he knew in town. Ed could fix him up with specialist help if he needed it. Ten minutes later he pulled on his clothes. He didn't usually eat breakfast at home: he picked up a coffee and low-fat muffin on the way to the office. This morning he planned to eat in at the café, and go straight on from there to the Sheriff's Office. He opened the curtains and looked out at the whiteness gleaming in the soft grey of dawn. It had snowed heavily overnight. As he busied himself putting on coat, hat and gloves and fetching a shovel, he thought that whatever happened, whatever chain of events he set into motion that day, he knew Cheryl would stick with him. He could face any future if it was with her. He smiled. He would get through the day.

The glimmer of morning light was just spreading across the snowscape when Uncle Yuri caught some movement from within the house. Sure enough, the side door opened and

Vikram appeared, bundled up against the cold, wielding a shovel. He was less than a hundred metres away.

Uncle Yuri pulled the trigger once. There wasn't even a cry as Vikram's body folded into the newly fallen snow. Twenty minutes later, as he climbed into the cab of his pick-up and started it up, Uncle Yuri turned to see a column of smoke rising above the trees half a mile away.

One target dealt with. One more to go.

Martel looked out of his window for a glimpse of the Tetons, but he couldn't see them. It was snowing over there, on the other side of the Snake River, and by the look of the sky it would soon be snowing again on his office building. Martel wished he could see the mountains on this day of all days. He needed their strength.

He had started off the morning in the trading room, but the atmosphere in there was so awkward that he had retreated to his own lair. There were one or two questions being asked about Vikram's absence, and he didn't trust himself in his current mood to maintain the correct façade of concern. With the weather as it was, it was quite possible that Vikram had been snowed in. But Martel suspected that none of them would ever see him again.

He smiled. Bodinchuk's man certainly knew his stuff. Soon, very soon, Alex Calder would finally be dealt with as well.

Cheryl would be devastated when she found out about Vikram. Serve her right. She would get no sympathy from Martel. She had forced him to spend another night in one of the guest bedrooms. There may be a few more of those, but he would win her back eventually. He wouldn't confront her about Vikram; he would wait until her grief had subsided and then he would be there for her. With her lover gone she would need his comfort and support.

Martel began to pace. He was severely wound up. Things were finally breaking his way. First the call from Stahl, that unbelievable stroke of luck. Three hundred million of new money just in time. Martel's chest swelled with pride. Sidney Stahl was acknowledging how great an investor he was: there could be no better accolade than to have one of the most important men on Wall Street fly out to pay him homage.

The cash position would be tight, but the market was up and implied volatility was down. If only Bodinchuk had let Vikram live a few hours more so that he could have run the new numbers. It all depended on the revaluation from Bloomfield Weiss, due any moment.

There was a knock at the door. It was Vikram's assistant, looking timid. 'Since Vikram isn't here yet, I thought you ought to see this.'

Martel snatched the fax bearing Bloomfield Weiss's logo from her trembling hand. The revaluation was there. A loss of twenty-three points. Four hundred and sixty million dollars. Which meant that Bloomfield Weiss was demanding three hundred and sixty-eight million of new collateral for their loan. With three hundred million from the Artsdalen Foundation, that left sixty-eight million to find. Fortunately, the market rises of the previous week had released nearly a hundred million dollars which was no longer required as collateral on his other positions. He would make it!

He bounded into the dealing room. 'Hey guys! We're there!'

His traders turned to face him. There was shock on every face.

'What is it?' he said, knowing the answer.

'It's Vikram,' Andy said. 'There was a fire early this morning. He didn't make it.'

Martel's elation was doubled, but he fought to control it. He froze his face. Then he manufactured a frown. Then he slumped into Vikram's chair. He put his face in his hands. '*Mon Dieu,*' he said. Then in a whisper: '*Merci, mon Dieu.*'

Under the guise of a desire for privacy to hide his grief, he stumbled back to his office. As soon as the door shut behind him he let out a cry of victory and held his long arms outstretched.

He was a genius. There was no other word for it. He had overcome overwhelming odds, odds that would have crushed lesser men, to come up with another brilliant trade. Vikram had doubted him. But where was Vikram now? Martel knew the Japanese equity market was going nowhere but up, he just *knew* it. And when it did, the profits would come rolling in. The Artsdalen Foundation would make hundreds of millions, so would Bodinchuk, and Stahl would hail Martel as a guru of the markets. The whole world would have to acknowledge his skills. He would eclipse George Soros, eclipse all other hedge-fund managers.

What would be next, he wondered. The US government perhaps? They had been cutting taxes and spending more and more on defence, letting their budget deficit spiral out of control, ignoring the mumbled warnings of the markets. Well, the markets would have to show the US government who was boss. And how would they do that? Through Jean-Luc Martel, of course. It was a brilliant idea. He would work out the details later.

He had been lucky, of course he had been lucky. But that was a part of his genius. He was special, someone was watching over him, helping him when all hope seemed to be lost. Perhaps it was God, Martel's own personal God. Or perhaps it was the mountain. He looked through the grey and white of the outside world to a miraculous streak of blue through which he could just glimpse the peak of the Grand Teton itself. Only for a second or two, and then it was gone. Yes, perhaps it was the mountain.

His phone rang. 'Yes?'

'Jean-Luc? It's Nils.'

'Ah, Nils. Good to hear from you. We have a great job waiting for you.'

'It's that that I wanted to call you about.'

'You're not having second thoughts, are you? I can assure you the performance fees here will be significantly higher than any bonus Bloomfield Weiss will pay.' Martel chuckled. 'Significantly higher.'

'There's been a squad of people crawling all over the Derivatives Group. There are rumours that the Teton Fund has notched up huge unrealized losses.'

'Don't worry about that,' said Martel. 'Sidney Stahl himself is coming to visit me this afternoon with three hundred million bucks of new money. We'll cover those losses.'

'It's a set-up.'

'What's a set-up?'

'Stahl's visit. He has no new money. He wants to ambush you into giving Bloomfield Weiss control of the Teton Fund. And, by the way, Alex Calder has found Perumal. Stahl is bringing him along too.'

'Perumal's alive?'

'Alive and singing.'

It took a few moments for Martel's brain to begin to take in what Nils was saying.

'You remember we discussed that up-front payment?' Nils went on. 'The signing-on bonus? I think I'd like that paid into my account now. Half a million dollars, we said, didn't we? I deserve it, especially after everything I gave you about what Alex Calder has been up to. *And* that dodgy info I passed on to him about Perumal sending those e-mails to Bodinchuk.'

Martel slumped against his desk.

'Hello? Jean-Luc? Are you there?'

Martel put down the phone.

He was being set up. Of course it made sense: he had been a fool not to realize it. Why would Sidney Stahl come in person simply to introduce a new investor? No reason. But to take over the reins of the Teton Fund? Now that was something that would tempt Bloomfield Weiss's chairman away from his Wall Street lair.

If what Nils said was true, then it was all over. After the euphoria of the previous half hour, Martel found that very hard to accept. But slowly he felt the inevitability of failure rise up over him, like a man caught in quicksand as the tide came in.

Like a drowning man, he struggled. His stomach howled in pain and fury, snapping something within him. He picked up his four-thousand-dollar leather chair and threw it across the room, cracking the whiteboard on the far wall. He slammed his head against the window. He turned to see his wife sneering down at him from her portrait on the wall. Searching for a sharp object he found a pen, and set about the canvas, slashing and stabbing until that knowing face of fake innocence was shredded into a dozen pieces. He launched himself into a flying drop-kick against one of her pieces of pottery, balancing on a plinth, and both he and the vase fell crashing to the floor. There he lay, sobbing.

He was dimly aware of the door to his office opening, and then shutting hurriedly. They would leave him to the squalor of his defeat.

As he lay there, tears running down his cheeks, a thought glimmered at the back of his brain somewhere, and then grew. This was the ultimate test. It would take a miracle for Martel to survive now. But Martel believed in miracles. They had served him well in the past, they would serve him in the future. He should trust to fate, or God, or the mountain, or whatever it was. Gain control. Be calm. Think.

He pulled himself to his feet, picked up his chair and sat facing the window, and the snow falling steadily outside. Over there somewhere, through all that white, was the enormous mass of the Grand Teton, immobile, invulnerable, permanent.

Think.

Slowly at first, then more rapidly, an idea began to form. It was audacious. But what was Martel, if not audacious?

37

Jackson Hole airport was small but efficient. They were used to dealing with snowstorms and this one was not troubling them unduly. Calder had to wait twenty minutes while the Bloomfield Weiss jet circled in a holding pattern several thousand feet above the Rockies, but as soon as the airfield detected a small let-up in the snow, the aircraft came in. It was carrying Sidney Stahl, Tarek and a few others. Most of the army of accountants, lawyers, traders and general hangers-on would be arriving on scheduled flights from New York and Tokyo a couple of hours later.

Through the window of the terminal building Calder saw the group of investment bankers scurry across the tarmac, hunching their shoulders deep into their raincoats against the snow, which had started again. Tarek gave Calder a broad smile when he saw him, and shook his friend's hand warmly. Stahl dusted the snow off his raincoat and jammed an unlit cigar between his teeth. Stahl was in his sixties and tiny, but with energy bursting out of every pore. He moved quickly as his eyes darted around him, taking in the no-smoking sign and the airport security guard watching him closely.

Calder had exchanged pleasantries with Sidney Stahl several times when he was working on the trading floor in New York, but that was a few years ago. He turned towards the little man tentatively to introduce himself, but Stahl had no trouble recognizing him.

'Zero! How you doin'? You come by car?'

Calder nodded.

'You mind if I smoke in it?'

'No, Sidney. That's fine.'

'I'm goin' with you then. Come on, Tarek. I'll see you guys at the hotel.'

Four lackeys of some height and seniority scurried off to find a taxi, while Stahl and Tarek followed Calder to his car. Over her protests, Calder had left Sandy behind at the hotel.

Stahl was already puffing away as he and Tarek climbed into the back of the Bronco, and Calder pulled out of the airport parking lot. Within a minute there was nothing to see out of the car window but sagebrush sugar-coated with snow.

'Great view,' said Stahl. 'They were right, this is a beautiful place. Reminds me of Chicago. Whenever I go to Chicago it's either snowing or it's foggy. Either way, it's white.'

'Everything ready?' Calder asked.

'Not quite,' said Tarek, 'but we're getting there. The meeting with Martel is at three o'clock. The local cops are all prepared.'

'Sheriff and his loyal deputies,' said Stahl with a throaty chuckle. 'Can you believe it? They got six-guns and horses as well?'

'Haven't seen any horses yet,' Calder said. 'But this is Wyoming, so you can bet they've got guns. And moustaches.'

'Can't be a cop without a moustache,' said Stahl.

'Actually, the sergeant I met seemed to know his stuff.'

'Well, he'll need to,' said Stahl. 'Because we got SEC, we got assistant district attorneys, we got FBI. All we need is Tarek's bomber brother and we'll have everyone coming to this party. Your guy Perumal will be there?'

'His plane is due in in two hours,' Calder said. Despite Sandy's fears, Perumal had been happy to appear as the star witness to shock Martel into admitting his guilt, although he had insisted that he be promised immunity from prosecution for wasting the Teton County's time. This had taken some doing. 'Who's going to be at the meeting with Martel? You can't bring all those people in.'

'Myself, Tarek, and Arnie Robach to start with. We'll give Martel the bad news that we haven't brought the Artsdalen

Foundation. Then you come in with Perumal, a detective from the Sheriff's Office, and the guy from the DA's Office in New York. And we take it from there. The hope is Martel will roll over and tell us everything. Once he lets us at his traders we can stabilize the situation. They should cooperate when they realize what's happening.'

'Any news from London?'

'Yeah, Simon Bibby's on the case. Carr-Jones is being very helpful, apparently.'

'I bet he is,' Calder muttered.

'The new reval shows the Teton Fund is down four hundred sixty million dollars on the JUSTICE notes. That means we need three hundred sixty-eight million of cash to cover our loan. They've sent off the demand to Martel.'

'Any pressure from the other brokers?'

'Actually, not that we know of,' said Tarek. 'We think that with the recent rally in the market the Teton Fund's losses elsewhere will have fallen over the last week or so. That means the brokers will need less security for their loans, and they'll be releasing cash.'

'No one seems spooked yet,' said Stahl. Then he chuckled. 'At least, not till I spook them.'

'When are you going to do that?'

'I'll make some calls when we get in. The hotel's gonna set up a conference room for us to use.'

'Speaking of which, we're nearly there.'

They had driven through town and Calder pulled off the main road and up some switchbacks towards the Armangani, the most expensive hotel in Jackson Hole.

Stahl puffed at his cigar, the smoke filling the enclosed space of the Bronco.

'About my brother . . .' Tarek said, a hint of nervousness in his voice.

'Forget about it,' Stahl said.

'But –'

'I said forget about it. My younger brother was busted for running a numbers racket when he was seventeen. Seriously. You can't help your family. Don't sweat it.'

Calder manoeuvred his Bronco between the fleet of grey Lexus SUVs that guarded the entrance to the hotel. It was a spectacular building, made of red shards of stone and timber squatting on the side of a hill.

'There's a great view of the Tetons from here,' Calder said.

Stahl looked up around him at the shifting whiteness of falling snow. 'Sure there is,' he said. 'I'll just go up to my room, and then we'll meet downstairs and see what they've got set up for us.'

Calder and Tarek waited in the lobby: wood-panelling, square log-and-leather chairs, granite tables, roaring fires and Indian artefacts casually strewn around the place – a canoe here, some snowshoes there – as if left by a tribe of Sioux who happened to be passing through the week before. A stone-rimmed pool lurked just outside some glass doors, steam rising up from it to do battle with the snowflakes falling from above. A family consisting of a youngish bespectacled investment banker, blonde wife and two yellow-haired small girls padded through in bathrobes, heading for the heat and snow.

'I'm sorry, Zero,' Tarek said.

'For what?'

'You know. For everything. For not backing you up over Jen. For not fighting harder to keep you on at Bloomfield Weiss. For not taking you seriously over Perumal.'

Calder shrugged.

'I admire you, you know,' Tarek said. 'Being able to walk away from a good career at Bloomfield Weiss. All those millions you would have made.'

'I can assure you, it's not that difficult.'

'Oh, I know it is,' said Tarek. 'Believe me, I know it is. For people as ambitious as you and me, it's very difficult to walk away.'

Calder looked closely at his friend. 'You'll do well at Bloomfield Weiss, Tarek.'

Tarek shrugged. 'Maybe. Sometimes I wonder whether I want to.'

'What was that about your brother?'

Tarek sighed. 'I don't exactly know. I haven't seen Omar for years. He was always a bit of a wild man. He's got involved with some lunatics.'

'And Carr-Jones found out?'

Tarek smiled ruefully. 'And threatened to tell Sidney. Sounds like he did, as well.'

'Bastard,' Calder muttered.

Stahl's helpers arrived in one of the grey Lexuses and set off to prepare the conference room.

'You know,' Tarek said, 'I've met Martel before.'

'Really?'

'Yeah. Freddie Langhauser tried to get my family to invest in the Teton Fund. Actually, my father was enthusiastic – he liked all that "Man Who Broke the Euro" crap. Fortunately, he asked me to look at it with him. We met Martel in Geneva a few weeks ago. It was clear to me right away he didn't have a clue what he was doing, although he gave no indication he was in quite such a hole. I'm not at all surprised he's blown himself up.'

'So you didn't invest?'

'No way. I was pretty firm with my father. He listens to me.'

'Does Sidney know about this?'

'Yes. I told him on the flight here.' Tarek checked his watch. 'He's taking his time.'

Then the elevator arrived in the lobby with a ping and as he and Calder turned towards it, out stepped a tall figure Calder was not expecting.

Jean-Luc Martel.

He was smiling, his bulging eyes shining. He raised his eyebrows when he saw Calder, and the smile broadened to a manic grin. 'Still here, Alex? I am surprised. Won't be long now.' A strangled laugh emerged from his lips as he strode towards the exit.

Calder felt a chill run through him. He knew what Martel meant. But before he could say anything, the Frenchman had gone.

'Come on,' said Calder, rushing to the elevator. Tarek followed him.

Stahl was on the first floor. Calder hammered on the door. It took a full minute before Stahl answered it. He looked dazed.

'Martel was here,' Calder said.

Stahl nodded.

'Did he do anything to you?'

'He didn't touch me.' Stahl sounded detached.

'But he threatened you, didn't he? He threatened you with something?'

Stahl's eyes rested on his cigar, half-smoked, lying in an ashtray. He picked it up, examined it, put it in his mouth and relit it. His hands were trembling. Calder had never seen Sidney Stahl anything but full of confidence before. The little man's ebullience had evaporated, leaving him small, thin and frail. Stahl puffed hard at the cigar. The smoke seemed to give him some strength. He glanced at Tarek and Calder and spoke. 'Martel said unless I do what he asks he'll kill either my wife or one of my daughters or one of my grandchildren.'

'He's bluffing,' said Tarek.

'He says he's good friends with the Ukrainian guy Zero mentioned, Mykhailo Bodinchuk. This guy is a big investor in the Teton Fund. He arranges things. He arranged Jennifer Tan's death. This morning, he arranged for one of Martel's own people to die. Vikram, his derivatives guy. Someone else you talked about. He says finding my grandchildren will be no problem.'

'Vikram's dead?' said Calder.

'That's what he says.'

Calder shuddered. He remembered Martel's comment only a few minutes before. 'It will be me next,' he said.

'Martel said that too,' said Stahl. 'Sorry.'

'What did he want?' asked Tarek.

'He knows we didn't come here with an investor. He wants me to agree to waive the requirement for the Teton Fund to provide collateral for the JUSTICE notes. Just for a week. He figures the Japanese stock market will have rallied enough by then.'

'Is he crazy?' Tarek said. 'What does he think will happen then? We'll all just go away and forget about him threatening you?'

'I don't think he's thinking that far ahead,' said Stahl. 'He knows about Perumal. But he says he's willing to take his chances on a murder rap. Pay for a squad of top lawyers and keep his mouth shut. It's worked before. I think he is crazy. But I do think he means what he says.'

'He's lost it,' Calder said. 'He's just going one day at a time, hoping something will turn up. What are you going to do?'

Stahl turned to face him, his expression, usually so forceful, now hesitant, uncertain. 'I don't know. I really don't know. I mean, if it was just me, I'd take the risk. But I got three daughters. And five grandchildren. I can't protect all of those. And these Russian nuts would happily blow away a whole family.'

A drop of moisture appeared in one of Stahl's eyes. He quickly touched it with a finger.

'It's difficult,' said Tarek.

'What would you do?' Stahl asked Calder.

'Me?'

'Yes, you. You're a brave man, I can see that. You've risked a lot just to come this far. What would you do?'

Calder moved over to the window and stared out at the white nothingness. Was he brave? Or was he just foolish? Someone was out there somewhere looking for him. He would be lucky to survive until the end of the day.

But he wasn't a father and grandfather. He wasn't innocent, either; he had come looking for trouble.

He turned to Stahl. 'People are always telling me I take too many risks,' he said. 'But I'd listen to Martel. He may be bluffing, or he may not, we have no way of being certain. But if he's telling the truth then I've no doubt this man Bodinchuk will be able to get someone killed, someone who shouldn't die. Anyway, three hundred and sixty million bucks is only money. It's a hell of a lot of money, but it is only money.'

Stahl smiled. 'Thank you.'

'What about all those people out there?' Tarek said. 'The police, the lawyers? Are you going to tell them all to turn round and go home?'

'I'll figure something out,' said Stahl. 'Give me a few minutes. I'll figure it out.' Then he looked at the two men in front of him. 'Can I rely on you not to mention this to anyone?'

'Of course,' said Calder. Tarek nodded.

'You should forget we ever had this conversation, especially you, Tarek. As soon as this is all over, I'll resign from Bloomfield Weiss. It would be a shame if you had to go too.' He sighed. 'Tarek, can you tell the others I'll be with them in twenty minutes?'

Tarek left the room. Calder was just about to follow when he was brought up short. 'Zero?'

Calder turned.

'Thanks,' said Sidney Stahl. 'It's not too late for you to go to the airport and take the first plane out of here. That way you might stay alive.'

Calder was about to reject the idea when something stopped him. 'I'll think about it,' he said.

As he took the elevator down to the lobby, he thought about it. Seeing a great conqueror like Stahl so scared had shaken him. Stahl was right, he could leave now, drive straight back to the hotel, pick up Sandy and go directly to the airport. Get a flight to anywhere. Stay alive.

But he had come so far. He had almost trapped Martel, but now Martel was fighting back; he was proving dangerous when cornered. Even so, Calder hated, *hated* the idea of letting him go.

The elevator reached the lobby and Calder stepped out. Something else was fighting for Calder's attention, some other piece of information. What was it? He frowned, thinking through Martel's conversation with Stahl. Martel had known that Stahl's trip was a set-up. He had known that Perumal had been discovered alive. That was why he had broken or bribed his way into Stahl's hotel room. Someone must have told him. Who?

Carr-Jones? Possibly, if Bibby had told him in advance what was going on. But Stahl had sworn Bibby to discretion. Calder didn't trust Bibby an inch, but Bibby wouldn't want to make himself any more exposed than he was already in this affair, so he would probably follow Stahl's orders on this. And Calder was still convinced that Carr-Jones's fear of Martel was genuine.

Then Calder knew. Nils! It had to be Nils. Which was why the story about Perumal's e-mail to Bodinchuk hadn't stacked up. Perumal had had no links to Bodinchuk at all, Nils had made that up as some kind of red herring. Calder moved over to a corner in the lobby, under a cradle made of buffalo hide, took out his mobile and dialled Nils's number at Bloomfield Weiss. He noticed his phone's battery was running low.

Matt answered.

'Can I speak to Nils?' Calder asked.

'Hey, Zero. Nils hasn't come back from lunch. And that was five hours ago,' said Matt. 'Do you know what the hell's going on here? He's been behaving very strangely, and Simon Bibby and Justin Carr-Jones are chasing each other around in some huge panic.'

'You'll find out soon enough,' Calder said. 'And Matt?'

'Yes?'

'Keep your head down, will you?'

'All right, boss.'

So, Nils had legged it. Slimy bastard. How had Calder ever trusted him? Calder had assumed that Nils had helped him for the sake of their old relationship. But personal loyalty meant nothing to people like Nils. Why should he help a former boss unless there was something in it for him?

Calder's phone rang. 'Hello?'

'Alex, it's Sandy. Where are you?'

'At the Armangani Hotel.'

'Well, you'd better come back here quickly.'

'What is it?'

'It's Cheryl Martel. She came by a quarter of an hour ago. She's in a hell of a state. She says –'

Just then his phone started beeping.

'Hang on, Sandy, there's something wrong with this damn thing.' Calder checked his battery indicator. Out. 'My phone's going to cut out in a moment. I'll be right there.'

Martel pulled up in the parking lot outside his office building and looked up towards the first-floor windows. He couldn't face going in and just hanging around waiting for the meeting with Bloomfield Weiss at three o'clock. All those long faces from the traders, the speculation about Vikram's death. And his own office would still be a mess from when he had trashed it earlier. He was alone now, he knew. Only he could save the Teton Fund. The people he thought he could trust, Vikram and Cheryl, had proven themselves his enemies. The staff in the office up there were mere mortals, without the imagination or courage to be of any use to him.

He pulled out his mobile phone and called Bodinchuk, perhaps the one man on whom he could still rely. 'Mykhailo, it's Jean-Luc.'

'Yes?'

'I thought I ought to tell you about an idea I've had.' Martel explained his threat to Stahl. 'Can you help?' he asked the Ukrainian when he had finished.

'I'm sure I can, Jean-Luc. I'll get my people in place right away.'

Martel put down his phone, gratified with Bodinchuk's cooperative attitude. It would be no problem for a man like him to deal with one of Stahl's grandchildren, if the situation arose, which Martel was pretty sure it wouldn't. His threat to Stahl had been credible. Stahl would give the Teton Fund another week, and a week was all that was necessary, Martel was certain.

He glanced up at his office and turned the car around. He called his secretary to tell her he would be at home for a couple of hours.

Calder found Cheryl and Sandy in the small hotel lobby. They were sitting together on a small sofa, both hunched over. As he approached them, Cheryl looked up. Her eyes were rimmed with red.

Calder sat next to her and touched her arm. 'I'm sorry about Vikram,' he said.

Cheryl's eyes widened in surprise. 'You know?'

'Very little,' Calder said. 'I believe he was killed this morning.'

'I mean you know about me and Vikram?'

'I saw him touch you when I came for lunch at your house.'

'Oh,' said Cheryl. 'We were so stupid. We should have been more careful. We were careful before. But in the last week or so we took risks. We couldn't help it.'

'And your husband found out?'

'If you knew, he must have,' Cheryl sniffed. 'And that's why Vikram's dead now.' She began to cry. Sandy put an arm around her shoulders.

'I came to you when I heard,' Cheryl went on. 'I wasn't sure what to say to the police. I knew you'd been asking questions about Jean-Luc, and I guess I trusted you. Your taste in pottery, perhaps.' She smiled nervously.

'I'm glad you did,' Calder said. 'What happened to Vikram?'

'There was a fire at his house this morning,' Sandy said. 'The police are refusing to rule out arson.'

'I bet they are. The Sheriff's Office know what your husband has been up to, Cheryl. Or some of it – at least, what I've been able to tell them.'

Cheryl sniffed. 'Vikram told me himself what he knew. Just a couple of days ago.'

'What did he say?'

Cheryl told Calder and Sandy all that Vikram had told her. All about the IGLOO notes and Perumal and Jennifer Tan and Mykhailo Bodinchuk. Cheryl said that she was sure that Martel had tried to kill Calder the week before on the mountain. And now, of course, she was sure he had killed Vikram, or at least ordered his killing.

'We talked about it on Friday. Vikram said he was going to go to the authorities with all this. And he would have done, too. I promised him I would stay with him no matter what. But now . . .' The tears came again. 'My husband's a monster. I can't believe I touched him, let alone married him.' She shuddered.

'It's all over for him now,' Sandy said. 'There's going to be a big meeting this afternoon. The Teton Fund is bust and there's a plane load of lawyers, accountants and policemen descending on Jackson Hole as we speak.'

'Good,' said Cheryl.

Calder sighed. 'It might not be quite that simple, Sandy.'

'What?'

Calder told both the women about Martel's threats to Stahl, and Stahl's inclination to do what Martel asked.

'He's totally right,' said Cheryl. 'If I were this man Stahl, I'd be careful.'

'Yes, but we can't let Martel get away with it,' said Sandy. 'Not now.'

Calder leaned back in his chair. 'My hope was to use Perumal to surprise Martel this afternoon. But he'll be ready for it now. He'll probably have his own lawyer at the meeting.'

'What about Cheryl?' said Sandy. 'What she knows is more damning. And if anyone is going to rattle him, it will be her.'

'That's true,' said Calder. 'But the key thing at this stage is to remove the threat to Stahl. Only Martel can do that, and there's no way he'll admit he threatened anybody when he's surrounded by lawyers and cops.'

'We could go and see him now,' said Sandy. 'With Cheryl.'

'We could,' said Calder. The more he thought about it, the better the idea seemed. 'We could. Would you do that, Cheryl?'

'I'd be glad to.'

'All right,' said Calder. 'Wait here. I need to fetch something from my room.' He still had Pohek's gun stashed away. He wasn't going anywhere near Martel unarmed.

38

Having drawn a blank at the Teton Fund's offices, they found Martel in the great room of his ranch, sitting motionless, staring out of the window at the snow.

'Is that you, *mon ange*?' he said.

'Yes, it's me,' said Cheryl. 'I've brought some people with me.'

Martel turned. His face, usually so full of expression, was taut and pale.

'Hello again,' Calder said.

Martel turned away, back towards the mountain, the biggest mountain, out there somewhere behind the snow. He was sitting very still; it seemed as if the energy which usually animated him had drained away, or frozen in his bloodstream.

'Vikram's dead,' Cheryl said.

'I know,' said Martel. 'And I'm sorry. I know you liked him.' His voice was low and flat.

'You had him killed.' Cheryl's tone was icy, but controlled.

'I heard it was a fire. Difficult for the fire trucks to get through the snow in time, I guess. Especially up that hill he lived on.'

'The Teton Fund's finished,' Calder said.

'We'll see,' said Martel.

'You need to find nearly four hundred million dollars.'

'I said, we'll see. We'll discuss it at the meeting with Bloomfield Weiss at three o'clock. Oh, but of course, you probably won't be around then, will you, Alex?' Martel turned to Calder and allowed himself a small smile.

'What do you mean by that?'

'You know,' said Martel. And Calder did. Martel was clearly

convinced that someone was going to kill him soon. Soon, as in the next couple of hours.

'I know about your conversation with Sidney Stahl,' said Calder.

'That conversation was confidential. I will respect that confidentiality, as, I am sure, will Mr Stahl.'

'We've found Perumal,' Calder said. 'He told us about the way you persuaded him to fake the revaluations of the IGLOO and JUSTICE deals. And about the e-mail you sent to him reminding him of how you had Jennifer Tan killed.'

'Me? I only met Perumal once. And that was only briefly during the week he died. Vikram dealt with him. You should ask him all about that. Ah, but of course! You cannot do that now.'

'Did you know Vikram and I were lovers?' Cheryl interrupted.

'I thought you were fond of him,' Martel muttered, his face impassive.

'But we didn't just make love. We talked. About you. About the Teton Fund. About Perumal and Jennifer Tan and Mykhailo Bodinchuk. We talked about securities fraud and murder and conspiracy to murder. And then he died, in a fire that the police find highly suspicious.'

'Cheryl, I don't care what wild stories Vikram made up to entertain you. But this afternoon the Teton Fund will survive. And then I will hire the best lawyers in the land to defend me. I have a lot of money. I think I can safely trust your wonderful American justice system to protect people with a lot of money.'

'Lawyers won't protect you from me, Jean-Luc,' Cheryl said, her voice building. 'You killed the man I loved. And you killed other people as well – you've even threatened to kill little children. I won't forget that. I'll never forget that. I will come after you from now until the day I die. I'll have my own lawyers. I'll have the police. And I'll fight dirty, believe me, I'll fight dirty.'

'You'll get over it in a few months,' said Martel.

'I will not!' Cheryl screamed, her face, usually so sweet and innocent, now red and contorted. 'You still don't understand, do you? You think you've just done a bad trade that will come right like all the others have. But you've crossed a line. You're not just a criminal, you're a murderer. Either they'll put you in the chair or you'll spend your life in jail. And after that? You're a good Catholic, Jean-Luc, you know about hell.'

Martel looked at his wife, the first traces of doubt creeping into his expression.

'It's over,' said Calder. 'Call Stahl. Call Bodinchuk. Give up before anyone else gets killed.'

Martel turned back to the window.

Cheryl fought for some self-control. Her voice became lower, laden with cunning and malice. 'I said Vikram and I were lovers. We saw each other many times. We fooled around a lot. At his house. And here, on that rug by your feet.'

Despite himself, Martel glanced down at the Indian carpet in front of the fire. 'Sometimes we made love three or four times in one night. Can you even imagine that, Jean-Luc? It was wonderful.'

Martel's shoulders tightened.

'It's pathetic being married to you. You act like you're this great trader, this six-foot-seven superman, when all the time you're like a timid little boy, scared of his own shadow. You remember that first time when we made love? When you lit all those candles and played all that music and huffed and puffed and grunted and jiggled up and down? Well, I had a much better time on my high-school prom night.'

Martel turned on Cheryl, a spark of anger flashing in his eyes. 'But I remember how you felt. It was magnificent.'

'I was faking it, Jean-Luc! Just like every girl you ever slept with was faking it. Believe me, if you're a girl and you find yourself in bed with an old guy who has problems getting it up, that's what you do. It's the kindest thing.'

The spark ignited an explosion. Martel sprang to his feet. Before Calder could stop him, he was pointing a revolver at his wife, his hand shaking. '*Tais-toi!*' he cried. 'No more!'

'Go on, press the trigger!' shouted Cheryl. 'Let's see if you can kill someone yourself instead of getting some Russki heavy to do it for you. I don't care. I'd rather be with Vikram than with you, wherever he is.'

'Cheryl, stop! I said stop!'

'Well, I won't! I'll never stop. I'll always be here, always accusing you!' Cheryl's face was filled with hatred and loathing and anger.

Martel raised the gun and held it with both hands. He tensed.

'Jean-Luc?' said a gentle, calm voice. It was Sandy, who was sitting on the edge of an armchair to Martel's left.

'Be quiet!'

'Jean-Luc?'

'Be quiet, or I'll blow your head off too.'

'Jean-Luc. Who do you love most in the world?'

There was dead silence in the room. The shake in Martel's arm seemed to spread to his whole body. Then he pulled the gun away from Cheryl. For a moment it looked as if he was going to point it at himself, before he swung round to Sandy.

'Stand up!' he shouted, aiming the weapon at her.

'Me?' Sandy said, her eyes wide.

'Yes, you. Stand up! We're going.'

'Where are we going?'

He reached into his pocket and pulled out some car keys. He tossed them to Sandy. 'Outside. The rest of you stay here!' he growled.

Sandy threw a worried glance at Calder and then slowly walked towards the hallway, Martel's pistol inches from her head. Cheryl and Calder stayed motionless in the great room, watching them.

*

Uncle Yuri was lurking in a bush in the Martels' neighbour's yard, his rifle resting against one of its branches. The snow was falling steadily and visibility was poor. But he did see a woman leave the ranch closely followed by Martel, pointing a gun at the small of her back. They climbed into Martel's Range Rover and sped off away from the house back towards the main road to Jackson. A moment later Calder sprinted out of the house, leapt into his own car and followed them.

Uncle Yuri picked up the Winchester. He'd been unable to get a clear shot, but this didn't disturb him too much. A getaway would have been difficult from this spot anyway, with only one road out, and he had an idea of where he might be able to get a better shot later on. He crept out of the cover of his bush, unnoticed in the snow, found his own truck and drove off to make a reconnaissance of the new position. He smiled. More time meant more preparation, which meant greater certainty. He should be on his way home by nightfall.

Calder was finding the driving difficult. It was snowing hard now and the Range Rover was really moving. Presumably it was Sandy at the wheel with Martel's gun pointed at her temple. Calder had never driven a four-wheel drive hard before, and the slight knocking in the engine of the Bronco that had first appeared after he rammed Pohek was getting worse. But he hurtled along the road from the valley, past the airport and towards the main road to Jackson. He could just make out the blur of the Range Rover in front as it came to the junction with the highway. To Calder's surprise it didn't turn left or right, but shot across the highway at full speed on to a small road that led God knew where.

Calder worked to free his phone from his trouser pocket, which he found tricky since he really needed both hands to drive at the speed he was going. He glanced quickly at the device. Dead. The battery was gone.

He considered turning back to get help from the police but

rejected the idea. He could not lose the Range Rover. He cursed himself for getting Sandy into this mess. He had to get her out of it. He hoped that Cheryl would have the good sense to call the Sheriff's Office herself, although the police would be unlikely to look for them up this road. Which was presumably why Martel had taken it.

They were hurtling across a plain, past cattle, horses and even a herd of bison. The snow was still falling hard, but Calder was slowly making ground on the Range Rover. They passed a small community of log huts and mobile homes before the plain abruptly ended and they entered some foothills. Here there were sharp, unexpected bends, one of which Calder took too fast, his tyres momentarily losing grip on the snow-covered road surface. But with the exception of that instance the tyres and the four-wheel drive kept the Bronco on the road.

They drove on, the snow becoming deeper with every mile. Whoever was doing the driving was pretty good. They passed a couple of ranch gates, but no other sign of habitation. They drove along the edge of a canyon, higher into the mountains, the snow thickening all the time and slowing their progress. Finally, Calder rounded a bend to see Martel's vehicle stopped in front of him, its nose shunting forward into a pile of snow, back wheels spinning. There was no way forward, even for the powerful Range Rover. The snow was piled at least four feet high.

Calder swerved the Bronco so that it blocked the way back down the road. Above was a steep slope, below the canyon. He pulled out Pohek's revolver and slipped out of his vehicle, taking cover behind it.

The Range Rover was now trying to reverse out of the drift, its wheels spinning the other way. Calder could see that Sandy was indeed at the wheel, with Martel's gun at her head. Martel's mouth was working, he was shouting at her, although Calder could not hear the words above the whine of the Range Rover's engine. Calder assumed Martel would have to abandon the car and fight his way through the snow on foot, dragging Sandy along as a hostage. If that happened, Calder decided to shadow them until the weather cleared and he could hope for help to arrive.

But Martel had different plans. The door of the Range Rover opened and Sandy tumbled out. Martel took the wheel and managed to reverse the car out of the drift. He executed a neat three-point turn, and pointed the vehicle downhill, straight at Calder's Bronco. Then he accelerated.

Calder fired two rapid shots at the oncoming vehicle. The windscreen shattered but the car didn't stop. It was going to ram the Bronco. Calder leapt to his left and clung to a sagebrush growing out of the steep hillside, hauling himself upwards just as the Range Rover hit the rear of the Bronco, spinning it through two hundred and seventy degrees so that it was facing downhill. Martel reversed and drove between the Bronco and the rim of the canyon, with so little room to spare that Calder thought he was going over the edge.

Calder slid down the slope and jumped into his own vehicle. Although the bodywork was badly dented, the engine still worked fine. He reversed up the hill to meet Sandy who was running down towards him. She grabbed the passenger door and flung herself in. Calder had hit the accelerator before she had a chance to close the door.

'You OK?' said Calder.

'Get that bastard!' she panted.

As they barrelled down the hill, they broke out of the cloud and snow into clearer visibility. They caught occasional glimpses of the Range Rover speeding down the road about half a mile ahead. Once Martel reached the highway north of Jackson he would be caught. Calder was sure that by now the police would be out in force, although with the weather as it was, they would be unable to put up a helicopter.

Calder lost sight of the other car as he rounded a bend, and a few seconds later, when once again a clear view of the road below opened up, there was no sign of it. But a couple of hundred yards down the road was a ranch gate, two tall lodgepoles with a third across the top. On one side was a sign for snowmobile rental. Martel's fresh tyre marks led up the snow-covered track, which climbed steeply uphill through small fenced-in meadows. The going was slow, and the Bronco's tyres could barely maintain their purchase, but after half a mile, they came to the ranch itself. The Range Rover was halted in the middle of the yard with the driver's door hanging open. There were half a dozen snowmobiles lined up beside a cabin, and the unmistakable lanky figure of Martel was climbing on to one of them. A man dressed in overalls and a baseball cap was standing a few yards away, arms stretched up to the sky.

Martel's snowmobile roared into life as the Bronco sped into the ranch. Calder aimed the car at the snowmobile, but Martel shot off ahead of it up a narrow track and off into the snow. There was no point in following him there.

Calder jumped out of his car. 'Keys!' he shouted at the man and pointed to the snowmobiles.

The man, who was about sixty with close-cropped grey hair under his cap, turned and ran into the cabin. He was out a second later and threw Calder a set of keys. 'Take the sled on the end!' he said. 'I'm gonna get my rifle.'

Calder jumped on the snowmobile, started up, and roared off after Martel, leaving Sandy to wait for the man.

The snowfall had thinned and Martel's tracks were easy to see. They headed up a steep slope towards the brow of the hill. Calder remembered that Martel had scoffed at snowmobiles, which suggested that he probably wasn't an experienced rider. But if he got away from Calder he could go for a hundred miles through the wilderness, and emerge where the Teton County deputies would never find him.

If he could get away.

Calder opened up the throttle. He fought to keep the powerful machine under control. Every time he came to a turn or a bump or some uneven snow, the machine tried to throw him, but he hung on. At the brow of the hill was an incline down to a shallow valley and some trees. Calder saw Martel's snowmobile speeding towards those. The tall man turned his head and almost fell off when he saw Calder. Calder opened up the throttle to the maximum as he shot over the snow. He was catching up.

Martel might not have had much experience riding a snowmobile, but neither had Calder, and both men were learning fast, taking risks, seeing how far they could push their machines. Martel was a great skier and his sense of balance served him well as he weaved through the trees and then along a creek. Calder tried to accelerate, but lost control as his snowmobile refused to turn and instead hurtled straight ahead over a bank. He just managed to stay mounted, and was very lucky not to wrap himself round a tree. But he had to stop and turn to resume his pursuit, by which time Martel was far ahead.

With no sun visible, it was hard to be sure of direction, but Martel seemed to be heading upwards and northwards. If they continued like this, they would eventually hit Twogatee Pass, where Perumal had faked his accident.

Calder was once again closing on Martel. They shot over the crest of a hill, and there in front of them was a meadow flanked by pines on either side, leading down to a ravine. Martel turned sharply, as did Calder, and accelerated along the rim of the ravine. They were hurtling towards the trees where Martel would have to slow. Calder's gun was in his jacket pocket, but there was no way he would be able to reach it without stopping his snowmobile. So he'd have to jump.

He timed it to a few feet before the pines, when Martel had slowed his machine. Calder accelerated and leapt off, catching Martel on the elbow. The two of them rolled over and over on the ground. Calder's machine crashed into the trees, and Martel's did a back flip and skidded over a heap of snow.

Despite the soft surface, at the speed Calder was travelling the breath was knocked out of him. He pulled himself on to his haunches and reached for his gun. He cocked it and saw Martel, only a few yards away, pointing his own weapon at him. Calder dived to one side and crawled for the trees. A shot rang out and then another. He reached the trees and turned to see Martel aiming at him with two hands. Calder fired quickly, as much to scare the other man as anything else. Martel was out in the open. He turned and ran back towards the rim of the ravine, sliding behind a small rock at its edge. Calder could just see the top of his head and a gun. Calder aimed, fired and missed. He checked the revolver. Although Calder had taken Pohek's gun, he hadn't taken his ammunition. He'd fired four of its six shots. He would have to get closer to Martel to be sure of hitting him with the remaining two.

Martel's gun was a semi-automatic pistol, probably with a magazine full of bullets.

Then Calder heard the whine of a snowmobile in the distance. The man from the ranch. With his rifle, no doubt.

Martel must have heard it too. His own snowmobile was perhaps twenty yards from him. It looked undamaged. He darted out from behind the rock and ran towards it, bent low, pointing his pistol in the general direction of Calder and pressing the trigger. With bullets passing harmlessly several feet above his head, Calder took careful aim at the running, crouching target struggling through the snow and pressed the trigger. There was a cry and Martel fell to the ground. But as Calder rose to his feet in the trees, so did Martel. With one arm hanging limp he fired a couple more shots in Calder's direction. Calder ducked back behind cover.

One bullet left. He couldn't risk loosing off that last shot and leaving himself defenceless. So he watched powerlessly as Martel ran to the snowmobile, pushed it upright with a cry of pain, clambered on and started it up. He was just pulling away when a sharp *crack* rang out and echoed around the mountains.

Calder looked up and saw a puff of smoke from the meadow above, where two figures were crouching by a snowmobile. Sandy and the rancher. Martel's snowmobile seemed to leap out from underneath him, throwing him off to one side, and rolled over a couple of times. Calder sprinted out of the trees towards the figure lying dazed in the snow. Just as Martel reached for his gun, Calder held out his own revolver and cocked it. One round left in the chamber. It would be enough.

Martel knew it. Still sprawled on the ground, with blood pumping out of his injured arm, he raised the other. His gun was lying harmlessly in the snow a few feet away.

Calder stood over him, breathing deeply, just managing to restrain himself from sending that one bullet on its way.

Uncle Yuri fingered the smooth wooden dragon in his pocket as he waited. He had found the perfect spot, in a clump of trees near the bottom of the ski-mountain on the edge of town. He had an unrestricted view down a couple of blocks to the Sheriff's Office. The weather was lifting nicely and the visibility was good. The range was a little further than he would like, he estimated it at between three hundred and sixty and three hundred and eighty metres, but he had practised sufficiently with the Winchester to be confident he could hit his target. If his target appeared.

He had calculated that either Calder and Martel would kill each other in the middle of nowhere, or at some point they would be coming back to the Sheriff's Office.

Then he heard it, the urgent blare of sirens, the triumphant cries of policemen returning to base with their quarry. He checked the two flags flying outside the building, the stars and stripes and the white bison on blue background that was the flag of Wyoming. They were flapping idly to the left. At this range, he would have to allow for the slight cross-breeze.

In a moment four white and orange SUVs pulled excitedly into the parking lot. Doors opened and people leapt out. Most were deputies, but there were two civilians. A tall girl with short blonde hair. And Calder.

Uncle Yuri examined Calder closely through the telescopic sights. He was smiling, and clasping the girl around the waist. A brave man who had found a criminal and was bringing him to face justice in the courts. Uncle Yuri smiled to himself. That wasn't the way things worked in his world, Bodinchuk's world. Myshko's instructions had been very clear.

The last SUV pulled up, the doors opened and the tall figure of Martel was bundled out and towards the door of the Sheriff's Office.

Uncle Yuri shifted the crosshairs to a spot just above and to the right of his victim's head to allow for distance and drift and pressed the trigger once. A flash of red appeared on the side of Martel's skull as he slumped against his captors.

Jean-Luc Martel and Vikram Rana were the two men who could have connected him and Bodinchuk to the death of Jennifer Tan. Now that connection had been severed. Uncle Yuri dumped the rifle and slipped away.

39

It was a few minutes past six and the last of the skaters were making their final circuits. Calder nursed his beer as he looked down on the rink in Broadgate Circle from the same spot he had sat with Jen a year before. They never had gone out on the ice together. Calder smiled as he remembered Jen's words. She was right, she would have shown him up.

He had done his best for her. He had given up his job at Bloomfield Weiss and he had brought down Martel, the man who had ordered her death. Could that make any difference to Jen now? The answer to that question was unknowable. But Calder realized that he had done what he had done as much for himself as for her. He couldn't face being the kind of man who stood by and watched while someone was beaten up on the street. Well, Jen had been beaten up all right. And then murdered. And he had done something about it. He didn't know exactly why, but he had felt more alive, more invigorated over the last couple of months than he had felt for a long time.

It was now two weeks since Martel had been shot and Bloomfield Weiss had moved in to take over the management of the Teton Fund. Calder followed it all in the financial press. The first few days were hairy as the Nikkei plunged in anticipation of the Teton Fund being forced to sell the trillions of yen of Japanese equities it owned. But Bloomfield Weiss, with the grudging support of the other brokers who had dealt with the Teton Fund, managed to steady the market by claiming that they would liquidate the fund's positions over the next twelve months, not twelve days. Although the positions were big, they weren't big enough to suppress the market for a whole year, and so prices had begun to rally. Martel had been right –

there were buyers out there waiting for their moment after all. The investors in the Teton Fund might even come out ahead.

It had been impossible to link Mykhailo Bodinchuk with anybody's death. He had the good grace to agree to be interviewed by both the British and American police on neutral ground, in Switzerland, but they were unable to prove a link with Martel beyond the relationship of fund manager and client. Nils had waited in vain for Martel's cheque for half a million dollars. Bloomfield Weiss had fired him and, according to Matt, the bookies were after him for massive unpaid debts. So far it looked as if he wasn't going to face any criminal charges, but his employment prospects were not good.

Calder threw himself back into the flying school with renewed energy. It was still making a loss, but a number of new students and aircraft-hirers were appearing as word spread. There was plenty of work to be done, but breaking even now seemed a distinct possibility rather than the implausible dream it had appeared to be only a few months before.

There had been an envelope from his father waiting for him when he got back home, as promised. Calder had sent it back to Orchard House unopened. Since then the two men hadn't spoken.

Sandy had begun her new job. Calder spent a night with her in a hotel in New York, but there was so much for her to organize that he knew he was in the way. He watched as she began to focus on the new work, and he could see how, despite all her complaining, it was desperately important to her. She was sorry to see him go; he was sorry to leave, and felt even sorrier now. They hadn't even discussed a future. A woman who couldn't keep an appointment for a date could hardly maintain a boyfriend three thousand miles away. That was so obvious it didn't need to be said. So it hadn't been said. Calder felt sad about that.

She had seen him off at Newark airport. They had been silent in the taxi on the way, their fingers touching on the seat between them. At the gate they held each other for a long time. When they finally broke apart and she looked up at him, her face had been damp, and so had his shirt where she had rested her head.

He remembered the tiny freckles on her nose. He would always remember those.

He hadn't called her. She hadn't called him. They were beginning to return to their very separate lives. But he missed her. God, he missed her.

'Hey, it's The Man Who Broke The Man Who Broke the Euro!' Calder turned to see Stahl approaching him, clutching a whisky. 'Don't look so miserable, you've got a lot to be proud of.'

'Hello, Sidney.' Calder forced a smile as he rose to his feet and returned Stahl's firm grasp. Stahl had asked to see him for half an hour before he went on to dinner with the chief executive of one of the major oil companies.

He raised his glass. 'I wanted to say thanks.' His voice was suddenly serious. 'Not just for the help with the Teton Fund. But for everything else too.'

Martel's threat to Stahl and Stahl's decision to acquiesce hadn't been mentioned by anyone. That was the closest it was going to get.

'I see the Nikkei is up again today,' Calder said.

'Seven thousand four hundred and rising. We're gonna be OK. Actually, it's been kinda fun. Showing the other guys on the street that when there's a real crisis Bloomfield Weiss can handle it. Tarek's doing a great job out there in Jackson Hole.' Stahl chuckled, his laugh turning into a rasping cough.

'How's Justin Carr-Jones?' Calder asked.

Stahl put down his drink. 'Justin's doing fine,' he said carefully. 'He's been very helpful getting us out of this mess.'

Calder remembered Sandy's comment about Carr-Jones being history. How wrong she'd been. 'What about Benton Davis? And Simon Bibby?'

'They're good.' Stahl held Calder's eyes. He knew what Calder was saying.

'And Perumal? I suppose you've fired him?'

'By no means. He's no longer in London. We've transferred him to New York.'

'And he's happy with that?'

'Very happy. He's got a good future at the firm.'

'So Bloomfield Weiss is all one big happy family then,' said Calder bitterly.

'No. It's a bunch of bright, overambitious sons-of-bitches who happen to make a lot of money,' Stahl replied. 'You know that.'

Calder watched the last skater being ushered off the rink. He was angry and he wanted Stahl to know it. 'The reason I left Bloomfield Weiss, the reason I started trying to find out what was wrong with the Teton Fund, was what Justin Carr-Jones did to Jen. It was wrong. And you're going to let him do it again.'

'He didn't kill her,' Stahl said. 'He didn't even get involved in faking the revals.'

'But he knew about them.'

'Maybe. Maybe not. But the guy's gonna make us a lot of money this year. And next year.'

'And that's all you care about?'

'It's what I care about,' said Stahl. 'It's what makes Bloomfield Weiss the most successful firm on the street. The thing is, guys that make money, big money, they've often got something wrong with them. Some personality defect. They've got some screwed-up childhood or they're trying to prove something to their fathers or their mothers or their friends, and they'll die trying. Dysfunctional, that's what the shrinks call them. Half of them, if they weren't on Wall Street, they'd be in prison. They're just not very nice people. My job is to manage these misfits, point them in the right direction and encourage them to make money.

'Take this guy Carr-Jones. Now he's an asshole. He's got all kinds of personal problems, and he's definitely not the kind of guy I'd want my daughter to date. But I don't care.'

'I do.'

Stahl smiled. 'I know. And that's the thing. You told me yourself in Jackson Hole there are some guys at Bloomfield Weiss who are straightforward decent people. People like Tarek. People like you. And if those people can make money too, I want 'em working for me.'

'Uh-huh.'

'So.' Stahl stared hard at Calder. 'I want you to come back.'

Calder couldn't believe what he had just heard. He glanced at Stahl: he was serious. 'No,' he replied simply.

Stahl leaned back, studying Calder. 'With most guys I'd be trying to work out how much to pay you. But that's not gonna work with you, is it?'

'No, it isn't.'

'Come on, Zero. You miss it. The excitement of the markets moving up and down. The thrill of running a billion-dollar position. I've watched you. You're a risk taker. If you stay at that airfield of yours you'll either kill yourself or die of boredom. Am I right? Say I'm wrong.'

Calder looked at Stahl. He was right. Stahl was bloody well right. But Calder couldn't admit that to him, or even to himself.

He remembered Jen sitting in the same spot where Stahl now was, saying that for the first time she was happy with her life in London. A minute later that had all changed.

He had to get out. Now. He stood up, leaving his half-finished beer on the table. 'Sorry, Sidney, I've got to go.'

'Stay a few minutes. Finish your drink.'

'No, Sidney. No. I have to go now.'

Stahl sighed. 'All right, then,' he said, standing up and shaking Calder's hand. 'But, Zero?' Stahl smiled the confident smile of someone who always gets what he wants.

'Yes?'

'I know where to find you.'

Author's Note

None of the characters in this book is based on a real person; any resemblance to a real person is coincidental. All the companies mentioned are fictional. The Teton Fund does not represent a real hedge-fund in Wyoming, or anywhere else for that matter.

A great many people need to be thanked for giving so generously of their time, among them Eric Wilson, Tony Main, Simon Davis, Stephen Dyer, Jon Graesser, Brian Lacey, Paul McNulty, Mark Aitken, Allan Walker, Toby Wyles, Kevin Whyman, David Craggs, Shantanu Bhagwat, Michael Mabbutt, Saheed Awan of Clearstream, Emily Rixinger, Jock Paton, Agnès de Petigny, Anne Lumsden of Charles Russell, Haim Merkado and Stuart Reeves at Panshanger Aerodrome, Monica Steidele, Judy Singleton, "Skinner", Dale Donovan of the RAF's corporate communications section and the unnamed Tornado aircrew at No. 1 Headquarters in RAF High Wycombe. If there are any factual errors in this book, they are mine. As always, I would like to thank my editor, Beverley Cousins, and my agent, Carole Blake, for all their help and support.